DESTINY'S EMBRACE

Picking up the lion's empty water pail, Lake Emerson started up the path to the stagehouse. The moon slid under a cloud. Halfway up the slope, head down in thought, he collided with a small body.

The water pail went clattering to the rocks, as Lake reached out with his arms to keep from falling. They landed around a tiny waist. To his delight, Lake found himself embracing Clover Sinclair.

"Oh-h," she gasped, her head flung back, her coal-black eyes wide with surprise.

But Clover made no attempt to move out of the lion-tamer's arms. They could have met by design. Her soft hands clutched his shoulders, then moved up to clasp behind his neck. She seemed almost in a trance.

Instinctively, his own arms tightened, drawing her close. She sighed, a whispery sound that sent prickles up and down his spine, and her lips parted.

All this Lake saw as if it were a dream. It was a dream, he knew, that had been long in coming, but now that it was here, he knew his fate. This girl, this night, this place, was all meant to be . . . Slowly, he bent to press his lips against hers . . .

MIDNIGHT ECSTASY
RITA BALKEY

ZEBRA BOOKS
KENSINGTON PUBLISHING CORP.

ZEBRA BOOKS

are published by

Kensington Publishing Corp.
475 Park Avenue South
New York, NY 10016

First printing: March, 1990

Printed in the United States of America

Chapter One

Fourth of July, 1876

When Clover Sinclair was five years old, she fell headlong, totally, irrevocably in love. The object of her obsession was not a little boy her age, but a lion cub just two days old. As often happens with wild animals, the mother lioness had not only refused to nurse her young, but had begun to eat him.

The cub had looked dead. Its tiny body was gouged with deep bite marks. It no longer quivered. Snatching the bloody mass of flesh from out of the lion cage, the ringmaster put it into a sack for burial. But little Clover, who was living with the ringmaster's family while her father was away on a long business trip, thought she heard a whimper from the sack.

"It's alive," she screamed. She pleaded for the cub's life. "Let me try to save it." The child began to weep violently. She had never wanted anything so desperately in her life.

"It's hopeless." The man shrugged, but he handed her the sack. "Do what you can." The girl was a problem, always moping about and getting in the way. Caring for the cub would keep her out of trouble until the inevitable befell the wretched creature.

Clover's mother had died when the girl was born. The ringmaster's children were all grown up, and Clover was very lonely. Eagerly she took the rejected cub to her tiny bosom and nursed the dying animal back to health. She fed him boiled milk from a bottle, and gradually spooned in whatever food his little stomach could bear. She dosed and prayed him through a terrible fever. She tucked him lovingly into bed with her each night to still his cries for his mother. The two warm little bodies fitted together like two spoons in a drawer. Both were very happy.

In an elaborate ceremony, Clover christened her cub Henry, and he became her whole life. Clover's father, Dr. Cedric Sinclair, who operated the circus medicine wagon, remained in the wild West where he was scouting out miracle Indian "cures" for various ailments. But Clover no longer yearned each day for her father's return. No longer did she stand in the dusty road, hand over eyes, looking for a medicine wagon approaching.

She had Henry.

Two years passed. Under Clover's loving care, Henry became a young giant, with sinewy muscles and a savage appearance, but—thanks to Clover's affection—a loving disposition. When the ringmaster told her the animal was ready, she began training him for performances. Henry showed great promise, the man vowed. He also promised that Clover could one day perform with her lion.

"You'll be one of the best in the business," he exclaimed, filled with admiration for what the child had accomplished with the beast. He shook his head with wonder. "In all my years with the circus, I've never seen such a rare combination as you and your Henry. It's as if you're almost one person."

As orphans often are, Clover was quite grown up at seven. She commented proudly, "He's more than a pet to me, he's all I got. I'll never love anyone the way I love Henry."

Shaking her hand in a verbal contract, the trainer said, "You'll have a job here as long as you live." He grinned. "Just make sure you marry a circus man."

"I'll never marry," the girl said firmly.

Many in the circus thought the closeness between the girl and her lion was almost magical, bordering on the mystical. But nobody worried about it. Everybody was happy. The tiny circus was struggling to survive. Henry's mother had died, and the outfit couldn't afford to buy a new lion. Clover and her marvelous Henry were bound to become star attractions, drawing crowds from everywhere. What's more, it didn't hurt that the girl was strikingly beautiful, with large, dark, compelling eyes and a wealth of jet-black hair that gleamed and shimmered under the circus flares.

However, cruel fate had other plans for Clover. Dr. Sinclair returned, and set out for California with Clover in his medicine wagon. He had come into some money, he informed his daughter. They would sail for his home in England from the port of San Francisco.

What could Clover do? Where on this earth could a seven-year-old girl run to, dragging along a four-hundred-pound lion? The heartbroken girl wept and wept, but to no avail. There was no room for Henry in the medicine wagon. Besides, he belonged to the circus, her father said, and he couldn't afford to buy him.

Parting from her darling cub broke Clover's heart. With the wisdom of the young, she knew that she would never love like that again. She grew up to be a beautiful seventeen, but she never forgot Henry. One day, her heart told her, she would find her lion again. She would never, *never* give up her search. One day she would leave Black Springs and travel all over the United States looking for Henry.

Tall and slim, Clover now lived with Molly Robinson, who had adopted the girl after Dr. Sinclair had been killed on the ill-fated voyage of father and daughter to California. Sinclair's medicine wagon had hurtled over a cliff in Black Springs, Nevada, where Molly ran a stagehouse. That was ten years ago.

Every summer, when one or more of the many circuses that toured the West came to town, the grown-up Clover ran to see if the circus lion in its cage could be — by some miracle — her long-lost Henry. She had never heard from the ringmaster who had sheltered her and given her the cub. Her many letters came back undelivered.

It was the day before Centennial Day, and everyone in the entire United States was getting ready to celebrate the hundredth birthday of the nation's freedom from England's tyranny. A traveling circus had come to Black Springs to cap the day's festivities. The music from the circus band had just begun to drift over the arid sagebrush hills as Clover raced down the dusty road toward town to see the circus parade. Molly had sent Clover for a tin of lard from the butcher in town.

"Now, mind, come right home once you've seen the lion," Molly yelled after the girl. "I need that lard for my pine-nut cakes."

Fried pine-nut cakes were Molly's specialty. She and Clover ran the stagestop and hostel at Black Springs. Molly and Clover served three meals a day to stagecoach travelers and provided beds of a sort in two large upstairs rooms. But business had been failing since the boomtown silver days. Sometimes days passed with no more than ten or twenty customers, most of them local bachelors who enjoyed Molly's cooking, especially her pine-nut cakes.

Happily, tomorrow—Independence Day—promised to be the biggest day in years, with hungry crowds expected from all over the silver-mining country. Just one day would make up for many week's losses, Molly was confident.

After a hurried stop at the butcher's for lard, Clover arrived on Front Street where the circus parade had just started to move. Attired in her customary trousers and boy's shirt, her thick black hair tucked beneath a boy's plaid cap, she mingled easily with the noisy crowd. She elbowed her way to the front row of spectators. Her blood stirred at the familiar circus sights and smells and sounds. Clover longed to join a circus as a liontamer.

But Molly was against it. "It's no place for a female," she said testily. "Only riffraff work in circuses."

Obediently, Clover quelled her ambition. She loved Molly more than anything in the world, except maybe Henry. Dr. Sinclair had died instantly in the wreck of his wagon, but Molly, out picking pine nuts on the steep canyon wall, had found the little girl cowering in an old mine shaft. When nobody showed up to claim the child, the childless old woman had joyfully adopted her.

Now, with Molly's filled lard bucket over her arm, and trying not to hope too hard, Clover watched eagerly as twelve red-and-gold painted wagons rattled past. Belly dancers, monkeys, a bearded lady, a sword swallower, clowns, a human pretzel who twisted about in incredible contortions—all cavorted energetically to titillate their audience.

Clover's heart sank. Maybe there wasn't any lion in this circus, for many of them couldn't afford a beast who ate twenty pounds of meat each day. But in a moment, a cageful of puny, dozing leopards was followed by a blue-painted lion cage. The crowd surged forward. Only a handful of them had ever seen an African lion in the flesh. Cougars, also called mountain lions, abounded in the Nevada hills, but they were half the size of this circus beast.

The young liontamer jerked the reins of his dappled horse to stop the wagon and give the crowd a good long look. The lion was the star attraction of the Grandiose Traveling Circus, and this one was a beauty.

A collective, indrawn breath, like the soughing of the devil wind in autumn, surged through the crowd.

"My God, he's gorgeous," a woman cried.

"Please, God," Clover prayed, walking into the rutted street, staring fixedly, hopefully, at the lion. "Let this one be my Henry."

Tawny as a honey jar in the Nevada sun, the beast lay on its haunches, massive forepaws outstretched. A luxuriant mane cascaded darkly over the massive head and throat, falling to the floor of the cage in undulating,

10

royal folds. A soft command from the trainer brought the animal slowly, sinuously, to his feet, like a giant cat awakening from an afternoon's nap on the hearth. As if aware of his beauty, he stretched to his full nine feet, tail extended. He filled the cage.

Lifting his head and yawning, the beast revealed a maw filled with long yellow fangs. His sandpaper tongue darted out hungrily. Panting, he flared his nostrils, surveying the crowd with slitted amber eyes, as if choosing a victim for his supper.

The trainer-driver spoke again, sharply. The lion growled, sounding like distant thunder from the encircling Sierras. A flick of the man's finger, and the lion roared—a rumbling, rolling sound that sent the crowd back in dread.

All but one.

Brazenly, Clover inched toward the cage, arms extended, palms up. Her dream had come true. The long prayed-for miracle was at this very moment taking place.

"Henry," she breathed, "it's really you."

"Hey, kid, get the hell out of there," the liontamer bellowed in a distinct English accent. "He'll eat you in two bites."

Seemingly deaf, Clover thrust a hand between the bars and began stroking the rough flank of the lion, who abruptly stopped his roaring and stuck a wet black snout between the bars. Leaning forward, the girl kissed the lion on his moist, warm nose.

Stunned, the crowd fell silent. Heads were shaking. Nobody in town was too surprised, though. What else could you expect from that loony Clover Sinclair who was raised by that half-savage Molly Robinson who had been raised by wild Indians herself? Molly dressed the girl in boy's clothes and hauled her off to live with the Indians every summer.

The liontamer's rawhide whip whistled over Clover's head, but she paid no heed. The whole world had vanished. She heard nothing but the thudding of her own heart, saw nothing but the liquid amber eyes that had filled her dreams for ten long years.

She had found her long-lost Henry.

"Goddam."

Madder than a hornet, Lake Emerson threw down his whip and vaulted off the wagon seat to stop the crazy kid. The lion was now rolling ecstatically on his back, rumbling in his belly like a pussy cat with cream on its whiskers.

Grabbing the thin shoulders, Lake yanked the kid away from the cage so forcefully the youngster sprawled onto the rutted street. A tin lard bucket clattered after him.

"Dammit, kid, let my lion alone."

Furtively, Lake scanned the crowd. Faces were gaping at him in wonder. Angry murmurs were heard.

"That lion is dangerous, I tell you," Lake reiterated, glaring at the boy, who was scrambling to his feet.

Henry was on his feet again, growling mildly. It was a happy, humming, animal noise, but it sounded threatening, and the crowd fell back, scared. Lake sighed in relief. Actually, Henry was the gentlest beast in creation—all that fierce roaring was done on cue. The big cat wouldn't harm a flea if it were crawling on his nose.

12

But the public must never, never know that.

Nobody pays to see a lion who is still a cub at heart, who adores playing with a ball of yarn and having his stomach tickled.

"It's Henry," the kid said flatly, brushing off his pants. Then—more defiantly—"He's my lion."

Struck dumb, Lake could only stare down into a pair of the biggest, blackest eyes he had ever seen. It was like looking into a coal mine. A head of magnificent, shiny black hair rippled around a pale, cameo face, the plaid cap once covering the glorious tresses now lying in the street.

By all that's holy, Lake thought, the pesky kid was a girl, and a very pretty one at that.

"What the hell do you mean, he's your lion?" he exploded.

A shout from a roustabout cut him short. "Hey, Lake, you're holdin' up the parade."

The crazy girl lunged forward again as Lake leaped back onto the wagon and flicked the reins. He had a fleeting glimpse of a shiny, tear-streaked face before a cloud of dust from his wheels enveloped her.

"Damn," he exploded. He'd have to do his wounded-arm trick tomorrow to convince the people of Black Springs that Henry was a genuine, savage man-eater. How in hell did the girl know the lion's name? Maybe she'd caught the show in another town. Maybe she'd even worked in a circus. From the familiar way she touched him, she obviously knew lions well.

Long ago, he'd known a little girl who had adopted a lion cub—

Lake's heart seemed to crash into his ribs. His brain began to whirl as the dusty town disappeared for him.

In memory he was inside a medicine wagon, gazing at a wide-eyed child in a flannel nightgown. She had a newborn cub in her arms.

The child was called Mary Anne and she had a mop of hair so black it shone blue in the lamplight. Her black eyes took up half her face. Mary Anne was the daughter of that bastard Sinclair who had run out of an Illinois bank twelve years ago, after robbing the place and killing a man. The scoundrel Sinclair had left a scared kid called Emerson to face the authorities alone.

Jerking back to reality, Lake whooped for joy. His quest was over. Who would have thought that here—in this godforsaken desert—he'd end his long search to catch up with Dr. Cedric Sinclair.

Vengeance will be sweet, Lake Emerson mused. He would return the living hell, fourfold, that the traitorous Sinclair had given him. Because of Sinclair's desertion, Lake had spent five years in prison for a crime he never committed. That black-eyed lion-loving girl, who was surely Sinclair's daughter, would make the path of revenge even sweeter.

The hot wind soon dried the tears on Clover's cheeks as she gazed numbly at the departing circus wagons. The crowd dispersed. Some followed the wagons to the campground behind Molly's stagehouse, others vanished into the clutter of storefronts and houses that was Black Springs.

In a daze of happiness, Clover picked up her lard bucket and headed for home, forgetting her plaid cap lying in the street. Following the crowd, she placed one booted foot in front of the other, like a child learning to walk. Her long, thick hair blew about her face in the desert wind. Not for a single moment did she doubt that the circus lion was her darling Henry. It made no difference that ten years had passed. It could have been yesterday that they had parted.

It was almost human, the way their eyes had met and locked. His had narrowed, then widened, turning a deep, dark gold. When he had rolled over, she'd seen the liver spot on his inner thigh, shaped like a question mark. Chances that more than one lion in the world had a birthmark like that one were one in a million, she told herself.

Somehow, she'd get the money to buy Henry. She'd keep him in a large pen out back of the stagehouse, with a tall wood fence to keep out intruders. Some in town might think it dangerously insane to keep a full-grown lion as a pet, but Spike and Molly, too, would see that nobody caused any trouble.

As if summoned by her thought, Clover heard heavy footsteps behind, followed by the feel of a man's strong arms around her waist. Spike lifted her off the ground from behind.

Pressing her tightly to his hard body, her fiancé splayed big hands over her abdomen, digging his blunt-nailed fingers into her tender private parts. Clover felt the hard manhood thrusting into the space between her buttocks.

She giggled. "Spike, stop that, people are staring."

"Let 'em stare," he muttered thickly, pressing moist, hot lips to the back of her neck. "You're my woman, I'll do whatever I please with you."

His hands wandered up to her breasts, which swelled small but firm and round under the thin cotton shirt.

15

Clover rested, limp in his arms. She suppressed a sigh. This was the price she must pay for marrying rich and powerful Spike Brant, heir to the biggest silver fortune in this part of Nevada.

She and Spike had known each other since childhood, when both had scrambled with the other Black Springs kids over the arid hillsides. They had hunted for sage hens and snakes, and despite the fact that Clover always looked more like a boy than a girl, Spike became her friend and protector.

"We'll get married when we grow up," he vowed. Nobody ever argued with Spike. Clover forgot about her childish vow never to marry.

His parents spoiled him outrageously. The Brants were very wealthy, having struck a rich vein of silver in the boomtown days. After she took in Clover, Molly Robinson never prospected again, continuing to struggle along with the stagehouse.

Ralph Brant, Spike's father, didn't care that Clover was dirt poor. He wanted his son to marry Clover for reasons of his own. Molly had great influence with the native Paiutes and Washos. With Clover as his daughter-in-law, Brant's plans to take over some valuable Indian land would have a good chance of succeeding.

Now, halfway to the stagehouse on the rocky path, Spike began to move his hips lewdly in and out. His tobacco-scented breath was hot on her neck. Clover quelled her revulsion at his obscene poking into her buttocks.

"You must learn to endure a man's passion," Molly had told her. "Children will follow. Children are the only joy in a woman's life."

When Clover's first woman's blood had spotted her

underthings, Molly had taken the twelve-year-old into her bedroom, shutting the door. The girl had listened, wide-eyed, as the older woman had outlined what it meant to be a woman.

"You must couple like the sheep," she'd said bluntly. "You must be a man's plaything."

There would be little pleasure, Molly said. "Only loose women enjoy the physical experience of coupling."

Clover had seen loose women hanging around the saloon in town. They were blowsy, tired, poor, mostly drunk, and allowed themselves to be fondled by any man with money in his pocket.

Better dead than to become like them, she had shuddered. In October, on her eighteenth birthday, she would marry Spike.

Now, as Spike's hands kneaded her buttocks, Clover snapped, "Spike, put me down. Molly will be wild if I don't get this lard to her for supper."

Spike yelped, loosening his arms. "Can't afford to get my future mother-in-law mad at me."

Impulsively, Clover whipped around and kissed him fully on the lips.

His broad face was surprised and pleased. "Hallelujah, I do believe my li'l virgin is beginning to ripen."

His lips came down on hers—brutally, possessively. Clover tried her darndest to respond, dutifully straining her lithe form against his hardness with all her strength. Spike was a good man, she told herself. He truly loved her, with a man's passion. Spike would give her the money to buy Henry. Just yesterday he'd asked her what she wanted for a wedding present. A silver service, a Paris gown, a horse and buggy of her own?

"Buy me a lion," she'd tell him.

But not just yet. She was not ready to share her precious, secret joy with anybody. Besides, her years with Molly at the stagestop had taught her to be cunning in business. If that foul-tempered liontamer found out how desperately she wanted Henry, he'd ask an outrageous price for him.

Arm in arm, the sweethearts walked up the rocky slope toward Clover's home.

Molly Robinson was slicing pickled buffalo tongue at the butcher block in the steaming kitchen when Clover and Spike entered from the back door, laughing merrily.

Wiping the ready smile from her weathered face, Molly barked, "Where have you been, you lazy girl?" She snatched the lard bucket from Clover. "Now quit your lollygagging and get your apron on. The dining room's full to bursting."

Chuckling, Spike slapped Molly's withered bottom and helped himself to a tall glass of whiskey from a bottle on the windowsill. Sipping happily, he lounged against the adobe wall, watching Clover as she tied a voluminous checked gingham apron around her slim waist. Donning a white mobcap, she carefully tucked in her windblown hair so that not a strand was visible.

Sliding out a platter of crispy fried potatoes from the warming oven of the gigantic cookstove, the girl swung through an archway into the dining room.

"Ah-h-h." Spike sighed, licking his lips as he gazed at her rounded buttocks straining at the tight blue serge trousers. "I can hardly wait."

"The girl is not to be touched until the wedding

18

night," Molly growled, noting his glance. "I want no so-called premature babies born six months after the wedding day."

But she grinned at the boy. He was perfect for her Clover. Virile, rich, good-looking, clean. A little too free with the ladies perhaps, but with Clover in his bed each night, he'd settle down. Molly would make sure of that.

Clover would never love him, but she'd be content. With a bellyful of baby every year, she'd have little time to brood about romance. Molly had no use for what passed as man-woman love. That kind of mindless passion had ruined her own life.

At eighteen, Molly had run off from the Indians who'd raised her as a captive and fallen headlong for the first man who talked sweet to her. He'd taken her to California to get rich, promising to marry her when he found a preacher.

Preachers were scarce in the gold fields. A year later, her lover had abandoned her, still unwed, with child. The little bastard had been stillborn.

"You did a good job raising Clover," Spike broke into her thoughts. He refilled his whiskey glass. "She'll make me a dandy wife."

Molly waved her meat cleaver at him. "See that you treat her right, mind, or you'll answer to me."

"Ye-es, ma'am."

Bowing deeply from the waist, Spike scuttled into the dining room. He was in no mood for still another of the woman's sermons on how to treat a wife. Spike knew how to handle women. Lordy, he'd had enough of them. He'd started poking under skirts at fourteen. Clover would be putty in his hands. He knew all the tricks to make her buck like a mare in heat.

But the crusty old dame was not to be toyed with, Spike was painfully aware. Everyone on the Nevada side of Lake Tahoe had a healthy respect for the woman who had raised Clover Sinclair. Reared by the savages as a white captive, Molly retained much of the implacable spirit of the red man. By her strong personality, she and she alone had kept the Paiutes and Washos from harassing the white men who had ruthlessly moved into their hunting grounds to pan for gold and dig for the silver that threaded the Sierra Nevadas.

After months of talks, Molly had persuaded the remnants of once-powerful tribes to remove themselves to a hidden valley a hundred miles to the south, called Eagle Valley by the white man. The Indians called it Wun-i-muc-a. Molly and her daughter had spent many happy months in Eagle Valley living with the Indians. Clover was happier there than she had ever been in Black Springs. The girl had many young friends among the Indians.

Alone in the kitchen, Molly absently lifted an aromatic slice of tongue to her mouth. As she chewed, she began to cough, a deep, hacking sound that brought Clover flying back from the dining room.

"Get back to your work," Molly gasped at the frightened girl. "It's just a nasty summer cold."

Tight-lipped, Clover picked up the platter of tongue and swung back out of the kitchen. But her black eyes were bright with tears.

Convulsed by coughing, the tall, gaunt woman fled through the lean-to pantry into the yard, snatching a cloth from a shelf. After a bit, she buried the blood-stained cloth under some loose rocks at the corner of the house.

It was fully dark when Lake returned from his bath in town. He had not eaten there, however, his excitement at finding Sinclair's daughter having driven hunger from his belly. But now, strolling round the circus camp, the aroma of roasting lamb from the stagestop set his juices flowing. He'd go up to the house, have a meal, talk to Clover Sinclair.

Casually. She must not suspect his intentions.

The man who had scrubbed him down at the bathhouse readily answered Lake's questions about the girl in pants who had petted his lion.

"Sure I know her. Everyone does. Molly from the stagestop found her at the bottom of a gorge ten years ago, along with her dead pa and his wrecked wagon. The poor li'l tyke was a bag of bones, hidin' in an old mine pit. She couldn't remember a thing. Couldn't even recall her own name. Molly called her Clover, and she growed up to be a right pretty gal, even in those boy's duds she always wears."

"Then Sinclair isn't her real name?" Lake's heart sank.

"Yep, sure is. Molly found some papers in the wrecked wagon that said the gal's name was Mary Anne Sinclair and that she was seven years old." By that time, the man chuckled, the girl had gotten so used to being called Clover, she wouldn't answer to Mary Anne.

So Sinclair was dead. Lake felt an instant of keen regret, but immediately a vast feeling of relief. Vengeance was a terrible burden. He'd never been sure anyway just what he would do if and when he ever found the old man.

Shoot him? Hardly. One murder rap was enough.

Turn him over to the authorities? Not likely. Lake Emerson himself was a wanted man for escaping from prison where he'd been serving a fifteen-year term for helping Sinclair in the bank robbery. He'd be strung up right alongside Sinclair.

But the English boy was determined to find out what had happened to twenty thousand dollars or so in brand-new golden eagles. The image of Sinclair throwing the bulging canvas bag on his shoulder and running down that cobbled street in Illinois was etched in acid in Lake's brain.

Pulling on a nickel cigar, Lake stared moodily at the craggy hills hemming in the town of Black Springs. A dismal sight — abandoned sagebrush shacks, rusting machinery poking into the sky, a few stunted piñon pines and junipers. The wind was still blowing, and Lake felt the gritty alkali dust between his teeth. Like much of the Comstock Lode country, Black Springs had run out of silver.

If Molly Robinson had found the bank loot in Sinclair's wagon, she wouldn't have stayed in a miserable town like this.

But on the other hand . . .

He glanced up at the stagehouse, a substantial two-story building of mixed brick, stone, and adobe, painted a firehouse red. At boomtown prices, ten years ago, it might easily have cost her twenty thousand dollars.

But then again, she just might have held on to the double eagles — coins that were worth a great deal more now than they were right after the Civil War.

His thoughts flew back to that dreadful time. At fourteen, he'd been gullible, eager to get rich quick. Orphaned at ten, he'd learned that life is kind only to the man who dares.

"Banks are robbed all the time, every day," Dr. Sinclair had stated flatly. "The bankers rob the people, we rob them back. Tit for tat. Nobody's ever caught. Jesse James is still on the loose, laughing at them all."

Lake's mother had died when he was a babe. After his father had been killed in a California gold field, the boy had drifted to Illinois to seek out his father's old friend Cedric Sinclair. The two men had come from England years before to seek their fortunes in America.

"You'll be rich. Rich is the only way to be in America." The man's cultured English voice echoed down the years as he had slyly persuaded the boy to help him rob a bank. The English boy had trusted the man implicitly.

Lost in the past, Lake was startled by a shout from a nearby wagon. "Ho there, Lake, glad you're back. That lion of yours is in a state. Can't get him to settle down."

Turning, Lake saw a roustabout who was splashing off the monkey cage with pails of cool water. "Henry won't even touch the slab of meat I gave him, and when I threw a bucket of water on him to cool him off, he lunged at me."

"It's the heat," Lake said wearily. "Henry always hates the heat. I'll settle him down."

The delighted squeals of wet monkeys followed Lake as he walked toward Henry's cage. The lion was in a royal tizzy, he found, nervously pacing in circles round and round the cage. His head was up, snorting, as if

23

catching an elusive scent. The amber eyes glittered almost feverishly.

"Damn," Lake exploded. That Sinclair girl had got the animal all riled up with her stroking and tickling. In his disturbed state, the beast would be impossible to handle in tomorrow's show. The trainer didn't dare enter the cage to soothe him. In his frenzy, the lion might run out on him, looking for a black-haired little girl.

"Mary Anne," Lake said clearly, suddenly inspired. "That's who you want, don't you, Henry?"

The lion growled deeply, stopped his pacing. The amber eyes narrowed to slits, glinting fiery gold.

"Blast if that beast doesn't understand every word I say," Lake breathed. "And they call them dumb animals."

Shaking his blond head in wonderment, Lake went on. "Okay, pal, I'll fetch your precious Mary Anne."

Picking up Henry's empty water pail, the liontamer started up the path to the stagehouse. The moon slid under a cloud. Halfway up the slope, head down in thought, he collided with the small body coming down.

The water pail went clattering to the rocks as Lake reached out with his arms to keep from falling. His hands landed on a tiny waist. To his delight, Lake found himself embracing Clover Sinclair. Her black hair was rippling over her shoulders, the silky mass laying heavily on his bare forearm.

The feel of the warm hair on his flesh jolted him all the way to his toes. He felt a beginning, answering warmth in his loins.

"Oh-h," the girl gasped, her head flung back, her coal-black eyes wide with surprise.

But she made no attempt to move out of his arms.

They could have met by design. Her soft hands clutched his shoulders, the sharp little nails biting down, then moved up to clasp together behind his neck. She seemed almost in a trance.

Instinctively, his own arms tightened, drawing her close. She sighed, a whispery sound that sent prickles up and down his spine. Her lips parted softly, revealing the tips of small white teeth.

All this Lake saw as in a dream. It was a dream, he knew, that had been long in coming, but now that it was here, he knew his fate. This girl, this night, this place, was always meant to be.

Like a thunderbolt it struck him. All these lonely years it wasn't Cedric Sinclair he'd been seeking.

No—it was the girl, the black-eyed daughter who had haunted his heart. Those deep, mysterious coal-black eyes had burned into his memory.

Too stunned to move, Clover studied the man looming over her. Aquiline nose, a fall of whitish-blond hair over a high-browed sculptured face.

Something leaped in the dark cave of her memory.

"I know you—from somewhere," she stammered. "Long ago—"

She fell silent, caught in the grip of the years.

"In a dream, perhaps," he said lightly, masking his own turmoil by a mocking laugh. "Women are always dreaming about me."

That laugh! Sharp, crisp, mocking. Clover stiffened. Suddenly the clouds of memory cleared. She was back on a bitter-cold night. The moon was bright, on a twisting, narrow mountain road. Wagon wheels were approaching fast, then overtaking them. At the last, in the split second before Papa's wagon hurtled into the ravine, Clover had heard a mocking laugh. Looking up in terror, she had seen a circus wagon with a name beginning "Grand—"

In the driver's seat, standing up, she'd seen a tall, muscular man whose whitish hair fell into a thin, angular face. At seven, she had sworn if she ever saw that man again, to kill him with her bare hands.

The man who was holding her so intimately, who looked as if he were going to kiss her at any moment, was her father's murderer. Her heart swelled up until it filled her breast. Clover shivered with excitement.

But was it the thrill of catching the villain at last, or the anticipation of his kiss that made her blood race?

"You . . . you killer," she exploded, letting her pent-up breath out in a whoosh. "Let me go, this instant."

Clover made a fierce but vain attempt to wriggle out of his arms.

Lake's gray eyes lightened, and he laughed again, this time to hide a pang of fear. She'd called him a killer. How much had her father told her of the bank robbery? If he revealed himself as her dear papa's young accomplice, the one who had taken all the punishment for the crime, she would promptly, without mercy, turn him over to the police.

"I've killed nobody in my life," Lake replied calmly, ignoring her struggles. Clasping his hands behind her waist, he held her fast. He grinned. "Except maybe a fly now and then who was pestering Henry."

"Henry . . ." she breathed.

"I love that lion," he stated simply.

"Oh-oo-oh," she sighed, "he's a lovely lion."

Lake felt a pang of jealousy. Ah, to be loved as she clearly loved that lion! But he must not tell her he knew

26

about her connection with Henry. Not yet. He couldn't risk spoiling his plans for revenge.

Lake's gray eyes took on a gleam. He'd seduce her before asking about the gold double eagles. Since he was a kid in the California gold fields, the handsome Englishman had known that females, without exception, were easily won over by masculine sweet talk.

Clover Sinclair promised to be an easy mark. He'd start with a kiss.

Himself fresh from his bath, Lake's nose wrinkled in the dark. The girl smelled of herbs, roast lamb, and lard. Tiny beads of sweat trembled on her upper lip. Aroused by her earthiness, he bent to press his lips on the salty drops.

His touch was feathery, but the effect on Clover was shattering. She tried to bring her lips together, to shut him out. But they seemed to have a will of their own, falling open for his invasion.

Groaning, Clover sank against the liontamer, her firm breasts in the sweat-damp shirt pushing into his broad chest.

Lake's lips parted, and he flicked the tip of his tongue into her open mouth. Her yielding warmth made him dizzy. Making love to this girl drove all thoughts of Sinclair and the money out of his head.

Responding helplessly, Clover's virginal body was in a ferment. Waves of heat washed over her. In her feminine region, she felt a sudden, startling moistness—a sweet, melting sensation that Spike, with his frantic pokings and proddings, had never induced.

She was kissing Papa's killer, and enjoying it enormously. Gasping, fearful, Clover managed to free herself from the man's iron grip.

The kiss ended, and, shocked, they were both silent for a long moment, then he picked up his pail abruptly. "My lion needs water, where is your pump?"

"Out back, in the yard. You'll have to pay. Water's scarce in these parts. We have to haul it in."

As the man raced toward the house, Clover hunched over on the path, hugging herself with her arms. Her limbs had turned to water, and she was afraid to move for fear of falling down. All of Spike Brant's kisses rolled into one had never had the sledgehammer effect the liontamer's single kiss was having on her.

Tarnation, what was she going to do with this liontamer? She had sworn to kill him for sideswiping her father's wagon ten years ago. But accusing him would serve no purpose. She had no proof.

Besides—a sudden, scary thought—he would get so angry he might refuse to sell Henry to her. She'd have to be sweet to the man, maybe even let him kiss her a few more times. Clover's stomach fluttered at the thought.

Eventually, she would have her revenge, she was certain. But not until she had Henry penned up securely safe in her own backyard.

The soft Nevada night was suddenly jolted by an earsplitting roar from the compound.

Henry!

Returning from the yard, Lake bolted past Clover with the full water pail, yelling at her, "Come on, that damn lion needs you."

Seconds later, Clover had reached the lion cage. She stuck a slender arm through the bars. "Henry, it's Mary Anne," she coaxed. "What's the matter, sweetie?"

Instantly, the pacing stopped, and the incessant

28

growl of an anxious lion became a kind of grumbling purr. Putting the tip of his snout through the bars, Henry reached for the stroking hand he knew so well in memory. His wet tongue licked hungrily at her sweet, salty flesh.

After a moment, when the lion's trembling ceased, Clover leaned her head against the shiny nose.

Without lifting her head, she ordered the liontamer, "Unlatch the cage, please, I'm going in."

"You'll be mauled," he replied sharply, shaking his head so vigorously the white-blond hair fell into his eyes. "Lions are as unpredictable as the weather."

"I know," she said testily, "I used to live with them." She must be careful not to reveal that she and this particular lion were old friends.

Shrugging, Lake opened the cage door, and Clover entered with the water pail. Turning from the bars, Henry reared up on his hind legs and placed both huge paws on her shoulders.

Amazingly, throwing back her head, Clover started singing, " 'Oh, my darling, oh my darling, oh my darling Clementine—' "

It was a song she used to sing to the suckling cub when he was restless. Sinking to his haunches, Henry settled down, his head between his paws, like a sleepy child.

The circus folk who had gathered to watch let out a collective, admiring "ah-ah-h."

"Give me some meat," Clover ordered, "and send for some beer."

Lake slid a long slab of beef between the bars. Sniffing at it, Clover grated, "No wonder he won't eat, this stuff is as tough as boiled shoe leather."

"Can't get fresh," Lake growled. "Nothing lives in this blasted desert."

"Give me your knife."

Snatching the trainer's knife through the bars, Clover started cutting the meat into smaller pieces, tossing them into the water pail to soften. Her breasts jiggled with her movements, and the tip of a pink tongue thrust out from between her teeth. Lake found himself staring. Several men from the crowd drew closer to watch this amazing girl.

What a bewitching minx, Lake reflected. He was going to have a devil of a time telling her that her old man had been both bank robber and killer.

The cage door closed softly. Clover Sinclair leaped out, holding an empty water pail. Henry had eaten the meat, water, and beer mixture, then curled up for a long sleep.

Filled with awe, the circus people clapped quietly, murmuring praises.

"We could use you in our circus," Lake said, chuckling. "You have a gift."

Her reply, when it came, was almost inaudible. "I'm only good with lions, actually. I had a cub once—"

"Henry?"

She paused, gazing at the crowd drifting away to the tents. "Ah, no. My cub died," she lied.

"Too bad."

Now, an inner voice urged Lake. Offer to give her Henry. Ask her about the robbery money.

Turning to start back toward the house, Clover remarked in an offhand way, "Besides, I'm to be married in October." She giggled. "A lion just wouldn't fit in."

Married! A sharp pang of loss pierced Lake's heart,

30

but quickly rallying, he persisted. "I'll give you a good price."

Turning back, she said, "Why would you do that?"

He sighed. "He's getting old. Cranky, much of the time. His appetite's enormous, and sometimes he's too lazy to do his routine."

"Maybe the trainer's at fault," she said tartly.

She'd been staring at the lion wagon which sparkled from a washing down after the parade. In shiny gilt letters across the top, she read, "Grandiose Traveling Circus." In her excitement yesterday at seeing Henry again, she had failed to notice the name of the outfit. "Grand—" was the partial name she had glimpsed on the wagon that had nudged the Sinclair wagon off the road. All doubts that this man was her father's killer fled.

Lake heard a sharp intake of breath, and the cameo face that now turned to his had gone stark white.

"How about it," he urged. "You'd make a far better trainer than me."

"No, thanks," she said in a strangled voice. Whipping around, she ran back up the hill to the stagehouse. Tomorrow, when she was in firmer control of her emotions, she would bargain for Henry.

First Henry, then revenge.

Chapter Two

The roaring started at dawn, an echoing, deep-bellied rumble, jerking Clover from a fitful sleep. Leaping out of bed she threw open the window, pushing her head out to drink in the sound she loved so much. The soft whinnies of the horses, the gibbering of the monkeys, the sight of the pitched tents, all brought back many happy memories.

Although it was now eleven o'clock, Henry's intermittent roars could still be heard all over Black Springs. Clover chuckled as she dressed. Henry was not on the warpath. Setting the lion to roaring, the elephants to trumpeting, and the leopards to screaming on the morning of the show was a timeworn circus trick. It always guaranteed a capacity crowd, eager to see the savage beasts for themselves.

Clover had yearned to visit Henry this morning but had to help with the overflow breakfast crowd in the dining room. Just as well, she mused. She dreaded running into that liontamer again. He was precisely the kind of man Molly had always warned her to stay away from.

As she stood before her bedroom mirror dressing for the Centennial festivities, Clover touched her lips with her fingers, remembering the heat of his masculine lips. Just thinking about that bold, searching kiss gave her the shivers. Through the night, it kept returning—that lovely warmth she'd felt in his arms.

Picking up a wide pink satin ribbon from the bureau top, Clover pinned it squarely in front of the swirly topknot of black hair. The ribbon hung down on both sides of her face, giving her the look of a bride.

The sprigged voile gown, with its alternating rows of embroidered violets and rosebuds, enhanced the virginal, dewy look. Clover grimaced at her image in the mirror. She looked like a bride.

For the first time since her engagement at Christmas, Clover was forced to face the imminent prospect of being a wife.

"You can't go on wearing trousers, darling," Molly had said. "Let's go down to the emporium and order you some dresses."

Clover wanted to weep. No longer would it be just her and Molly. Each morning when she awoke, Spike's heavy, masculine form would be at her side.

Sudden tears choked her throat. She put both hands over her eyes as if to shut out the harsh reality of the world.

"Do you have a headache, dear?"

Molly's voice sounded from the doorway, and as Clover uncovered her face and looked up, the older woman rushed into the room to enfold the girl in her arms.

Kissing her adoptive mother soundly on the lips, Clover laughed. "No, of course not. I was just resting

33

my eyes for a moment. They say it makes them sparkle."

Drawing back, Molly surveyed the girl. "Your eyes are lovely, as always. In fact—" she broke into a wide smile—"you're as pretty as a picture in that gown."

"I hope Spike likes it," Clover caroled, waltzing around the room to make the wide, gored skirt flare out around her white kid shoes.

"He'll adore it, you look very . . ." Molly groped for a word.

Clover arched a brow. "Seductive?"

Frowning, Molly snapped. "Hardly. A husband need not seduce his wife."

The dancing had brought a flush to her cheeks and a warmth to her blood, and Clover instinctively cupped her bosom, sweetly outlined by the snug bodice. She did feel different this morning—softer, rounder. Her breasts seemed fuller, the nipples more rigid than usual.

"Somehow, though, it's sad, leaving girlhood behind," Clover mused. "Did you feel that way when you were my age?"

There was no answer from Molly, who had sunk into a chair and was gazing out the window. Her face was white as chalk, her blue eyes sunken into her head. The telltale red spots of tuberculosis stained each gaunt cheek. The woman was not yet fifty but looked seventy.

In her Sunday-best black dress and hat to match, this wonderful woman seemed to Clover like an apparition of death. Clover's heart contracted. Long before her wedding day, she might lose the only mother she'd ever known.

The doctor from Carson City had given the woman a

potion to help her sleep. But there was nothing else he could do.

"Her only hope is to lie flat on her back for at least a year. Drink lots of milk, eggs, butter. No work, no beer, no talking," he'd said.

"I'd rather die," Molly had told the man tartly.

Her casual tone masking her anxiety, Clover remarked, "Now that I'm to be married, why don't you go to Eagle Valley to live? Chief Red Hawk wants you there. He's promised that you'll be treated like a queen."

"Indians don't have queens," Molly whispered weakly. "An old squaw is just an old squaw."

"If Spike and I got married right away, would you go?"

"Hmm." Molly's faded blue eyes gleamed. "Getting anxious, are you?"

Clover blushed. "Maybe." If Molly only knew how much she dreaded the wedding night.

The clock in the dining room struck the half hour. "Where's Spike?" Molly bolted from the chair with false energy. "We should get started. The parade starts at eleven."

"I imagine he overslept. He and his father had an appointment last night with a man in Carson City about some sheep. Mr. Brant wants to give Spike a ranch for a wedding present."

Slipping on a brand-new pair of long white gloves, Clover added, "Don't worry, they'll show up. Mr. Brant is making a big speech after the parade."

"Sheep?" Molly shot the girl a sharp glance. "The Brants have never been sheep men."

Clover shrugged. "Now that the silver's played out . . ."

She lowered her eyes, hoping that Molly wouldn't see the lie in their dark depths. Sick as she was, the older woman would go into a tizzy if she knew that Spike and his father were meeting with some malcontent Indians from Eagle Valley. The Brants had been trying for years to buy the valuable, silver-rich land from the tribes.

But it might also send the sick woman flying off to Eagle Valley, to keep the Washo and Paiute Indians from selling their last remaining Nevada land. Clover's heart lifted. Once with the beloved friends of her youth, Molly might stay there.

"Ladies, you both look bewitching," Spike boomed as mother and daughter came downstairs and entered the kitchen. Setting his coffee mug on the cold stove, he grabbed Clover by the shoulders and kissed her on the cheek. "You, my bride, look good enough to eat."

The trio started off for town, Spike manfully linking arms with the two women. Except for the old Indian Pedro, who stayed behind to guard the place, the stagehouse was deserted. Everyone in town would be at the Centennial celebration.

A short way from home, Spike's mother, Mrs. Brant, joined them, and the two older women walked ahead, chatting. Spike and Clover lagged behind. Clover didn't worry about being late. Nothing could start without the Brants; they were the town's leading family.

"Everyone's staring at us," Spike murmured, squeezing her arm with his. He looked proud enough to burst.

Clover simpered. "We *do* make a handsome couple."

She was proud to be seen with Spike. In blue pinstriped trousers and creamy, ruffled shirt, a dapper straw hat on his head, which he lifted for every passing female, he was a veritable fashionplate.

More than one brow shot skyward, though, as if to say, "Is this pink-and-white vision our Clover, who always looks like a ragamuffin boy?"

Her heart beat proudly. As Mrs. Ralph Brant, Jr. she would be somebody in this town. Keeping Henry would pose no problem. A Brant could do no wrong.

"Spike, let's move up our wedding day," she said, abruptly. "Why wait until I'm eighteen?"

Whirling in surprise, he faced her, grinning. "Is my little virgin getting anxious?"

She colored. "It isn't that—well, not completely. It's Molly. I want her to retire—"

Pulling her roughly to him, Spike held her close, kissing her feverishly on the neck, below her swept-up hair. "Mmm," he mumbled, "you're hot. We'll tie the knot tomorrow. Can't wait to get you between the sheets." He pulled away. "Tomorrow. I'll fetch the judge from Carson City."

Two girls walking by giggled loudly, and, embarrassed, Clover said softly, "Next week, Spike. Molly and I need a few days to prepare the wedding supper and fix up the stagehouse."

To cover up her inner turmoil over her sudden decision to marry, she asked, "Were your talks in Carson City successful?"

"Papa feels good about it, though no settlement was reached. We're cheered by the fact that not all the Indians in Eagle Valley want to stay there, sitting on all that gold and silver."

"I guess not," she said faintly, feeling an inner chill. Until now, she had not taken seriously Mr.

Brant's attempts to get the paradisal valley away from the Indians.

Front Street looked festive. American flags were everywhere, flapping crazily in the hot wind. Everybody in town and many outsiders as well, swarmed about in their Sunday best. Hawkers peddled lemonade and seltzer water.

They reached the grandstand. "If we can get that land," Spike said confidently, "you and I won't be raising any goddam sheep."

Spreading his white hankerchief on a front-row bench for Clover to sit on, Spike furtively looked around, then hissed, "Before the year is out, we'll be silver mining in Eagle Valley. Papa says the man wasn't born who doesn't have his price. That includes Indians."

A blare of horns from the brass band coming down the street cut off further talk. A straggly parade of Civil War vets from both sides in shined-up uniforms were joined by a small U.S. Cavalry unit from a nearby fort. Nevada had been courted by both North and South during the war for its wealth in silver. But in 1864, they were made a state, becoming part of the Union.

A fife-and-drum corps in red-and-white colonial uniforms brought up the rear, stopping before the grandstand on which Mr. Brant and other dignitaries were already seated. Molly was there, too, as a pioneer citizen, right next to a United States congressman, who looked hot and bored.

The band struck up "Yankee Doodle" and everyone joined in the singing. After a boisterous "My Country 'tis of Thee," the crowd sat down, noisy and restless. Mr. Brant, resplendent in silk top hat and bright blue suit, gave a long speech, in which he took full credit for making peace with the Indians and for the future prosperity of Black Springs.

"The silver is gone," he said, "but Black Springs will flourish as a crossroads. I, Ralph Brant, will get you the railroad."

Cheers from the crowd. A few Indians stood silently, arms folded on chests, at the edge of the crowd. Obviously, they were not happy about the railroad, which would gobble up even more of their ancestral lands.

Except for a few sheep and cattle ranches, most in the town made their living from a continuous flow of stage and wagon traffic from the south and east toward California. Brant was dickering with the Central Pacific for a railroad spur. If that happened, Black Springs would be as populated as Carson City.

At the mention of the Indians, Molly flinched but stared stonily ahead over the crowd. After the last massacre at Tahoe, it was Molly who had risked her life to parley with the tribes. She had persuaded the Indian agency to set aside Eagle Valley for the remnants of the Paiutes and Washoes not already on reservations.

The congressman spoke, drawing cheers again about the new unlimited silver coinage policy. Molly got up to say a few words to wild applause. The band played again, and in the silence, Henry's roar could be clearly heard. When she left the house with Spike, Clover had noticed that the big tent was not yet erected. She had wondered how they would drive the stakes into the hard ground.

She got her answer. Brant rose to his feet, and waving his arms for quiet, called out importantly, "The circus will be staged on the flats behind Molly's stagehouse. There will be no big tent. Come one, come all, it won't cost you a red cent. Ralph Brant is paying for all of you."

As he finished, Henry roared again, as if on cue. The crowd erupted into laughter, and then pandemonium broke loose, as men, women, children, raced to get front row seats for the circus. A bench would be reserved for the Brants, so Clover strolled lazily with Spike toward the flats behind the stagehouse.

"By the way, darling girl, I heard you petted the raging lion yesterday." Spike was frowning down at her.

"He's not really raging, he's trained to seem that way. Don't forget, I lived with circus animals for years. I love them, I go every year when the circus comes to town."

"Stay away from that beast today," Spike ordered. Then, more gently, "If you want a lion of your own, I'll buy you a cub. We can declaw it and keep it penned up for you to play with, until our children come along."

Whipping around, Clover faced Spike angrily. "An animal needs its claws, it's cruel to cut them off."

Spike's heavy brows came together, and his lips tightened. "Well, then, no lion, my girl. It's high time you forgot all this circus nonsense, anyway."

Clover was still fuming inside at his domineering tone as they took their seats at ringside beside Spike's parents. Molly had gone home after the speeches, pleading that she'd had enough excitement for one day. Spike and his father immediately put their heads together, launching into a whispered conversation about Eagle Valley.

As the acts began, the magic of the big ring began to work on Clover. Spotted dogs jumped through hoops, danced to a tune on a fiddle, and then obediently leaped on each other's backs to make a shaky pyramid.

Clowns cartwheeled around the ring, conducted a silly baseball game, and yelled bad jokes through a megaphone. A bareback rider in spangled pink tights brought disapproving clucks from the ladies of Black Springs. With effortless ease, she struck one graceful pose after another, swooping, pirouetting, balancing on one leg atop a snow-white steed. She galloped off amid thunderous applause, and calls for more.

Though far from fierce, the leopards were energetic, making a pyramid, leaping through fiery hoops, jumping up and down from stools at their trainer's commands.

After a short intermission, the three-man circus band struck up a tune, and four roustabouts dragged in large sections of wire netting, which they speedily set up to form a large cage.

Running off, they returned immediately with the blue lion wagon from the parade. The music stopped, but the drum continued to roll, with dramatic intensity, as the ringmaster mounted his stool. Doffing his hat with a flourish, he bowed from the waist.

"Ladies and gentlemen, you are about to see a death-defying feat of courage. Captain Lake Emerson, late of His Majesty's British Grenadiers—"

Clover started. So that's his name. Lake. An unusual name for an Englishman. Oddly, though, she knew she'd heard it before. Perhaps from her early circus days.

At mention of his name, the liontamer sprinted from the opening in the crowd. He was truly resplendent in yellow trousers, a high, cockaded hat with yellow feathers, and a military jacket with gold epaulettes. There

41

was an evil-looking whip in his right hand.

"If he so much as touches Henry with that whip," Clover gritted under her breath, "I'll run out there and strangle him."

Spike threw her a curious glance, but did not interrupt his conversation with his father.

Captain Emerson cracked his whip on the bars of the blue cage. After a moment, the lion obligingly yawned, baring its fang-like teeth. After another moment, he roared. The audience rippled with anticipation.

Up went the ringmaster's arms for silence. "Please, good people of Black Springs, I beg you not to make a sound during the lion act." He pointed at Henry. "Witness the ferocity of the beast."

Henry yawned again. Clover giggled. Her sweet, lovable lion might fall asleep if that longwinded ringmaster didn't hurry up.

"Do not applaud," the stentorian voice went on, "no matter how much you are tempted. You might startle the savage beast or disturb the concentration of brave Captain Emerson."

Brave Captain Emerson smiled bewitchingly at the enthralled spectators. Dammit, the man was devilishly charming, mused Clover. She had a lightning vision of that blond head on the pillow beside her.

The ringmaster shuddered audibly. "Terrible accidents have happened—"

It was the usual hokum. Clover smiled to herself. But the faces of the audience were dead serious, even scared. Mr. Emerson had done perhaps too good a job with the forced roaring all morning.

"I give you without further ado the daredevil Captain Emerson and the King of Beasts from Darkest Africa

42

—" the ringmaster shouted.

"Nee-eer-o!"

"His name is Henry," Clover spoke aloud.

"What's that, sweetheart?" Spike turned from his father.

"Nothing."

Spike and Mr. Brant both sat up straight, giving full attention to the show. As the liontamer opened the door of the blue wagon, Spike instinctively slid his hand to his gun in its holster at his belt.

A crack of the liontamer's whip brought the lion into the open door of the larger cage. With Henry safe inside the netting, Emerson slammed the cage door shut. There was a latch but no lock, Clover noted.

Trainer and cat faced each other. There was a tense silence, neither moved a muscle. Suddenly, the man hurled the whip aside, picking up a wooden stick with a tassel on the end from the cage floor.

Henry growled. Emerson flicked the tassel under the lion's chin. Baring his teeth tiredly, the lion sat back on his haunches, waiting for the trainer's next move.

Clover stole a glance at Spike. His eyes were wide, and his mouth half-open. His right hand was still on his gun beneath his light jacket.

Then, slowly, to the rapt attention of the onlookers, the liontamer started to undress. The feathery hat came off first, then the epauletted jacket and the golden trousers. He flung them into a corner of the cage with a kind of regal contempt.

Tall and muscular, Lake Emerson faced his lion and his public. Flesh-colored tights outlined powerful legs and thighs. His bare chest was covered with a whitish fuzz of hair. His arms were long and sinewy.

A gasp, followed by a sigh, came from every feminine mouth. Clover's heart fluttered, and her stomach began to warm as she recalled the feel of those strong arms last night, crushing her against him.

Another touch of the tassel started Henry trotting round and round the cage, his hairy tail swishing, his massive head held high. He growled deep in his throat. The animal was obviously enjoying the act. What an actor!

Clover's eyes misted. She had taught Henry how to walk that way—seemingly indifferent, but loving every minute. Not all lions were trainable, but her sweet, adorable cub had been an unusually clever lion.

A standard repertoire of lion tricks followed, Henry going through his paces dutifully. A growl and a snarl now and then kept the audience alert.

He sat down, stood up, rolled over, played dead, forepaws up in the air. There was wild applause, despite the ringmaster's warning. He was certainly no captain, reflected Clover, but Lake Emerson, Englishman, was good—very good. She found herself wondering what he was doing with such a small outfit as the Grandiose Circus.

Man and beast rested, the lion being held at bay with the extended stick. A roll of drums brought the ringmaster back into the ring.

"Captain Emerson will now attempt the most daring and death-defying feat of all. After opening the lion's jaws with his bare hands, he will put his head, totally unprotected, into the killer animal's mouth."

The audience gasped in amazement. Even Clover felt prickles of fear tearing up and down her spine. No matter how well trained or docile the animal, this was a dangerous trick. Idly, thoughtlessly — or even play-fully — the lion might clamp down.

Only one piercing of those sharp fangs could sever a man's neck.

Stalking slowly toward the animal step by step, Lake Emerson dropped to one knee, putting both hands on the lion's mouth. Thrusting his head in without hesitation, he turned sideways to look at the audience.

He grinned, devilishly, then, after a moment, he pulled out his head, bounding upright.

Theatrically, with one hand holding the stick pointed at the lion, the other thumbing his belt, Lake Emerson bowed deeply to the enthralled audience.

But, instantly, the cheers became shrieks of horror. Stretching out his massive neck, Henry clamped down on the trainer's forearm. Writhing, grimacing, Captain Emerson yanked his free arm from the belt of his tights, fastening on his bitten arm, prying it loose from the vicious teeth.

Blood spurted from between his fingers.

Rising to his feet at Clover's side, Spike cocked his pistol, aiming it at the ring.

"No," Clover screamed, striking his forearm with a gloved hand. "It's all a trick, the trainer's not really wounded."

But her words were lost in the general pandemonium. Women screamed, pulling their children to their breasts, running for their lives out of the arena. The men pulled out guns and rifles. The air was peppered with gunshots.

Wild with fear, Clover ran into the ring to protect her sweet Henry from being slaughtered needlessly. It was an old-time circus trick. A sausage skin filled with pig's blood from a butcher was slipped under the liontamer's tights before the performance.

Surreptitiously, in the thunder of the applause, Captain Emerson had tugged the blood bag from his tights, pouring the contents on his arm.

Cursing her billowing skirt, Clover lifted it high as she raced to save her lion. Bullets rang about her ears. The ringmaster stood on his stool, calling for calm.

"Stay back, do not shoot your guns. You may hit Captain Emerson or some innocent child." But the warning shout was lost in the din of screams and yells and gunfire.

Men were bandaging the trainer's arm. Blood was dripping on the rocks. Captain Emerson swayed, as if about to faint.

In his cage, Henry sat back on his haunches. His act was over. He yawned, then sank to the ground, forepaws out.

"Hey, what the hell—"

The ringmaster took hold of Clover's skirt as she flew by, but she tore loose.

Spike yelled frantically, "Clover, Clover!"

Captain Emerson stuck out a booted foot to stop Clover, but leaping past him, she bolted to the cage. Catching Spike instead, who was in fast pursuit, the trainer knocked him down.

As the men fought, Clover opened the cage door. At sight of her, Henry reared up, amiably trotting toward her.

"Run, Henry, run," she hissed.

Picking up the trainer's discarded tasseled stick, she struck the animal smartly on the rump. Gracefully, he bolted out of the cage, Clover running at his side. The guns fell silent. People shaded their eyes against the broiling sun to see what their heads refused to believe. That crazy Sinclair girl and the African lion became specks on the horizon.

Nobody noticed the wide grin on Lake Emerson's face.

At eight o'clock, the liontamer was no longer smiling. A morose scowl wrinkled his handsome face as he stared into his third tankard of beer at Walter Hill's saloon on Front Street. A thick ham sandwich sat alongside a fat dill pickle on the plate before him. Both were untouched.

His thoughts were black. That damn girl was in trouble. Lions—even the tamest of them—were unpredictable. You can never take the jungle completely out of a wild animal. Fooling around with Henry securely locked behind bars was one thing—but creeping around in those dark hills with a frightened, hungry beast was asking for a bloody death.

Shuddering, Lake closed his eyes, trying to blot out a sudden image of that lovely head in Henry's giant maw. Even now, the savage beast might be tearing her limb from limb and dragging her tender parts into the bush.

Lions always ate the stomach first, burying the heart to enjoy later. Lake shuddered, imagining the still-pulsing, tender heart of the girl he had kissed beneath a layer of forest dirt.

The saloon was jammed. Every able-bodied man in Black Springs—and some not so able—had gone into the hills after Clover Sinclair and the African lion. Now, hours later, driven home by nightfall, they were in the saloon, drinking, eating, and oiling their firearms for the big lion hunt scheduled to start at first light.

Spike Brant was drunk and loud. "Walter, ol' pal, how would you like a nice li'l ol' lion's head to hang behind your bar?"

"Fine, Spike, fine, it'd be a real tourist attraction," replied the saloonkeeper. Walter turned, one elbow on the worn oaken bar, gazing rapturously at the spot now adorned with a moth-eaten elk's head with arching antlers.

"It'll be the only African lion ever killed in the wild in America," the saloonkeeper added enthusiastically. "We'll be famous."

Yanking his rifle from his lap, Spike aimed it over the man's head and pulled the trigger. There was a thunderous roar, and shot splattered the bar and wall, narrowly missing the astonished barkeep and filling the stuffed elk's head with pellet holes. The massive head plunged to the floor, where it broke in half with a sharp crack.

"Merciful Jesus," a female voice yelled and Molly Robinson tore from the door she had just entered. Grabbing Spike's gun, she roared, "You're drunk, Spike. Go home and sleep it off." She wrenched the weapon from his hands.

"Nope, gotta find my sweetie." With a cry of anguish, the young man laid his head on the bar. Great wracking sobs shook his brawny shoulders.

"Nothin' to do but go into every damn one of them ol' mines," Walter muttered, grimacing as he picked up his fallen elk's head. "Even the ones that's unsafe."

He shrugged. "Must be fifty of 'em, most with rotten

timbers."

Molly whirled angrily. "My little girl's got more sense than to go into an abandoned shaft."

Tugging at Spike's shoulders, she yelled crossly, "Somebody give me a hand with this man."

Two strong men half carried the inebriated Spike to the far end of the long room, where they stretched him out on a bench. Others called out sympathetically.

"Don't worry, Spike, we'll find your gal."

"She raised that lion from a cub, ain't that so, lion-tamer? It wouldn't harm a hair on her head."

All heads turned to the table where Lake still leaned, eyes closed, against the adobe wall. Molly had sat down opposite, gratefully accepting the mug of steaming coffee fetched by Walter.

"Tell them, Lake," she urged, touching the Englishman's arm to rouse him. "Tell 'em all there's no danger."

"That's right," Lake mumbled. "Henry thinks she's his mother. Nobody eats his own mother."

He'd been forced to tell the town about Clover as a little girl and how she'd tended Henry for two years in a circus. Wisely, he had not disclosed the truth about his wounded arm. Only Clover must know that Henry's attack on his trainer was all an act. Lake had his future to think about.

"Clover's found her Henry after all these years," sighed Molly happily. "She just wants to spend a little time with him alone. She'll come home when she's good and ready, not a minute before."

Raising her voice, she shouted over the din. "No use goin' on any damn fool lion hunt."

Lake's head came up, his light gray eyes glazed with worry. "Her sweet cub is no longer kittenish, he could

49

turn nasty—"

Molly silenced him with a look, shaking her head. "She's okay," she said. "I know it. I raised Clover to take care of herself."

"We must stop this hunt," Lake yelled, turning to face the men. But nobody was listening. The men of Black Springs were afire with hunting fever. It had been many years since any critter bigger than a weasel had been caught in the nearby hills. Once, back in Indian times, when the gold rush had just begun, elk, bear, cougars, and the like had filled the forests. But soon the white man's voracious appetite for meat had killed them all or driven them to the higher Sierra mountainsides.

Some of the men had wandered outside to stand on the dried-mud street in front of the saloon. They stared at the hills. Beyond the arid flats and foothills rose the majestic peaks of the Sierra Nevada range, clear into California.

"She's out there somewhere," one said.

"We'll get the beast if it takes a month—"

A fear that no one had dared to express in Spike's hearing now surfaced.

"There's still Injuns out there in the mountains, livin' wild—"

"Nah, the Injuns know she's Molly's kid. They won't touch her—"

"I wouldn't put any money on it," commented Ralph Brant, who had just climbed off his horse. "Lots of Injuns heading west from Idaho and beyond, looking to settle. Drifters, outlaws—none of them ever heard of famous Molly Robinson, the peacemaker."

Laughing dryly, he joined the men, turning his eyes

to the hills. "A pretty scalp like Clover's could be mighty tempting." He rubbed his chin. " 'Course, some of 'em might prefer her live and kicking."

"Up to your old tricks, eh, Ralph?" Molly rasped, throwing her shawl around her shoulders as she exited the saloon and rushed past the clump of men.

Whirling, Brant put a staying hand on her arm. "What's that you said, Molly?"

"Injun baiting, that's what. Nevada Indians don't rape white girls. You know damn well there ain't a warlike Indian left in these parts. Any trouble in the past was caused by greedy landgrabbers like you."

Brant laughed dryly, then turned serious. "This is no time to be arguing about that, my good woman. I have here—" he rustled in his trousers pocket and drew out a paper—"a search warrant from the sheriff in Carson City, Black Springs having no law officer of its own."

"More's the pity," Molly grumbled.

In the moonlight Ralph saw the woman's consumptive face tighten as she scanned the paper. "Just what do you intend to search, Mr. Brant?"

"Your stagehouse, ma'am." He addressed the men outside, who had suddenly grown into a crowd. "I'm of the opinion that your gal and her lion are right here in Black Springs."

He pushed his face into Molly's. "Sure as I'm sitting on this horse, you know damn well where that gal is, Molly Robinson, and if you don't turn her over, I'll slap you in jail."

Glinting on his vest in the moonlight was a brand-new deputy sheriff's badge.

"Humph. I see that a search warrant wasn't the only thing you picked up in Carson City," Molly snapped, flipping the badge with her finger. Although she had planned to marry Clover to his son, she had never been overfond of Ralph Brant.

Walking at a rapid clip up Front Street the old woman set a smart pace for the parade of men marching toward the stagehouse. A half hour later, Ralph Brant admitted defeat. He and his men had poked into every corner of the sprawling structure and outhouses. A few hillside caves where fruit and meat were stored were also cleaned out.

Standing in Molly's front door, he scratched his head. "I still think you know where she took that beast," he said. "But no way on earth can I force you to tell us, you being so sick and all."

As if confirming his remarks, a hacking cough wracked the woman's skinny frame. "Now get out of here and leave me in peace. I need my rest." She covered her face with a blood-spotted handkerchief.

Her loud coughing continued until the men and horses were out of sight. It stopped suddenly as she turned inside and spoke in low tones to Pedro, the old Indian who worked around the place. After a brief, spirited discussion, with Pedro clucking and shaking his pigtailed head, the old Indian nodded "yes."

Molly was going out into the night to find Clover, she told the old man. No one must know. Samson, the Chinese cook, and two lads who helped out and slept on the hearth at night were put on guard.

"Make certain nobody follows me," she hissed.

The moon was high, and coyotes were yapping in the hills as the old woman walked rapidly away from the stagehouse toward the hills. The Grandiose Circus had already packed up and left for its next engagement, and the flats beyond the town were deserted.

Molly was ninety-nine percent certain where Clover and Henry were hiding. She had to find them before Spike or some other drunken, trigger-happy fool stumbled on them.

Chapter Three

Her chest still wracked from the two-mile run from town, Clover sat outside the old mine entrance leaning on the rotting post. Blood ran in scarlet threads from numerous scratches on her arms where the thin voile had ripped on thorny shrubs along the way. Her delicate white kid slippers were in tatters from climbing rocks. Tearing them from her feet, she tossed them into the air with a mighty swing.

"So much for being a lady," she muttered. The whole business of dressing up like a fancy woman was comical, but she was too exhausted to laugh.

She had not taken the well-worn trail, but a winding, torturous, hidden way, known only to herself and Molly. It was safe, she decided, to rest in the open air for a few minutes before entering the dark tunnel of the mine, where she could hide from any pursuers. Hopefully, they would expect her to escape through the heavily wooded eastern slopes leading to Lake Tahoe.

Though winded himself, Henry trotted busily in a wide circle, establishing his claim to this small bit of land. He did this, in the jungle way, by urinating freely at various points — against a wrecked shack, on a sage bush or stunted juniper trunk the wind had twisted into grotesque shapes, now partially cloaking the mine opening.

After sniffing his "marks" again to make sure his animal magic was strong enough, the lion trotted to Clover and squatted companionably at her side.

"My brave protector," she smiled tearfully, reaching out to touch his moist snout. Rumbling, he shook his head, lifting it high, tucking his hind legs tight to his body, and curling his bushy tail around his haunch. Henry loved being touched by Mary Anne, who now was Clover.

He gazed regally toward the canyon walls, once heavily wooded with pine, cedar, aspen, mountain sage, and manzanita as if posing for a portrait. Laughing with delight at having him to herself at last, Clover chucked him under the chin, digging vigorously into his whiskers with her fingers. It was like old times. The years rolled back. She was a girl of seven, he a growing young giant, trustful, happy.

Alas, now they no longer dwelt in the safety of a small circus. The two of them were in mortal danger from trigger-happy men. Clover was certain that a fear-crazed gunman would not hesitate to shoot her down if she tried to defend Henry.

The slope they sat on was called Superstition Hill, because so many miners had died here, both in cave-ins and at the hands of angry Indians whose land had been usurped. It was also rumored to have been an ancient Indian burial ground. The terrain was rocky, littered with shacks and debris, crisscrossed by rusting rails which had been used to haul supplies by cart in the boom days.

The day-long wind had died; everything was still. She would hear a footstep long before any intruder appeared over the brow of the hill. Henry would certainly sense danger before she did.

The sky turned gray, then blue, then purple and red, bathing the rusting summit clutter in a rosy hue. She rose from the hill holding out the liontamer's tasseled stick and made a scissoring motion with both arms. Promptly obeying the familiar command, Henry followed her into the dark tunnel of the mine. Inside, it was cool and dark. There was a distant sound of water trickling, vestige of the spring that had once run black from heavy silver deposits.

Stumbling at a point where the roof dropped suddenly, she felt for the plaid circus blanket she always kept there. A wall of boulders stopped further progress. They'd been placed there to keep coyotes and other scavengers from the bodies of ten men who had died in a cave-in years before.

Henry waited as she settled herself on the blanket. It was the same blanket she had dragged from her father's shattered medicine wagon right after the accident.

She'd kept it here, as a remembrance, and in the early years in Black Springs, she had come here often to think of Papa and the circus and Henry.

Clover curled up in the blanket. Molly would come soon, with food and water.

"It's all right, Henry," she murmured sleepily. "You stand guard."

The blanket had never been washed, and it smelled wonderfully of circus straw and animals. Henry stretched out across the mouth of the cave, barring entrance. His heavy breathing was the only sound in the night. Clover felt safe, transported back to her childhood when she and Henry had been a family.

Her stomach rumbled with hunger. So excited at seeing Henry performing again, she'd put nothing in it but some coffee all day. Long ago, on that terrible night when Papa had been killed, she'd been hungry, too. He'd been in such an awful hurry to get to San Francisco and the boat that they had not stopped to eat. Tiredly, she thought about that time and how she'd stumbled from the rocks where she'd been thrown from the tumbling wagon trying desperately to wake up Papa who sprawled nearby, his eyes half-open, staring. She had known he was dead.

That first night she'd curled up in the blanket beside Papa's body, huddling close, waiting for him to come back to life. The second night she spent in this very mineshaft.

Molly would surely bring meat for Henry. Maybe she'd bring that Captain Emerson with her to help handle the lion. Clover's hand clutched the stick that she'd taken under the blanket with her. In her heart was a cold resolve. If that murderer dared take Henry, she would command him to charge. Lions will do anything for their original trainers, especially if that person had supplanted its natural mother.

Her heart warmed by hate and vengeance, Clover fell asleep.

A pale moon moved in and out of shifting clouds as Molly started her climb up Superstition Hill. She did not pause for breath but made steady progress, setting one foot in front of the other doggedly, as she had been taught when a child with the Washos. Those who did not keep step were often left behind to die on the trail or fall prey to the invading white men.

"Let me carry this," Pedro had pleaded as he lifted the heavy woven basket into place on her shoulders. In the basket was a ten pound chunk of fresh lamb for the lion, a jug of water, a flask of coffee, some cooked meat and fried piñon cakes for Clover, and a change of garments for the girl.

Gruffly, but with affection, Molly shoved her Indian pal away. "Carrying burdens is a woman's work." Thoughtfully, she gazed at the man's strong, weathered face. "Follow me, but do not show yourself until Clover has the lion under control."

Lowering her voice, she added, "I mean to persuade Clover to flee to Eagle Valley. You will take her there, White Hawk."

The Indian grunted; he was obviously pleased at being called by his Indian name. The two were of an age, having grown up in the same tribal family. Their early years were spent in a snug wooden house along Pyramid Lake. They had been promised to each other, but White Hawk's manhood had been torn off in a skirmish with settlers. He could neither marry nor fight as warrior. Shamed, he had left the tribe, wandering for many years in the West. A mission priest in California had converted him, christening him Pedro. Stumbling into Black Springs one day, he had met Molly again and settled in with her at the hostel.

Molly would trust her life to the old brave. And Clover's, too, if necessary. Drawing her cloak tight around her head, Molly mumbled grimly, "Clover is in real danger."

As she neared the summit of Superstition Hill, Molly heard Henry's soft growl. Pedro slunk into the shadows behind the rocks.

Molly took a few more steps before calling out, "Clover, Clover."

Growling, the massive animal emerged from the tunnel, followed by the girl herself. Clover ran to Molly, sobbing, and embraced her fiercely.

"Oh, Molly, Molly, what are we going to do?" she wailed, tears gushing from her black eyes. "Now that Henry and I have found each other again, I will never give him up."

Clover threw back her head, staring fiercely at the moon. "I'll die first," she vowed.

"No need for such drastic action," Molly said, dryly. "No one is going to harm Henry if Pedro and I can help it."

Drawing back from the girl, Molly lowered her basket to the ground. Fearfully, she glanced at the lion, who had crept up too close for Molly's comfort. Crouching, he opened his jaws wide, baring his canines, and pulled back his upper lip in a hideous grimace.

Molly stiffened. "That beast may think you're his mother," she quipped in an attempt at humor, "but I don't think he considers me his grandmother."

"He smells the meat," Clover laughed. "Give it to him quick."

Reaching into the basket, Clover pulled out the bloody stump of fresh meat, removed the cloth wrapping, and threw it on the rocks in front of Henry. After sniffing it a long minute, he clamped his jaws on it and dragged it off to the mine entrance to eat.

"It's got a long bone in it," Molly said. "It'll keep him busy for awhile."

Drawing out the warm garments, she said tersely,

"Here, change quickly, before you eat."

Gratefully, Clover tore off the flimsy embroidered Centennial Day dress, slipping into sturdy woolen pants and shirt and sweater. A warm knitted cap fit snugly over her tied-up hair. Happily, she pulled on her old, dusty boots. Then, as she settled down with Molly against a rock to eat, a small noise caused Clover to jump up nervously.

"Sit down, child, it's only a sage hen. The men who started out after you and Henry at the circus are now all back in Walter Hill's saloon, getting drunk and talking about the big game hunt tomorrow."

"Then Henry and I must leave tonight." Clover glanced fearfully at the sky. The fitful moon had disappeared again and the land was completely dark.

Clutching Molly desperately, Clover urged, "Pedro can take me to Eagle Valley. He knows these mountains as none other."

"That is our plan," Molly responded, adding, "But Spike must be told where you are and that you're safe."

Flaring up, Clover spat out, "No. Nobody must know. Spike hates lions. He said I could have Henry only if I declawed him. That's cruel, I'll never do it to him."

"Spike can change his mind," Molly said tartly. "Make him build a nice big pen for your lion, with a high fence. A man will do anything for a wife he loves."

Pausing, she looked slyly at the girl. "Provided that wife keeps him happy every night in bed." She laughed dryly. "Men are fools where a lovely woman is concerned."

Clover was silent for a time, listening to Henry's loud chewing. Finally, she said flatly, "I don't want to marry Spike. He will never love Henry. He might pretend to at

60

first, but eventually he will shoot him."

"No man will love that lion as you do," snapped Molly impatiently.

"Some would . . . that Captain Jack Emerson would . . ."

"Emerson?"

Molly rose up, arms akimbo, staring down at her adopted daughter. "What is that man to you?" Her eyes narrowed in suspicion. "How many times must I warn you to stay away from no-good drifters?"

"Calm down, Molly, I hardly know him." She wrinkled her brow. "But somehow I have this eerie feeling that I've seen him somewhere before." She shook her head, as if to shake out the answer to her puzzlement.

"Circus people are the very worst kind to marry," the older woman persisted. "Worse than Gypsies."

Clover sighed. If Molly knew that the liontamer had kissed her last night, she would have an apoplexy.

Seeing that the lion posed no threat, Pedro emerged from the rocks, standing a few feet away. "It is time to go . . . We must leave this place before the moon wanes," he said softly.

Molly lifted her hand. "A minute, Pedro."

Rising to her feet, Clover moved toward Henry, who was happily gnawing the sheep bone. "I have decided that the man I marry must love Henry as much as I do. One day he will come along, I'm sure."

"But the animal's not even legally yours, child," Molly persisted. "What if the handsome captain refuses to sell him? Stealing such a large animal is grand larceny, I'm sure."

But Clover appeared not to hear. Moving swiftly to where Henry was contentedly gnawing on his bone, Clover lifted the stick again. "Come, Henry, time to go."

The lion growled briefly, obviously upset at having his meal interrupted. Then, as Clover remained still, looming over him, stick extended with authority, the animal got to his feet and carried the bone into the mine for safekeeping. Returning, he trotted happily between his Mary Anne-Clover and Pedro as they headed for the dark mountains.

Running into the shaft, Molly emerged with the old circus blanket. "Here, you'll need this," she said, arranging the musty wool on Clover's shoulders, Indian fashion. "It'll bring good luck."

The two women embraced silently. Molly stood a long time looking after the Indian and the girl before starting back to the stagehouse. Her heart was heavy, but it was for the best. Clover would be safe with her beloved Indians.

Saloonkeeper Walter Hill hadn't sold so much hard liquor in one night since the bonanza boomtown days of the sixties. His stock had already been depleted from the circus crowds. The circus had already left town, in the predawn dark, and the crowds of Centennial visitors would soon dissolve. He was happy as a clam at the unexpected business from the lion hunters. His shelves were bare, and he had to send his oldest son to Carson City to fetch more whiskey.

Most of the men who were going on the lion hunt at dawn were asleep on the floor or outside on the hard dirt. Ralph Brant had sent jugs of hot coffee and half a ham with bread and biscuits to help feed the hunters.

As for that damn fool Spike Brant, he had passed out

cold on the hearthstones after a prolonged crying jag. "Leave him be till morning," Daddy Ralph had said. "I'll be back before we start lionhunting."

Cold sober, Lake Emerson watched Brant leave, then walked to the hearth and stood gazing down with contempt at the man Clover Sinclair was pledged to marry. A girl like that deserved better, he reflected glumly. The man was soft, a rich kid pampered by his rich father. Spike had so much whiskey in him he'd be no use at all on any hunt — in his condition, he couldn't even bag a weasel.

A girl like Clover needed a man who could at least hold his liquor, Lake thought.

"A man like me," he muttered.

Jolted by the vagrant thought, Lake refilled his mug at the coffeepot, then walked slowly, three times, around the long adobe room, thinking.

Restless, he bolted outside and stared at the pale, lightening skies, then down at the sleeping men. None of these louts was fit to use a gun. Maybe in two or three days when their heads cleared up. But not at dawn. He groaned aloud, draining his coffee mug. To think that they would march out of town gunning for Henry.

And Clover.

Lake's heart leaped into his throat. Until this very moment, he had not dared to admit to himself that the dark-eyed daughter of his enemy Sinclair had become important to him for reasons having nothing to do with the stolen bank gold.

That kiss last night had left him shaken. Her sweet, naive passion had startled him. She was so terribly beautiful, yet vulnerable, trusting — exactly the kind of girl he'd always yearned for.

63

If one of these drunken fools shot her by mistake —

Running inside, Lake slammed his pottery mug on the oak bar, shouting, "Get up, you drunken bastards, I have something to say."

A few of the men grumbled in their sleep, but nobody moved. Like a man possessed, Lake dashed from one to the other, kicking them awake. The saloonkeeper came out of a back room, yawning.

"Hey, stop that." He grabbed Lake's arm. "Do you want to start a brawl?"

Lake viciously slammed into Spike Brant's hard buttock with his booted foot. "No. I want to stop a tragedy. There can't be any lion hunt."

"And why not, liontamer," Walter Hill sneered.

Ralph Brant's commanding voice sounded from the doorway. He entered the saloon, and drawing a revolver from his belt, pointed it at Lake. "I was afraid we'd have trouble with you, liontamer. What's the matter, scared of losing your investment in that savage animal?"

"No," Lake replied. "Hunting big game with a crowd is dangerous. Clover and Henry will be together, probably sleeping curled up, side by side. A wrong shot might hit her."

Spike's heavy hand on Lake's shoulder turned him around. The young man's face was flushed with anger and drink, and, without warning, he shoved his fist into Lake's face, knocking the Englishman to the floor.

Straddling the prone body, Spike gritted, "I'll protect my own sweetheart, you damn foreigner, nobody else."

Lifting his head, he shouted to one and all, "Hear that, everybody? Nobody's going on any lion hunt but me."

Lake tried to rise, but Spike viciously knocked him down again, delivering a hard kick to the groin. In agony,

Lake rolled round and round on the sawdust-covered floor.

Spitting in the downed man's face, Spike growled, "What right has a damn fool English liontamer got to be calling my gal by her Christian name? He leered, standing back with arms folded. "I know your kind. The whole town saw you manhandling her yesterday at the parade."

Struggling to his feet, Lake held on to the bar edge for support. His genitals hurt like hell, but he had to win this battle. Ignoring Spike, he spoke to Ralph Brant in urgent tones, "I can get the lion safely back here without firing a shot. Nobody else must go out. Men with guns will only antagonize the animal, maybe cause him to charge."

Pausing for breath, he sucked in deeply to ease his pain. "I know this for a certainty: Clover Sinclair will die to protect her Henry."

Someone guffawed. "What a name for a lion!"

Pushing off his still-belligerent son, Ralph Brant pursed his lips. "You've got a point, Emerson."

Slipping his revolver back into his belt holster, he put a restraining hand on his son's arm. "The man's dead right, Son, I say the liontamer goes out hunting alone."

Spike's eyes were slits in his puffy face as he spat out thickly, "Don't listen to him, Dad. The bastard's not really interested in saving his lion. He wants to get his cock under Clover's skirts.

Laughing lewdly, Spike moved his hips obscenely. "He'll fetch his lion back all right, I betcha, but not until he's had his British pole in my tight little virgin a couple of times."

"That's a lie!"

The words fell like bullets in the now-quiet saloon.

Wide awake, and eager for a fight, the men encircled Spike and the stranger. Calling a man a liar was a challenge to battle. Spike was good with his fists, and from the look of his muscles, the liontamer would put up a rousing fight.

Without warning, Spike lunged at Lake with his head, butting him in the stomach and knocking him flat on his back on the hearthstones. Rolling over quickly, the Englishman sprang to his feet, and swinging widely, delivered a powerful punch to his attacker's face as Spike crouched in front of the long mantel, one foot on the andiron.

The blow sent Spike spinning. Struggling to keep upright, his one free hand swept along the mantel, sending various items of pottery hurling to the floor. He fell, striking his head on the andiron.

Grimly, fists still clenched, Lake gritted, "Come on, big man, on with the fight."

There was no answer from his opponent. Spike Brant was out cold. The saloonkeeper started counting. "One, two, three—"

"Stop, damn you."

Ralph Brant bent over his fallen son, his ear to Spike's chest. Feverishly, unbuttoning the flannel shirt, he placed two fingers at the unconscious man's throat. The roomful of men was deathly silent, waiting. After a few tense moments, Mr. Brant got slowly to his feet. He turned to Lake Emerson, who had unclenched his fists and stood soberly near the fire, his blue eyes bright with fear.

Touching the deputy sheriff's badge pinned to his vest, Brant said quietly, without a trace of emotion, "Captain Emerson, you are under arrest for murder."

"Murder!" Lake exploded, "You're mad. It was an accident."

Squatting quickly, he touched the andiron against which Spike had fallen. He held up his hand. "See, here is blood. Your son died from hitting the andiron, not from my punch."

His face remaining impassive, Brant barked to his men, "Luke, Tom, Jake. Take him."

Stunned, Lake put up no resistance as men came forward to grab his arms and drag him out of the saloon. His pistol was yanked from its holster.

"Put the killer in the shed behind my house until we can fetch the marshal from Carson City to take him there for trial," Brant ordered, mounting his horse.

"Trial!" yelled one of the men who held Lake. "Hell, a hangin's a lot more fun. He's guilty as sin, we all saw it."

"Yeah," called out another. "Why waste time?"

Lake's blood ran cold. He'd seen a lynching once, in Wyoming. The poor man had been strung up and strangled with a rope in minutes. Never had a chance. Wildly, he shouted at Brant, "It was an accident. You can't kill a man for that. It was a fair fight."

The bereaved man's craggy face could have been carved from stone. In the early-morning light, his eyes were flat, like pieces of dull glass.

"You killed my son," he said tonelessly. "The Good Book says, an eye for an eye."

His captors tied Lake's arms behind him and hoisted him on a horse. Followed by a cheering crowd, they all started at a gallop for the Brant homestead in the foothills.

Clover lay on a pile of rabbitskins in a corner of a smoke-filled Indian hut constructed of cattail reeds. An old squaw squatted by a fire humming and turning a spit on which two plump mudhens were roasting to a golden crust. From time to time she dipped her hand into a jug and sprinkled water on the birds. Beneath, on the coals themselves, a mess of blackfish wrapped in cattail leaves was cooking.

The mingled aromas, combined with her day-long fast, made Clover wildly hungry. Pedro had permitted her to stop only long enough to drink from an occasional stream. But the exhilaration at escaping Henry's pursuers drove all exhaustion from her body. She'd never felt more alive. Clover was accustomed to long tramps in the mountains. She and Molly had often traveled for days in the forest, searching for unharvested piñon nut trees.

"Eating will make us sluggish," Pedro had said. "At my brother's house, we will feast."

Henry would feast, too, he promised, and be allowed to sleep through the night at the hut on the shores of vast Pyramid Lake. In the morning they would resume their journey on mules. They had skirted the lake most of the day, doubling back often, taking a roundabout route, being careful to remain in the thick pine and juniper woods. They could have easily crossed the lake by boat in an hour, but Clover was afraid her lion would not take to traveling by water.

A lad entered, smiling, holding aloft a very fat muskrat. He walked across the long hut to where Pedro and his brother Falling Rock were chewing the succulent meat of skinned cattails and talking quietly.

Pedro called to Clover, "Take the fresh kill to your lion." The boy was given a chunk of sugar by the Indian woman, who was his grandmother. He was one of numerous children in this remote part of the Pyramid Lake reservation.

Rising eagerly, Clover followed the lad outside to a large wire enclosure once used for chickens where Henry had been placed on arrival. Three stalwart braves stood guard. A crowd of adults and youngsters surrounded the cage, gazing in awe at this massive African beast. Henry sat on his haunches, his handsome leonine head regally uplifted, lapping up the admiration.

Clover opened the cage and entered with the muskrat. Trotting toward her, Henry waited, sniffing. He had withstood the journey well, she thought with pride. A circus lion gets little real exercise, compared to his jungle brothers. She had worried about Henry's stamina, but she felt that he was smart enough to sense the danger they were in and had decided to cooperate. Like the big cat that he was, he had trod the often-rough terrain with an almost dainty agility.

Tossing the muskrat to one side, she called out, "Come, Henry, eat." Then she quickly left the cage.

The sound of his canines tearing into the fresh meat brought squeals of terror from the children, exclamations from the men, several of whom ran off.

Clover laughed. "Henry is hungry," she said. "We have traveled all day without food."

She lingered at the cage door, staring at the animal she loved so much, marveling at the luck that had reunited them after so many years apart. With fresh resolve, she turned back to the hut, cautioning the youngsters not to disturb the lion by loud noises and shouting.

As Clover entered, the old squaw rose, respectfully bowing and sweeping a hand to point out where the young white girl should sit for eating. Pedro and Falling Rock were already seated, awaiting her presence. To eat with the men was a rare privilege for a woman.

"Your power over a massive beast will strike awe into my people's hearts," Pedro had told her. "To them you are a magical person, like a shaman."

"There's nothing mystical about it," Clover retorted "It's all a matter of training, and of long practice with an animal. Henry has learned to trust me."

"No. It is more than that. The lion may be only an animal to you, but to my countrymen, he is from the spirit world, a kind of messenger from beyond." He shook his head. "The Paiutes believe that ancient warriors often return to earth in the form of beasts and birds."

After she had eaten heartily of the fish and mudhens, Clover went out to take one more look at Henry, who had fallen asleep with his paws on the muskrat carcass. Back in the hut, she fell upon her rabbitskins, covering herself against the cold night with a massive skin blanket. But sleep eluded her. All day she had not thought of anything but escaping, but now that she and Henry were safe, images of Lake Emerson filled her mind. As warmth from the skins crept through her veins, she felt her breasts tighten as they had last night when he had kissed her. Once more, her loins grew deliciously warm and moist.

Positive that he was the man who had so callously killed her father, she tried to will away the rush of passion that swept over her. She had sworn to avenge Papa's death. But that would be impossible, for now she and Henry would be in Eagle Valley. She would never see the liontamer again.

This wanton emotion she was feeling for the Englishman would eventually go away. Molly always told her,

"Man-woman love never lasts. It is lust."

A night bird hooted distantly. A wind blew across the lake, rattling the leaves on the hut. They sounded like lost souls murmuring for help. The old squaw was snoring mightily. Pedro and his brother were sleeping outside the hut entrance, the better to guard her and the lion. *How blessed I am*, mused Clover, *to have such devoted friends*.

Turning on her side, she drew up her knees, placing her hands between her trembling thighs. Willfully, she gave her self to dreaming about Lake Emerson, imagining his strong body pressed on hers, as his fierce, hard manhood invaded her private places. Clover's heart beat like a hammer, but she did not stop the rush of feeling. This one night she would give to love. Tomorrow she would thrust the man out of her mind forever.

At dawn, Clover woke to find Pedro bending over her. His hawkish Indian face was grim.

"Come, we must return to Black Springs. Your young man is dead."

Bolting up, Clover stared at the man, unable to speak. Her mouth seemed filled with cotton and she had a headache from the sagebrush smoke. She must be in a dream.

At last, she squeaked, "Captain Emerson is dead?"

The old man snorted. "I thought Spike Brant was your sweetheart."

"He is," she said weakly. "The liontamer has been on my mind, that's all."

"That liontamer killed him in a fight. With one punch, they say. Mr. Brant will see that the man hangs." Pedro turned to the door. "Without a trial. The English stranger may be dead before we reach Black Springs."

"A lynching?"

But Pedro had left. Stunned, Clover drank the hot

herb tea handed her by the squaw. She had slept in her clothes, and, running out to join Pedro, she climbed into a fishing boat to cross the lake. There was no need for secrecy now. Henry would remain here with the Indians. No harm would come to him. As Pedro had said, they would revere the lion as a kind of god, a reincarnation of an ancient warrior. He would be given fresh-killed meat every day and guarded like a pile of gold.

"Now you may keep your lion without fear of the liontamer chasing you," Pedro remarked, picking up an oar. One of the boys who worked for Molly manned the other oar. He had come with the doleful message.

"Molly says to hurry so's you can watch the hangin'," the boy grinned. "She'll try to make them wait until you come."

Rambling on excitedly, the lad told her also that Spike and Emerson had been fighting over her. "Spike hit his head on the andiron and never got up."

"It was an accident then," Clover said. "The stranger did not mean to kill Spike. It was an unlucky punch."

"Nope, not accordin' to them that saw it," the lad responded. "Spike said that the liontamer wanted to get under your skirts. He was pretty mad."

Clover groaned. What could she say? She had actually led the liontamer on, allowing him to kiss her.

"Holy cow, I've never seen a hangin'," the boy went on. "My old man says there used to be a hangin' most every week in the boomtown days. Folks kinda looked forward to it."

Seeing that Clover was upset, Pedro bade him to shut his big mouth and Clover drew her old circus blanket tightly round her chilled body at the horrible image. Mists hung over the lake; they seemed to be in another world. The happy, normal life of yesterday was gone forever. Strange, how life works out, she thought morosely. Fate was avenging Papa's death. Captain Emerson would die. Henry was hers, free and clear.

But deep within, Clover could find no joy. Her heart was like a millstone in her chest, choking the breath out of her. It was all her fault—Spike's untimely death and Lake Emerson's imminent lynching. She was an evil woman. A vampire who had destroyed two men. Spike had been so good-natured, so full of life and energy. And the liontamer had been so virile. She had loved him for his kiss, she had lusted after him in mind and body.

She hated herself. How could she live out her life with the dreadful knowledge that she had caused the death of two men? They had been fighting over her. She was no better than a loose woman who pleasures herself in goading men to madness.

A kind of demonic rage at herself and the quirks of a mindless, whimsical fate possessed Clover. Her whole body was on fire. She had craved to kill the man who had pushed her father's medicine wagon off the road. But now, he was to die for another crime.

She must save Lake Emerson. But whether she wanted him alive to wreak her own revenge on him, or to have him love her, she could not tell.

"Hurry, hurry," she screamed at Pedro. "We must stop them from hanging Captain Emerson."

Tormented almost to madness, Clover moved her body back and forth in the boat, as if to move it faster toward the shore.

Chapter Four

Blinding clouds of gritty alkali dust from the desert billowed down the narrow, dried-mud streets of Black Springs as Clover and Molly rode into town. But the townspeople huddled around the hanging tree looming heavenward from a pile of rocks at the end of Main Street seemed undaunted by the blasts. Debris of various kinds flew through the air. A sharp piece of tin roofing from a downtown store flitted past, glinting and crackling and evoking a few shrieks from the women, shouts and cackles from the men.

The crowd cheered. It was in a rowdy mood. A hanging meant an undeclared holiday for most.

The hanging tree was not a tree at all, but a rudely built scaffolding consisting of a tall, upended log and a crossbeam. When Clover saw the thick rope loop dangling from the beam, ready for Lake Emerson's neck, her heart trembled. She'd seen hangings as a child, and remembered with horror the sight of a limp body twirling in the wind.

The brash young liontamer did not deserve to die, especially in such a barbaric way. But then, she mused, trying to nourish the bitterness in her soul, Spike Brant should not be dead, either.

The two women were greeted lustily as they moved their horses through the crowd.

"There she is, and Molly, too. Now we can get on with the hangin'."

A loud voice yelled, "Hallelujah!"

Other voices chorused, "Amen."

Most of the men were drinking whiskey, bottles passed freely from hand to hand. Little children darted about, playing tag. There would be no school today. For the most part, though, the women's faces were grim. Lynchings like this did not bode well for the future of law and order in Black Springs.

But they had come to keep an eye on their children who should have been in school, leaving their breakfast dishes on the table, their laundry soaking in the tub. The people of Black Springs were hungry for a hanging. It meant excitement, a relief from the monotony of existence in a sleepy town.

Many longed for the bonanza days of the Comstock Lode, back in the sixties when the surrounding hills sprouted silver and every man who could wield a pick got rich quicker than he had ever dreamed. But it had been a bloody time. Gun battles raged on the hills, in the streets and saloons.

Walter Hill walked toward Molly and Clover. The saloonkeeper's genial face was troubled. He put a comforting hand on Clover's arm. "Sorry about your loss, gal. Young Spike was a fine man. He would have made a crackerjack of a husband for you." He shook his head mournfully.

"Thank you, Mr. Hill," Clover whispered, covering his

big hand briefly with her own. "I . . . I still can't bring myself to believe it."

Clover bent her head low, causing the thick fall of hair to cover her face. She'd had no time to braid it this morning, and as the wind played with her loosened tresses, it blew about her head in long black ribbons.

"Look at the poor young thing," she heard a woman say, "she can hardly keep her head up."

Clover said no more to Mr. Hill, though her brain was full to bursting with words of protest. Molly had preached at her all the way down from Superstition Hill on how to behave.

"Button your lip, Clover, if you want to save Lake Emerson from being hanged unjustly. Leave it to me. The town respects me. They'll listen to me. Just look griefstricken — a few tears won't hurt."

She had shot Clover a sidelong glance. "And for goodness' sake, whatever you do, don't let anyone guess that you are soft on the liontamer."

Despite Clover's vehement denials, her adoptive mother was convinced that the towheaded Captain Emerson meant more to her daughter than Spike Brant ever had. A woman truly in love would want to kill the man who had caused her lover's death with her bare hands.

Instead, Clover had pleaded with Molly to save the liontamer's life.

"The man can't die," she had wailed. "I can't have the deaths of two men on my conscience." Her dark eyes had blazed in anguish.

"This hangin' must be stopped," Molly snapped at the saloonkeeper. "There was no proper trial." Sucking in a deep breath, she proclaimed, loud and clear, for all to hear. "In 1864, when President Lincoln brought Nevada into the union, we got law and order. That means you can't hang a man without a proper trial by a duly constituted judge and jury."

"Brant brought in a justice from Carson City," Walter said softly. His tone was defensive. "He swore in a kangaroo jury. The foreigner was sentenced at midnight."

"Bullshit," Molly gritted, "and you well know it. From what I hear, the killing was an accident. Spike was knocked down in a fight and hit his head on—"

A wild shout from the crowd caught her up short. The condemned man was being led to the hanging tree. Clover peered at Lake through her tangled hair. Her heart contracted, and dread coursed through her veins like liquid fire. What if Molly was unable to stop the death of the young man who had ridden into town never thinking that he was soon to die?

Tears choked her throat as she recalled how cocky, how fearless, he had been, driving his lion wagon through town as if he owned the whole world. He had seemed to her the embodiment of life. How angry he had been with her for pestering Henry. She almost smiled at the memory.

Now a prisoner, the virile liontamer sat atop a dappled roan from Brant's vast stable. His hands were tied behind his back. His chest was bare, ragged trousers covered his long legs. He wore no shoes. His whitish hair blew in the wind, framing his head like a halo.

He did not speak, apparently resigned to his death. As Clover lifted her head, his gray eyes caught hers. He stared at her, fixedly, unblinkingly, inscrutably.

Clover closed her eyes against his stare. She felt as if she were in a nightmare. What cruel, puckish fate had brought this man into her life to change it so completely?

He had returned her sweet Henry to her and kissed her

in the night outside a lion's cage. She'd had a brief glimpse of love, a night of soaring, expectant joy of bliss to come. In those few hours of knowing Lake Emerson, Clover the girl had become Clover the woman.

Then the same cruel fate had taken love away with one unlucky punch.

Her eyes flew open once again as she studied the condemned man's handsome, tanned face. Memory teased. She'd known that face all her life, it seemed.

"He killed my lover, he killed my dear papa, he deserves to die." Clover's lips moved silently, as she sought to assuage her agony.

The dappled roan was led to stand directly under the noose, which dangled over Lake Emerson's head. The crowd grew quiet, waiting for the signal from Ralph Brant, who had walked to Clover and Molly.

A chant arose. "Get on with it, Brant. Let's see the foreigner swing."

"Swing, swing, swing," a man sang drunkenly.

Holding up a hand for silence, Brant nodded to Molly, but spoke to Clover. "To you, my dear, whom I had fondly hoped would become my sweet daughter, goes the great pleasure of kicking the horse from under the man who murdered your sweetheart."

Spike's father reached out to grab her hand, to help her down from the horse.

Clover uttered a strangled shriek, her hands flying to her face.

"You damn fool, Brant," Molly yelled. "Can't you see that the girl's near collapse?"

Drawing out a long kitchen knife from her saddlebag, Molly dug her heels into her horse's belly. She rode up to the liontamer, holding the knife aloft, ready to cut the

78

rope.

Whipping around to face the crowd, she shouted, "You all know this man's innocent of killing by intent."

Pausing to let that sink in, Molly guffawed, "why, Lordy, if every man who killed another in a fair fight was hanged for it, this town—land's sake, all of the west— would be full of widows."

Some laughter was heard, and a murmur of assent from the crowd. The women's heads nodded solemnly. "She's right," they hissed to each other. The men looked troubled, pursing lips and rubbing chins. Molly Sinclair could always make them stop and think.

Everyone in town knew that the consumptive old bitch was to be reckoned with. She knew President Ulysses Grant personally and there was talk of a very intimate relationship between the two when the general was serving in western forts.

His florid face beet-red with rage, Brant strode to the scaffolding. "This Englishman was tried fair and square. We brought in eyewitnesses."

He glared at Molly. "You weren't there, madam. This is none of your affair."

Brant's hands reached up to slip the noose over Lake Emerson's head. Craning his neck over Brant's shoulder, Lake shouted at Clover, who was secretly staring at him through her hair. "Has any harm come to Henry? Where is he, Clover?"

Clover sat up straight. Molly be damned, she was going to be heard. An inspired idea struck her.

"I—I—oh, God, I don't know where he is, Captain Emerson," she lied. "He's lost. He ran away in the night."

Her head swiveled, viewing the people on all sides with stricken dark eyes. She lifted her hands to the hills, as if praying. "He's out there, in the hills, wandering around, getting hungrier by the hour."

She bent her head again, despairing. She let a sob escape. "My lion is lost, lost, lo-s-s-st."

After a moment of surprise, Molly picked up the cue. Clover's shrewdness surprised her. She pointed to Lake. "And there sits the only man who can track down and control the savage beast." She paused dramatically. "In minutes he'll be dead, and we'll all be at the mercy of the savage beast."

She whirled her knife theatrically around and around her head. "Who's for cutting the noose from this poor boy's neck?"

The crowd roared. Molly neatly slit the rope above the noose which dangled loosely around Lake's neck.

Brant cursed roundly, but did nothing, seeming at a loss.

Ignoring his sudden release, Lake moaned to Clover, "Oh, my God, Clover, you were so confident that you could master the lion as you had been able to do long ago."

"I was wrong. It's you—only you—whom he acknowledges as master." Clover broke out in a torrent of weeping, swaying back and forth on her horse until a woman behind her reached out to hold her in the saddle.

Molly's face was a study in torment. She groaned inwardly. Hanging the rascal would get him out of Clover's life for good. Why in tarnation was she fighting for his life? The crowd was murmuring, their faces telling her that they were clearly afraid of the runaway lion.

Lake continued to stare at Clover, his heart in his eyes. He could think of only one reason she and Molly wanted to save him from the noose.

Clover loved him.

Suppressing a grin, he remarked, in a half-joking way, his English accent crisp, "I'm a prisoner accused of murder." He slipped a long finger under the noose, rubbing his neck. "But I doubt that I can catch that lion."

Brant's face worked convulsively. His eyes darted over the crowd, who were observing his reactions to this new development. It was obvious that he felt he was losing the battle of words.

Lake continued solemnly. "Once a beast like that reverts to the wild, he'll stop at nothing to feed his appetite. He requires eighteen to twenty pounds of meat each and every day."

"Our sheep won't be safe, our dogs, our mules," a man said gloomily. "There goes our livestock."

"Lions crave horsemeat," Lake said flatly.

"Our children—" shrieked a woman.

"For the love of heaven, set the man free to find his lion," another sobbed.

Finally, Brant spoke up, waving his shotgun in the air. "There's fifty of us here with shotguns. We can track that lion down before sundown. What say, men? Who's with me?"

There wasn't a sound from the men. One and all, they stared down at their boots.

Sighing deeply, then breathing out explosively, Brant removed the dangling noose from the liontamer's neck. "Just as well," he muttered, "From the drunken looks of you, you'd all end up shooting each other."

Much relieved, the men tittered.

"I brought the goddam circus to town, I'll see that no other man's son dies for it," Brant continued.

Sliding off the horse, Captain Emerson stood erect, rubbing his wrists where the rope had bit in.

"Five days is all you get to find the beast," Brant said grimly to the reprieved man. "If I don't see that lion carcass in that time" — he swung the noose with his hand — "the rope will still be ready for you."

Lake faced the man squarely, his high-boned face a mask. "Here are *my* terms, Mr. High and Mighty — my freedom for the safety of the town."

Facing the crowd, he addressed them in a clear, firm voice. "Ralph Brant, I demand that you swear to these people that I will be freed in five days, whether I bring back the lion or not."

"You've been tried and found guilty," Brant said coldly. "Don't push your luck."

"Swear, " Lake persisted.

"He's risking his life, Brant," Walter Hill put in. "He's a stranger in these parts. Finding his lion won't be easy in these canyons." He peered at the horizon. "That animal could be clear across California by now."

"Okay, okay, you win," Brant grunted, remounting his horse. "I swear by God, in front of all the good Americans of Black Springs, that you'll be a free man — whatever happens."

A posse of five men were picked, who, along with Brant would ride with the prisoner on the lion hunt and keep him from escaping.

Mounting the dappled roan, Lake pushed through the crowd, the posse surrounding him. As they passed between Molly and Clover, Lake jerked the reins. He met Clover's eyes. "I'll bring Henry back to you," he said. "Alive."

"Thanks," she choked, "I know you will." She kept her head downcast, her lovely face cloaked by her tangled hair. No one, not even Lake, must see the love in her eyes for this man. He must have guessed that the lion was safely tucked away, but she was confident he would not betray her to the lionhunters. How gallant of him to go along with the game.

Lake's hand lifted, moving forward as if to touch her arm, but, with a jerk, he withdrew it instantly.

Clover's gaze fixed on the strong brown hand, the blunt-tipped fingers, then drifted up the broad, muscled chest, the airy mat of golden hairs.

Her blood sang with the sheer joy of knowing that he was still in the same world with her. Beyond that she did not dare to think.

She and Molly watched the eight riders moving out of town toward Brant's ranch to get supplies for the hunt.

"What if Brant kills him anyway while they're in the mountains," she said fearfully to Molly. "A stray shot, an accidental slip off the trail down a cliff—" She shrugged. "No one will dare question Ralph Brant."

Her adoptive mother shook her head. "The cowardly fool is afraid of the lion himself. Like everybody else in town, he wants Henry dead. If he comes back to town with no Henry and no liontamer, there'll be the devil to pay for Ralph Brant."

Molly was glum. The worst had come to pass. She had freed the man Clover was desperately in love with. Now her precious, sheltered daughter would be prey to the scoundrel. She wondered how many in town had already guessed the truth.

They turned their horses toward the stagehouse. "Ah, well," she sighed. "It's stupid to cry over spilt milk."

Clover turned. "What's that you said, Molly? Do we need milk?"

A snort from Molly. "Nah, gal, what we need right now

83

is for you to get the hell out of town and back to Pyramid Lake to grab your lion before the posse finds him."

"Yes," Clover sighed happily. Then, frowning, "But Eagle Valley's such a long way. Brant and his men are sure to find us along the way."

"Not with Pedro guiding you," Molly assured her. "That Indian knows these mountains like the back of his hand." She chuckled. "Sometimes I think he was right there alongside of God when he put them here."

Clover shaded her eyes, staring at the peaks of the Washo Range and, beyond them, the long dark line of the lofty Sierra Nevadas and some of her fear evaporated. Pedro had spent his boyhood here on these thickly wooded slopes and deep canyons. He had hunted antelope and deer in the ancient hunting grounds of the Martis and Washo tribes.

"I'm not afraid for myself," she said finally, "but Henry has lived his life in a cage. He's fat and lazy. He doesn't know how to hunt his own food." Her voice caught. "My sweet lion will die or be shot by Brant's posse."

"That's as may be," Molly responded cryptically. "Fate will decide. But you can't bring your animal home. He wouldn't last a day in Black Springs. Without Spike to protect him, someone would shoot him."

They had reached the stagehouse, where Pedro awaited with fresh mules for himself and Clover. Mules were superior to horses in the craggy hills and steep valleys.

Samson the cook, his slanted Chinese eyes spilling with tears, was packing jerky, cured bacon, corn cakes, and shelled piñon nuts into the saddlebags. Two skins of water were hung alongside.

"Young Missy never come back from desert," he wept. "You be lost—" His slender hands cupped his face in horror. "Your bones will lie there—"

"Shut up, you fool," Molly yelled, dragging Clover inside to dress her for the journey. She would travel as a squaw—black hair in a single, thick braid down her back, face smeared with dirt lathered on with rancid bear grease. A shapeless calico garment of Molly's covered her slender form and a scruffy pair of her mother's old boots would protect her feet from rocky mountain slopes.

When she emerged, Samson wrinkled his nose. Pedro laughed, nodding his approval. "Now if you can only remember that Indian women don't talk when their men are present."

"I know," Clover replied meekly, "I'll speak only to you and Henry."

The excitement of changing clothes had served to banish some of Clover's fears and her heart began to pound with anticipation. As a child, she had dreamed of living in the wild with Henry, away from people, circuses, and cages.

Freedom lay ahead. Freedom with Henry in Eagle Valley. In a way, the hidden place south of the desert was her second home. As a child, she and Molly had often spent summers there. During the last such summer, when she was thirteen, Clover had been inducted into the tribe and had been given the name of Flying Bird because she raced about the valley as if her feet had wings.

Secretly, unofficially, she had traded blood by slitting wrists with an Indian lad named Gray Falcon. He was also thirteen, and in love with Clover. She loved him, too, and had pledged to be his wife when she was eighteen.

That was long ago, she thought now, and all in fun. Gray Falcon was a stalwart young brave by now and had surely taken himself a comely Indian maid to wife.

But she found herself looking forward to seeing him and all her old friends in Eagle Valley again.

That other—the man who had stolen a piece of her heart, and whom she and Molly had saved from hanging—she would never think about again.

But as she hugged her mother, and turning her face to the south, she found herself saying, "What do you think will happen to Captain Emerson?"

Molly stared at the rocky ground. "I'm sure Ralph Brant will see that the foreigner pays with his life for killing Spike. That one is out of your life forever."

Clover's heart lurched. "But he promised Lake his freedom. You heard him. Everybody heard him."

"Baloney. Since when did Ralph Brant pay attention to what other people think? He'll know by tonight that you have Henry safely in your charge. He won't need Emerson anymore."

She patted Clover's hand resting on the bridle. "That unlucky young man will more than likely end up in jail. A couple years or so—for manslaughter. There will be no lynching. Brant has had his day."

"Let's get these mules on the trail," Pedro grumbled, impatient with the woman-talk.

But Clover did not move. The anticipation of being with Henry had fled. She had been so firmly convinced that the liontamer was the man who had pushed her father's wagon into the canyon. But now, she faltered. Once again, her mind swarmed with doubts. She had seen that face before, of that much she was positive.

But where? If not on that lonely, twisting mountain road, then where?

Clover was filled with agonizing doubts. Molly could ease her heart. Molly was her tower and her strength.

Now that Spike was dead, there was no one left to lean on but her beloved foster mother.

If only she could empty her heart to the older woman, Clover thought.

"I love him desperately, Molly," she would say. "It's the most wonderful feeling in the whole world."

But Molly Robinson did not believe in love. As a girl she'd given her heart to a man who betrayed her, who had left her without a care, after he'd had his pleasure with her firm, young body.

"Love is for fools, girl," Molly would scoff. "It's a cruel trick of nature. Forget it. Run, run, run, my child, as fast and as far away as you can from that good-looking lion-tamer."

Well, that's exactly what Clover was doing. But, oh God, why did it have to hurt so much?

"Hug me one last time, Molly," Clover pleaded, bending in the saddle.

Instead of reaching up to clasp the girl to her bosom, as Clover expected, Molly stepped back, arms folded to hug her own skinny chest. "You're a woman now, Clover. All grown up," she said sternly. "You must bear this trial alone." She paused, before adding grimly, "One day I will not be here to comfort you."

She turned to enter the house, calling over her shoulder in a more cheerful tone, "Besides, I've got to stay here and work my backside off with the authorities to keep Ralph Brant and his greedy cohorts from raping Eagle Valley for its silver."

Feeling duly chastised, Clover urged her mule after the rapidly disappearing Pedro.

The Nevada night was filled with stars when Molly started back up to Superstition Hill, a wide-brimmed and very decrepit straw hat on her gray head, a filthy Indian blanket falling from her shoulders. A basket woven of river tules hung from her arm for collecting piñon nuts and artemisia seeds which grew profusely on scrubby bushes in dry lake basins and barren hillsides. The seeds were rich in oils and, when ground, provided life-sustaining meal.

Indian women, alone and in groups, were a common sight in the lower hills, foraging in the few woodsy patches and clumps of brush. Even if she met Brant and his posse, Molly would arouse no suspicion.

But this was no seed-gathering sojourn for Molly Robinson. She had ventured out this scorching summer day for another purpose.

The impending rape of Eagle Valley was not all that prevented the woman from joining Pedro, Henry, and her precious girl on the long trek to the south as she longed to do. Despite her glib reassurances to Clover, she feared for their safety. So many dangers could beset them. Bandits, cougars, scorching heat, bitter cold. Clover might catch a chill and die without her Molly there to care for her.

Since Molly had found her, near death, beside the body of her father, Clover Sinclair had never spent a night away from her side.

One thing was certain. She must ensure that the girl never met up with the Emerson lad again. Something about that one troubled her. Molly had been a gambler in her gold rush heyday, and she figured it for a one-in-a-million chance that an orphaned English lad had rolled into Black Springs with Clover's lion accidentally after ten years, going on eleven. With all the miserable little towns in the vast expanse of the West, it seemed too incredible that the Grandiose Circus had landed here in Clover's town carrying Clover's lion.

The Englishman was here for a purpose. What could it be? How did he come to have the beast? Clover's hunch that she had seen Lake Emerson somewhere in the past nagged at Molly. Her intuition warned her that the man who had captured Clover's heart in a day was after more than the girl's love.

Sinclair had left a letter along with the bank loot. He had mentioned a young boy. Molly had read the letter but once and she'd forgotten the details. Could Emerson have been that young boy? Had Clover seen him then, years ago, in her father's medicine wagon or working about the circus?

The twenty thousand dollars fetched by selling the gold double eagles she'd found in a metal box under the wrecked wagon was snugly tucked away in a San Francisco bank. She and Clover had lived on the interest, leaving the capital intact.

Clover would never have to fret her pretty head about money. With a handsome dowry like that, she could settle in a big house in San Francisco with a solid kind of man. A banker, maybe, or a shipping tycoon.

Not a circus roustabout like Lake Emerson, who would squander it before Clover had the stars out of her eyes.

At the summit, Molly paused and looked around, breathing a sigh of relief. Deserted. Quickly, she moved toward a stunted cedar that had grown against the shale hillside. Once it had served as a wickiup, or summer wigwam, for a nomadic Indian family. Rushes, animal bones, and rabbitskins and twigs had been woven in and out of the petrified branches of the cedar to form a dense, weatherproof roof.

Setting her basket and wide-brimmed straw hat on the rocks, Molly fell to her knees, and cautiously inched into the shelter through a narrow opening against the granite. She swore roundly as a jackrabbit darted past her out of the shelter, nearly knocking the wind out of her.

Squatting—for the wickiup was not high enough to stand in—she dislodged a flat piece of shale to reveal an opening behind. She grimaced, remembering the painstaking work she'd done to rout out a hole big enough for Dr. Sinclair's metal box. Hiding the thing in a cave would have exposed it to underground water and vermin.

Removing the oil-soaked rag she had wrapped around the box, she gazed a moment at the ornate cover. Circles, squares, triangles, and miniature sunbursts surrounded a snarling, writhing dragon. Her father had told his gullible little daughter that the box held magical powers.

"I thought a real live dragon would jump up and eat me up," the child had shuddered, telling Molly about it.

Well, the so-called magic had not saved the man from being killed, Molly mused wryly. She had saved it all these years to give to Clover along with her inheritance when the time came.

Opening it, she extracted an envelope containing a piece of heavy, watermarked paper, leaving in the box some legal papers relating to property in England and Clover's birth papers, bearing her actual name of Mary Anne. The mother's name was listed as Marguerita.

Dr. Sinclair had penned a confession on the heavy paper, addressed to the governor of Illinois. It was dated 1865. Since she'd found the box, days after she'd found Clover herself, Molly had not read the letter. Now, as she scanned the one page document, her heart began to race.

Her memory had served her right.

"Dear Sir,
   When you read this, I and my little daughter will be on the high seas bound for my home in England, there to claim my patrimony and establish my daughter in society.
   "This will inform you that I, and I alone, am the man who robbed the bank in Flat Rock, Illinois, in August, and killed the man who accosted me. It was an accident, my finger slipped, I was nervous.
   "The lad who was with me is altogether innocent. He was my dupe. The lad worked for me, he trusted me as his father's friend. I betrayed him most cruelly.
   "A bank president absconded years ago, taking with him to Mexico my fortune, along with that of many others. *Lex talionis*. Eye for an eye. I have no remorse. But the lad is innocent. He is not yet sixteen, an Englishman, as I am. He is not to be held to account. In a moment of cowardly panic, I thrust the gun into his hand and fled for my life."

Molly folded the letter with shaking hands and inserted it back into the envelope. It all fell into place. Lake Emerson had most likely been under sixteen ten years ago. Lake Emerson was English. Lake Emerson had probably been in prison for years after being caught in the robbery. Consumed with vengeance for the wrong done him, Lake Emerson was in Black Springs for the bank loot. And revenge.

Clover *had* seen the man before. But not at the scene of the accident. He could not have sideswiped the Sinclair medicine wagon, because he was in prison at the time.

Caught with the gun in his hand at the scene of the robbery, the youngster had rotted in jail. His heart would be black with vengeance. With Sinclair dead, that vengeance would certainly wreak itself on poor, defenseless Clover. A man who has wasted years of his young life for a crime he didn't commit would stop at nothing to get revenge. Sinclair was dead, beyond his reach. But Clover was not.

Fear for her sweet Clover wound an iron band around Molly's heart. The liontamer could destroy Clover's virtue, her reputation — Molly sucked in an agonizing breath — maybe her life itself, if that is what was needed to get the money.

I've got to warn her, Molly thought wildly as she hurriedly shoved the box and concealing stone back in place. But as she crawled toward the opening in the wickiup, the sound of horses approaching reached her ears.

Men were on the summit, their voices were angry, argumentative. Her heart jumped. It was Brant and his posse.

"Waste of time," a man was yelling. "I'll lay you ten to one that Sinclair gal's got that lion with her right now and is hightailing it for Eagle Valley with him."

"By herself?"

"Naw, that old Pedro that lives at the stagehouse is most likely with her. He knows all the old Injun trails."

"Don't be a fool," Brant replied. "That circus lion was raised in a cage. A tame animal like that won't last a week in the mountains."

Another voice. "They'll never be able to keep him fed with fresh meat. Not enough large animals round here anymore." He snorted. "Take about five jackrabbits to make a meal for a lion the size of that one."

Lake Emerson's clipped English voice broke in. "The

man is right. The girl would never take Henry on a journey like that. He's not with her at all. She was telling the truth when she said that he ran off."

From her hiding place, Molly peered out through the tangled branches. The men had dismounted, and the mules wandered off to a clump of sagebrush to graze. Molly could see Emerson's face clearly. He rubbed his chin and gazed at the clutter of abandoned mines. "Henry's in one of these caves. He won't wander far from where people are."

Brant again, fearful. "You said he might charge."

"Only if threatened."

Emerson broke off, staring at a clump of fresh animal feces on the rocks. "There's his spoor," he said flatly. "The animal is here."

"Spoor?"

"His droppings," Lake said, squatting to examine the spoor more closely. "Yes," he said finally. "There's no doubt, it's lion spoor."

That the droppings were a day old, Lake kept to himself. Henry and Clover had been here all right but were long gone.

The men cocked their guns. "Call to him, he'll come to you."

"Too risky," Lake responded. "With so many strangers around me, he could very well charge. I say we wait until he's hungry enough to come out and look for meat and water."

Angry voices erupted again.

"I'm for headin' south and catchin' up with the Sinclair girl."

"Me, too. There ain't no lion here."

"Whatta you say, Ralph? You're the boss."

Brant's broad back was toward her so that Molly couldn't see his face, but his voice was quiet, confident. "Let's listen to the liontamer. If the lion doesn't show at daybreak, we'll pack up and start combing the hills."

"By then the gal will be halfway to Eagle Valley with the critter," Seth grumbled.

Brant was undaunted. "We'll track her down if she's run off with her Henry. Pedro's not the only Injun who knows these hills. I got plenty of my own Injuns who'll find our runaway gal and the lion, if it comes to that."

The men unrolled blankets and squatted in what shade they could find, talking quietly and smoking. Two of them gathered sagebrush for a fire to cook their supper.

Dismayed, Molly realized that she might have to stay here all night, stretched out in the wickiup. If she fell asleep, she would surely cough and betray her presence. How could she explain hiding in the wickiup? And what if they found the box with the letter in it?

Lake Emerson strolled close to her hiding place, pausing so that his broad legs straddled the opening in the wickiup. Molly's hat and basket brushed his boots.

"See anything over there, liontamer?" Brant asked. "No. Just an old Indian basket somebody left here, I guess, along with a hat." Lake called back. "No Indians in sight, though."

But instead of joining the others, Emerson remained standing at the wickiup. From her hiding place Molly studied the long, masculine line of strong legs and thighs, the narrow waist, the swelling chest. His hands were splayed on his hips, the strong, blunt fingers firm and brown. Molly could tell a lot from a man's hands. This liontamer was a man to trust in, she mused. Dependable in a crisis. He was proving that right now by not revealing her presence to the others. He was passing up a chance to get into Brant's good graces by pretending to hunt for a lion he knew was safely hidden.

Molly was known for her strong opinions, but she was not averse to admitting she could be wrong. And she *had* changed her mind about this circus man.

Resting from their climb, the posse men began telling barroom jokes and laughing. During an especially loud outburst, the liontamer bent and hissed, "Come out, woman."

Startled, Molly slid out quickly, slapped her hat back on her head, and picked up her basket.

Lake spoke loudly, "Well, look what I found!"

Taking her arm, he pulled her toward the others. "It's the woman who saved me. But without her crazy lion-loving daughter."

"I've been looking for Clover," Molly said, distractedly. "The fool gal's gone off looking for her lion." She coughed, then gasped, "She often comes up here."

"She's lying," one called out. "She knows where the lion and the gal are." He grabbed her seed basket. "She carried up food in this, I warrant."

Molly studied Lake Emerson's face in the dying sun. Strong lines, fresh, clear, guileless gray eyes. For a face like that she had once sold her soul. Could this be the face of a killer? Did vengeance lurk in the heart of this man who had saved her from being discovered in the wickiup?

Lake Emerson was well aware that Clover and the lion were together. At the risk of his own life, he was obviously dallying here on Superstition Hill, giving Clover and Henry valuable time to get away.

Brant strolled up, laying a big hand on each of Molly's skinny arms resting beneath the blanket. "Perhaps we can get the truth out of her." He chuckled. "Eh, men, whatta you say we have some fun?"

Brant and Molly had once been friends, but it was clear that the man hated her now for interfering with the hanging of his son's killer.

Emerson's voice was deadly, replying, "You'll have to kill me first, Brant, provided you have the guts."

"Oh? What's she to you, then? Your mother?"

"No. She's only a sick old woman. True-blooded, honest-to-god Americans don't torture old women."

The men giggled, waiting. Emerson strode forward, pushing his face into Brant's. "Care to fight about it? Maybe I'll land another unlucky punch."

"Let the old one alone," one of the men murmured.

Red-faced, Brant loosened his grip on Molly, and in the ensuing silence, she scuttled off the summit.

Chapter Five

Clover sat against an alder tree, somewhere high up in the Goshute mountains north of Virginia City. The moon was bright, in its third quarter. Pedro squatted beside her, his blanket slung across his shoulders. Henry sprawled on a nearby rock, licking his paws clean after a hearty meal of fat beaver that Pedro had caught for him in the river tules. The two mules munched contentedly on a bit of green pasture, finding it a refreshing change from their usual sagebrush fare.

The fire over which Clover had cooked two fat trout on sticks had gone to embers. Her body reeked of sweat, her face itched from the smeared-on paint and dirt. But Clover was content. It had taken them two days to reach the timberline and some of her initial fear of being caught by Brant's posse disappeared as they had headed north from Pyramid Lake.

"When the liontamer does not find the lion, Brant

will know that Henry is with you," Pedro had explained. "He will expect us to head south toward Eagle Valley."

They would continue to take a northerly zigzag route for at least a week to head off any trouble. Though Henry's presence was security against attack by bandits or wandering Indians, a man with a shotgun and a good aim could pick off the lion from a nearby knoll.

Her chin in her hands, Clover mused, "Do you really think Brant will kill Captain Emerson when Henry isn't found?" She tried, vainly, to keep the dread from her voice.

Pedro grunted. "No. The man is certainly angry enough at losing his son, but there's something else he wants more than revenge. Killing the Englishman without a fair trial would bring Molly's wrath down on his head. Many in the town would not like it either, especially the women. Brant wants Wun-i-muc-a. He needs Molly's help. He needs the help of the people if another Indian war is to be avoided."

"Wun-i-muc-a . . ." Clover softly echoed the Indian name for Eagle Valley. The name meant "giver," for the lush valley gave generously of nature's bounty.

"I love it there. Sometimes I think Henry and I will stay there forever," she said.

Henry got to his feet, stretched, paws out, like a big cat, and ambled leisurely over to the stream to drink. His long tail swung back and forth contentedly. Clover watched proudly as the tawny form bent gracefully to the water, then slid in to lie, half submerged. Henry rumbled, a low sound he always made when he was happy. Her fears that Henry could not stand the trek through the mountains had proven groundless.

As a child, she had traveled often to Eagle Valley with Molly. The life was hard, simple, but somehow free of care. She'd worn moccasins and a rude skin garment. Her clear skin had turned brown as a berry and her long black hair blew free. She and other Indian girls had frolicked in long summer days, bathing in the streams, often tending the fat papooses for their busy mothers.

She'd been thirteen the summer Gray Falcon had grabbed her, kissing her as she gathered firewood with the other young girls in the woods.

"I could marry an Indian brave," she mused aloud to Pedro. "There were many handsome boys. One named Gray Falcon was quite taken with me, as I recall."

She giggled. "He taught me how to kiss. His lips were so warm—"

"Foolish talk," Pedro grumbled, gathering up the fish bones and hurling them almost angrily into the water.

Clover fell silent. He was right. How Molly would scold to hear such talk from her sweet little girl.

She could hear Molly's sharp voice: "Being a squaw is not the romantic life you imagine. It's work, work, work from dawn till dark. Your handsome brave will beat you, then put a papoose in your belly every year."

"Indian women are slaves," muttered Pedro, who had lived many years among the white men.

But so is any woman who loves deeply, Clover thought bitterly, thinking of the helpless, warm, limp feeling she had experienced in Lake Emerson's arms. As for work, work, work—wives and mothers of Black Springs also worked themselves into an early grave, cooking, cleaning, washing, producing many babies, many of whom died in infancy. Being a woman like that meant a lot of unhappiness, she reflected.

Emerging from the water, Henry shook himself, then trotted up the embankment to sidle against Clover, inviting strokes and caresses. She buried her face in his thick mane, inhaling the strong animal smell of him. Henry would be happy in Wun-i-muc-a. There was game aplenty in the well-watered valley. Deer, bears, buffalo still roamed the hills, driven there by the incursions of the white man in the north.

"Your people regard my lion as a god, Pedro," she said, stroking Henry's wet flanks. "No one would harm us."

Pedro let out a loud laugh. "That is foolishness and superstition." Then, sharply, "God or not, that beast is going to hunt for his own food. I'll do no more of it."

"He will soon, Pedro, I promise," Clover replied meekly. "He has to become accustomed to the wild."

"If we're not careful, that voracious beast will attack our mules," he continued to grumble. "Then what will we do?"

The old Indian had been bagging weasels and rabbits, with native traps, had even brought down a coyote with arrows to feed Henry's ravenous appetite. Pedro carried no gun, for an Indian caught with a firearm was instantly arrested as a troublemaker.

When darkness fell, Clover and Pedro wrapped themselves in blankets and lay on the leafy ground beneath the cottonwood. Henry stood up and roared a few times, as lions like to do at night. The travelers had no fear of coyotes or other predators who heard the ear-shattering noise. Henry, after all, was their best protection.

True to his word, Pedro provided no meat for Henry the next day, or the next. As they prepared for sleep the third night of Henry's fast, the lion began to pace around the campsite frantically.

Suddenly, the largest jackrabbit Clover had ever seen emerged from the woods. It stopped, staring at the huge African beast, obviously too surprised to move. Lightning-fast, the lion lunged, trapping the rabbit in his mouth. Much to Clover's relief, Henry dragged his kill into the woods to consume it.

She and Pedro roasted and ate a fat squirrel and sat for a long time gazing into the fire, talking of earlier days in Black Springs. They had reached the end of their northward journey, the Indian told her, and now must turn east before heading south.

"It will be desert much of the way," he warned. "Fresh water will be hard to find, and trees for shade. Game will not be so plentiful for the lion, either."

They would also meet many other travelers, he said, and must be prepared for trouble.

Henry did not return until daybreak. Clover was not concerned about him, for a lion can always find another territory he has marked as his own.

At dawn he reappeared, dragging a half-eaten carcass of a young deer and dropping it at Clover's feet as if to say, "There now, aren't you proud of me?"

Pedro was proud, too, and for the first time put out a hand to stroke the lion's flanks. Henry didn't seem to mind, sensing instinctively that the Indian was a friend. Pedro sniffed, wrinkling his long brown nose. "The animal smells of blood," he grinned. "That is good."

After his night of hunting, and a bellyful of fresh meat, Henry slept until noon. Then, rising, he drank from the stream, and, at Clover's command, joined them eagerly. He seemed a different lion, livelier, more confident, as he trotted alongside the mules, growling now and then as if to scare the brutes and remind them that he was master here.

Clover thought she had never been happier in her life. All fear of the desert journey evaporated. Henry would protect them. Her night beneath the trees had been filled with dreams of Lake Emerson. But as she led her mule down along a steep and rocky path, she put him out of her mind forever.

A new life lay ahead.

Lake Emerson sat on a velvety, cushioned chair in the house of the Indian agent in Carson City, wondering for the hundredth time in the past week what the hell he was doing in this godforsaken part of planet Earth . . .

Without his lion, to boot. Bloody, bloody, bloody, he swore under his breath. He missed that beast like the very devil. Man and lion had grown close through the years together as they'd toured the untamed American West. Like man and wife, they had learned to sense each other's moods.

Blast the girl for a nuisance, the young man inwardly raged. She acted as if Henry were hers, that only she could love him properly. Just because she'd weaned him as a cub. Why, hell, he loved that lion as much as that female ever could. When he'd bought Henry, cheap, from that two-bit circus in Illinois, Henry had been so starved his ribs had been showing. He'd nursed him, too, feeding him fresh meat, expensive beef, lamb, pork.

That was only three days after he'd escaped from prison. Lake traveled with that circus for a year, figuring it for a good blind from the authorities. A man on the run needs to be just that — constantly on the move.

A pretty Indian girl in her teens entered the room with a feather duster and began swishing it on the layer of dust that covered the dark furniture in the room. The chalky dust blew into the house, blanketing a mahogany piano, a velvet settee, assorted chairs. The agent for Indian affairs in western Nevada was not a poor man, from what Lake could see. He suspected that the Indians got little of the money allotted them by the government in Washington.

Everyone in America was free, Lake reflected wryly, everyone but the natives who had been here to begin with.

He nodded, smiling in a friendly manner, but the girl ignored him. He rose from the chair and paced the carpeted room, keeping out of her way, stopping to stare out the window overlooking the town. Lake began to worry. What in blazes was Clover giving Henry to eat out there in the desert? If they stuck to the High Sierras, though, there'd be plenty of game.

Brant and his posse had been overjoyed when the news came that the lion had been spotted. Last evening, as they were setting up camp beside still another watering hole where Lake told them the lion might be lurking, an Indian had run up out of the trees. The roar of a lion had been heard up north in the lower mountains, he reported. The lion had actually been seen by Brant's scouts.

"You're free, dammit, Englishman," Brant growled. "The beast has been found." He didn't look too happy about it. "I'd sure as hell like to gun you down right here and leave your carcass to the coyotes."

The older man's hand caressed the six-shooter at his belt.

Lake was silent. He understood that the man was suffering. The loss of a son is a pain that lasts a lifetime.

"I never meant to kill your son," he said.

They rode all night out of the mountains, and as the town watched, cheering, Brant and his posse paraded their released prisoner down Front Street in Black Springs. The rancher was a hero now. He had proven to be a man of honor and law and order had been restored. Everyone appeared to be satisfied with how it all turned out.

All but Molly, Lake found out. "That landgrabber has got the town under his thumb again," Clover's mother grumbled as she fed Lake a roast beef dinner in the stagehouse dining room. "Brant can do what he wants. He has a free hand to grab what Indian land is left, including Eagle Valley."

The Central Pacific Railroad had gobbled up all the Indian land along its route, even from what was supposed to be set aside for reservations. The Paiutes had submitted meekly, the Washos and what was left of the ancient Martis put up no fight, either. Like lambs to the slaughter, they had been herded like sheep onto reservations far away from their ancestral lands.

"Our Indians of Nevada are not a warlike people. With their trees cut down, their streams dried up by dams, their game driven out, those who stayed behind are starving," she said grimly. Tears filled Molly's eyes and she longed to ask the Englishman, "Are you the lad who helped Sinclair rob that bank? Have you come back for my sweet Clover's gold? Will you seek revenge against her?"

But she didn't. The handsome Captain Emerson would soon be out of their lives. No need to betray her secret now, Molly thought. Brant, playing the role of benefactor to the hilt, was making sure that the man who killed his son left Nevada for good. He was putting the Englishman on the Central Pacific Railroad up north along the Truckee. The train would take him to Salt Lake City, in Utah, then on to St. Louis.

As the town cheered, the freed prisoner had been presented with the ticket for St. Louis and ten dollars in cash.

But instead of heading straight to the train, Brant had stopped their horses in Carson City. He had to see the Indian agent, whose name was Parker, about urgent business, he explained.

Brooding, Lake placed both hands on the sill and leaned his head out the window, gazing up and down the main street of Carson City. A dismal sight it was.

Not a tree in sight. Powdery alkali dust covered the line of stores, coated the faces of the people.

His heart ached to be in England. The outlines of his native village sprang to mind. It's raining there at this very moment he thought. Everything is green, wet, glistening with life. His body itched and he scratched idly. He'd had no bath since the night he'd arrived in Black Springs.

He'd never forget that night. He'd smelled of lavender soap, the girl he'd kissed had smelled of lamb and herbs. Clover Sinclair would love England, he thought. So would Henry. Henry loved the water. He used to splash in every pond and river along the circus route.

Stop it, Lake told himself sternly. Tonight you'll be on a train out of here, away from the dark-eyed minx whose sweet kiss had left a permanent imprint on his lips.

"Go back to England," his father had groaned as he lay dying in that miserable damned gold-mining town in California.

And so he would, Lake vowed now as he viewed the ugly, dusty town of Carson City. He'd had a bellyful of America. Reluctantly, Lake gave up the memory of gold double eagles . . . and vengeance for the great wrong done him.

Nevada had brought him nothing but trouble. Forget the girl, forget the money.

The voices from the adjoining room where Brant and Mr. Parker were in conference behind the closed door grew louder. Lake had glimpsed them, on opposite sides of a huge oaken desk, when another Indian girl had carried in a tray of whiskey. There was a lot

106

of laughing, both were in high spirits.

The door opened suddenly, and the two men emerged, red-faced, smiling broadly. "I've given these Indians the best years of my life," Parker was saying. "Yet they are ungrateful. They are children, and need to be strictly controlled."

"I agree," Brant sighed. "If we let them have Eagle Valley to set up a free state, there'll be war and massacres, as before."

So they've settled it between them, Lake mused, feeling a kind of nausea in the pit of his stomach.

"Here's one of my children," Parker laughed, placing an arm around the waist of the girl who was raising a cloud of dust as she plied a broom to the thick carpet.

The girl blushed as the old man squeezed his coarse hand on the soft flesh of her breast. It was obvious that the agent had more than a fatherly interest in her, Lake thought angrily.

It was dark when Lake boarded the train at a waterstop just south of the northern Nevada-Idaho border. The five coaches were packed, mostly with Indians who, by a governmental edict, could ride free, since the railroad had stolen their land. Two flatbed coaches were also swarming with Indian families, going from place to place.

Despite the heat and the strong odor of unwashed bodies, including his own, Lake fell asleep, stretched out on a wooden bench.

The train stopped with a lurch, and Lake stared bleary-eyed out at a gray dawn. The air outside was cold, and Lake gratefully bounded out of the car onto a lush, green pasture surrounded by green hills.

A narrow river skirted the foot of steep mountains. Several other white men joined him as he splashed river water on face and hands. There was no depot, the train was merely taking on water from a tall wooden tower.

The pasture swarmed with more Indians than Lake had ever seen in one place at one time. Naked children ran screaming around their crudely built sagebrush lean-tos built against the lower mountain slopes. Fires burned all about, sending smoke into the morning air.

A group of Indian women stood knee-deep in a shallow river pounding garments on the rocks with broad sticks. They sang a high-pitched song as they worked.

"Beads, baskets, you buy?"

An old Indian squaw with a leathery face, so stooped she seemed bent in half, thrust a red bead necklace into Lake's face as he stood drying his face in the nippy air. Grinning at her, he began to inspect her wares.

Instantly he was surrounded by other women, hawking trinkets, bolts of calico, and reed baskets of a multitude of shapes and sizes.

"Damn Injuns, they belong on reservations where they won't bother decent white men," one of the men from the train gritted, aiming a large glob of tobacco juice at the feet of the old woman, splattering her.

She took no notice of the insult, apparently accustomed to being abused by the white man.

"They look half starved," Lake commented, noting the bone-thin children, the gaunt, hollow-eyed mothers.

Instinctively, Lake had put his hand in his trousers pocket, fingering Brant's ten-dollar bill. The tobacco-chewing man put a hand on his wrist. "Don't waste your money on the savages," he said. "They'll just buy whiskey with it." He glanced at the group of Indian braves around a fire looking on with stern faces. "Or guns," he added.

The Indian men's chests were brightly painted with crimson-and-yellow stripes and white clay paint covered their long-nosed faces. Stone tomahawks hung from their belts, and one Indian cradled a long-barreled rifle in his arms.

Another man from the train spoke up. "Guess they're fixin' to make heap big war again to get their land back." Then he laughed derisively.

The train whistle tooted, and his companions rushed to board the train, but Lake did not move. His feet seemed rooted to the ground. Brant and his threats seemed far away. He was a freeborn Englishman. No tinhorn American Indian-hating rancher was going to tell him where he could or could not live.

There was also the matter of Sinclair's gold that Lake was determined to get his hands on. He'd had time to think and he was having second thoughts about forgetting the money, half of which was rightfully his.

The train started up again and, dimly, Lake heard a shout from the train. "Hey, kid, get on board."

A young girl walked slowly toward him from a crowd of women and children. She was young, slim, pretty, and was leading a mule with a rope.

"Buy my mule for two dollars?" she asked, displaying white teeth in a broad smile. Her English was only slightly accented. A richly colored beaded band encircled a shapely head. Jet-black hair fell in glossy folds over slim shoulders. The breeze from the mountains lifted gossamer strands into the clear morning air. Full, upstanding breasts lifted her pink calico dress and beaded rabbit-fur moccasins covered tiny, slender feet.

She reminded Lake of paintings he'd seen of Pocahontas, the legendary Indian maid who had saved the life of Captain John Smith hundreds of years ago in Virginia.

In a curious way, she also made him think of Clover. There was that freshness, a virginal look, an expectancy of joy about her that caught at a man's heart.

Clover's creamy face might well be as brown as the Indian maid's by now, he mused, after a week in the open air. Lake felt a fulness between his thighs as the girl, noting his stare, sidled up to stand close.

He heard a muttering from the braves around the fire. He turned to glare at them, pretending to be unafraid. Would they scalp him, he wondered, if he refused to buy the girl's mule? Fearfully, he reached up to run his fingers through his white-blond hair. Sometimes, he'd heard, the Indians liked to roast a white man over coals. On a spit, turning, turning, still alive. It often took days to die that way.

"Please, good mule, you buy?"

Turning around again at the girl's plea, Lake stared at the mule thoughtfully. A man needed transport in this wild, uncivilized part of the universe. Mules were cheaper and more dependable than horses in the rugged Sierras.

Frowning in concentration, Lake stomped heavily around the beast, his boots making prints in the dew-wet grass. The animal had bent to crop the long grass of the meadow.

"How old is he?" he asked casually, laying his hand on a somewhat withered rump. He spoke in a loud and clear voice, wanting to seem brave and manly to the Indians looking on. He knew little about Indians, but knew they despised cowards.

Giggling, the girl replied, "Oh, two years. Very young."

He opened his mouth to laugh, but shut it again. The beast had seen five times two years, he reflected. The coarse black hide was scarred and patches of skin were missing from the tan flanks and legs where the beast had probably been caught by thorns. A large chunk had been bitten off, it seemed, from a long ear.

"Looks like it's been through a war," he muttered, half under his breath.

The mule was so thin its ribs were showing. But its legs looked sturdy, and it seemed gentle enough. Though you never could tell about mules. Ornery, people said. Black-and-tan mules were reputed to be sturdier than the gray ones.

"Good mule, take you to silver." Pocahontas pointed to the hills. Bending gracefully, she pulled up the animal's long head, putting slender hands on its mouth, forcing it open.

Large yellow teeth, good color to the gums, he thought. The mule seemed to be laughing at the curious young white man; the beast's bloodshot eyes seemed almost human.

What the bloody hell, Lake thought, laughing to himself. When he had bought Henry from that fleabitten circus, he'd known absolutely nothing about lions, either. Mules were smart and survived almost anything nature threw their way.

A crowd had gathered, chattering noisily in their dialect to each other, pointing at the white man and laughing with obvious glee. The painted braves had moved from the fire. No longer menacing, their faces were smiling.

Without thinking about it another moment, Lake reached in his pocket and thrust the ten dollars at the girl. A delighted squeal rose up from the women.

Pocahontas handed him the frayed rope that served as reins and left, returning almost immediately with a thick, very dirty blanket, folding it on the broad back as saddle. To Lake's amazement, within minutes others supplied him with two skins of water, some dried meat, and ground corn in old flour sacks. One of the warlike braves smilingly strapped a fresh-killed and gutted rabbit to his saddle. Standing back, the man beamed and reaching out, Lake shook his hand.

Pocahontas had left again, returning this time astride a second mule. "I go with you," she smiled. "Help you gather seeds, keep you warm on cold nights." The girl offered herself unblushingly, simply.

More giggles swept the women. Even the men were smiling broadly now, gleefully hopping up and down and poking each other in the ribs with their elbows. Struck dumb with amazement, Lake rallied quickly, shaking his head vigorously from side to side. He didn't stop to worry about possibly offend-

112

ing the Indians for spurning one of their women.

"No," he raised his voice. "I have wife." He swung his hand to the south. "She is in Carson City, with many children." Folding his arms across his broad chest, he made a rocking motion. Everyone laughed again, uproariously.

The girl's face clouded, but she smiled bravely as she dismounted and led her mule away. Mounting himself, Lake jerked the rope and turned the mule toward the south. He felt happy. There was a lightness to his body, a zest for life such as he had not felt since he'd been a child in England.

Lake's passion for Sinclair's daughter goaded him toward the south, where her adoptive mother had sent her. Once he had made her his own, Clover would gladly tell him where the bank loot was hidden. He would be doubly blessed. Penniless but free, Lake Emerson began to sing as he entered the mountains.

His ten-dollar mule proved to be sturdy, taking him patiently, surefootedly up and down steep trails as he followed a narrow riverbed in the low foothills. As he rode steadily through the sizzling day, he pondered the events of the morning. It seemed an omen—finding the meadow, buying the mule. Lake had not believed in God since early childhood, when his mother had read to him from the Bible every night.

But now, he mused, some Great Spirit seemed to be hovering over him. Both Clover and the gold seemed very near.

On the second day, he stopped by a small spring to fill his waterskins and worry about how he could snare a rabbit, or maybe a squirrel. He was hungry for fresh meat. His luck held out, and at dusk he came to a small plateau where a band of Indians were camping. They looked healthier than the ones up north by the railroad stop. Many of them spoke fair English, having been sent to reservation schools.

The men carried quivers filled with stone point arrows, and within an hour they had brought down ten fat rabbits from the nearby wood, which the women quickly skinned and put on sticks to roast.

Since Lake carried no gun, and had never shot an arrow in his life, one old man was happy to show him how to make a rabbit snare of sticks.

"Have you seen a white girl with black hair traveling with a lion?" Lake inquired of the group.

Heads cocked, some laughed. Others stated, "Lions gone from mountains, shot down, bang, bang."

What a fool I am, Lake thought, as they departed. *The only lions they've ever heard of would be cougars.*

The third day he caught his own rabbit and roasted it on a sagebrush fire. That night he lay wrapped in his saddle blanket, gazing at a star-filled Nevada sky. His mule grazed nearby, contentedly munching sage. This feeling of content would soon vanish, the old Indian had warned him.

"Now you must go into desert," he had said. "Very hot, much sand, water too salty to drink."

Lake woke to find a toothless old squaw squatting by the still-warm fire, gnawing on his rabbit carcass. A hawk-nosed Indian man sat cross-legged under a tree, staring at Lake and chewing on peeled cattails. Their two mules had joined his tan-and-black prize, grazing in the sage.

114

Struggling to his feet, Lake nodded a greeting. "Hello. Welcome." He extended his two hands widely.

The man grunted, handed Lake a white cattail spear. Lake sat down politely and bit off a piece. It was sweet, and satisfying.

After the Indian had smoked a pipe filled with an evil-smelling weed, he began to talk in almost perfect English.

"I am called Loud Thunder. My squaw is Sweet Bird. We go to Wun-i-muc-a Valley, where there is game and pasture for our sheep. I once had a ranch, with wooden house and many sheep. But railroad took my land, my sheep died."

"Wun-i-muc-a?"

"The white man calls it Eagle Valley."

That wonderful Wun-i-muc-a Valley will soon be the most crowded place on earth, Lake thought privately. But he said nothing. Let them dream—for now. Brant would have silver-rich Eagle Valley before the snows came, and these same Indians he met along the way would be heading to the Pyramid Lake Reservation.

Instead he asked, casually, as he had asked everyone he had met. "Have you seen a girl with a lion?"

Immediately the man shot up, and throwing out his chest and arms, emitted a roar. The woman rocked on her haunches and cackled.

Sitting down again, the man said, "We have heard the lion roar at night. Many say he travels with a girl and the Indian White Hawk. The girl is White Feather's daughter, she who is called Molly Robinson, and they go to Wun-e-muc-a."

Much relieved to know that the two people dearest

115

to his heart were safe, Lake traveled with the Indians, who, despite their age, kept pace with his mule.

They came out of the cool, shady canyon onto a rocky plateau, thick with scraggly sagebrush and sharp rocks. Alkali dust blew into their faces. High, rocky crags overhung the road. About noon, they stopped at a hot spring where the water had boiled up into a basin. It was unfit to drink, but Lake washed his face and arms and neck in it.

Whitened skulls and abandoned wrecks of wagons lay all about. They were on a once heavily traveled route to the gold country. Sand-covered skeletons of men and beasts lay all about, and hastily constructed graves piled high with rocks bore grisly evidence of travelers who had foolishly started across the desert without adequate food and water.

Lake took a leather harness from a horse whose carcass lay near its rider's skeleton. With a few adjustments, it replaced the rapidly deteriorating rope on his mule which served as reins.

As he mounted once again, Loud Thunder picked up a wide-brimmed felt hat that lay alongside the man's skull and handed it to Lake.

Grimly clapping the hat on his own sun-baked head, Lake muttered, "Thanks." But he couldn't help muttering a silent prayer for the poor bloke who had perished in this hellish place.

At Carson Lake, they stopped for water. A passing Indian family riding by on a horse told Lake that the holy lion was at Ragtown with the white medicine girl.

"She is big medicine woman," said one. "She is master of lion. Great Spirit speak through lion.

116

White girl speak for lion."

"Ragtown?" Lake asked.

"It is where the river empties into the lake," Loud Thunder offered. "Two, three hours' ride."

Whooping for joy, Lake remounted. "Let's go."

Visibly, with some help from his wife, Loud Thunder restrained him, pulling him off the mule. "You'll get lost in desert in dark, soon become skeleton yourself."

Lake woke up fitfully through the night, thinking that he was hearing roars from the nearby hills. He lay tense, waiting for more. Silence. Perhaps he was only dreaming of Henry, he told himself.

But at dawn the roaring was clear and unmistakable, heard by Loud Thunder and Sweet Bird also. After a quick breakfast of jerky and water, they all started for the hills. Within the hour, the roaring stopped.

"We'll never find him," Lake groaned.

"He is close. The mules are nervous, they know," Loud Thunder said.

At midday they came upon a flock of sheep wandering around on a grassy meadow. A man came out of a shepherd's hut. Seeing Lake and Wild Thunder, he mounted a horse and approached them.

Eagerly, Lake asked the shepherd, "Have you seen an African lion in these parts? With big mane?" Lake swept his hands over his head and shoulders to demonstrate. "Like this?"

Spitting a large glob of tobacco juice on the grass, the man replied angrily, "Seen him?" He shook his fist. "Took one of my sheep, he did. By the time I heard the ruckus and got down here from the shack, all I saw was him hightailing it thataway. Down to Ragtown."

He pointed down the hillside. Digging his boots into his horse, he grunted, "You'll pardon me for bein' unfriendly, but I gotta go after the critter afore he gets too far."

Lake's heart swelled in his chest with fear for Henry, and the shepherd, as well, if Henry charged. But he said calmly, "I hope you get him on the first shot. A wounded lion is the deadliest weapon on earth."

Riding up, Loud Thunder put in, in ominous tones, "This African lion is holy to the Paiute nation. Any man who kills it will pay with his life." The Indian made scalping motions with his hand around his head.

The shepherd had gone a few paces but stopped, turning around. "What the hell do you mean, sacred lion? Bullshit. This one stole one of my best ewes."

"Holy lions have to eat, too," Lake said impassively, repressing a chuckle.

The shepherd's face paled. "Do you, a white man, swallow all this holy-lion nonsense? Will the Injuns really come after me if I shoot the critter?"

Lake nodded. "I'm sure as hell. I've worked with lions in a circus. They're often regarded as having special powers. I'll speak to its owner, the white medicine woman. I'll see that you are given another sheep.

Scratching his gray head in puzzlement, the now-frightened shepherd pursed his lips. "The whole thing sounds crazier than a hoot owl in a thunderstorm, but I've no hankerin' to tangle with an African lion."

"Now you're being sensible," Lake said lightly. "Foolish to lose your life for one sheep, when you've got so many."

Still not completely mollified, the shepherd squinted at Lake. "How can I be sure that so-called sacred lion won't kill all my sheep?"

"You can't. But I'll try to persuade the owner to sell him to me immediately. I want him for my circus in San Francisco."

He chuckled wryly. "This one's no ordinary lion."

Amazingly, the shepherd seemed to believe Lake's wild story and rode back to his hut. Loud Thunder and Lake and Sweet Bird pointed their mules downhill to Ragtown.

Halfway down a steep, heavily wooded slope, they came across Henry, right on the trail, a freshly killed sheep dangling from his maw. Hearing the mules, the lion stopped, turning around. He began to growl deeply in his throat at the interlopers.

Loud Thunder and his old wife instantly led their mules into the trees by the side of the trial, but Lake dismounted.

"Henry, you old so-and-so. It's me, your old pal," Lake exclaimed in a loud voice. He walked slowly toward the lion, who blocked the trail with his huge body.

Dropping the bloody ewe, the lion crouched in a charging posture, baring his yellow canines. His ears drew back, and the snarls that emerged from his half-open mouth were not the friendly sounds that Lake had expected.

Henry's amber eyes slitted alarmingly.

The damn beast doesn't even remember me, Lake

thought. I've also disturbed him with his kill.

Thoroughly frightened for his life, Lake backed up, remounting quickly. Slowly, he inched the mule toward the tree cover. After a few more menacing rumbles, Henry warily picked up his kill once more and turned to trot rapidly down the hillside.

After a long time, Lake and his Indian companions followed Henry down to Ragtown.

Chapter Six

For the third time in less than an hour, Clover pushed aside the rabbitskin door covering and stepped outside into the glaring sun. The wooden door of the abandoned blacksmith shop that she and Pedro — and Henry — were living in had long ago been torn off for firewood by previous owners.

The early-morning desert cold had yielded to a hot wind, and Ragtown shimmered with dry heat. Shading her black eyes with a work-worn hand, she frantically scanned the mountains to the west. Green slopes with snow on top, the hills looked inviting. Maybe Henry had decided to stay up there in the cool. Not even a dumb animal would want to return to a furnace like Ragtown, she reflected sourly.

Hearing a footfall behind her, she moaned, "He's never been gone this long before, Pedro, I'm so afraid."

"One day your lion will not return to you," the Indian said flatly. "You can't fight nature."

121

Old White Hawk sighed. He had promised his old pal Molly to guard her girl and the silly lion with his life, but while he loved Clover, he felt only exasperation for the lion. He and Henry had made a sort of peace with each other. At least the lion was killing his own meat now, but Henry was still more trouble than Pedro needed.

Clover worried constantly about him, like a mother with a sick child. No good could possibly come of this crazy business of Henry being a "holy" lion. If she wasn't careful, the girl could get herself involved in a nasty tribal war, with all sides claiming rights to the lion.

Seeing Clover's distress, though, Pedro laid a comforting hand on her shoulder. "Your darling pet will show up soon. He can't live without you any more than you can live without him."

Then, mildly, "I think I heard some roars at dawn."

A dry wind whipped Clover's calico dress against her swelling bosom and curving, womanly hips. Although Pedro had been castrated by an enemy's lance in his youth, he had not lost his keen eye for a lovely woman. Molly's little girl needed a man, a husband, to sleep at her side at night. Not a lion.

A pity, he thought, that the good-looking English liontamer had come to a bad end. Captain Emerson had the look of a man who could fill Clover's bed in a manly fashion. What's more, the girl had seemed taken with the Englishman, too. Pedro had witnessed, unobserved, the kiss near the lion's cage the night the circus came to Black Springs.

The Indian White Hawk stood a moment longer

gazing at the near-hillside down which Henry would have to come before turning away from the doorway. "I've got to see to the mules," he said.

In his heart Pedro prayed to the god who watches over animals to set the lion free somewhere in the heights of the lofty Sierra Nevada. Only divine intervention could break the almost unnatural bond between the girl and her Henry.

A few days earlier, a falling rock had struck Clover's mule, hurling both animal and rider to the ground. Pedro thought it best they stop in Ragtown until the mule was strong enough to travel again. Luckily, Clover had been unhurt, only shaken up. She welcomed the week of rest from constant traveling. Ragtown was perfect for it. Once a thriving crossroads for gold-rush emigrants, it now lay empty of permanent residents. The Carson River flowed nearby, providing fresh, clean water and welcome shade from the willows and cottonwoods on its banks.

Ragtown's clutter of houses were falling apart from disuse and weather. Debris littered the white alkali sand—rusting wagon wheels, bleached animal bones, chains and harnesses from long-gone horses.

"A watched pot never boils," she thought grumpily. Staring at the mountains wouldn't bring Henry back any sooner.

Two small Indian children ran up to Clover as she turned to reenter the blacksmith shop. "We want to see Henry," one of them said.

Clover smiled down at a little girl dressed in dirty pink calico. If she made her life in Eagle Valley, she might marry Gray Falcon and have a sweet little girl

123

just like this black-eyed charmer.

"Where is he?" her boy companion shouted as, stark naked, he raced like the wind around the long adobe dwelling, hoping to find the lion in his usual resting place beneath a sprawling sagebrush behind the house.

The children were Paiutes, and Clover answered them in their language, which she had learned as a child from Pedro and other Indians who visited the stagehouse.

"Henry is hunting food for himself," she said.

Disappointed, the children ran off, back to the motley assortment of tipis and wickiups set up on a grassy place against the lower mountains. About a hundred Indians were also resting from the long, arduous journey south to the valley of their dreams.

In the house, Clover took two neatly folded frocks from an iron-bound wooden chest, left behind by a female traveler. One was a plain blue calico with long, close-fitting sleeves, the other a soft, flowered pink, with ruffles edging the V-shaped neckline. Unfolding them, she held them up, trying to decide which to wear today.

The sturdy chest was filled with exquisitely made frocks and undergarments. Miraculously, the Indians had never discovered it. Clover hoped that the woman who owned the chest had abandoned it to lighten the load on her wagon.

"The woman who wore those dresses is probably lying in the rockpile that marked the emigrant graveyard beyond the town," Pedro had ventured gloomily.

Slinging both frocks over her arm, Clover stepped to the huge stone firepit, removing last night's trout bones from the spit, then wrapping them in a bit of old cloth.

At the door she paused to survey the long room. She and Pedro had worked a full day clearing out debris and animal droppings. Clover had swept the dirt floor with sagebrush brooms, scrubbing the walls with pails of river water until they smelled almost fresh.

The old shop was cozy and unexpectedly spacious, she thought, consisting of two sleeping rooms in addition to the shop. The forge stood outside. She and Henry slept in one room, Pedro in the other.

The smith had surely made a fortune, she mused, shoeing oxen, horses, and mules for the thousands of wagons that had crossed the plains to California during the big gold rush. In the sixties, they had crossed for Nevada silver. Now the man was probably living in high style in a San Francisco mansion, Clover reflected.

At the river, Clover hung the frocks over a willow branch, lifting the sweaty one she was wearing over her head and dropping it on the ground. Her single undergarment, a cotton shift, joined it. She'd scrub them later in the river.

Naked, Clover happily slipped into the shallow water by the reedy bank. The water was icy, and she quickly swam along the shore, stroking vigorously. Her daily swim was her salvation; it kept her sane in this desolate place. Pedro was not given to idle chatter, and Clover was lonely. She missed Molly horribly.

When the mule was fit to travel, her life would be dust, alkali grit, and sweat once more. Thankfully, though, she need not wear the smelly squaw clothes anymore.

"It's useless to keep up your disguise," Pedro had commented. "Our passage south is public knowledge. Brant is no longer interested in killing your lion now that we are far from Black Springs."

But her late fiancé's father had surely killed Lake Emerson, Clover reflected bitterly as she stroked steadily through the water. Her loosened hair made a black halo around her face and shoulders. Idly, she ran her fingers through the tangles, and set her thoughts on Lake.

Stop it, you idiot, she scolded herself. The man is dead. Brant is not a man to keep his pledge to spare the man's life. Who could blame him? The liontamer had killed his son, the apple of his eye. And Mrs. Brant . . . what about her? The poor woman was probably prostrate with grief.

Clover felt a deep shame that she had not grieved for Spike. He had been very fond of her for many years. But the dazzling new love that had struck with Lake Emerson's kiss had driven the faithful Spike clean out of her mind.

"You never forget your first love," Molly often said. Many times in odd moments, Clover had caught the yearning look in her mother's eyes when they talked about love. Clearly, Molly had not forgotten the man who had loved her and left her bitter.

Clover grew warm just remembering the feel of the virile liontamer's arms around her. He had seemed so strong, so completely in charge. She had wanted to cuddle forever against his broad chest.

Loud noises from the Indian camp jolted her back

to reality. She heard shouts and greetings; newcomers had apparently arrived. Pedro warned that war was brewing. Indians from tribes as far east as Utah and Montana were pouring into Nevada to help save Eagle Valley.

As she climbed out of the water, Clover heard a chant: "Wun-i-muc-a, Wun-i-muc-a, Wun-i-muc-a!"

Quickly, she slipped the pink, ruffled frock over her wet body. Her nipples were dark points in the thin fabric. The hot sun would dry the frock in minutes, but now it fit snugly across her breasts and thighs, clinging like a second skin. The feel of the fine gingham against her bare, wet flesh was so sensuous, she caught her breath, feeling a stirring in her lower regions.

If Lake Emerson came riding up right now, she thought, she might just throw herself into his arms. But of course he couldn't, for he was either dead or rotting in the Carson City jail.

The sun was climbing in a cloudless sky, and everything seemed unnaturally still. Oddly, the racket from the Indians had stopped, too. Maybe they were eating. Clover started to pull at her dripping hair, fingering out bits of river weeds and bringing the heavy mass to the front over one shoulder. As her fingers tried to separate the hair into strands for braiding, she found them slow, clumsy.

An eerie aura of strangeness came over her, the kind of feeling a person gets when lost in a thick forest. Her bare feet sank into the soggy riverbank, but when she tried to move back to firmer ground, they felt like lead weights. *Someone or something is watching me,* she thought. But she was too frightened to turn around.

A split second later Clover heard a distinct roar behind her. It could not be—but it had to be. Nothing on earth but a lion could produce a noise so powerful.

Her fingers froze in her hair as Clover lifted her glistening face to listen. A second roar brought a flush of sheer happiness to her veins. She turned around.

"Henry!

But the lion was not there. Instead, Clover saw a single rider advancing toward her on a mule.

A beautifully radiant Clover was what Lake Emerson saw as he led his black and tan mule to the river. A wet pink dress clung tenaciously to her maddeningly curvaceous form and she appeared to be wearing no undershift. Her nipples were dark points against the pink cloth, and a distinct dark shadow marked her feminine mound. Obviously she had not expected anyone to catch her in such an immodest state.

Her dark eyes were wide and inky black in a flushed face. The full lips he'd kissed were half open in surprise. There was a disarming, completely unconscious sensuality about the girl, an erotic aura that struck him like a blow to his solar plexus.

The usually self-possessed young Englishman was totally unprepared for this. The girl had filled his dreams for weeks, but all dreams paled before the reality of her.

His lower body began a kind of revolt. His loins

grew warm, then, helplessly, he became aware that his sexual organ was swelling. Instantly, he lowered his hands, still on the mule's reins, to hide the embarrassing bulge.

Bloody hell, a sight like this would drive any man with any blood in him clean out of his senses. Desperately, Lake clung tightly to the bridle to keep himself from leaping from his mule to crush this vision to his overheated body. She was already scared out of her wits at seeing what she probably would think was a ghost. To move rashly now would spoil his plans to win her over.

When they came together in love, it must be perfect—a blissful harmony of soul and body.

"Tarnation!" Clover shrieked. "You're supposed to be dead." The heavy braid she'd been working on fell from her fingers, to spread over her breasts and waist.

Lake playfully pinched his arm under the rolled-up sleeve of his plaid shirt. "Ouch," he yelled. Then, breaking into a wide grin— "Sorry to disappoint you, Miss Sinclair, but I fear that I am very much alive."

"Oh-h-h, my God—"

She took one step toward him, her bare feet pulling out of the muddy bank with a plopping sound. Her arms stretched out invitingly. The man was dazzling, she thought, more heartbreakingly handsome than in any of her dreams. His high-browed face was deeply suntanned, the dove-gray eyes were smiling at her wickedly.

Before she took another step, a second giant roar was heard. Clover came out of her trance. "It's Henry," she breathed, her black eyes becoming limpid pools. "He's with you?"

Cursing the lion for interrupting what might have been a tender reunion, Lake nodded. But his heart leaped at bringing her such joy. "We met by accident, he and I, on the trail." Cocking a blond brow, he added, "I'm afraid, though, that your lion is in a spot of trouble."

She looked stricken and her hand flew to her throat. "Is he hurt?"

A laugh erupted from Lake Emerson's throat. "No, he's bouncing with health. But there's a sheep that's hurt badly, in fact mortally wounded, I'd say, because of Henry."

Wailing at the top of her lungs, Clover streaked past Lake and his mule toward the blacksmith shop. Behind the adobe building, she came upon a very angry Pedro glaring—at a safe distance—at a very hungry lion, who sprawled in his favorite spot under the sage, avidly devouring a sheep.

"You naughty, naughty boy, what have you done?" Clover yelled as she ran up to the scene. She turned to Pedro. "We passed some sheep ranches on the trail, but I never dreamed . . ."

Joining her, still on his mule, Lake commented dryly, "Meat is meat to Henry." He shook his head. "Our darling animal has got the sheepmen in an uproar."

Glancing up at the hills, he continued. "I stopped them from storming down to Ragtown with shotguns cocked for Henry by spinning a tale that he was some kind of 'holy' animal to the Indians, who would kill him if he killed their totem animal."

"Hell's fire," Pedro broke in, enraged. "That superstitious nonsense won't stop them for long. By night-fall we'll be surrounded by trigger-happy sheepmen out to shoot the beast dead."

The Indian stalked off, muttering, "Hope they do. The sooner we're rid of that pesky lion, the better for all of us." He glared at Clover. "Especially you."

There was nothing to do but draw back and watch that nobody disturbed Henry at his meal. Tears streaked down Clover's cheeks as she leaned against a nearby rock. Dismounting, Lake slapped his mule's rump, sending it off to graze.

"We'll have to tie our lion up, maybe build a cage," he said. "Do you think we can find any sturdy lumber in this dried-up place?"

"The willow grove by the river has some thick branches," Clover replied absently. Then, as if suddenly realizing what was happening, she jerked her head up, staring with blazing eyes at the liontamer.

"I have no intention of caging up my lion, Captain Emerson. He's already had a lifetime of imprisonment." Balling her hands into fists at her side, she raged, "Anyway, what do you mean, *our* lion? I raised that animal, he's all mine." She glanced at Henry. "Why, he's forgotten all about you."

Grim-faced, Lake snapped back, "We'll see about that, young lady. I paid good cash for that lion. He was never yours to begin with."

Lowering himself to the ground, Lake squatted against the shop wall, several yards from the eating lion. "No need for you to stand guard here, too, Clover. You must have other things to do."

Thinking briefly of the soiled dress and undergarment left by the river to launder, Clover said testily,

"No, thanks. He's my lion, and I'm responsible for him. He cannot be allowed to wander into the Indian camp. The children may taunt him . . ." She inhaled, deeply. "Tame as he is, he could become dangerous."

"Well, we can't let that happen, can we?" Lake smirked. "Henry's already a wanted killer."

Ignoring his attempt at humor, Clover shrugged. "I'm not leaving until he's finished with his meal. Then he goes inside the shop with me."

Pursing his wide lips, Lake squinted at the now molten sky, then lazily slid his eyes downward to meet hers. "We could tie him up to a tree," he said thoughtfully. "I'll make a collar for him."

Sliding his glance from hers to sweep the barren landscape surrounding them, he inquired, "Got any scraps of leather around this graveyard of a town?"

His gray eyes returned to hers, catching her unawares staring at him unabashedly.

Flushing with annoyance and embarrassment, Clover replied, "I think I can find some. But Henry isn't going to like being harnessed like a mule."

"All of us, including a pampered lion, have got to tolerate things we don't like." Lake's tone was more pensive than angry.

Irritated at herself for allowing him to unsettle her so easily, and going nearly mad at the nearness of sweating biceps, not to mention strong thighs straining the blue fabric of his dusty trousers, Clover bolted to her feet. She started to pace back and forth nervously on the baked dirt. A minor panic in her midsection was beginning to make her dizzy.

Although her dress was nearly dry, she self-consciously folded her arms across her bosom, hiding her nipples. The effect, however, was to push her breasts up into the low-cut neckline so that a distinct, mounded cleavage was alarmingly visible.

Appreciating the sight, as well as her obvious discomfort, Lake chuckled, "Pretty dress. Where the devil did it come from? I heard that you were going around disguised as an old squaw."

Struggling for control, she replied weakly, "I gave it up. Everybody in three states knows where Henry and I are, it seems." Unfolding her arms, preferring the revealing damp dress to an exaggerated cleavage, she said, casually, "As for the dress, some poor woman left a clothing chest behind in the shop."

"Hmm. How fortunate for you. But you're right about your whereabouts being public knowledge. Soon as I got free of Brant, I came after you immediately."

"Why?"

For a brief moment, the sharp question caught him short. But then he said softly, "You know why, surely."

Lake's clipped English words slurred a little, and his clear eyes clouded to a new softness. Rising himself to conceal his returning erection, he stood tall and quiet, gazing down at Henry, who was gnawing a bone, completely oblivious to everything.

"He's almost done eating," he said, in a queer kind of stifled voice, "now he'll bury the heart and liver for a snack later on."

At that moment, Lake wished fervently that the lion had been shot by the sheepman. At the river she had come to him with open arms, ready to surrender—until the damn lion roared again.

"You've come for Henry, haven't you?" she whispered, suddenly terrified. Coming close, she groaned, "You're going to take him away, aren't you, you heartless Englishman?"

To her chagrin, Clover was helpless to stop the scalding tears from coursing down her cheeks into her mouth, dripping off her chin. Furiously, she pounded her fists against his broad chest. "You want to put him in a cage again, for people to stare at. You—you murderer—you can't have him." Clover's eyes narrowed to slits. "You'll have to kill me first."

Snatching her flailing fists, Lake held them against his hard body with one hand. With the other hand he cupped the back of her head, pulling her tear-wet face close to his. She smelled of fresh water and gingham. His erection pushed painfully against his trousers.

He himself reeked of sweat, dust, mule, and the forest creatures he had caught and eaten on the trail.

Clover sniffed disdainfully. "You even smell like a skunk."

But she did not pull away. She seemed to be waiting, her mouth open wantonly, tears glistening like diamonds on her upper lip.

"Oh, God," he moaned, bending his head to cover that alluring mouth with his own. Gently, he swept his tongue across the trembling tears, swallowing them.

Clover uttered a strangled sob.

"Kiss me, little one, my sweet, adorable Clover," he hissed, pushing his tongue into her mouth. Her inner body warmth flowed into his mouth, mingling with his breath.

As a mind-searing heat scorched her every muscle, Clover felt that she was a living flame. She fell against him, straining with all her might. Her nipples became hot and dry and stiff.

Releasing her with a jolt, Lake pushed her away almost violently. "I want both you and Henry," he muttered hoarsely. "The three of us belong together."

Lightning swift, her mood changed. Her black eyes widening in horror, she brought her hand to her mouth, wiping away his kiss with vigor. "Never. I despise you. How can I live with a man who's killed twice?"

Lake's tanned brow furrowed. "That's the second time you called me 'killer.' I've been cleared of blame in Spike's death." Taking her by the shoulders, he shook her angrily. "Now, who else do you think I murdered?"

Her eyes grew hot and her nostrils flared. But it was with more sorrow than anger that she cried, "My father."

Too astonished to speak, Lake could only stare. The girl was stark raving mad.

"You were at the reins of a circus wagon that sideswiped my papa's medicine wagon off a cliff," she wept. "I've never forgotten your face and your devilish laugh as you drove away leaving us to our fate."

"Wha-at?" he finally choked. Smacking his brow with the flat of his hand in disbelief, he exclaimed, "What a damn fool notion, what a goddamned cockeyed idea!"

Throwing back his blond head, Lake Emerson hooted at the mules nibbling at some brush at the far end of the house. "D'ya hear that, you jackasses, this

135

loony female thinks I killed her precious papa."

His face convulsed with merriment, he paced rapidly back and forth in front of a white-faced Clover, who had not expected this reaction to her accusation. The liontamer looked absolutely flabbergasted, and not a bit guilty.

"Why, you silly goose, I was a thousand miles from Nevada back in the summer of 1865."

Clover narrowed her eyes. "How did you know that my papa died in 1865?"

"Because Molly told me about how she plucked you half-dead off a mountainside when you were seven."

Mollified, but still unconvinced of his innocence, she inquired, "Where were you in the summer of 1865?"

"In prison, Mr. Prosecutor," he said tartly.

She stepped back. "Oh, really? What for?"

Taking a few steps himself, Lake closed the distance between them once again. "Until we are a bloody lot closer — as in marriage, Miss Clover Know-it-all Sinclair — that information is strictly my own affair."

Childishly, she persisted, desperately wanting to believe him but unable to abandon just yet her long-cherished dream of vengeance.

"Why should I believe you," she said flatly.

"Because you love me," he replied swiftly, pulling her close again. "That kiss, added to the first one by the lion cage, tells me everything I want to know. Grinning wickedly, he added, "Shall we try another for good measure?"

With a shriek, Clover struggled to free herself.

Molly was right—all handsome men are scoundrels. At her scream, Henry lifted his head, and, leaving his sheep bone, bounded toward the embracing pair. Crouching dangerously close to Lake, the lion bared his teeth and flattened back his ears. His amber eyes stared menacingly at Lake as a rumbling growl came from his throat.

Startled, Clover hissed, "Let me go. He thinks you're hurting me."

Genuinely scared, the liontamer who once was master of the beast now threatening him, sprinted toward the river. Henry made no move to follow him.

Straightening up to her full height, Clover broke off a leafy branch from the sage bush. Calmly stripping off all but the endmost leaves to make a replica of the customary tasseled lion stick, she held the branch over the animal's head, advancing forward cautiously.

"Up, Henry," she said sharply.

Whether the tasseled branch did the trick, or the rapid disappearance of the man from his mistress, the lion got to his feet and ambled back to his sheep bones. After she watched him bury the heart and liver under the sand, a distance from the house, Clover led him inside.

The carrion birds would no doubt clean up the bloody mess her lion had made of the poor sheep.

Splashing around in the chill water of the Carson River, Lake Emerson soon recovered his equilibrium. Fickle lion, he fumed. Just like his mistress. He laughed aloud. Serves me right, he thought, for being so bloody cocky. Less than a month ago, he had been lord and master of the beast. Henry had been his puppet, his slave. When Captain Emerson, brave liontamer, had snapped his fingers, the massive beast had obeyed.

Now a mere snip of a girl had Henry mesmerized. *Me, too,* reflected Lake wryly. Swimming lazily to ease his tense muscles, he relished the sting of cold against his fevered body. His erection had gone limp when the damn lion crouched. He'd have to make sure he didn't try such rough-man tactics again if the lion was anywhere nearby.

But blazes, what's a man to do? He wanted her so savagely. No woman had ever got under his skin like Clover Sinclair. Plenty he'd known had been prettier, more desirable — certainly more willing.

I'm in love, the real thing this time, Lake admitted grudgingly.

It was obvious that Clover remembered him from the time he'd worked for her father, several years before Sinclair had devised the robbery scheme. His striking white-blond hair and his distinctive laugh must have impressed her as a child. Molly said Clover had been confused for a long time after the accident. He could readily understand how she had merged his face with that of the man who had brushed against the medicine wagon.

But her haunting memory of his face was not likely to go away. One day soon Clover herself would put two and two together and start asking him other questions. She would surely investigate his prison record and uncover the story of the robbery and her father's part in it.

Somehow, he had to stop her from doing that. It would break her heart to be told that her dear papa was a thief and a coward who had run off, leaving a boy to face the punishment for him.

Lake cringed inwardly, imagining the deep pain in her beautiful eyes. One day she must be told, but not until she was his wife and he could ease her hurt.

Climbing out of the water, Lake hastily pulled on his trousers, and, after a quick scrub on the rocks, he left his filthy shirt to dry on a willow branch alongside a blue calico dress of Clover's. Whistling with confidence and anticipation of the conquest he planned for the night, the liontamer ran toward the blacksmith shop.

As for that fickle lion, he vowed, he'd have to train him from scratch again. Henry would soon learn that he had more than one master.

Chapter Seven

Lake glanced up from the floor, where he sat cross-legged piecing together scraps of old leather to fashion a harness for Henry.

"Why would anyone want to push your father's medicine wagon off the road?" he asked. "Unless it was a rival doc trying to get him out of the way?"

Clover shook her head, which was bent low over two skinned rabbits she was chopping up for tonight's stew. "No. My papa was the dearest, kindest man in the world. He never had a single enemy. Besides, the killer's horses were pulling an animal cage, and the name across the top of it began with Grand—."

"For Grandiose Circus." He grinned. "So that's why you thought it was me. Rather flimsy evidence."

She lifted her head, looked him directly in the eyes. "The driver looked very much . . . like you."

Lake spoke sharply, in a scolding tone. "For God's sake, girl, it was dark, you were a mere child, there must be millions of tall blond young men in the world."

"Of course," she murmured, her thoughts far from the memory of that fatal night. The heat of the fire and his hard work cutting and knotting the thick leather had brought out beads of sweat on Lake's bare chest and muscled liontamer's arms. Light from the open door danced on his fine white-gold hair. Clover's heart jumped into her throat. She loved and desired this man even more than the first day she had laid eyes upon him.

She threw the last of the rabbit chunks into the simmering iron pot, setting the mess of animal bones on the hearth.

Shrugging, he stood up, too, dangling the harness. "It was an accident, pure and simple. It's a miracle that anyone ever survives these beastly mountain trails."

"I suppose."

Clover gazed vaguely at the harness, seeing instead the two strong, brown, very masculine hands clutching the bits of leather. She imagined those hands clasping her lower body to his, pressing tightly, tightly —

"Well," he prodded, "what do you think? Will Henry take to being led around like a dog on a leash?" He walked to the open doorway of the adjoining room where Henry lay sleeping off his meal of stolen sheep.

Clover banished her erotic daydreams and with effort threw him a scornful look. "You seem to have forgotten what happened this morning when Henry saw the two of us together." She laughed contemptuously. "That lion will make mincemeat out of you if you go near him with that harness. He won't have to kill any sheep for days."

"Hmm." Lake looked thoughtful. Then, bowing deeply, he handed Clover the harness and long leather leash. "You put it on. If I hear a growl, I'll come to the rescue."

With lifted brow and skeptical face, Clover squeezed past him in the narrow doorway. Lake felt the press of her firm bosom against his chest and a tremor shot through his body. As she took the harness from his hands, their fingers touched, interlocking at one point.

She hesitated, facing the darkness of Henry's room. The desire that welled up between them was so strong, it was almost palpable.

The moment passed, and, quickly, Clover moved toward the lion. Lake strode back to the firepit, savagely attacking the sagewood coals with the poker. Peering into the pot, he sniffed hungrily. He'd been so anxious to catch up with the girl at Ragtown, he hadn't eaten anything since yesterday morning.

So this is what's known as love play, he thought, lying down on the hearth propped up on one elbow, staring into the fire and smelling the cooking rabbit. I know she wants me, she knows I want her, but yet—it can't happen too soon. A certain amount of tension and uncertainty seemed necessary in this circumstance.

He had seen circus animals brought together for mating. Elephants, lions, hyenas—the pattern never

142

varied. The female danced around, played coy, ran away, pretending to hate the male.

He bolted up at a startling thought. All that nonsense about his driving the wagon that killed her father had been just that—a female trick to put him off.

Falling back down again, Lake chuckled softly, pleased with himself. Except for a few loud snuffles and a single irritable "uh, uh, uh," everything was quiet in the next room. A marvel of a girl, he thought. Then he corrected himself. She was a woman. His loins tingled in anticipation of possessing a woman who could master a lion.

A deafening clap of thunder announced the start of a short and violent desert storm. In seconds, rain was hitting the packed brush roof at a punishing clip, drowning out the noise from the Indian encampment where a tremendous powwow was taking place. Indians from all over the Far West had been singing, chanting, and whooping for hours, and the smoke from their fires had laid a thick haze over Ragtown.

"They are working magic for one last battle against the white man," Pedro had said. "This mighty battle will be held at Eagle Valley when Brant and his men come to take it from us."

"No place for Clover to be," Lake had commented.

The old Indian had mutely pursed his lips, shaking his pigtailed head from side to side.

But here, in this dim, warm house, all was cozy and content, Lake reflected. They were safe, for a while, from the rain, the world. There would be an end to their personal man-woman battle when Clover returned from tying up Henry.

Home to twenty-six-year-old Lake Sinclair was only a word. He'd never known what others call home. When he was three, his mother had died of a fever, and his grieving father had brought him to the California gold fields. Life there was a dismal chain of filthy shacks and houses where thin curtains divided one room from the other. At ten, he'd become a circus roustabout; at fourteen, home became an Illinois jail.

Now, as an escapee, he could never settle down like other men and allow himself to be caught and dragged back to jail.

A lump of unshed tears rose in Lake's throat, and he pressed his face into the hearthstones, half sobbing with self-pity. He'd wasted his young life in a desperate search for wealth and revenge. The heart that had known little love had been consumed by greed. Greed had driven him to join Sinclair in the bank robbery.

"You may be only fourteen, as you claim," the judge had said sternly, "but you've a man's body, and a man's conscience. You were not led blindly into sin."

The judge had glanced at Lake's long legs. "You could have run away."

A sudden wetness at his back caused him to jump up. The rabbitskin at the door had blown off, and rain gushed into the room. Grabbing a reed broom from the hearth, he began to sweep the water vigorously out the door. He peered out. Rain was coming down in sheets. No sign of Pedro. After fetching the rabbits, the Indian had left to join the powwow. The hoopla might go on all night, despite the rain, Lake mused, leaning on his broom, forgetting to sweep.

His mind spun dreams. First, they would eat the rabbit stew. He needed strength. He imagined the two of them sitting by the hearth, close, chatting. Then, when she was full, and maybe a bit sleepy, he would guide her to the pile of skins in the corner. His blood grew hot, his hands clenched the broom handle.

"You idiot, the floor is covered with water!"

Clover rushed into the room, jolting him out of his fantasy. Grabbing the broom, she began to sweep. "Another five minutes and the water would have reached the fire."

"Blimey," Lake exclaimed, gazing stupidly at the water sloshing around his boots. "Bloody hell!"

"The skin," she yelled, dropping the broom and darting past him into the rain.

Lake looked out. The rabbitskin door covering lay in a sodden heap in a puddle. He ran out after her, and as she turned to run back, they collided, both falling down in three inches of water.

"Oh-h, you stupid—" Choking with rage, Clover sat, straddle-legged, her beautiful face red with rage. "You utter fool," she spluttered.

She looked so ravishing in the very wet, very cling-ing pink dress that Lake threw back his head and laughed uproariously. He opened his mouth wide, lapping up the cool, sweet raindrops.

"Life with you, Clover Sinclair, is . . ." He paused, reaching for a word to describe the deliciousness of his feelings at that moment. "Exciting," he finished. "Very exciting," he repeated under his breath as he lunged forward to pull her to her feet. The movement was so swift that Clover froze, surprised. Cupping her wet head in one hand, Lake bent to kiss her soundly on the mouth.

When he released her lips but not her head, she peered into his eyes. There were drops of rain on her long black lashes.

"Are you sure," she asked, breathlessly, "that you were in prison in 1865?"

"You hang on to a notion like Henry with a juicy bone," he chuckled. "The very minute we get to civilization, you can wire the prison and verify my story."

The warden will also inform her that her father had robbed a bank and run off with the money, leaving me to be caught, he thought. But by the time she learned that devastating news, they would be man and wife. When all was revealed, he could ask her what happened to all those double eagles. They were probably gone, spent by Molly for house and food, but he'd be damned if he was going to forget about them.

The punishing rain had stopped, and the waning day grew chill. "Let's go inside," she said, shivering in his arms. Childlike, she leaned against him, as if trying to warm herself.

Scooping her up in his arms, Lake turned to reenter the house. The rabbitskin covering lay forgotten in the puddle. He strode to the fire, where he gently set her on her feet. They kissed, quickly, feverishly. Clover felt her blood grow hot, warming her as it flowed through her body.

With a tiny moan of pleasure and anticipation, Clover stood back, and grasping the gently flaring skirt, started to lift the wet dress over her head. In her haste, she forgot to unfasten the buttons in the back, and the clinging fabric covered her face and head like a hood.

"I'll help," Lake laughed, leaping behind her to fumble with the tiny buttons.

"Hurry, I'm suffocating," she pleaded.

Pedro's loud voice sounded from the doorway. "Put your garment back on, Clover, I fear your lovemaking will have to wait."

Startled and embarrassed, Clover eased the wet frock down again over her shoulders. Her lovely face was beet-red as she smoothed the pink gingham out again around her breasts and hips.

"Why, Pedro, what have you done to yourself?" she gasped when she could finally look at him.

Molly's old childhood friend looked like a painting of an old Indian brave. Instead of his customary plaid shirt and dungarees, he wore a smelly buckskin garment, embroidered with brightly colored beads. His long black hair hung down around his shoulders and in place of his battered felt hat, a feathered headdress shone brightly in the firelit room. His hawklike face bore streaks of red and yellow paint.

"What the devil," Lake exploded. "Are you on the warpath?" His face showed concern.

"Not at the moment," the Indian grinned, "but the sheepmen are." He glanced toward the room where Henry slept. "Runners bring news that a posse of ten sheepmen are riding down the mountains with guns, vowing to shoot the lion dead."

Clover blanched. Her fevered body grew cold with fear. All thoughts of love and passion fled as she ran to protect her beloved Henry. "Hurry, we've got to get him away."

In the next room, the lion slept soundly, peacefully, stretched out to fill the room from wall to wall. He snuffled, grunted, and moaned, as if dreaming of fat sheep in the mountains.

Kneeling at his side, Clover spoke softly. "Henry, Henry, wake up." Gently, so as not to startle him, she touched his velvety nose.

"My God, Clover, be careful. A lion awakened before he's ready can be dangerous," Lake whispered from the doorway. Remembering Henry's snarling attitude toward his former trainer that morning, he had no intention of approaching the beast.

"It's okay." Clover replied sharply. "I've had to awaken him this way many times on the trail."

"There's no time to escape," interrupted Pedro, who had slipped past Lake to loom behind Clover. "The sheepmen will be in Ragtown in minutes. Get the lion on his feet and follow me to the Indian powwow."

Clover stared. "But—"

"Don't argue," the Indian shouted. "Come!" Whipping around, he strode into the main room and out the door.

Awake but groggy, Henry trotted meekly at Clover's side. If he were even aware that a harness encircled his muscular chest, he gave no sign. Holding tightly to the leather leash, Clover listened intently as Pedro outlined his scheme to save the animal from the sheepmen's wrath.

Many of the tribesmen gathered for the powwow believed that Clover's lion was the reincarnation of an ancient warrior. Clover herself was regarded as a shaman, who could speak to the beast and transmit messages from the dead warrior. If the sheepmen point their guns at Henry, the Indians will threaten to kill the sheepmen, Pedro assured her.

"First, you must show your mastery of the beast by making him perform as in the circus. Then, you must speak words of hope and comfort to my people. Tell them not to make war against the white man. Tell them that the sacred Eagle Valley will be theirs for all time. Tell them they must wait for help from Molly Robinson."

He swore an oath in his Washo language, as he ran beside her. "Another war will mean extinction for my people. A once proud and mighty nation will be lost forever."

Some children came forward from the powwow to meet them. "Stand back," Pedro yelled. They entered the crowded firelit meadow. Many men were dancing in circles, whirling about madly, chanting in high-pitched, frenzied tones.

"It is a dance of war. The men are invoking the demons of battle to give them strength," Pedro mourned.

"Ho, Raging Bear, have the sheepmen arrived?" called Pedro to an old Indian, one of a group of old men sitting around a fire, smoking pipes and talking.

"No, White Hawk," the man responded, rising respectfully as Clover approached with Henry.

Lake, who had run quietly at her other side, spoke urgently to Clover. "Don't be afraid. The crowd will not disturb Henry. He will think it just another circus."

She turned to face him, her dark eyes wide with fear. "I can't remember the routines, the signals. What if Henry won't obey?"

The dancing stopped, and the singing. A silence fell upon the vast throng. White Hawk stepped forward, shouting in a loud voice for all to hear.

"The sacred lion who was once a holy warrior will perform and speak to you through his shaman, the dark-eyed girl who was called Flying Bird when she became one of us."

Lake was whispering softly to Clover as Pedro spoke. "Key words are 'place,' 'high,' 'low,' 'dead,' 'jump.' Speak sharply. Don't forget, you are master here. Whatever happens, show no fear."

As their eyes met and locked, Clover felt the lion-tamer's strength flow through her body. He placed her sagebrush branch training stick into her hand. "I grabbed it from the house as we left," he said.

She gazed at it dumbly, flicking the dried leaves at

the tip. A pang of fear chilled her heart for a moment. She was well aware that if Henry did not obey her, if she brought no messages from the spirit world, her own life would be forfeit. An enraged Indian mob might very well rise up and kill her for being a fraud. And her lion with her.

Her heart beating furiously, Clover faced the throng. Lake stood at a distance, in the shadows of a tall yucca tree. Slowly, she opened up her hand, and watched the leash slide through to fall upon the ground. Henry sat upright, his furry paws neatly brought together, his tawny flanks glistening in the light of many fires. He exuded strength and power.

"Henry, come here," Clover said firmly in a low voice. The animal's mighty head came up, proudly, as his amber eyes locked with the girl's. Leisurely, he got gracefully up on four paws, walked slowly to her side.

A kind of sigh rippled through the assembled Indians. Not a child whimpered, as all watched, breathlessly, it seemed. Bending from her waist, Clover caressed her lion, stroking his heaving flanks, running her hand through his long tawny mane. He raised his head almost erotically, exposing his long neck for her caress. Then, falling down, Henry rolled over on his side, lifting his leg for Clover to stroke his inner thigh.

There were distinct giggles from the old pipe-smoking men around the fire. Henry made happy noises in his throat. Bending to his head, Clover whispered into his ear, "Roar, Henry, roar."

Scrambling quickly to his feet, Henry spread his legs, opened his big maw, and emitted a long, ear-shattering roar.

The crowd cheered, no longer fearful. Children squealed, jumping up and down with glee.

The lion roared again, and, stepping back, awaited his master's instructions. Filled with soaring confidence, Clover said, "high," and held her stick out at arm's length in front of her.

After trotting in a circle several times, Henry sat up on his haunches, forepaws lifted high.

The Indians cheered again, and Henry roared again.

Her heart nearly bursting with happiness, Clover made her lion roll over, paws up, playing dead. This trick caused a bit of pandemonium among the spectators, quelled only by Pedro whom they knew as White Hawk, who got up on a rock and shouted for quiet. Three young men, under Lake's directions, had rolled three boulders into a circle. Henry would be commanded to jump from one to the other, so the distances between the rocks must be carefully calculated.

"Up, Henry," Clover had just ordered, when a noise of horses came from the edge of the meadow. Instantly, ten white men with shotguns tucked under their arms rode through the throng, knocking down women and children recklessly.

One of the men rode close to the boulders, and lifting his gun, pointed it at Henry, already up on one of the rocks. Clover heard the cock as the man prepared to fire. Two others joined him, all pointing guns at Henry, taking careful aim.

"Out of the way, girl, unless you want your pretty brains splattered all over this meadow," the first man yelled.

A shot rang out, and the sheepman who had threatened her tumbled from his saddle. His horse had been shot and fell heavily on the ground, keening in pain and flailing about in his death throes. Lake and two of the braves who had been helping him pulled the unhurt sheepman from beneath his horse.

A tall young brave on a white horse emerged from the shadowy fringe of the meadow. He faced the sheepmen, his long, double-barreled rifle moving menacingly back and forth, ready to shoot. "The next man to aim at the sacred lion will receive a bullet in his own heart," the brave said in a cold, deadly voice. "I, Gray Falcon, swear it by the spirit of his father."

Whipping around, the Indian stared at Clover, and at a very agitated Henry who had leapt down from the boulder to stand at her side. Sneaking around behind Clover, Lake picked up the end of the leather leash lying on the ground. In the circus, many trainers used weapons in their animal acts, and Henry usually ignored the sound of gunfire. But in his present, excited state, a second sharp report might set him off.

It came, immediately. "Put the horse out of his miserable death throes," Gray Falcon ordered a young

Indian, without removing his eyes from Clover. A second shot rang out, the sheepman's horse screamed once, raised its head, then fell back, its misery at an end.

Henry bolted. Holding desperately to the leash, Lake was pulled out of the encampment. The sheepmen scattered.

Whirling to follow, Clover found her right wrist held fast by Gray Falcon, who had leapt from his horse to her side. "Stay, foolish woman, the lion will return when — and if — he pleases." He laughed, dryly, scornfully. "He is of the spirit world, is he not? So the Indians say. No harm can come to him."

"The sheepman would have shot him. You saved his life," Clover exclaimed, stunned by the man's sudden appearance. "I am grateful."

The Indian pulled her close with an iron grip. Their eyes met, and held. Memories of her youth at Eagle Valley flooded into Clover's mind and heart. As a girl of thirteen she had loved this man. They had slit their wrists and traded blood, sealing their youthful troth.

"Perhaps I, too, am an instrument of the Great Spirit," grinned Gray Falcon wickedly. He was poking fun at her, Clover knew. He did not think that Henry was sacred. Like the old Pedro, Gray Falcon had been sent to the white man's school, and had lived among them many years. Both regarded the superstitions of the red man as nonsense.

Tears welling up in her dark eyes, Clover moaned, "Henry is lost. I will never see him again."

Gray Falcon's grin faded, and his eyes grew mild. He was of mixed blood, and his eyes were a deep, lovely sea-green. His white father, a captain at a remote military post, had been captured in a raid. The tribal chief's daughter had wanted him for her mate, and so his life was spared. After the babe was born, the captain escaped back to his former life and his white wife. Since he was a strapping boy, the chief of the tribe had adopted the boy, naming him Gray Falcon.

He gazed intently into her eyes. "Do not weep, Flying Bird. I will see that no harm comes to your lion. I will be your champion. Are we not of like blood?"

Twisting her arm, he laid his own wrist against hers. "Have you forgotten our pledge, made so long ago?"

She flushed. "No, Gray Falcon, I have not forgotten. But much water has flowed to the sea since then," she whispered, suddenly aware that all around them had become still and were enjoying the intimate scene. The old men with the pipes were snickering and slapping their knees in glee.

"It is said that all water will return to the place from whence it started," he replied huskily. "We are truly one in the river of life."

The green eyes smoldered, and his fine nostrils flared with desire. "You are more beautiful than the morning star, Flying Bird. One day—sooner than you think—you will be mine."

Erotically, the handsome brave ran the tip of his

tongue around his lips. "You will yield your woman-liness to me and bear my children on a bed of willow rods."

His thumbnail dug into the soft flesh of her wrist. Clover cried out at the little pain. When he let her go to remount his horse, she saw that her blood flowed from the cut onto the meadow. But Clover felt no fear of the man. Gray Falcon had always been moody, becoming violent when crossed. But he cared for her deeply, and she for him. He would never force her to his bed like a slave.

For a few hundred yards Lake was dragged along behind the lion, his body jostling on the rocky ground before he was forced to let go. A lion in panic or closing in a kill is probably the swiftest thing on two feet, he'd been told.

Blood streaming from his bruised face and bare chest and arms, Lake sat up, watching helplessly as Henry vanished into the lower wooded slopes, his leash flying behind him.

Clover would be in despair, he thought, his heart aching for her. She would want to search for the beast again. Damn, he'd like to ship the pesky lion back to Africa and be done with him.

But then—like a fresh breeze from the distant sea—a distinct feeling of euphoria overwhelmed him. Happy thoughts tumbled around in his head. An animal who runs like that is scared enough never to return. Henry was gone forever. He might well live out his allotted span in the lofty peaks of the Sierra Nevada range.

"Can't blame him," Lake chuckled. "Everyone likes freedom, even dumb animals."

His cuts were bleeding onto the ground. He might have been killed, but he'd never felt happier in his life. His heart swelled with joy. Without Henry, Clover would turn to him for love and comfort. There'd be no blasted lion sleeping in the next room like an old lady chaperone. After they were married, she would probably have had the smelly thing sleeping right beside their bed. Or even in it, God knows.

Lake recalled the animal's resentment that morning when he had merely put his arms around Clover. As he rose, dusted himself off, and headed back for the powwow, Lake mused, with horror, "Why, I might have been eaten up like that poor little sheep on my wedding night." Whistling, he entered the encampment.

Seeing the liontamer return without Henry, Clover rushed to meet him. "Quick, we must go after him, before he gets too far."

He shook his head. "The lion can go to hell, for all I care," he grated. "I'm bleeding to death, woman."

Pedro stepped forward, examining the young man quickly. "Go home and bathe your wounds. I will get some healing leaves from a woman in the camp and bring them to you."

Later, before a leaping fire, Clover tended Lake's wounds. She had no soap, so she bathed the numerous cuts and bruises with river water and fine sand.

With exquisite care she applied a dainty fingernail to the bits of rock and gravel that had become embedded in some of the cuts.

Lake winced, but did not cry out. But when she was forced to grope slightly beneath the belt of his dungarees to reach a wound, he felt a leaping in his loins. To his dismay, his male organ became erect, bulging obscenely between his thighs.

What the hell, he thought. An hour ago, she'd been ready to tumble to the floor with me.

Curiously, with Henry gone, something had changed. Their embrace in the rain had been spontaneous, natural. But now they both sensed that their lovemaking was inevitable. They would be together through the night.

Both were nervous as cats on a backyard fence.

To cover her nervousness, Clover rambled, chatting about this and that. "Henry will be home at dawn," she said cheerfully, "just like always."

"I hope not," Lake replied. "The sheepmen are still hanging around, waiting for him to do just that."

"Oh-h," she moaned. "I'd hoped the Indians had scared them off." Agitated, she dug deeply into a cut to remove some packed dirt.

"Ouch!" Lake yelled, jumping back from her. "Keep your mind on your work, girl."

"Sorry." Red-faced, she mixed some leaves brought by Pedro with water to form a poultice. "These leaves are guaranteed to keep out the blood poisoning," she said. "A mix of angelica and prickly pear."

Lake gazed down at his chest, and ran a hand over

158

his face. The aromatic poultice lay thickly on most of his upper body. Blast! How could the two of them lie close together, as they must to make love?

"Now I think we should both stretch out on the hearth and get some sleep," she said casually, washing her hands in a basin of water. "Sleep on your back, so as not to disturb the poultices."

Lake's erection immediately went down. She was right. His scheme to possess her now, to spend the night in glorious, soaring passion was ruined. Cursing under his breath, he fell down on the hard dirt floor, turning a grim face to the fire.

"You and that Gray Falcon seemed awfully friendly," he remarked. "I saw the two of you billing and cooing like lovebirds when I came back from chasing Henry."

She sat down beside him, her arms wrapped around her upraised knees. After a time, she replied, "We were friends as children in Eagle Valley. Molly and I used to spend months there in the summers. I loved it there."

She laughed. "They took me into the tribe. My Indian name is Flying Bird."

Lake rolled over on his side, facing her. "Indeed. And were you promised to this handsome Gray Falcon as a child? Will he come to claim you one day and sweep you into his tipi as his bride?" He chuckled. "I can picture you with a papoose on your back. They have a lot of children, you know."

Embarrassed, she said quickly, "What an absurd idea! Your imagination is running away with you."

"Maybe not," he said, noting her violent blush. Then, "Do you love him, Clover," Lake asked quietly.

"No." Her prompt answer convinced him. "But he is very brave," she continued heatedly. "He saved Henry's life by shooting the sheepman's horse. He could have been shot himself. He risked his life for me."

"While I stood by like a helpless idiot," Lake mourned. "Worse, I couldn't even catch your lion when he ran off."

Clover sat deep in thought, seeming to be far away. Glumly, she gazed at the thick brown patches of drying herbs on his chest and face. How could they ever get close enough to make love? The healing leaves would be rubbed off, the passion of their embraces would aggravate his wounds. He would start to bleed again.

The intimate scene, the breaking of her maidenhead that she had envisioned through the day—the pain, the ecstasy, the fulfillment—would have to wait.

How long? Two days? Three days? A week?

Clover closed her eyes, pressing them tightly to keep from weeping. How frustrating. During this past hour she'd been working on this wickedly handsome man, touching the warm, resilient, muscular flesh, a flame had grown within her. Chills and hot flashes had alternated in her own flesh, so that she felt as if she had a fever.

She'd noticed immediately the telltale bulge under his dungarees. He, too, was more than ready to join her body to his. *How shameless I am,* she thought.

Molly would be shocked. Molly had told her that women did not feel this way.

"Love lasts but an hour, then it's gone," her adoptive mother had warned. "But the consequences may last a lifetime."

"I want that hour," Clover mumbled to herself.

Rolling back again, so that his face was hidden from her, Lake muttered angrily, "No woman on earth wants to make love to a coward."

Clover's eyes flew open. "This one does."

"What did you say?" Rolling back again, he propped up his head on one hand. "Did you say you wanted to . . ." Stumbling, he fumbled for the right words.

"I want us to pick up where we left off before we went to the powwow." She grinned, giggling a little, shocked at her own words spoken so brazenly. "I like to finish what I start."

He hesitated, thinking hard. He should be surprised, he thought, but somehow wasn't. Miss Sinclair the lion-lover was the most passionate woman he had ever encountered.

"Even if your lover is an ex-prisoner, and maybe—just maybe—the man who pushed your papa's wagon off the road?"

He leaned forward for her answer.

Unclasping her hands from her knees, Clover slid across the few feet separating them. "Tonight I don't care if you killed ten men or was going to be hanged tomorrow for torturing your grandmother."

Before he could reply to this outrageous statement,

161

she quickly pressed her mouth to his. Her lips were hot as burning coals, and he felt his blood roar up as if torched.

She kissed him long and hard. Lake lay still, startled, but enjoying this aggression by a woman. When she withdrew, she was breathing raggedly. So was he.

"What the hell are we going to do?" he groaned, pulling her close to him. "I can't even hold you against me."

"There must be other ways," she said pertly, pressing him back against the hearth. Slowly, she unbuttoned his dungarees and pulled them down past his hips. Quickly, he lifted himself up and let her pull them completely off.

"Some things are instinctive," she said, gasping, as she put her hands on his swollen organ.

He bolted up. "Don't do that, it will be too fast," he barked. Then, laughing, "Take it slowly. You're a virgin and don't know that a woman's touch can speed things up so that she gets no pleasure."

"Tell me, dearest, tell me what to do," she breathed wantonly. "I want to be possessed, totally."

"First, remove your dress," he said, "I want you naked."

Quickly, he undid the top few buttons at her back, and she pulled the pink frock over her head. He groaned as her breasts bounced into view, and he viewed without covering cloth her sweet, delicious, feminine mound.

Lake drew a rabbitskin from the corner pile to spread on the floor. Then, lying prone again on the skin, he said, "Sit on my legs, right below my hips."

She did so, and began instinctively to stroke his trembling flesh on either side of his organ, then his belly, which was free of wounds. His arms, covered with poultices, lay limp at his side.

He sat up then, and being careful to keep inches between their chests, Clover offered her breasts to him. Capturing a nipple in his mouth, he caressed it until she begged for mercy.

Their lips met, and as his mouth surrounded hers completely, Clover felt the exquisite agony of a desire she had not even imagined. She placed her hands beneath his hard buttocks, lifting him up. Lake's hands stroked her body; his long, blunt fingers stroked the tender parts of her that he would enter to make her his own forever. He felt her grow warm, and moist.

Her sweet mound began to pulse. "Oh darling, darling," Clover panted. "Please, please show me what to do. I cannot bear it any longer."

Once again, he pushed her back onto his hips, then, sitting up, his hands on either side supporting him, guided her to sheath his manhood in her soft inner warmth. Falling back again, he began to move gently inward, lifting up as he pressed ever more tightly toward her virginity.

In seconds, she cried out at the tiny pain. Then, with total abandon, Clover moved her hips instinctively, swiveling, circling, pressing against his hardened flesh. Sensations of utter pleasure filled her. If the sky had fallen on them, she could not have stopped this wonderful coupling, she thought.

Dizzily, she soared, until she thought she would surely faint. Her flesh throbbed around this manhood that filled her, and she felt herself swelling, too, to match him. Then something within her exploded, as if a volcano that had been simmering for many years had finally found release.

Clover felt spiraling spears of pleasure mount and mount and mount, until, unable to bear the peaking pleasure that was half pain, she cried out, as an animal does when being mated.

Wide-eyed, bewildered, astonished at the delicious feelings that rocked her, she felt him burst within her. At the same moment, he shouted out, and flailed his arms about as if some terrible thing were pursuing him.

For a long time, they were still, Lake lying prone, Clover sitting on him still, feeling their flesh diminish and cool. "Darling Lake," she moaned. "I will be your slave. You have but to love me every night. Just this way."

At that he laughed aloud, and, sitting up, held her close. He kissed her gently. "Every night and every day," he vowed. "Until we are old and gray."

His impulsive embrace had disturbed some of the poultices, and Clover had to repair them. It was half an hour before they slept, side by side beside the fire. The cold desert night crept in through the open door, cooling their waning passion.

Drowsily, she pulled the edges of the rabbitskin to cover them both, enfolding them as one.

Chapter Eight

Clover woke to a chilly desert dawn. The rabbitskin blanket had slid off and, shivering with cold, she instinctively tried to curl her naked body up into a ball to gain warmth. But a strong arm was flung across her breast, holding her fast. Turning her head, she bumped her chin into Lake's shoulder. He lay on his stomach, fast asleep.

The poultices!

Jabbing Lake fiercely in the ribs with her elbow, Clover yelled, "Wake up, you idiot, you've ruined the dressings on your wounds."

Groaning, he rolled over and immediately pulled her to him with one hand, while flinging the skin over her with the other.

"To hell with the poultices," he muttered. Then before she could reply, he kissed her passionately on the mouth.

As their lips met, Clover felt delicious warmth filling her cold body. Last night's lovemaking returned to her in all its glorious detail. She pressed against him sensually, wanting it again. Then, as she remembered his wounds, she pushed away.

"We must repair the poultices," she insisted, bolting up, and, from force of habit, heading toward the bedroom to look in on Henry.

She had not gone two steps when Lake spoke behind her. "He's gone, darling, remember?"

She stopped and waited for the sudden shaft of pain to subside. Turning around, she fell back onto the hearth, reaching out blindly with her arms for comfort.

Fearing to ruin his poultices, Lake touched her face with his hand. "He'll come back, darling, I promise."

"I want to go home," she sobbed. "Take me home to Molly. When you find Henry, bring him home to me there."

"I can't," Lake replied, brushing the top of her head with his lips. "Brant put me on a train and ordered me out of Nevada. If I show up in Black Springs, he'll have me shot. He still blames me for killing his son."

Pedro's tall shape filled the doorway. His headdress was gone, and his face was scrubbed free of paint. "The powwow is over, and I regret to say that the chiefs have set their minds on putting up a fight to the end at Eagle Valley, even if Brant calls out the entire United States Cavalry." Ominously, he shook his head. "It will not be safe there for any white woman." He glanced at Lake. "Or man, either."

"But I am Flying Bird," Clover protested. "I am one of them, just as you are, White Hawk."

The old man shook his head. "You are white, and a white man's woman now."

"What if Henry returns . . ."

Angrily, Pedro started out the door. "I swore an oath to Molly that I would keep you from harm. My sacred oath does not include lions. Please obey me. Prepare to head north again." He glanced at Lake again. "Without or without your man."

Obediently, the lovers walked to the river and bent to splash water on their faces. Lake said to Clover, "Pedro is right, you know. There will be a terrible war. Brant intends to have Eagle Valley if he has to massacre every Indian in Nevada to do it. I overheard him and the Indian agent talking in Carson City."

"I won't go back," she said stubbornly. "Take me with you. We could cross the mountains to California."

He shook his head, holding her face in his, kissing her lips. "Go back to Molly, I'll head for California and send for you."

Putting both hands on his muscled upper arms, Clover pleaded, "No. I cannot bear to be apart from you, not for a minute, not after we . . ." Her face got beet red. "You must think me a wanton, like one of

167

those loose women in Black Springs who live in the shacks behind the town." She hid her hot face in her hands.

Throwing back his blond head, he laughed uproariously. "Sweetheart, you are nothing like those harlots. You are a woman in love, the dearest, most wonderful thing in the world."

"What will Molly think?" she mumbled, sidling up to him again and kissing him on the lips softly. "She's always told me that a woman who enjoys lovemaking is headed for trouble."

A shout from Pedro sent them running to pack their saddlebags and mount their mules. Lake refused to let her renew the herbal dressings, maintaining that fresh, clear air was nature's best healer.

The journey back home would take them less than a week, Pedro said, because now they could travel a more direct route. There was no longer any need to shake Brant and his lionhunters off their trail.

The imminent Indian war was not the only reason Clover had no wish to continue the journey to Eagle Valley. That lustful, hungry look in Gray Falcon's green eyes last night at the powwow frightened her. Little did she know that once she was in Eagle Valley, he planned to make her his woman, even if he had to kill Lake to accomplish it!

It was decided that Lake would veer off the trail to head west at a crossing fifty miles from Black Springs. Refusing to dwell on the dismal prospect of separating from her love, Clover instead vowed to thoroughly enjoy the few nights they would have together. When Molly discovered that her "little girl" had slept with a man for almost a week, she would be forced to accept the itinerant no-account liontamer as her son-in-law.

Before leaving Ragtown and heading for the mountains once again, Clover regretfully packed the pink dress—a tangible reminder of her first joy with Lake—in her saddlebag and donned the worn dungarees and a wide-brimmed reed hat she'd bought from an Indian woman.

On the first two nights of love under the Nevada stars, the lovers came together as they had their first time in Ragtown—Clover on his thighs, Lake on his back. But by the third night, Lake's wounds had healed sufficiently to allow them to make love in a more traditional way—his arms tight around her, every part of his body touching hers.

"Sitting on top of me must not get to be a habit," he grinned. "After all, I am the man here, I am the master.

While she thrilled at his manly words, Clover discovered that Lake had no objection to lying on his back, his brawny arms flung out, wantonly accepting her erotic strokes and caresses. She experienced a new and dizzying kind of ecstasy as she kissed his sinewy throat, his long English nose, his sweeping brow. With her slender fingers, she traced the sinuous body line from just under his broad shoulder, down along the swelling chest, in again at the slim waist. Flattening her hands on his rock-hard hips and buttocks brought chills of pleasure to her own body.

When they were both aroused beyond the point of endurance, they came together with a violence that left her drained and shaken.

Lake was the first man she had ever seen undressed. He seemed the most wonderfully ingenious combination of human parts she could ever imagine. Compared to other men she knew—their cook Samson, old Pedro—the liontamer was a new creation. Her heart lurched in a new kind of terror. She worshipped him. Was this madness overwhelming her heart and mind the terrible thing that Molly had always warned her about?

"A woman in love will break her heart," the embittered old woman had said over and over again.

As their faithful mules picked their way among the rocky slopes and down steep canyons, Clover had no eyes for the spectacular scenery that she had enjoyed coming south. She could not keep her eyes off Lake. When they stopped to eat, she sat so close to him at the fire that Pedro finally went off in disgust, muttering in Paiute.

Clover translated for Lake. "He called us moon-touched, and does not wish to catch our disease."

About a hundred miles as the crow flies, they came to a canyon called Hell-gate for Wagons. While Pedro conversed with some passing Indians headed for Eagle Valley, Lake and Clover fearfully peered over the rim of a sheer drop from the narrow road. The bottom of the gorge was littered with wagons that had tumbled over the edge. Whitened bones of men and animals were strewn all about the rocks.

170

Clover gasped, pointing. "Look, there's a medicine wagon just like Papa's." She blinked back tears. "I hope and pray that nobody was killed."

"The side is still intact," Lake said, reading off "Nostrums, Patent Medicines, Indian Cures." After a moment, he said, "This one's much bigger than your papa's. The so-called doctor who drove this wagon probably put on a big show for the folks, with trained monkeys, a parrot, maybe even a dancing girl or two."

Clover's blood froze in her veins. Whirling, she blazed out at Lake, "How could you possibly know what my papa's wagon looked like. Unless . . . un-less—"

"Unless I pushed your wagon off the road?" Lake put in. His gray eyes saddened, and he took her by the arms. "It's obvious, darling, that you still think I am a killer."

White-lipped, Clover persisted. "Answer me. How could you know how large my papa's wagon was?"

"Simple. From all you've said about your early childhood, I assumed that Dr. Sinclair did not have an elaborate outfit like that wagon down below. Your papa went from town to town selling door to door, didn't he? He never stopped to put on a show."

Averting her face to keep him from seeing the doubt in her dark eyes, Clover responded weakly, "I'm sorry, Lake. Forgive me."

Whew, that was close, Lake reflected. She had almost caught him up. He had almost revealed the fact that he had known both her and her father before the

171

robbery.

As they remounted, Clover berated herself inwardly. Would her doubts about this man haunt her forever? Her heart was heavy. She would live out her life with him, bear his children, perhaps, he would possess her body every night. But deep in some dark inner portion of her mind, she would always think he was a murderer.

There was only one way to be sure. She must write to Illinois about his prison record. It must be done secretly. He must never know the full extent of her mistrust.

When they stopped to eat ground squirrel with some Shoshones, those Indians reported that Ralph Brant was riding for Eagle Valley with a band of men. "They are hunting for an African lion who has been heard and seen in these parts. His roars are very loud," said one.

A mixture of joy and fear struck Clover. Obviously her lion was tracking her and Lake's progress from a safe distance. For the first time since leaving Ragtown, she began scouring the hills again with her eyes, listening for Henry's roar, looking for a flash of tawny brown among the greenery. Sometimes she imagined that he was bounding down the slopes into her arms.

Noticing her preoccupation, Lake remarked, wryly, "I'm jealous. I thought I had pushed that lion out of your heart."

She spun around, quick anger mottling her deeply tanned face. "Understand me, Captain Emerson, nobody will ever push Henry out of my heart. That lion was my first love and a part of me will always belong to him."

That night, as they rolled up in their rabbitskins under a towering piñon-nut tree heavy with snow, Lake drew her close, warming her with his body heat. He bent to kiss her nearly frozen lips. "I'm so sorry, sweet. Please forgive me for being a jealous idiot. Your love for Henry is something rare and should be cherished."

Sadly, she returned his kiss. At dawn, Lake would leave her and Pedro to head west. They were a bare fifty miles from Black Springs.

A short time later, they were awakened by Pedro's explosive yell. "Five men are headed our way from the north. I'm almost sure it's Brant."

"What rotten bloody luck," Lake cursed, bounding up. Without another word to Clover, he mounted his mule and spurred the beast westward through a thick grove of trees.

Gazing after him, Pedro muttered, "Sure hope he gets away."

Mounting also, without breakfast, Clover and Pedro had not gone a hundred yards to the east when a gunshot shattered the wilderness quiet. Her heart in her throat, Clover whipped around to see Ralph Brant dismounting from his mule. He loomed above, on a narrow ledge, his revolver still pointed upward. Six men on mules were strung out on either side of him.

Brant swung his gun at two of his men. "Take care

173

of the Indian," he barked. Dismounting, the men picked their way carefully down the rocky slope toward the old Indian.

Drawing a red-tipped arrow from his quiver, Pedro yelled, "White Hawk dies fighting." One of the men fell, hit in the shoulder. Nostrils flaring with rage, Brant ordered all his men to descend the slope on the hapless Indian. They rolled down swiftly before White Hawk could draw another arrow.

The faithful old brave was knocked to the ground and besieged with kicks in the groin and side and fierce blows to the head.

Shrieking "murderers," Clover leaped off her mule and ran to Pedro's aid. "Stop beating this old man. What has he done to you?"

Two powerful bronzed arms encircled her before she reached the spot and pulled her back. "Don't get in their way, Flying Bird. I have no wish to bed you with your beautiful body bruised and battered."

The man pulled her around to face him, drawing her close. It was Gray Falcon, dressed in beaded buckskin.

He smiled, revealing a mouthful of gleaming white teeth. "I warned you that we would meet again soon, did I not, Flying Bird?" Gray Falcon's green eyes became slits of desire as he bent to capture her lips in a passionate, biting kiss. When he released her, Clover felt hot blood trickling down her chin from a wound to her mouth.

"That's enough," Brant shouted to his men from above. "Leave the bastard to the vultures."

Pointing his lighted cigarette at Gray Falcon, Brant added, "Let the girl alone, you randy redskin bull. You'll have the rest of your life to enjoy your luscious prize."

Clover went rigid, nursing her bitten mouth with her fingers. "Prize," she squealed, "what do you mean—prize?"

Brant's answering smile was mirthless. "You are my prisoner, Miss Sinclair. When you have served my purposes, I will give you to anyone I please." He winked broadly, swaying his hips obscenely. "Right now, my pal Gray Falcon has the edge on who gets to enjoy your sweet body."

"Never! I'll die first."

Clover's head lifted defiantly. "When Molly hears of this, you'll pay dearly, Ralph Brant. Her Indian friends will roast you over a slow fire, with pine slivers in your cowardly body."

"Not a chance," he replied silkily. "You are my trump card in a little game old bitch Robinson and I are playing for Eagle Valley. That paradise of silver is my ransom for her sweet little girl."

Clover gasped. "You couldn't do such an evil thing."

"I already have. She should have my ransom note in hours."

Slowly, as his words sunk in, Clover's blood filled with ice. She was being held hostage to force Molly to cooperate with Brant's plans to rape her beloved valley.

Filled with loathing, Clover spat upon the ground.

"You are a slimy toad, Ralph Brant, and to think I almost married your son—"

The rustling noise of mules breaking through the brush caused her to pause. Three mules drew up. One of them held Lake, his hands tied behind his back, his face was a mass of black and blue bruises.

"Lake," she cried. "Oh, darling—"

"I'm fine, sweetheart," Lake replied softly, attempting a weak grin. "These cowards won't kill me as they did poor Pedro. His eyes flicked to the Indian's bludgeoned body spread-eagled on the rocks. "Seems I'm worth money to Brant."

"What a lucky young woman you are," Brant interrupted. "You've not one but *two* men lusting after you. My, my, what would old Molly say?" His eyes swept her from head to toe. "Even in that smelly outfit, I'd not be averse to a taste of you myself." He chuckled. "Never thought that son of mine was nearly man enough for you."

"You bastard," she gritted. "You have no right to kill Lake Emerson. He was cleared of Spike's murder."

"True," he replied snidely, "but your precious liontamer will hang for other crimes."

"He served his time in prison," Clover said heatedly, trying to go to her lover. But Gray Falcon held an iron grip on her arm.

"Not exactly." Brant laughed uproariously. "The rascal decided to leave jail a bit early. Seems he served only five years of a twenty-year term."

Frozen with horror, Clover looked up imploringly

176

at Lake. "Is that true?" But even as she asked the question, she had a dreadful intuition that he indeed was an escaped convict.

He nodded. "Yes. I escaped because I was innocent and wanted to clear my name by finding the real criminal."

One of Brant's men hooted derisively. "That's what all the bank robbers and murderers say. To hear 'em talk, not a soul in jail is guilty."

"Why didn't you tell me," Clover wailed, burying her face in the warm neck of her mule. "I trusted you, I gave you my body, when all the time you were hiding this terrible secret from me."

Lake's reply was cloaked in agony. "I couldn't, my darling, I could not bear to tell you that your father—"

She interrupted, flaring out, "What has Papa to do with all this awful business?"

He remained silent. Even from a distance, the suffering in his face was palpable.

"Your old man held up a bank, with the help of a kid named Lake Emerson," one of Brant's men put in cheerfully. "When they ran off with a bag of golden double eagles, a lawman was dead, shot by the trigger-happy kid. Both your pa and his accomplice were accused, but your pa got clean away"

"No, it isn't true, it can't be true," Clover screamed. "It's all a filthy, rotten lie, a monstrous mistake."

"Cut out the palaver," Brant barked impatiently. "Luther and Slate, you two take the prisoner to Carson City and lock him up good and tight." He pointed to two of his men, whom Clover knew to be ruthless characters, capable of the most cold-blooded killing.

"Those two are jackasses in every other way," Brant smirked, "but they're crackerjacks with a gun. Your clever lover might have gotten out of an Illinois prison, but he won't get away from me."

Accepting another freshly rolled cigarette from one of his men, Brant stuck it between his thin lips. "But don't shoot him dead. He's worth five hundred dollars alive, only two hundred dead."

Brant pulled a reward poster displaying Lake's picture from his saddlebag. "This valuable piece of paper was sitting on a pile at the Carson City jail office. I was lucky enough to see it there, and wrote to the authorities."

He grinned expansively. "They sent a telegram to Carson City. Two deputies are traveling all the way to Nevada to fetch the prisoner back east by train. Your liontamer will be hanged for breaking out."

Slate and Luther were busily roping Lake's mule to theirs so that he was forced to ride between them. "Listen to me, you two," Brant cautioned once more, "this Englishman is slick as bear grease on a July day. If he gets away, I swear I'll personally plug you both with my own gun and throw your bones to the coyotes."

Brant twirled his revolver to emphasize his point.

"You can count on us, boss," Slate yelled back, jabbing Lake in the ribs with his fist.

As he jogged along between his captors, Lake was curiously calm. Once he was dead, Clover need never know that her dead papa, and not a hapless boy, had killed the man at the bank.

"Don't hate me forever, darling," he prayed silently. "Just try to remember the few nights of love we had."

Death did not frighten the young Englishman. Part of him—the best part—had already died when he lost Clover's love. She despised him now for a thief and murderer. He had betrayed her innocence and trust.

Luther and Slate joked as they rode along. Frequently, they reined in to quaff whiskey from a bottle, which Lake was overjoyed about. Even crack shots could miss when they were drunk. His depression lifted. He'd gotten out of that gray pile of an Illinois prison. Any man with half a brain could outsmart Brant's saddle bums.

Her mind a jumble of confused emotions, too shocked even to weep, Clover watched as Lake was led away, northward to Carson City, then on to Illinois—and death. She bent her body almost double in grief, clinging to her mule with one hand. How could she survive two terrible losses—her father accused of a heinous crime, and her lover led off to his death?

A triumphant Ralph Brant led his party directly south. After lifting Clover onto her mule, Gray Falcon solicitously wrapped the rabbitskin snugly over her shoulders. He fingered a length of rope. "Do I have to tie you to my mule?" he asked.

179

"No." She shook her head dejectedly. "I have no place to run to."

She could not go home to the stagestop. She could not bear to see Molly's face when she heard that history had repeated itself, as she had so often warned. How would she take the news that her carefully reared waif had been despoiled by a no-account lawbreaker?

She gazed full-eyed at Gray Falcon hovering over her. "I will willingly go anywhere you wish to take me, old friend."

The handsome Indian playfully chucked her under the chin, "We go to Eagle Valley. There you will be happy as we were in our youth."

"What about White Hawk? Are his old bones to lie unburied?"

She glanced with stricken eyes at the bludgeoned body sprawled obscenely on the rocks.

For a moment Gray Falcon's green eyes softened, and a shadow of pain crossed his hawklike face. Then it vanished. "The old man was in our way," he said curtly.

It was apparent to Clover that Molly's faithful Pedro had been slaughtered as an example to Molly. If she refused to persuade the Indians to sell Eagle Valley, she might receive the same fate. And her adopted daughter, the light of her life, was being held captive for the same cause, given as booty to a man she had once loved as a boy, but whom she now detested as a traitor to his people. She was Gray Falcon's reward for working with Brant.

Although she had set her mind to forgetting about Lake Emerson, from this moment on, Clover could not keep from dwelling miserably on the crime her father was said to have committed. She still refused to believe it. Had her papa been so desperate for money that he was willing to break the law, to take other people's money?

He had talked endlessly about taking his little girl back to England. "Where we both belong," he had reiterated.

Why was the young Lake Emerson with her father at the time? When Lake was fourteen, Clover had been seven. Her mind seethed with tormenting questions. Had Lake worked with Dr. Sinclair at the circus?

Closing her eyes, she wracked her memory. Had she seen that patrician English face, that wonderful whitish-blond mop of hair long ago in the medicine wagon? There had always been so many boys hanging around the circus, boys who had run off from home to find their fortune.

Young and orphaned, Lake had been one of them, she was now sure. He would not have instigated the crime. Her father had talked him into it. But gold double eagles had been taken. Where were they now?

That wild ride to the West came back to her. "We're on our way at last to England," Papa had told her joyfully. "I've had an unexpected windfall from an old mine I'd given up on. We've got more than enough money to set you up in society there."

Huddled in the stifling rabbitskin, Clover broke

out in a sweat. The money for England had been stolen from the bank. It was probably in that fancy gilt box he had always forbidden her to open because he said it was magic.

She suppressed a cry of pure agony. Everything was crystal clear now. Cruelly, piercingly clear. That unlucky boy had come to adulthood in prison, had made his way west to find Cedric Sinclair and the money and wreak revenge for the great wrong done him.

Finding Sinclair long dead, he had figured to get the money or what was left of it from the daughter.

An iron band of pain clamped like a vise around Clover's heart. She could hardly breathe. Lake Emerson had made love to her, since it was the best way for a good-looking man to get something out of a gullible girl.

He had even proposed to marry her. Everything she owned would then be his. That he would leave her soon after, as Molly had been left, was sure as sunlight in a Nevada summer.

Clover sobbed aloud, causing an alarmed Gray Falcon to ride up alongside, his green eyes anxious. "Do not weep, Flying Bird, you will know great happiness again. I swear it by my life."

Smiling at him through her tears, Clover reached out a hand to touch his on the reins. "I will make you a good wife, Gray Falcon," she said firmly. "I vow that I will never push you out of my mat of willow weeds."

It was a vow she had heard many an Indian bride

swear before taking a mate to themselves.

Her childhood Indian friend, now her lover-to-be, resumed his place behind her on the trail and they rode steadily toward the desert under a brilliantly moonlit sky.

Chapter Nine

On the third day out, Lake and his two captors camped at a frigid but well-watered spot near the timberline, about thirty miles from Black Springs. They were forced to avoid the more direct route along the Truckee River, because bands of Indians were holding powwows at numerous places along the way. The spirit of war against the white man was yet again in the air over Nevada.

"If any of those Injuns spy us, we're sure to be recognized as Brant's men," Luther commented to Lake.

Slate chuckled, shivering with mock apprehension. "We'd be roasted on spits, slo-o-wly, all through the night."

Lake was silent, thinking hard. The men had told him that Molly had been sent a note by Brant, demanding that she cease and desist in her efforts on behalf of the Eagle Valley Indians. Clover was the pawn. Somehow he had to help Molly. Somehow, although she hated him now, he had to free Clover. He clenched his fists, hitting one against the other, trying not to dwell on his darling with that brutal Gray Falcon.

The intrepid liontamer, who had cowed a four-hundred-pound savage jungle animal for six years, was utterly confident that he could elude these country bumpkins.

Lake's hands had been freed in order to eat. Luther's gun lay on his lap, Slate held his weapon high in one hand, pointed at Lake directly opposite. They were chewing on dried rabbit and piñon cakes, and Slate was having trouble eating with one hand. As he concentrated on his rabbit leg, the gun in the other dipped dangerously low.

"For God's sake, Slate," snapped Luther, "put the damn pistol down. If he runs off, we'll shoot him before he gets very far." He gazed around at the jagged cliffs surrounding them. "Besides, where's he going to go in these peaks? If he don't freeze to death first, he'll be eaten up by mountain lions."

Slate's gun dropped on the ground. After they had eaten, the three men sat around the sagebrush embers, Lake's two captors smoking and taking gulps from the whiskey bottle. They had tied him up again, at wrists and ankles. He leaned against a tree trunk, eyes closed, pretending sleep. But his brain was working on an idea to frighten the men, for, if

185

frightened, they would drink more, and make his escape easier.

Brant's men were fantasizing about the land their boss would give them in Eagle Valley, once it was won from the Indians.

"I'm to get ten acres of bottom land," Luther said, smacking his lips in anticipation. "With lots of streams to pan in."

Slate was not so optimistic. "Don't count on it, pal. Brant's a sly one. You'll be lucky to get rights to one piddlin' li'l creek."

A gasp came from Lake, causing the men to turn his way. "What's the matter, boy, got a pain?" Luther asked.

"I thought I heard a lion roaring," Lake replied. He paused a long moment, then said, more firmly, "There it is again. Can't you hear it?" He sat upright, head cocked, seeming very tense.

All three were silent, listening hard. "Naw, don't hear a thing," Slate said. "How about you, Luther?"

Luther took a swig from the whiskey bottle, "The boy's been with lions so long, he thinks he hears them in his sleep." But he cocked his head again, screwing up his eyes. "Sometimes the wind makes noises like that goin' through the trees."

They relaxed again, and Lake said nothing for a long time. Then, very softly, "You know, if Henry—that's my lion's name—if he's anywhere within twenty miles of here, he'll catch my scent and come find me."

"That so?" Luther sounded scared. "Then what'll

he do?" He picked up his gun, held it in his hand.

"Well," Lake replied slowly, "if he sees me tied up like this, I wouldn't want to predict." He yawned. "No point worrying about it, I guess. If he comes, he comes. I guess there's worse ways to die . . ." He chuckled. "Like being roasted on a spit over a slow fire."

Luther twirled his revolver. "Reckon six of these bullets can stop any lion, 'specially if I get him through the heart. I'm a light sleeper, I can hear a grasshopper creepin' up on me."

Lake slid down beneath the tree to sleep, and Luther covered him with a rabbitskin, checking the knots on Lake's ropes. Luther stepped back, satisfied. "Even a lion can't chew these knots apart," he grunted.

Lake's keepers drank some more, and after a time, sprawled beside the dying fire, fell immediately into a drunken sleep. Lake waited a few minutes, then rolled his body over and over until it bumped against a boulder. Finding a sharp edge, he placed his wrists against it, rubbing to fray the rough hemp.

As he labored, his mind slid back in time. At eleven, he had been apprenticed to a circus strongman who had gotten himself out of tight steel chains with ease. The man, a swarthy Armenian, had instructed him in his ancient art.

"You must relax your muscles," he had ordered the boy. "Let your whole body go limp. Think of something cold."

Desperately trying to recall the Armenian's exact

instructions, Lake sat very still for minutes, then slowly expelled all the breath in his body until he went limp. He was eleven again, without a care in the world. He was cold enough at these heights, no need to imagine it.

Miraculously, without straining, he felt the ropes loosen. *Don't give up,* an inner voice admonished. *Think of Clover with that blasted Indian. Think of hanging in Illinois.* His imagination took over. What seemed like centuries later, he managed to work one wrist free.

Luther's "lionproof" knots came apart with ridiculous ease, and Lake found himself completely free, gazing down at the sleeping men. There was absolutely no danger of their waking up before dawn and chasing after him. To be safe, though, he could kill them easily with their own guns.

But Lake Emerson was no killer. The poor blokes were only following orders.

However, he took both guns, stashing them in his saddlebag. As an afterthought, he also picked up the almost empty whiskey bottle. Leaving them in their drunken stupors, he mounted his mule and rode off toward Black Springs.

The Nevada sky was a pearly gray when Lake heard the delicate tap-tap of mule hooves behind him. He turned, to see a mule with the body of man slung across it. Lake veered off the narrow trail to stand behind a small outcropping. As the mule passed his line of vision, he saw that the man on the mule was Pedro.

Dismounting, he ran toward the man he had thought dead. Had a passing Indian placed the body on the old Yellow Hawk's mule, trusting the faithful animal to carry the carcass back to Black Springs for burial?

But there were no ropes around the body to hold him fast. Bending low, Lake spoke into an ear that was caked with dried blood. "Are you alive or dead, old man?"

His answer was a faint but distinct grunt, followed by a barely discernible nod of the head. Moving swiftly, Lake eased the man off the mule and laid him on the ground. Pedro was a pitiful sight. His Indian blanket was torn and bloodied, the once-proud hawkish face was nearly black with dried blood and bruises. Both eyes were slits beneath obscenely swollen lids. His legs appeared to be broken. Lake prayed that there was no internal bleeding. Brant's men had administered some vicious blows to the body, Lake recalled.

"You're a lucky bastard," he muttered.

"I played dead, they stopped hitting me," Pedro grumbled thickly.

"How in blazes did you get up on that mule?" Lake asked in wonderment.

Pedro's blackened lips moved in a kind of smile. "I imagined my muscles were young and strong again."

Lake whooped, bringing another smile to the battered face. "Well, that makes two of us tricksters, I guess."

After a few drinks of water from Lake's saddlebag,

and a few sips of whiskey from Luther's flask, the Indian seemed greatly revived.

"You must not enter Black Springs," he said, "Brant will know of your escape by now. You will be captured again."

Lake shook his head. "I don't think so. Luther and Slate will never face him after losing me. They're probably halfway to California by now," he chuckled. He squinted at the rapidly rising sun. "On wings, I imagine."

With Lake's considerable help, Pedro climbed back on his mule, as before, holding the reins loosely in his hands to guide the beast. They resumed their journey to Black Springs.

For an old man, Pedro seemed to be in surprisingly good shape. With Molly's expert nursing, he might be good as new in a few weeks, Lake figured. If only Molly had not gone after Clover before they got to the stagehouse.

They would stop over at Ragtown, Brant informed Clover, there to await Molly Robinson's reply to his ransom letter. "If that woman loves you as much as she claims, she'll stop her campaigning against me for Eagle Valley."

A large contingent of Indians sympathetic to Brant's cause would also gather at the town Clover had so recently left in happiness. Gray Falcon was not the only one of his people in league with Brant. Many hoped for big financial rewards eventually.

Some hours before the party was due to arrive at the old crossroads town, Gray Falcon went into the mountains alone to bag a deer from a secret place high in the mountains where they liked to water.

With her protector gone, Brant's men taunted Clover unmercifully. She would be known as a "redskin's woman" now, she was aware, and as such would be treated with contempt.

"Them Injuns has bigger cocks than white men," jeered one. "Like a stallion. I heard of a young gal who was taken by an Injun and was ripped apart their first night together."

"That Gray Falcon will make you a slave, he'll give you to his pals, and when he's through with you, he'll more than likely sell you for a pretty penny to one of them San Francisco fancy houses."

Brant merely laughed, enjoying the banter. Gray Falcon would enjoy the Sinclair girl only until Mrs. Robinson agreed to his terms. Then Clover would be sent back to Black Springs. He was puzzled, though. The Indian had not touched her since that first brutal kiss.

As for Clover, she paid no heed to the lewd talk. Nothing could hurt her now. Her heart had turned to stone.

But she was wrong. Gray Falcon returned from the mountain, not only with the carcass of a tender young deer, but with a bloodied leather harness, a long leash dangling from it, which he offered to Clover.

"They say it was taken from an African lion," he

said. His green eyes were full of compassion. "They tell me a band of sheep men finally tracked him down and shot him."

"Somebody's got himself a dandy lion skin," Brant commented. "Good riddance, I say. Now nobody's got to worry about that damn lion."

The harness that Lake had made at Ragtown to keep Henry from killing sheep could only have been taken off Henry if he were dead. Or by Lake. But Lake was in the Carson City jail, awaiting transfer to Illinois.

The pain that wracked Clover's heart and body as she clutched the bloody harness to her breast seemed like all the pain in all the world wrapped into one. She had survived from day to day with the hope that Henry was out there somewhere in the high mountains and at any time would climb back down to her.

Her life was over, she felt. Her future lay with Gray Falcon. He was good to her. She need not love him. She threw herself into working at the abandoned blacksmith shop in Ragtown where Brant had decided to headquarter. Fashioning a new broom with rushes from the river's edge, she set about sweeping out the stone floors of the place. She cleaned out the firepit, scouring it with white sand until it shone like new.

Once the deer was skinned and placed on a spit outside over a bed of sage coals, Clover set the hide to soak in the river, to make it soft for scraping, and, eventually, tanning with the liquid from the boiled brains. She had learned to do this during the summers at Eagle Valley.

Gray Falcon found her there, bent low over the river. "We cannot take the skin with us to Eagle Valley, Clover. It will dry out before we get there." Fishing the skin out of the water, he said, "I will give it to one of the women in the encampment to make into garments."

Stooping to lift her up, he kissed her on the mouth. His touch, unlike that first time, was sweet and gentle. Husbandly, she thought.

Clover let him lead her back toward the blacksmith shop where the others were already feasting on the roast venison. Brant and his men, together with a large crowd of Indians, were crowded into the house, drinking whiskey and talking in loud voices.

"That's no place for us," Gray Falcon commented as he led her to the fire where two Indian boys were turning the spit. The meaty aroma of the venison set Clover's juices stirring. Since her capture, she had barely eaten enough to keep alive.

Suddenly ravenous, she watched eagerly as the Indian cut two thick slabs of venison and placed them on a flat piece of shale. She gazed at him through veiled eyes. The young brave was strikingly handsome, with light skin and green eyes from his white father. From his Indian mother he had been given a wealth of jet-black hair, which he wore in two thick braids falling over his broad chest.

His shirt and leggings were of softest buckskin, heavily fringed. Clover imagined a shy young Indian maid chewing on the deerskin to soften it, then, delicately, laboring with needle and leather strips, binding the pieces together in a handsome garment for the man she hoped would come to her tipi and give her sons.

With a start and a thrill in her loins, Clover imagined the children she and this half-Indian would have.

Even as a boy, Clover remembered, the green-eyed lad had been coveted by most of the girls in the tribe. He was bold and arrogant and liked the girls as much as they liked him. Clover herself had bestowed on him all her adolescent sexual fervor. How ecstatically happy she had been when he had kissed her in the wood and traded blood with her at the wrist-slitting ceremony.

"Now we are one forever," he had murmured.

Molly had been furious when she discovered their pledge. "Nonsense. I'd rather see you dead than wed to an Indian."

At this moment, though, instead of the raging passion she had felt for Gray Falcon as a girl of thirteen, Clover felt only a kind of death. Inside, deep in her heart, where it really counted.

"Come," Gray Falcon beckoned to Clover. "We will eat our wedding meal down by the river."

My time of reckoning has come, Clover thought. This night I will become a wife by Indian custom.

Curiously, she felt no anguish, only a kind of emptiness. She accepted her fate calmly. She had loved only one man, and he had brought her brief joy, followed by great sorrow. Like a dutiful Indian wife, she trotted after Gray Falcon as he loped away from the fire toward the willow grove.

At his request, she had donned the pink gingham dress upon their arrival in Ragtown. "I do not want my woman to look like a squaw," he had said.

The day was hot, and they sat at the river's edge with their bare feet dangling in the water. Clover's dress was lifted to rest upon her knees.

"Remember how we loved to do this when we were children," he murmured.

Silently, she stared at the two pairs of feet, one small and delicate, the other long and strong. He was obviously attempting to break down her resistance by bringing up the past. Taking her piece of venison, Clover bit off a crusty chunk. Pink juice flowed down her chin, and Gray Falcon put out a swift hand to wipe it off before it reached her dress.

"Bend your head over the river," he ordered. "Let the juices flow into the water."

She obeyed and finished the venison quickly, then she looked up at him, grinning. "That was delicious." Cupping her hands in the clear, sweet water, she scooped up a handful to drink. Then another. Wiping off her wet face with the sleeve of her dress, Clover felt content. Perhaps, she mused, one *can* live in the past — for a while. She longed to be a child again. Being a woman meant only pain and the end of dreams.

Having finished his meat, her bridegroom walked to the trees and brushed some fallen leaves and branches aside to pull out a whiskey bottle.

Returning, he laughed. "I hid it here from the others earlier."

Unscrewing the cap, he drank long and heartily. Then he offered it to her. Quickly, eagerly, Clover took the bottle and swallowed a large gulp of the amber liquid. It burned all the way down to her stomach. She was not a whiskey drinker, having sampled it only a few times in her life.

But whiskey brought oblivion, she knew. She lifted the bottle again. After a few more drinks, Clover's whole body was aflame. Her heart was drumming in her ears. She felt her nipples harden with passion. The secret, womanly place between her thighs became wonderfully warm and tingling.

Her heart eased. It was going to be all right, she thought. Yielding herself to this man would not be the torture she had envisioned. A woman can feel desire even for a man she does not love.

Rising, he loomed over her. His huge manhood strained the soft fabric of his snug buckskins. Frightened for a moment, she recalled the banter of the men along the trail. Would she bleed to death from his violent lovemaking? She shuddered.

She lifted her face, and he bent to kiss her, taking both her hands in his and pulling her up. Then, placing one brawny arm beneath her buttocks, he carried her deep into the willow grove. Setting her down gently on a blanket he had obviously prepared for her, he quickly pulled his shirt over his head, revealing a hairless, truly glorious chest. A tiny image of a gray falcon was tattooed over his left nipple.

"Like it?" he asked huskily, noting her stare. Raising his arms, he made two fists, flexing his rock-hard biceps.

Clover gasped, then giggled. "You must be the strongest man in your tribe," she exclaimed.

"In all of Nevada," he replied proudly, testing his muscles with his fingers.

He's still a boy at heart, she thought, amused by his antics. As children, the Indian boys in Eagle Valley had spent long summer days wrestling, displaying their muscular prowess to the admiring girls.

Swiftly stepping out of his leggings, he stood before her tall and naked. His manhood thrust out almost like a weapon. Clover caught her breath, and her heart stopped for a moment. She again recalled the story of the girl who had bled to death on her wedding night to an Indian.

By now the liquor had overwhelmed Clover's brain. *I must be drunk*, she thought. She could not see the man in front of her, she heard nothing but a roaring in her ears. She felt as though she were in a dark tunnel, falling, falling, with no end in sight.

Consumed with desire, she rose up on her elbows, arching her body upward. "Take me, take me," she murmured. In desperation for relief from the pain of lust, she sat up and reached for Gray Falcon's legs, pulling him down to her.

He fell upon her, knocking her down to the skin. She heard him curse, and grate "slut" a moment before he reared back on his haunches and slapped her cruelly, sharply, on the face. She whimpered in pain and shock. Lake had loved her sexual aggression. Gray Falcon obviously detested it.

Viciously, he tore at the front of her dress, ripping the thin fabric to expose her breasts. His lips came down on one hardened, tender nipple, his sharp teeth biting into the rosy tip. Once again Clover cried out in pain and tried to twist free of him. Enraged at her resistance, the Indian grasped both her hands in his and held them above her head.

She was helpless. He placed his knees upon her legs, pinning her down. After he had feasted on her nipples, he drew back and placed his free hand beneath her buttocks, raising her up. She felt the cool night air on her thighs as he lifted up her dress.

She cried out again in fright and pain as his enormous manhood pierced her savagely. The playful boy of moments before had been transformed into a maniacal fiend. As he thrust in and out of her tender parts with animallike fury and intensity, Clover knew that she was being raped.

"Slut, slut, you're a white slut," he kept muttering, as though it were a term of endearment. When he reached his fulfillment he shouted out a cry of triumph. When it was done, the man who had sworn eternal love to her loosened his grasp, releasing her hands and hips before falling upon her heavily.

She must have lost consciousness for a while, for when she opened her eyes, her tormentor was standing over her.

"Get up, Clover, and wash yourself in the river."

Dully, she walked to the banks, and jumped in

without removing her dress. The icy water jolted her to her full senses. She swam vigorously toward the center of the swift stream, desperately wishing she could drown. After she had swum a bit, however, her spirits revived.

He joined her in the icy water, splashing about and chatting in a lively manner. "I hope I satisfied your desire," he called out, swimming around her in circles. "You are not only beautiful but also passionate. Few men are so fortunate. I will be the envy of all the chiefs in the valley."

Benumbed with shock that he could be so obtuse about her true feelings, Clover remained silent. Men of mixed blood were often said to be irrational, torn as they were between two worlds—despised by the white man, scorned as bastards by the red man. Many—like green-eyed Gray Falcon—harbored bitter hatred at the white man for rejecting them.

I must not aggravate him, she thought, touching her bruised cheek with her fingers. Despite the dismal prospect of life with this man, Clover discovered that she very much wanted to live.

When they climbed out at last, her new Indian husband tore off the wet pink dress and threw it into the water. Bemused, Clover watched it floating downstream. It seemed that all her girlish dreams were disappearing with it.

Then Gray Falcon took her back to the willows and bade her wait for him. Tenderly, he covered her naked body with the rabbitskin, tucking in the edges like a concerned mother. Exhausted, Clover fell asleep.

When she woke, he stood over her, holding a beaded buckskin dress in one hand, some mocassins and a beaded headband in the other. "I got them from a woman in the encampment," he said.

Clover put them on, thanking him politely. The cured skin carried another woman's scent, but was marvelously soft against her flesh. Now she was a full-fledged Indian squaw. Her childhood friend, now her husband, gazed at her a long time, extending a hand to touch the curling tendrils of her jet-black hair beneath the band.

"You are very comely," he commented. "But when we reach a trading post, I will buy you a white woman's dress of calico. Many of them. All must know that the brave Gray Falcon's wife is not a redskin."

When she walked back into the yard of the blacksmith's shop where Brant and his men were still drinking and carousing with several Indian girls, she received sly looks and winks from all directions.

"Well," Brant remarked, "I see the half-breed has put his stamp on hoity-toity Miss Sinclair." He laughed. "Good thing, too. There's been no answer from your Molly to my ransom letter. Guess she doesn't care whether you live or die."

Clover's heart was heavy as she walked to the embers of the fire and poured strong, hot coffee from the tin coffeepot into a chipped china cup. Molly would certainly abandon her now, she reflected, now that she was married to an Indian.

She drank her coffee slowly, savoring every swallow. The strong brew brought new energy. Clover Sinclair would meet life's challenges, whatever lay ahead. That much she knew for certain.

Chapter Ten

Night had fallen before Molly was ushered into the private office of the Indian agent at Carson City. She'd been sitting, dozing now and then, on the velvet settee in the parlor for two solid hours while people went in and out of the important man's office.

When she entered, she disdained the straight-backed wooden chair in front of his desk for a cushioned armchair by a window. The agent did not glance up from his papers. Molly coughed politely.

She had to cough a second time before he deigned to look up at his visitor. Smiling apologetically, he made a great fuss over shuffling the papers and straightening them into a neat pile before he inquired, pleasantly, "Now what can I do for you, Mrs. Robinson?"

Molly stiffened in her chair. "Mrs. Robinson, indeed! Don't go highfalutin on me, Aaron Parker,"

Molly sneered, "I've been Molly to you ever since you were a shave-tailed, snot-nosed kid in torn-off breeches running barefoot around Black Springs." She chortled. "Though I must admit you look a mite more respectable in that expensive city suit you're wearing."

Parker grinned, sticking his thumbs beneath his gabardine lapels as he gazed admiringly down at himself. "I've come up in the world since then, my friend. That's what America's all about, isn't it?"

Acutely conscious of her own dowdy wearing apparel—faded calico frock and worn woolen cloak on her thin shoulders—Molly nodded. "That depends," she replied sourly, "on the color of your money, doesn't it?"

Laughing again, he leaned back in his chair. "My money's mostly green, some gold, which suits me fine."

Deciding to change the line of talk, Molly rubbed the small of her back with a work-worn hand, commenting, "That settee of yours is mighty pretty, Aaron, but it's a torture to sleep on."

With a wide swing of her hand, the old woman swept her dusty, wide-brimmed felt hat from her gray head and set it on the polished end table at her elbow. Parker eyed the hat uneasily, then rang a small brass bell on his mahogany desk to summon the Indian servant.

When she appeared, the girl smiled prettily at Molly, greeting her in the old Washo tongue. Molly grinned, replying in like manner. Removing the hat, the maid walked back to the door.

"Give Mrs. Robinson's hat a good brushing," Parker called after her.

Molly turned a stern face to Parker. "How much you paying that girl, Aaron?"

Startled, he blurted out defensively, "Enough. She has a good home here, lots of good food, clean bed."

"Any cash money by way of wages?" she prodded.

Annoyed, he snapped, "Injuns can't handle cash. She'd only buy whiskey with it, and maybe some fancy duds to snare a white man into marrying her."

Selecting an expensive cigar from a box, the agent bit off the tip, spitting it into a woven basket at his side. "I treat my Indians well, Molly," he said coolly. "They're lucky to have such a comfortable home."

Molly's faded blue eyes narrowed. "I hear you're sleeping with that innocent girl."

Parker blushed, but remained unruffled. "No Injuns are innocent—man, woman, or child. They're born liars."

She let that pass. She was here to reason with the man, not argue. She launched directly into the purpose of her visit, keeping her own voice level. "I'm here to ask you one last time to call off your plans to chase the Indians from their rightful land at Eagle Valley. I know full well, as does everyone else in western Nevada, that you and Ralph Brant have divided up that silver-rich land between you."

She let out a breath, took out her handkerchief from her large handbag to stifle a cough.

"Nonsense," he barked, blowing a cloud of heavy

tobacco smoke in her face. Ignoring her sudden fit of coughing, he leaned over the desk, glaring at her. "Those Injuns are causing trouble. Serious trouble. The damn rascals have been holding war councils up and down the state."

Furious, Molly bolted up, turning her face from the path of the smoke. "The Paiutes and the Washos have always been the most peace-loving tribes in all the West. If they've suddenly become warlike, it's because your dirty spies have infiltrated the tribes, giving them whiskey and guns and agitating them to fight the white man."

Parker's eyes narrowed to slits and his lips became a thin, pale line in his long face. His jovial tone vanished abruptly. "Lies, all lies. You can't prove a thing, Molly Robinson."

Tilting his swivel chair all the way back, the agent blew a string of smoke rings into the air. "Nobody in Washington City will pay any attention to the wild ravings of a woman who was raised among Indians." He grinned widely. "You know what they say—you can't lay down with dogs and not catch fleas."

Convulsed with rage and contempt, Molly rose to go. "It's a waste of my valuable time trying to reason with you." She inhaled deeply behind her handkerchief. "I warn you, though, high and mighty Aaron Parker, there is one man in our nation's capital who will respect my word. I have the ear of the chief himself—the President of these United States."

Parker leaned forward. "And what will you tell General Grant, my good woman?"

Approaching the desk, Molly flattened her hands on its polished surface, bent her gaunt frame toward the man. "He will believe me when I tell him that you have abused your power for years. Many respectable citizens will testify that you have diverted money and goods meant for the Indians to line your own pockets. They're starving on the reservations. They have no land to raise crops, no forest to hunt game in, no trees to pick their nuts from."

Rising, too, Parker walked around the desk to face her. Grabbing the handkerchief from her hand, he shook it out to display the spots of blood. "You're an old fool, Molly Robinson. You're dying. Everybody knows it. Those Injuns don't give a damn about you anymore. Your power is gone. All they want is a full belly and a bottle of whiskey every night."

Gently, he handed the handkerchief back to her, put his hands on her skinny shoulders. "Give it up, woman. Spend your last years with your sweet Clover, sitting in a rocking chair dandling grandchildren on your knees."

"Never," she spat out, shrugging him off. "I will not yield to your crooked schemes. I'll fight you tooth and nail, and, before I die, I will win."

She stopped to cough again, a long spasm. Parker waited patiently. They were on opposite sides of the Indian question, but he admired this woman. Her kind had built the West.

Wiping her mouth, Molly resumed. "My Indians will get what is rightfully theirs." She pounded her fist on the shiny wood of the mahogany desk, upset-

206

ting a small bottle of black ink on the green blotter. "They will *not* . . . I repeat, they will *not* be driven out of Eagle Valley."

Hurriedly retrieving his papers from the spilled ink, Parker righted the bottle. Sighing deeply, the agent sat down heavily in his chair and picked up the ink-stained papers, riffling them with his finger.

"See this? It's my formal request to evacuate the redskins from Eagle Valley, transporting them to various reservations in Nevada and Utah. There's at least thirty sworn and notarized accounts of specific incidents of trouble caused by these Indians whom you love so much."

He paused, adding softly, "Indians in Nevada can live freely only if they are peaceable and cause no trouble. That's the federal law, and you know it."

He shoved the top page of the sheaf across the desk. Molly picked it up and read, with sinking heart: "To the Secretary of the Interior, Department of Indian Affairs—"

Slowly, she put it down. "It'll take them a year to push this thing through. You know how slow the wheels turn in Washington City among the bureaucrats."

He grinned. "Not this time. I have friends in the department. They assure me that the deposition will be read and acted upon with dispatch."

She turned to go. "Well, Aaron Parker who once had a snotty nose, I, too, have a high-placed friend—right in the White House. He can overrule, by executive order, all your damn lily-livered bureaucrats."

His laughter echoed as she sailed through the door. "If you refer to President Ulysses S. Grant, the talk is that he's drunk twenty-three hours out of twenty-four. You'll have to catch him sober."

Turning, she shouted back, "He can sign his name dead drunk. I've seen him do it often."

But the agent had the last word. Standing up, he shouted out the open window at her, causing heads to turn on the night-dark street.

"Well, it's sure as hell you can't go to bed with the general, like you did in the old days in San Francisco." He laughed uproariously. "You ain't got the body, woman, you're a dry well."

Ignoring his nasty jibe, Molly walked at a rapid clip down Main Street toward the stagestop, her fast-beating heart pushing the blood through her old veins. It was Saturday night in Carson City, and the saloons were crowded, the streets noisy.

But she heard nothing. The exhaustion of the long day had disappeared. She felt rejuvenated. Nothing like a good fight to make an old woman feel like a girl again, she mused. She did not realize she had spoken the thought aloud until she noticed a harlot on a street corner staring at her and making circular motions with her hand around her head to her companion.

Her brain teemed with a bold new plan. She had spoken in anger when she'd threatened Parker with seeing President Grant, but now she resolved to actually board a train for Washington City.

At her last talk with Doc Jackson, he had warned,

"Slow down, or I'll give you no more than a couple of months."

That's all she needed, Molly thought happily as she climbed on the stage for Black Springs. She'd fetch Clover back from Eagle Valley to accompany her. That damn lion could live without the girl for a month or two.

The stage was nearly empty, the lone passenger besides herself being an Indian, fast asleep and reeking of whiskey. The night had turned cold and windy, the bright moon had slipped behind a dark cloud. They were in for a summer storm, she thought as she pulled the leather curtain down over the open side.

Leaning back, she closed her eyes and thought about General Ulysses S. Grant. She'd met him — how long was it now? — a quarter century ago. He'd been a mere captain then, and very lonely — far from the great national hero he was to become.

Her mind slid back. Lordy, what a time that was. Aside from finding Clover, it had been the happiest experience of her life. In those years, young Molly Robinson, abandoned by a no-good husband, with the mark of Indian-lover on her, was prospecting on a small claim some miles from San Francisco. Her claim was on a stream off Humboldt Bay in the redwood country.

The closest town was Eureka, where a company of United States cavalry was stationed. The men and officers came to town when off duty, seeking company. They had little to do, since the local Indians were remarkably peaceable.

A lonely, frustrated, downhearted young captain offered to buy her a drink at a saloon, where Molly herself liked to sit and talk after a long day of panning for gold on her claim.

Sam Grant was easy to talk to, and good-looking, well set up with a nice little beard and kind eyes. With visions of becoming an army wife, Molly invited him home to her skin tipi, which she had built on the banks of her stream. She was totally alone, except for a few Indian families who also kept to themselves.

When he arrived, she feared that he would expect what any man did — an hour of pleasure with her body. But to her surprise and delight, the captain was not interested in physical love; though, to tell the truth, he took in so much liquor, he would have been unable to perform anyway.

"I'm lonely as hell," he had confessed to her, sitting cross-legged on her rabbitskin-covered dirt floor. Thereupon he hauled out a cameo portrait of his lovely wife Julia, far away in New York State, with their newborn son.

"I've never seen him," he had mourned. "I cannot send for her. We are not permitted to have families on the base."

For months, Sam Grant and Molly Robinson met and talked, both in town and in her tipi. They were two lonely people finding comfort in each other. Everyone figured they were lovers, for most of the soldiers had a woman, Indian or white, tucked away somewhere.

Molly let the notion persist, denying it would do little good. As the years passed, and the young captain made his indelible mark on history, she enjoyed the vicarious fame of having once been loved by Ulysses Grant.

But poor Sam's excessive drinking soon got him in trouble with his superiors, and eventually he was forced to resign his post. He left Eureka, and it wasn't until months later that Molly tracked him down to a San Francisco flophouse, alone and broke and near despair.

She had just cashed in a bag of nuggets and gold powder and purchased him a steamship ticket for New York to rejoin his beloved Julia. He never kept his promise to repay her.

"Now is the time to settle your debt, Sam Grant," she muttered to the sleeping Indian, who immediately woke up and cursed at her in Paiute.

As she got off the stage and headed for home in the wind, Molly realized for the first time that she had left her hat with Agent Parker. Well, she'd buy a new one, darn it, for her Washington City sojourn.

Molly also realized with a pleasant shock that she hadn't coughed at all during the long trip.

She was walking up the stony hill in a light rain to her stagehouse when she heard a shout. The front door opened wide and Samson tore down the hill, waving something wildly in the air.

Molly stepped aside before the man knocked her over. Samson stopped so fast, he fell down on the rocks, then, picking himself up, he gasped, "Here, read it, it's something awful."

His narrow Chinese face looked scared to death. "Awful, awful," he kept repeating.

Annoyed at his dramatics, Molly snapped, "And just how do you know what's inside?" She turned over the heavy parchmentlike envelope with Ralph Brant's name printed in one corner.

Shaking the cook, she said tartly, "Up to your old tricks, eh, Samson, reading my mail?" But her smile was broad. The man had no living relatives outside of China. He loved reading other people's mail.

They had reached the house, and, going inside, Molly sat down at the table and pulled the letter from the envelope. She recognized Brant's bold, clear script from previous correspondence. Holding it close to the kerosene lamp, she read aloud:

"My dear (and I hope we remain dear friends) Mrs. Robinson,"

She snorted. Ralph Brant had been once a schoolteacher and tended to be high-flown in his letters.

"Abandon, I beg you, your misguided efforts to save Eagle Valley for the undeserving Indians. I hold high cards here. Your darling daughter Clover, the light of your life, is in my hands. Her paramour, the rascal Emerson, should be back in Illinois by the time you read this. He will be hanged for breaking out of prison years ago. I accept your thanks for getting him out of Clover's life. Good Lord, what if they had married?

212

"If you desire to see Clover alive again, send a message by Festus Jones. He will deliver it to Ragtown where I am stopping with Clover and others.

"Here are my terms: Persuade the Indians—use any influence you have with them—at Eagle Valley and elsewhere, to stop their war councils. They will lose their valley in any case, and making war will only impoverish them all the more—those who are left alive, that is.

"If you refuse to cooperate, Clover will die. But not quickly. I will make her available to every man I employ, any others who will pay, and when we get to Eagle Valley, she will be given to my favorite Indians as well. Eventually, I might sell her to the highest bidder to live out her life in a San Francisco brothel. Sometimes white slave girls are shipped to Mexico.

"Your old friend, Ralph Brant, Esq."

Stunned, unable to believe the horrible things she had just read, Molly dropped the letter on the table as if it had suddenly caught fire. Her pale-blue eyes stared vacantly at Samson, who wept noisily in a chair across the table, his pigtailed head shaking uncontrollably from side to side.

Neither spoke for a long time. Then Molly sighed wearily. "It's a joke, of course," she said. "Nobody could be that inhuman." She paused, reflecting. "If that man hurts Clover in any way, he'll have the wrath of the whole town down upon him."

Bolting up from the table, Molly stormed, "Ralph

Brant is just trying to scare me into doing what he wants. He's been at it for years. Why, Pedro would never let Clover be captured. He would die first."

"Oh, dear God," Molly shrieked, clapping her hand to her mouth as she realized the obvious. Raising a tearful face to hers, Samson said it for her: "Pedro must be dead."

Molly did not respond. Her tall, skinny body seemed turned to stone. Her face was a mask of denial.

"The lion, too," Samson persisted. "Henry would rip anyone to shreds who tried to harm Clover."

"I don't believe a word of it," Molly said flatly, picking up the letter once again and tearing it across, then across a second time. She walked to the fire to throw the pieces into the embers, but when she got to the hearth, she changed her mind, shoving Brant's letter into the pocket of her cotton frock.

Moving briskly, she walked into her bedroom, just off the dining room. "I'm going to sleep for a few hours, Samson. You go into town and round up a few good men, preferably red ones, to ride with us to Ragtown. Now, scat."

Some time later, Molly was jolted from a heavy sleep by the sound of voices outside her open window. Instinctively she reached for the revolver on her bedside table. Creeping silently to the window, she peered out into the night. It was still raining, and the sky was thick. She saw nothing.

"Who's there?" she yelled out, cocking the revolver noisily and pointing it into the night. "If you're

214

stealin' chickens, I've got a bead on you."

A reply came promptly from the murk. "Would you shoot an old friend who has traveled many moons to see you?"

The voice was old and cracked and very weak, but there was no mistaking it. "Pedro," Molly squealed, lowering the gun. "Are you a ghost?"

A laugh rang out, strong and clear. A young laugh. "No, but he might be soon, if you don't come out and help us inside."

"Is that you, Lake Emerson?" she cried, amazed. The Englishman was supposed to be long gone from Nevada by now. Puzzled, but delirious with joy at finding her old friend White Hawk alive, Molly tore into the yard in her bare feet. At the corner of the house, she came face-to-face with two mules riding close together. Lake was holding the reins of Pedro's mule, on which the old Indian lay facedown across the saddle blanket. He was frighteningly still.

In seconds, the old woman and Lake had carried the wounded man inside and laid him on his cot in the pantry room off the kitchen. Peeling off Pedro's filthy, bloodstained garments, Molly quickly surveyed the damage to his body. Her large, capable hands prodded and kneaded gently, from the man's head to his toes. The Indian seemed totally unembarrassed that a woman was touching his private parts. Old White Hawk seemed content to lie back on his familiar bed and let his pal Molly here do her will on him.

Gazing at Pedro's mutilated manhood, Molly said

215

softly, suppressing her tears, "Young White Hawk, whom I was pledged to marry, was the strongest man in the tribe. Once I saw him wrestle a cougar who had attacked us as we gathered nuts."

She turned a smiling face to Lake. "The fearless brave pinned the animal to the rocks and strangled him with his bare hands."

When she'd completed her thorough examination, Molly commented with relief, "Lots of bruises, but no bones broken that I can detect. I find no soft masses to indicate bleeding in his organs."

Her lips tightened as she added angrily, "Somebody sure gave him a helluva beating."

"Three of Brant's bruisers worked on him," Lake said. "I saw it. If the poor fellow had not played dead, they would have finished him."

Molly whirled. "Were you there at the time?"

Lake nodded, accepting a cup of hot coffee from Samson, who had returned from his errand. "I'll tell you the whole grisly story later."

"Then it's true," she said, seemingly without emotion. "Clover actually *is* in Brant's hands."

"Yes," he replied hurriedly, placing a hand on her arm, "but she's well. They have not harmed her."

"Praise God," she muttered. Content with that much for the moment, Molly returned her attentions to the gravely wounded man. Samson was ordered to fetch hot broth and feed it in spoonfuls to Pedro. With Lake's help, she bathed the wounds with water and mild soap, then applied salves and ointments from her ample stock.

216

Molly's Indian upbringing had taught her the lore of herbs and poultices, and as she mixed and applied the healing paste to the open wounds, Lake turned away to hide the sudden rush of feeling.

That wonderful first night of love with Clover as he had lain covered with poultices seemed a lifetime ago. He dreaded telling Molly that he had deflowered her sheltered virgin daughter while he was covered with herb paste. His mind whirled with words to tell her how it had been with them. "I love your Clover more than life," he'd say.

But love meant nothing to Molly Robinson, Clover had informed him. Lake Emerson was a stranger, a nobody, completely untrustworthy to this fiercely protective mother.

Samson was sent back to town to tell the men he had alerted that Mrs. Robinson would not ride tonight. Pedro was given a sleeping draught in his broth and promptly fell sound asleep. He had not uttered a sound since being brought inside. Now and then he reached for Molly's hand.

Molly and Lake sat at a table by the hearth, sipping coffee and talking. Lake briefly filled her in on events of the past weeks since he had left Black Springs.

"I decided that Brant could go to hell with his train ticket. Nobody on earth is going to push me where I don't want to go. I went after Clover and Henry and Pedro, finding them easily enough at Ragtown. Henry ran off into the mountains our last night there."

He grinned wryly. "We didn't get very far before Brant surprised us with his men. They captured me again, but I escaped."

"Hmm." She pursed her lips, but her faded blue eyes gleamed with admiration: "The whole affair sounds a lot easier than it was, I warrant. I presume you wanted your lion back from Clover."

The young liontamer smiled. "Of course, but not enough to risk my neck for him. I wanted Clover."

He appeared unruffled at her look of surprise, but his heart was beating wildly. He was determined, come hell or high water, to have Clover for his wife, regardless of Molly's opposition. Life would be simpler with this woman on his side.

After a moment, Molly laughed. "I don't know why I'm surprised. I saw it coming. Handsome circus man, gullible young girl." She grinned. "Just like a story book."

"We . . . we—" Lake began. His fine English face turned the color of a ripe strawberry.

Raising one hand to silence him, Molly snapped, "Don't bother to tell me." She smiled, a strange, faraway look coming into her eyes. "You became man and wife under the stars in God's great cathedral."

Lake burst out laughing. What a grand old lady, he thought as their eyes met over the table.

Dipping into her dress pocket, Molly pulled out Ralph Brant's ransom letter. She shoved the four fragments across the table. "Read this, and tell me if you think he's serious. Does the greedy bastard mean what he says?"

218

Fitting the pieces together, Lake read quickly. Lifting his eyes to hers, he said, "No. It's a lot of bombast, empty threats. Nobody's going to sell Clover. Brant won't give her to his men, or to a brothel dealer, either."

Molly's eyes narrowed. "How can you be so sure?"

Leaning back in his chair, Lake eagerly ate from a plateful of food Samson had left for them. He took a generous bite of cold roast lamb, chewed it thoroughly, and swallowed before replying to the anxious Molly.

"Because he's already given her to Gray Falcon."

Molly's lined face cleared. She paused to cough into her handkerchief. The relief on her face was evident.

"He's a very handsome Indian, and looks at Clover like a starving man would look at this delicious lamb," Lake continued gloomily. "I'm sure he's already taken her by force and will guard her with his life."

Smiling, Molly began to spoon up the bowl of hot piñon-nut soup. Her appetite seemed unusually hearty for a woman whose daughter was in the hands of a lusty Indian, Lake reflected.

"Stop worrying. I can get her back from Gray Falcon," Molly said as she emptied her bowl. "Just like that." She snapped her fingers in the air. "I helped bring that young warrior into the world on one of my visits to Eagle Valley. Gray Falcon is a self-indulgent so-and-so of a spoiled child. He never wants anything—even a woman—for very long. After the conquest, he soon tires of his prize."

She clucked her tongue. "He's a child at heart."

Filling up her bowl with a second helping of the soup, she added, winking broadly, "His father is Red Hawk, one of the big Paiute chiefs in Eagle Valley, and, I might add, a longtime friend of mine. A word from him will force his son to surrender his prize."

Placing a comforting hand on Lake's tanned arm, she said, "Don't worry. Clover will survive. She's been raised to be strong. She's a fighter."

"I hope so," Lake said miserably. "I can't sleep for thinking about my Clover with that brutal man. She's almost a virgin."

"But she isn't," Molly said flatly.

"No, I saw to that, thank God," Lake breathed, reddening.

Rising from the table, Lake lifted his arms in a wide stretch. "Show me a bed, please, Mrs. Robinson. After a good night's sleep, I'm going after Clover. She may be a fighter, as you say, but something terrible might happen to her." He groaned. "That beast could get her with child."

"Don't even think about it," Molly muttered, angrily, because she herself feared the very same thing. Half-breeds did not fare well in the white man's society.

Leading the exhausted young man to Clover's pleasant room upstairs, Molly remarked, "You'll sleep well in your sweetheart's bed, but you're going nowhere in the morning." She chuckled. "Unless you want Ralph Brant to catch you again and haul you back to Illinois for hanging."

"Oh-h, that!" Lake exclaimed, falling back on the bed fully clothed. "That's another story . . ."

"In the morning, boy, in the morning. Let today's trouble suffice for the day."

"That's from the Bible," he mumbled, and promptly fell asleep.

Moving to the window, Molly opened it a crack. Hearing his steady breathing, she smiled to herself. This was the man who had just claimed he couldn't sleep for worrying about his sweetheart.

Covering him with Clover's afghan, which rested at the foot of the bed, Molly stood a long time gazing down at the handsome face. Bending slightly, she gently pushed a lock of platinum hair from his eyes. My Clover has chosen very well, she mused. This one was easy to love.

Not until after the midday diners had left the stagehouse dining room could Molly and Lake slip away to Superstition Hill. Pedro was still asleep. "He'll sleep for days," Molly explained. "Sleep—and nature—are the best healers."

She refused to tell Lake why they had to climb the rocky bluff before he was allowed to tell her why he'd been in prison.

"I need some exercise," she informed the mystified liontamer. "I've got to think."

When they reached the summit, Molly immediately retrieved the gilt box from its hiding place. She handed it to Lake.

"Why, I know this box," he said, amazed. "It belonged to Clover's father. Where did you get it?"

Silently, she took out Sinclair's unmailed letter to the governor of Illinois. "Read it."

When he had read the contents, which absolved him from blame for the killing of the policeman during the robbery in which they had both participated, Lake said quietly, "So you knew all the time that I was that unlucky boy."

"I suspected," she replied.

"Where are the double eagles?" Lake glanced into the empty box.

"Cashed in. The money is in a San Francisco bank, earning interest," she said quickly. "It helped raise Clover."

She failed to explain why she had not returned the gold coins to the Illinois bank, and Lake knew better than to ask her. Lake began to pace round and round the summit, gazing thoughtfully at the clutter of abandoned mines and shacks. The sun was high and hot, and, nervously, he ran his fingers through his blond hair. Molly sat down against her wickiup hiding place. Lake was a man with a problem of conscience. He had to work it out for himself.

She waited patiently.

At last he stopped and faced her. "You also know, I'm sure, that I came here for my half of the money. I wanted to kill Sinclair for the great wrong he committed against me. When I discovered he was dead, I wanted to get the money from Clover." He groaned. "I intended to seduce her." He emitted a yelp of frustration. "But instead I fell head over heels for her."

He sighed, but not unhappily. "It's not fair."

"Life is never fair," Molly murmured. "The rain falls on the just as well as the unjust. We poor humans got to make the best of it. We got to keep dry enough to live."

Lake struck his brow with the flat of his hand. "Oh, my God, when I think another day or two and the letter would have been mailed . . ." His voice was anguished.

Tall and slim, the young Englishman gazed directly up into the sun, as if seeking answers.

"Clover can have the money," he said finally. "Now let's get out of here, I want to go after her."

"You can't go alone," Molly scolded. "Brant's men will hunt you down like a dog. We'll all go—you, me, Pedro, a couple of Indians for insurance."

"The money belongs to both of you," she stated, getting to her feet. "Man and wife always share."

"Clover will have to be told that her father was a criminal," he declared. "It will break her heart."

Molly shook her head. "Molly is a woman now. She can face it."

Thinking of their nights of love in the mountains, Lake smiled. "Nobody knows better than I how much of a woman she really is."

They could not embark on the journey to Eagle Valley until Pedro was well enough to accompany them, she told him as they descended the hill. A week or two, she figured.

Since Molly had expressed a desire to remain on Superstition Hill to "meditate," as she put it, Lake fairly raced down the hill to the stagehouse. He felt light as a feather. The burden of years had been lifted. At long last his heart was cleansed of the cancer of hatred and revenge.

Chapter Eleven

The last leg of the journey to Eagle Valley passed through the fearsome desert called the Valley of Death. Crossing it normally took four days, but Brant forced his party to do it in two.

To accomplish this, he secured fast horses to replace the slower mules. Stops for physical needs were limited to ten minutes. At night, men and horses were allowed four hours' sleep. Food and water were consumed while riding, but Clover had no stomach for eating. Her wide-brimmed hat was ripped apart by the wind, and her face became severely sunburned. The skin from her face peeled off in strips. Her eyes burned like fire from the glare of the salt-encrusted desert floor.

Exhausted, weak from hunger and thirst, with no future in sight, Clover was in despair. For the first time in her seventeen years, she fervently wished she could die.

Upon their arrival in Eagle Valley, Gray Falcon took her directly to the lodge of his mother, Sweet Briar. Too weak to stand, Clover sank in a heap on the cool earthen floor. Her mind and body were numb. She was in Eagle Valley at last, the place she had thought of as heaven. But she felt as if she were in hell.

"White Feather, come here," Gray Falcon shouted, looming tall and fearsome in the middle of the lodge. A pretty girl ran from the hearth, shouting his name. She stood before him with beaming face. Even in the half gloom, Clover saw that the girl's dark eyes shone with happiness.

Ignoring White Feather's smiling greeting, Gray Falcon swung his proud head around the long room, announcing in a loud voice, "This white woman is to be my chief squaw." He flung a long arm toward Clover. "Care for her well until my return from powwow."

Clearly shocked and enraged, White Feather screamed, "I am to be your wife, I have your pledge." Rushing forward, she pounded her fists on his broad chest.

Drawing back a powerful hand, Gray Falcon slapped the girl so hard that she reeled back. "Silence, woman, you will be my second wife." He laughed coarsely. "Even that is an honor many would envy."

He left without a word to Clover, who huddled in a dark corner of the one-room lodge. Gray Falcon, along with most of the able-bodied men in this end of the valley, had been summoned to war powwow with

Ralph Brant. Already taking charge in the paradisal refuge, Brant was headquartered in a spacious suite of lodges, built into a cliffside miles away.

Two weeks later, Clover sat, hugging her knees, her head bent low, in her corner of the crowded wooden lodge. It was raining. The lodge was damp, and being farthest from the fire, she was cold. And she was dejected. The single ray of brightness in her life was the fact that Gray Falcon was gone and he could not abuse her with his savage lovemaking.

The unrelenting pounding of the rain on the tin roof was driving her mad. She dreaded the moment of Gray Falcon's return.

For three whole days and two nights it had been raining in Eagle Valley. The ground outside the lodge was a sea of mud. The women and children who lived in the long, narrow one-room building became quarrelsome. Nobody ventured outdoors, except the women assigned to fetching water and emptying wicker chamber pots into the ravine behind the line of lodges. Inside, the air was stifling and reeked of unwashed bodies.

White Feather, who was in charge of dividing the work among the younger women, had promptly added the new white woman to her stable of unwilling slaves.

"Here, whore, take these," White Feather had ordered on Clover's first day in the lodge, thrusting two overflowing chamber pots at the exhausted girl. As Clover dragged herself to her feet and took the vessels from White Feather, the girl added, "If you spill, it will make no difference to your filthy buckskin."

She'd put two fingers to her nose in a gesture of disgust and narrowed her eyes to slits. A soft, velvety brown, White Feather's eyes would have been lovely if they had not been filled with hate, Clover thought. In fact, the Indian maid was beautiful to look at, tall and slim, with flawless honey-colored skin and a shining fall of jet-black hair which she wore in a thick braid down her back.

Born and raised on the Pyramid Lake reservation, Gray Falcon's rejected sweetheart spoke impeccable English. She wore a pretty blue-print store-bought calico, as did most of the other girls in the lodge. Old and senile, Sweet Briar spent the long days and nights in a rocking chair by the enormous hearth and had delegated her responsibilities as chief squaw to White Feather.

The women in the lodge were Sweet Briar's daughters or wives of her many sons. The men whose wives lived in the lodge slept apart in the tipi of their chief, Red Hawk, who was Sweet Briar's husband. This peculiar arrangement was part of their ancestral code, Clover understood. For privacy and lovemaking, couples went to still another dwelling.

Nobody had given Clover anything to wear to replace the Indian dress Gray Falcon had given her in Ragtown. She was forced to wait until all were served before she was given her plate of food. Worst of all, nobody spoke a word to her—except White Feather, and then only to order her about like a commanding officer.

228

All looked at her with contempt, whispering behind their hands to each other. It broke her heart. Many of the girls had been her friends in the happy summers she'd spent in the valley. Now they regarded her as scum.

Clover didn't mind the hard work, nor even White Feather's vindictiveness. She felt pity for the girl. How terrible, she thought, to be pushed aside to second place even before the bridal night.

Hard work took Clover's mind off the misery her life had become. Lake was probably dead by now. There was usually no trial when an escapee was captured. Molly probably didn't even know where her daughter was. Or that she was married to an Indian. No matter that Gray Falcon was of mixed blood, Molly would disown her. She'd said so many times. "I love and respect the Indian people," Molly often affirmed, "but marrying white with red makes outcasts of the unfortunate offspring."

Suddenly, Clover's moody reflections in her corner were interrupted by a gleeful shout. "It's stopped raining!"

Housebound women and children poured out of the lodge. Clover, too, ran out into a gloriously bright sun. The entire village bustled. The children darted about wildly, like little mice suddenly released from a cage. They leaped into the many puddles, splashing and laughing, covering themselves with mud. Many started to fashion houses and animals from the pliable mud.

The squaws began to hang damp garments on trees and fences, and spread their damp bedding on rocks to dry. Everyone threw open their doors to let the sun pour inside.

Clover lifted her face to the glorious sun and prayed for courage.

Drawn like a magnet to the happy children, Clover knelt and spoke to a little girl of five or so.

"What are you making, little one?" she asked. Clover adored children. She'd always regretted being an only child. Placing her hand on the child's warm, glossy hair, she said, "It looks like a lion."

The child glanced up, smiling, but before she could reply, Clover felt a blow from behind on her head. Stunned, she fell back on the muddy ground. White Feather stood over her, her beautiful face contorted with fury.

"Take your whoring hands off that innocent child," she raged. "If I ever catch you even looking at any of these little ones again, I'll have you whipped and driven out of the valley like a dog."

Angered at the sudden, unreasonable attack, Clover flared back. "Is it not dangerous to treat Gray Falcon's chief squaw like a dog? Are blows and revilement the kind of care he demanded that you give me?"

Getting to her feet, she flashed, "When my husband hears of how you have treated me, you are the one who will be driven out, White Feather." She smiled. "If he does not kill you with his bare hands."

"No, white whore, Gray Falcon will do none of those things," the girl sneered. "Once his lust for you is sated, he will take me into his tipi as his

230

bride—his only squaw." She drew close. "I promise you that, you slut."

Gathering her spittle, White Feather spat directly into Clover's face. "You are nothing but a tool of Ralph Brant. He kidnapped you to get Molly Robinson down here to keep my people from going to war."

A crowd had gathered to watch. "Fight the white bitch, White Feather, you are stronger," someone called out.

Clover made her hands into fists. "I'd love to," she said loudly, raising her fists into the air. An exchange of blows between quarreling women was a favorite way to settle fights among the Paiutes, she recalled. The men loved to watch. They would come from miles around to see the amusing and blood-tingling sight.

Throwing back her beautiful head, White Feather laughed. "I wouldn't touch the filthy bitch," she said. "Does one fight with a dog?"

The spectators dwindled away, and White Feather returned to the lodge. Clover raced down to the stream, and ignoring the women who were pounding garments on the rocks, she leaped into the fresh, clear water.

She swam about vigorously for a time, cleansing her body of sweat and grime. The chill waters set her blood to racing and her brain to working clearly. She would find a way to escape the closely guarded valley. Better death in the desert than life in Eagle Valley as a captive.

If she could not manage to escape, she would go to live with the Diggers, a primitive tribe who were shunned by the other tribes. They dwelt in the farthest reaches of the valley where the land was poor. They ate grasshoppers and worms and wore skirts of grass.

She was climbing out, hair and buckskin dripping wet, when a lad came running up. "The white woman is wanted at the tipi of Red Hawk."

Clover followed the boy to the spacious rabbitskin tipi where Chief Red Hawk lived with some of his sons. She stepped inside. At first, she saw nothing in the gloom and smoke from the roaring fire. The smell of tobacco was strong.

A smooth voice called out, "Come forward, Clover, Chief Red Hawk wishes to see you."

"Ralph Brant!" she gasped.

Instantly, the tall figure of her kidnapper loomed over her. Placing his hand beneath her arm, he drew her toward the fire. An Indian, very old and shrunken, sat in a velvety, flowered armchair by the fire. The chair was obviously ancient and the smoke and grime of many years had darkened the original bright hues.

"Welcome, my daughter, to Eagle Valley," said Red Hawk. His mouth opened in a toothless smile. "I am told you are to be my son Gray Falcon's squaw. I adopted him when his white father deserted him, but I love him more than the many sons from my own loins. He is brave and true."

Clover was silent. Telling this doting father that she was unhappy would do no good.

"Are the women treating you well?" Red Hawk asked in the northern Paiute tongue.

Drawing herself erect, Clover answered in a loud voice, also speaking in Paiute. "Chief Red Hawk, I thank you for your concern. But I am forced to relate that the women of Sweet Briar's lodge regard me as the lowest dog. They despise because I am white and Gray Falcon has chosen me for his squaw."

Casting Clover a look of consternation, Ralph Brant broke in hurriedly. "She does not mean what she says, Chief Red Hawk." He spoke in English, for although he understood the Indian tongue, he could not speak it.

Brant's hand tightened on Clover's arm, as if in warning. "The girl is sick for home. She misses her mother and she is distraught." He grinned slyly. "She is anxious for the return of her bridegroom from powwow."

The old chief said nothing to this. He bent his grizzled head, as if in meditation. After a minute of silence, he spoke again. "Our friend Ralph Brant tells me that you will speak to my people, telling them they must not make war."

Clover laughed dryly. "How else than by making war can they prevent this greedy landgrabber from carting them off to reservations?"

Another Indian stepped forward. He was wrapped in a blanket and wore a hood over his face, with holes for eyes and nose. "I am shaman here. Chief Red Hawk is not well. Do not speak strong words to him."

As if to verify the medicine man's words, the aged man immediately began to cough. His frail old body bent nearly double in his frantic efforts to breathe. If

233

the shaman and another Indian had not supported the chief on either side with their arms, he would have toppled out of the chair.

Under cover of the disturbance, Brant hissed to Clover, "Your mother has not replied to my demands for your release. Gray Falcon is not here to protect you. I have sent him on a mission of many weeks to tribes in Utah."

"Praise the Lord," Clover said fervently. "May he never return."

Ignoring her comment, Brant continued. "There is but one way to save yourself from being sold by me to the highest bidder. You must go about the valley preaching against making war. They will heed you because you are Molly Robinson's daughter and are the handmaiden of the sacred lion."

"Who is dead," said Clover flatly.

"Do not tell them that, you must tell them that the lion is in the wilderness, gathering strength from the Great Spirit."

Clover snorted. But the notion made sense. "I will preach peace," she said heatedly, "but not to save myself from your wicked schemes. I will do it for the Indian people, whom I love. Another war will annihilate the Paiutes and the Washos. Their whole civilization will crumble under the white man's fire."

"Take her out," the shaman ordered, angrily. "Chief Red Hawk must rest."

The aged chief lay back in the flowered chair, as if dead. His arms and legs sprawled out obscenely. If this old man dies, Gray Falcon will be chief, thought Clover, trembling at the thought.

As Brant led Clover to the open flap of the tipi, the cracked old voice of the chief called out, "Treat Molly's daughter well. Give her a tipi, and a maid to be her servant and companion."

That night Clover left Sweet Briar's lodge for a small but snug tipi. Inside were two cots with warm woolen blankets from the government store set up by Ralph Brant for the use of Eagle Valley residents. One cot was for Clover, the other for Mia, the young Indian girl who had been chosen by Brant to be her servant.

Like Pedro, and many others, Mia had been sent to Jesuit school, and had kept her Christian name. She had come to Eagle Valley to care for her ailing mother and after her mother's death, she had remained. She had fallen in love with a young brave, who was in prison for wounding a man severely in a drunken brawl.

"Big Turtle will come home in three years," she told Clover. "Until then, I must work for my bread."

Though more highly educated than many white girls, Mia was naive in the ways of the white man. The girl was very fond of Mr. Brant. "Many of the old ones do not trust the man," she told Clover. "They think he will have the Great White Father in Washington City imprison us in reservations so that he can have our valley to himself."

"I believe so, too," Clover replied. "I do not trust him."

"Ah, but you are wrong. He wants only to be permitted access to the silver in our hills," Mia replied. "In return, he will give us food and goods from the government stores."

Like a child at Christmas, the girl gleefully showed Clover the wicker chest of frocks, shoes, and bonnets given her by Mr. Brant.

"Those who are given too much without hard work become weak and spineless," Clover replied, but under her breath. Further argument would only antagonize the girl, who would be her constant companion.

But she said no more of Brant's real intent. She was certain that the unscrupulous scoundrel was already working on obtaining a decree from the Bureau of Indian Affairs to move the Indians out of their last refuge in Nevada. It was easily done—a few trumped-up charges and a chunk of money in the right palms had accomplished it in the past.

A shooting war would ruin Brant's plans. A war would turn the Bureau against him. Brant himself might be killed, and many of his men, too, who were slated to help him found a silver empire.

That night brought little sleep to Clover, as she tossed and turned, her mind filled with uncertainties. She would gladly preach peace to the Indians of the valley, but how? What words could she use to convince them that she was not laboring on Brant's behalf.

Oh, Molly, where are you? she groaned inwardly. You vowed to work to keep this green valley for the Indians. What could possibly interfere with a sacred vow?

It was not like her foster mother to be so silent. Brant's ransom letter had told her of Clover's capture. She might not want to see her Indian squaw daughter, but she would never abandon her crusade to save the valley from being raped by Ralph Brant.

A dreadful thought brought a frightened Clover straight up in bed. Molly was dead, the consumption had killed her. That was the only logical explanation for her foster mother's continuing silence.

Comfort, some peace of mind, and sound advice came from an unexpected source. Chief Red Hawk summoned her at dawn. As Clover entered the tent, she thought it reeked of death. The old man called out to her from the armchair, which he apparently never left.

"Come forward, Molly Robinson's daughter."

Upon her capture and adoption by the Paiutes, the child Molly had been given the Indian name of Bluebird. But when she left the tribe to rejoin her own people, she never again answered to that name. "Answering to two names," she had explained to Clover, "splits a person in half."

As Clover neared the fire, the sick man extended two bony hands to grasp hers. His sunken eyes glittered with fever. The clawlike hands on hers were icy cold.

Alarmed, Clover said, "Should the chief not be in his bed?"

He shook his head. "I cannot breathe with my body flat."

She glanced around. "Where is your shaman, and your nursing men? Have your many sons abandoned you?"

"My sons are at powwow. I have sent out the sha-

237

mans, for I wish to speak alone with Molly's daughter."

Glancing at the array of bottles and powders on a nearby shelf, Clover said, "I will survey the medicines to see which nostrums might be of help. There is one that Molly uses when she is coughing badly."

She tried to extricate her hands, but with surprising strength, the sick man held her fast. "Stay, I am beyond medicine, except that of the Spirit."

Beckoning her to sit on a high stool at his side, Red Hawk began to speak, pausing frequently to catch his breath.

"Many think that Red Hawk is addle-brained and that the white man Brant has hoodwinked him. Red Hawk is old and wise. Red Hawk knows that Brant means to drive my people out of our beloved valley. Molly Robinson's daughter must preach peace to my people and assure them that they will not be driven out like dogs from their land."

"But how can I preach what I do not know to be true, wise Red Hawk?" Clover asked. Her beautiful face was troubled. "The yearning for battle is strong in many hearts."

"Red Hawk promises that help will come from the Great White Father who lives by the eastern sea," he replied sternly.

"How has such wisdom come to you, old chief?" Clover inquired gently.

Red Hawk's glittering eyes rolled back in their sockets until they were completely white. Releasing her hands, he stretched both arms upward, as if in prayer. "The Great Spirit speaks with the dying. He has told me that our great and loyal friend Molly Robinson will bring help from the Great White Father in Washington City."

Leaping to her feet, Clover wailed, "Pray, wise chief, tell me, why has my mother not come to us? Where is she? Brant will move swiftly, for he has friends in high places."

Rising up also, with new energy, the dying man took a great fortifying breath, then stormed at her, fiercely. "How can a daughter of Molly Robinson have such little faith?"

Overcome with shame at her doubts, Clover fell at the old man's feet, her arms encircling his knees. "Bless me, oh, Great Chief," she sobbed. "Give me your strength to believe."

His two hands came down to rest on her head. "Faith will come, and salvation." He paused, as if listening to an unseen voice. "The Spirit also tells me that help will come from still another source. Your blessed lion is alive and will return to you in good health."

"Henry is dead. I saw the bloody harness—"

Impatiently, with a quick movement, the old chief lifted a neck ornament on a leather thong over his head. Handing it to her, he said gently, "Take this totem of my clan for a totem of your faith."

Clover held it in her hands, feeling the warmth from the old man's body. A downward soaring eagle was carved in great detail on a bed of turquoise.

"I will treasure it forever," she said with reverence, slipping it over her own head.

But Red Hawk was not listening. He had sunk

into his armchair once again and, throwing back his head, fell into an exhausted sleep.

That very night, the old chief ordered that an elaborate ceremony be held in a meadow bordering Ralph Brant's lodge to bid farewell and call down blessings on the peace ambassador Clover Sinclair.

Mia would accompany her, as well as four stalwart young braves to act as escort, to defend the women if necessary from warlike tribes. They came from several tribes, and would also act as interpreters when Clover addressed those who were not Paiutes or Washos.

Not all in Eagle Valley looked upon this venture with favor, and there was danger of real harm to the two girls.

Defiantly, Clover faced the man who had destroyed the man she loved and had given her in slavery to a man she now despised. She and Brant stood in the shadows behind a large circle of Indians who were dancing and chanting around a huge fire.

"I intend to win this battle for the valley," she said grimly. "Molly is in Washington City at this moment, seeking help from her old friend President Grant."

He laughed uproariously. "Your doddering old mother is dying. Without her darling daughter and her old Indian at her side, she has given up the ghost."

Clover paled. "That's a lie. Molly Robinson will not die until her valley is saved."

Another man stepped forward, whom Clover recognized as the Indian agent Parker from Carson City. "I, too, heard before my departure from the north that your mother has taken to her bed," he said in his smooth, oily voice.

"You're simply trying to frighten me," she replied. "If Molly were dying, she would have sent for me."

"Perhaps she has," Brant sneered. "But you are now an Indian squaw and hardly free to go where you please."

As Clover returned to Mia's side to watch the dancing, she broke out in a cold sweat. Could it be true that Molly was dying? Raising a trembling hand to touch Red Hawk's silver eagle under her buckskin, she forced herself to say his words aloud. "Have faith."

Brant and Parker were not Clover's only enemies. White Feather was among the dancers, and as she passed the place where Clover and Mia were standing, she went into an elaborate body contortion, striking her breast with her fist and falling down.

"She means to kill you," Mia whispered. "That movement is part of the dance of death."

Smiling at the vindictive woman's gyrations, Clover once again pressed the totem at her breast.

"She's mad," Clover replied, with a laugh. "One day the two wives of Gray Falcon will settle their differences in the old way. Hand to hand."

Mia giggled, too. "Do you mean what I think you mean?" She put up both her fists in a fighting posture.

Clover nodded. "I do. It will be a pleasure."

Since the white man's pretty cloth dresses might antagonize many of the tribes, both Clover and Mia had been given newly made fringed and beaded

241

buckskin garments to wear on their journey. Lovely beaded headbands of brilliant colors crossed their brows, and they carried moccasins in their saddlebags. But only for ceremonial occasions. Sturdy leather boots would be their daily footwear, for they would have to do much walking.

They would also answer to their Indian names. Mia was most unhappy with this. "Your name of Flying Bird is beautiful, but who wants to be called Little Chicken?" she wailed. "All will laugh at me."

Assuring the girl that the name was most endearing and suited her perfectly, Clover embarked on her mission of peace.

Red Hawk's assurance that faith would come to her bore fruit very quickly. As they went from camp to camp, village to village, in the green, well-watered valley, Clover found herself afire witch a new fervor for life. The scenes of her youthful visits here brought back many happy memories. Unlike the women in Sweet Briar's lodge, many old friends made her and Mia welcome, holding feasts and dances in their honor.

All listened politely to her message for peace. The men nodded in agreement when she warned them that to fight was a sure way to lose their valley.

"The Great White Father in Washington City does not like war," she preached. "If you attack his people, he will drive you onto the reservations."

She was pleased to learn that the vast majority of Indians in the valley were not preparing for war. The few that were warlike, though, were fashioning mountains of arrows, some of them with poisoned ends. Guns and ammunition were being brought in and stockpiled. Tomahawks, knives—both of stone and steel—also lay ready in large quantities.

To her dismay, Clover saw many braves with gaudy war paint on their chests and faces.

These warrior clans mistrusted her. "You work for Brant," they accused her. Not even the sight of Red Hawk's sacred eagle around her neck convinced them otherwise. "That foolish old man has the brain of a child," they grumbled. "Nobody heeds his words anymore."

One night, about three weeks into their travels, Clover and Mia walked back to their tipi after long hours of feasting on roast lamb and succulent ears of corn. As they prepared for sleep, Clover felt herself grow suddenly restless.

"The autumn moon is bright and the night is soft," she told her companion. "I need to walk off some of the heavy food I ate. Want to come?"

Mia's answer was a drowsy grumble. The girl was already sliding under her cozy rabbitskin. Flinging her own warm blanket around her shoulders, Clover crept out quietly, closing the tipi flap behind her.

Lifting her head to the sky, she breathed in deeply. A canopy of stars glittered overhead. The whole world seemed at peace.

The Indians who occupied the sprawling camp were mostly Shoshones from Utah, with a sprinkling of runaway Sioux and Crow. Situated on a rocky mountainside, punctuated by steep defiles, they raised sheep and goats to sell to other tribes in exchange for wood and seeds.

Eagle Valley was hemmed in by mountains, but here and there openings to the surrounding desert could be seen. Climbing a jutting rock with a flat shale top, Clover looked out on a brightly moonlit vista of rocks, hummocks, and convoluted alkali formations.

Hunched over, with her hands around her knees, Clover filled her lungs with the cold, bracing air and let her thoughts meander. She felt more content than she had in a long time. Perhaps her message of peace would take root in many Indian hearts. She had tried to convince the elders that sacrificing themselves and their children in a bloody, hopeless war against the mighty white man's army would amount to extinction.

For herself, she had achieved a special kind of peace on this journey. She had come to terms with her life as it was. For now. Somehow — she had no clear idea as to how — she would escape the hell of being Gray Falcon's wife.

As for happiness, the kind of joy she'd known with Lake, she could never hope for bliss like that again.

A coyote keened its melancholy song. Seconds later she heard an answering call. Lifting her eyes to the dark shapes of snowy peaks, Clover thought of the happiness she had known in the forested hills. Henry had loved it, too, as he gamboled among the thick trees like a cub.

She steeled her heart against the pain of knowing that Henry was dead, lost to her forever. The lion had been a part of her for so long, he had become more than a pet. He had been the family she could not even remember.

A chorus of coyote howls made her shiver. The scavenging animals lurked around the camp, coveting the sheep and goats. Constant vigilance was needed to keep the hungry packs out of the camp. There was a ten-dollar bounty on the predators. She should go inside to bed, she told herself. Tomorrow she and Mia would head even farther into the hills to visit the camp of the Diggers, who kept themselves isolated from the other tribes.

But something held Clover on the rock. Every nerve tingled and she felt as if an invisible hand was pressing on her shoulders. Red Hawk's heavy silver totem lay heavy on her throat. A strange notion struck her. Perhaps the old chief had died, and the Great Spirit was trying to speak to her in the old man's place.

She waited for the feeling to pass but seemed paralyzed in her hunched-over position on the rock. She waited — for what, she did not know. Her dark eyes were fixed on the horizon. Was that something moving out there among the rocks?

Fearfully, Clover glanced at the tipi where her escort of four warriors were sleeping. Her scream would fetch them in a moment. They would be angry at her for being out here alone at night.

Returning her gaze to the desert, Clover saw a movement. In her sudden terror, she imagined that a pack of ravening coyotes was moving toward her. Clover leaped to her feet, straining to see more clearly.

There was no sound, save her own quick breathing. Could it be a shadow of the giant yucca that

245

dominated the landscape? As the shadow moved steadily forward, Clover relaxed, began to breathe more easily. A large animal, probably a sheep or cow, was walking slowly between two men on mules. Weary travelers, she decided. Indians, most likely, migrating to Eagle Valley from the north. They must have lost their way, she reflected, for travelers always entered at the Paiute village, where food and shelter were given.

Greatly relieved, Clover crept off the rock and waited for the travelers to approach. She would take them to the lodge of Raging Waters where they would be given guidance as to where to settle.

Seconds later, a resounding roar split the desert silence. In a moment, there was a second roar, and over the thunder of her heart Clover heard the wonderful sound of Molly's harsh voice calling to her.

"Clo-ov-er, darling, we are here to save you."

Chapter Twelve

Sucking in her breath, Clover closed her eyes, and, after a moment, opened them again. The vision was still there. It was no mirage. The rabbitskin had fallen from her shoulders as she'd climbed down from the rock, and she shivered in the cold night air. But the shivering told her that this was no dream. Henry's roar, Molly's call, the chill night air were very real.

Molly's strong voice was closer now. "Clover, Clover. Oh, my God."

Jolted out of her trance, Clover stumbled blindly into the rocks. Her bare foot struck a sharp rock and, crying out, she pitched forward.

Painfully pulling herself back up, Clover waited, wild with impatience. Henry reached her first, at a fast trot, slipping among the rocks with his usual grace. A man holding on to the lion's leash was forced to run also. As they neared the rocks where

she waited, Clover saw that there were three people —
Pedro, Molly, and the man with Henry.

Dimly, Clover wondered that Henry had permitted
a stranger to get that close to him. Probably one of
Molly's many trusted Indian friends. But how could
her lion be alive? Her brain whirled. Gray Falcon
had handed her Henry's bloody harness. But suddenly, as she realized the truth, her blood ran cold.
Her Indian husband had tricked her. It was a simple
matter to have a new harness made and bloodied.

Scenting Clover, Henry started to trot, and in moments girl and lion were wedged between two high
rocks. Falling to her knees, heedless of the pain in
her toe, Clover wrapped her arms around the animal's warm, hairy neck. His massive body throbbed
with pleasure.

Between sobs of joy, she murmured, almost inco-
herently, "Oh, you darling, you're alive, alive, and all
the time I knew you couldn't be dead. Red Hawk
knew, he vowed that you would return."

Boisterously returning the girl's affection, Henry
wiggled like a cub, nuzzling Clover's neck and hair
with his wet nose. From his throat came soft, guttural noises of contentment. He tried to roll over to
tussle with her as they both loved to do, but the
space between the rocks was too narrow.

"I suggest you two lovebirds wait until you have a
meadow to romp around in", came a cool voice from
above.

Clover's eyes flew up to the tall figure a few feet
behind Henry, his strong hand still clutching a long

leash. A riotous head of white-blond hair gleamed like platinum in the moonlight. Her heart plummeted. This *had* to be a dream.

"Lake! I thought you were back in Illinois—"

"Being hanged?" he broke in sardonically.

"Well . . . yes," she replied, flustered. Then, angry that he had put her on the defensive, she said, with spirit, "I'm glad you're alive. No matter what your crime, you don't deserve hanging."

A wide grin crossed his drawn, exhausted face. But all he said was "thanks," for Molly and Pedro, who had lagged behind, were now upon them.

It was all too much to take in at once, Clover thought, resisting the impulse to hurl herself into her lover's arms, to feel the solid, masculine warmth of his sinewy body. But he seemed so distant, standing there, so silent, so aloof.

Instead, she hugged Henry for reassurance that it was not all a dream. Miraculously, Lake had escaped from Brant's crack shots. But why was he here, instead of sailing for England to escape the Illinois prison?

Her heart swelled with joy. He truly loves me, she thought. He is risking his life for me, when he could easily be halfway to England by now.

With Lake's help, Clover and her lion backed slowly out of the rocky crevice onto the packed-earth clearing in front of her tipi.

Awakened by the commotion, Mia stood in the half-open flap of the tipi, clutching a blanket around herself. After one look at Henry, she shrieked in terror and ran back inside, closing the flap tightly behind her.

Clover giggled. "That's my companion, Little Chicken," she explained. "Her name is apt, she frightens easily."

Lake led Henry to a nearby giant yucca and tied one end of the leash securely to the trunk. If charging, or in a panic, a lion of Henry's strength could possibly uproot the shallow tree roots. Either Clover or he himself must remain with the lion constantly, ensuring that no disturbance upset the animal, he cautioned the small crowd of Indians who quickly gathered.

Noting the guns of four young braves who had run out of a nearby tipi, he said, "Do not fire your guns, no matter how much you fear the lion. He will not harm you. Keep your distance."

He'd hated having to harness the lion again, but once having found him, he was taking no chances of gunfire or other loud noise scaring him into the hills again.

As for Clover and himself being together with Henry, Lake had no plans in that direction. His brave words to Molly in Black Springs that he wanted to marry Clover now seemed foolhardy. He was a hunted criminal. What girl would want to marry a wanted man?

"Clover must be told fully, in every detail, of her father's crime," Molly had insisted.

But seeing the girl again, and witnessing her happiness at having her beloved Henry back again, Lake could not renew her pain. He could not tell her the truth—that her father was not only a criminal, but a dirty coward who had left a young, trusting boy to the mercies of the law.

First chance he got, he would beg Molly not to show the girl Cedric Sinclair's last letter confessing to the bank robbery and killing.

After a bit of rest, Lake resolved to disappear from Clover's life. The brief love they had shared could never be put to rights again. He'd work his way back to his native England and try to pick up the pieces of his life.

Both animal and man were weary and gladly settled down to wait for Clover and Molly to finish their tearful reunion. The four young men were soon joined by others, who whispered among themselves as they gazed with awe at Henry, peaceably lying beneath the tree like a large, friendly dog at the hearth.

The lion himself did not gaze back, but, tucking his snout between his paws, fixed his amber eyes at Clover. He seemed unperturbed at the growing crowd, having lived in a circus all his life surrounded by large numbers of people.

Lifting Henry's left paw, Lake examined it closely. The puncture wound inflicted by a thorn was healing nicely. The animal's soft pad looked healthy.

One hand on Henry's back, Lake gazed happily at mother and daughter in front of the tipi, arms entwined around each other, swaying back and forth and weeping loudly. After a few minutes of this, they began to talk. Shamelessly, Lake eavesdropped. He had helped get Molly across the desert. He had saved Pedro's life. He had found Henry. He was part of this family now. There were no secrets anymore.

In her loud, grating voice, Molly began to babble. "Oh, darling, I hated to take so long to come after you, but we stopped over for three days at Ragtown. Everyone told us that a lion had been roaring in the mountains, and that the sheepmen were after him again, so we went to look for him. Then we found him wounded, and waited for him to heal enough to travel."

She peered into Clover's eyes. "I felt that you were in no immediate danger—" She stopped, her blue eyes suddenly fearful. "Were you?"

Laughing, Clover shook her head. "No, you old dear, not at all. In fact, I've been busy being a good citizen."

Molly looked puzzled.

"Chief Red Hawk sent me on a tour of the Eagle Valley to preach peace," she said briefly. "Didn't they tell you when you got here? How else did you know where I was?"

Molly passed a tired hand over her eyes. "There was a lot of talk in the Paiute village, a lot of confusion. They simply said that you were at the Shoshone Sheep Ranch."

Pausing, she grabbed Clover's two shoulders. "But what about Gray Falcon? You are his squaw, by Indian custom. Has he—" She looked stricken. "Has he exercised his marital rights?"

Clover laughed aloud. Any suffering she had endured from her Indian "husband" evaporated from her mind in the face of all this joy. "Yes, he has, darling, but only one night when we were still at Ragtown. I've hardly seen him since arriving at Eagle Valley."

Visibly relieved, Molly hugged the girl so tight that Clover squealed. "Lordy, but you feel very strong, just like the old days," Clover said happily. "Does this mean you're well again?"

Pedro spoke from behind them. "It is the false strength of happiness, Clover. Molly is not strong at all. The long journey has weakened her. She has been spitting blood. She must be put immediately to bed and given nourishing broth."

Grabbing Molly's arm, the Indian gently nudged her away from Clover. "Come, old woman. I will take you to the lodge of my old friend, Raging Waters. Though he is a Shoshone and I am Paiute, we have hunted and fought together and are blood brothers by oath."

He chuckled. "Raging Waters has three squaws who will tend you as a newborn babe."

"Nonsense. All I need is a good night's sleep, without the damn coyotes yelping all around me."

Molly's voice was as sharp as ever, but as the two went off together, Clover noticed that her adoptive mother's step was much slower than she remembered. She leaned heavily on Pedro's arm.

Like a revelation from heaven, the thought came to her in terrible clarity and truth: *She's dying. My sweet*

253

Molly is dying.

But this was the day for miracles, she thought, offering up a silent prayer. Henry was alive, Lake, too, had managed to escape Brant's henchmen. She had seen with her own eyes Pedro left for dead. Yet here he was, looking hale and hearty.

Maybe—just maybe—she prayed, being back in her beloved Eagle Valley and with the Indians she loved so much would work a miracle on Molly Robinson.

Lake spoke from the tree. "I've known people who've spit more blood than Molly and recovered fully."

She whirled. "How did you know what I was thinking?" She moved toward him and Henry. But before she reached them, she noticed the crowd.

Laughing, Clover told them, "This is my very own lion. He's come back from the grave."

At these words, many lifted their hands to heaven, as if in worship. All had heard of the sacred lion, who listened to the voice of the Great Spirit. Soon it seemed that the entire village was gathered under the yucca tree.

Alarmed that Henry might grow restive, Lake rose up. "Do not come too close to the holy lion. He is weary from his long journey to the land of the Great Spirit and may snap at you."

In the ensuing hush, Clover called out, "The holy lion needs food and fresh water."

Henry reinforced his lady's request with a roar, then another. The fearsome sound was enough to send all but the bravest scurrying back to their lodges and tipis. Within minutes, an old, bent squaw brought fresh-killed meat and a large reed tub of water to the lion.

"The meat is that of a cougar," the woman said proudly. "It was killing my sheep, and I brought it down with my own rifle."

"The Great Spirit will smile upon you and your children and grandchildren," Clover beamed at the woman as she set the meat in front of Henry.

It took some persuasion to send the people back to their dwellings, but at last it was accomplished, Clover promising all that tomorrow the lion would perform his many marvels for them.

"At high noon," she announced, dimpling. "At the place of powwow.

Clover's heart was bursting with happiness. Everything was as it used to be in the happy days. She and Henry and Lake. Together again. But not quite. Lake was not the same. He was no longer a handsome liontamer who claimed to love her. He was a hunted criminal, just two steps from the hangman.

Turning back to the tree, she decided to have it out with him. She would demand to know the full story of the bank robbery and her father's part in it.

"We must talk," she said, standing over him as he leaned tiredly against the tree watching Henry eat.

Nodding, he rose, obviously with reluctance. Henry was chewing voraciously on the fresh meat and wasn't likely to go anywhere at present, so they moved a distance to a place behind the tipi to talk.

They stood face-to-face in the moonlight. A few fading stars twinkled overhead. We should be making love, not talking, Lake thought distractedly.

"Time is precious," he said absently. His arms ached to embrace her, but they seemed glued to his sides.

"I want to know all about the bank robbery," she demanded, ignoring his remark. "My father escaped the police, why didn't you?"

Placing her arms on her hips, she drew close. Standing there so defiantly, arms akimbo like an avenging angel, she seemed the most adorable thing in the world, he thought. Her glossy black hair blew gently in the predawn breeze. The black eyes that had first ensnared him blazed up at him. Just as they had that first day in Black Springs when she'd run up to the lion as he drove the circus wagon through the rutted street.

"It's a long story," he said dully, averting his eyes from her steady gaze. "This is not the time for it. Go back to your tipi and get some rest. I'll sleep out here, to keep an eye on Henry."

So we will not make love tonight, he thought miserably. Throughout the long journey from the north, he had envisioned their reunion. It was not like this cold meeting.

He glanced up at the hills. "Lots of sheep in these rocks. Even with a bellyful of cougar, Henry might just decide to go after some dessert."

Lake tried to laugh, but it came out more like a sob. Recovering, he turned his face away, shutting out the beautiful sight of her. "There's really no need to bore you with what happened eleven years ago," he said quietly. "What does it matter now? Soon I'll be gone out of your life forever."

"Without the money you came for?" she asked sarcastically.

Whirling back, he grated, "Who told you there was any money involved?"

"Nobody. I guessed." She smirked. "You don't seem to have the bank loot, and why else would you come to Black Springs?"

Hesitating, she continued in a low voice, her eyes trained on the hills. "Why would a cultured, well-traveled Englishmen, who could get any girl he wanted, ask a simple, uneducated girl like me to marry him?" To her own consternation, Clover broke into loud weeping. "I should have known better. Molly warned me against men like you. All you want is my fortune—"

"What in blazes!" Lake blew out explosively. "Of all the stupid, silly notions I ever heard."

The rage that had been building up in Lake at her cruel words dissolved as he saw the weeping girl fall upon the ground, convulsed with grief. Overwhelmed with love and bewildered by Clover's quixotic behavior, the young man could think of nothing else to do but comfort her.

Instinctively sinking to the hard, dry ground beside her, he took her in his arms. "Clover, Clover, darling, I love you truly, with all my heart. I don't want any of your money, wherever it comes from. I simply want to make you happy."

She lay a while in the circle of his arms, her sobs subsiding. After a time, Lake lifted her face from his chest and kissed her sweetly on the mouth. Her tears were salty, and he tasted them with sadness. How desperately he wanted her. But he pressed her no further, and taking her two hands, he pulled her to her feet.

"We are both too exhausted to talk with any sense. Now go back to your tipi and get a few hours' sleep. I'll keep watch on Henry."

Meekly, she obeyed, walking slowly back to the tipi flap. Lake noticed that she was limping, but he resisted the urge to run after her and inquire if she was hurt.

Inside the skin-covered tipi, Clover saw that Mia's cot was empty. The girl had apparently decided to sleep elsewhere, as far away from the lion as she could get.

Clover lay rigid on her cot, staring fixedly up at the smokehole. The village was still asleep, those who had come to gape at Henry having gone back inside. All was quiet, except for the faint bleating of sheep in the rocks.

To her alarm, Clover felt desire racing like a river of flame through her body. The dark place between her thighs was throbbing madly. Molly was right, she thought. Physical love is a snare. Right now, Clover wanted nothing so desperately as to hurl herself into that man's arms and have him appease her hunger. Her lips curved softly, yearning for his warm mouth.

Pulling the heavy blanket over her head, Clover shut her eyes and tried to think of something else. What routines would she and Henry perform tomorrow? She had promised the Indians a marvelous show. Would Henry perform as he once did—meekly, obediently? Perhaps his taste of the wild life had spoiled him for tricks and routines.

Furious at herself, Clover lay perfectly still. Maybe some cold water on her body would help. But that meant going outside again, past Lake to the barrel behind the tipi.

She sat up, flinging off the stifling covers. She felt that she couldn't breathe. The clear sound of Henry's loud chewing came to her ears. She began to worry. If he ate the whole carcass, he would want to sleep all day at least. There could be no show. The Indians would be angry, but she and Mia were scheduled to move on.

Molly had said the lion had been wounded. She must see if he was all right. If infected, the wound must receive immediate attention. Molly was too sick to think about Henry, and, as for Lake Emerson, he was not to be trusted. Lord only knows what the wound looked like now.

Clover bounded out of bed, dragging the oversize rabbitskin behind her. She was determined to sleep outside, by Henry's side. Captain Lake Emerson could sleep in the tipi. After all, he had been with Henry for weeks while she pined away, thinking the animal dead.

Lake lay on his side, asleep, under the yucca.

Nudging him in the ribs with her bare foot, Clover said sharply, "Where was Henry hurt?"

Sitting up groggily, he squinted up at her in the pale light. "What did you say?"

"Where was Henry hurt? What happened—a thorn in his paw?"

He nodded, wiping his mouth with the back of his hand. "It's fine, I just examined it."

Her bare feet were inches from his face. He saw that the big toe on one of them was black and slightly swollen. Impulsively, he reached out and lifted it up. It was cold and dirty from the ground.

"I see Henry's not the only one who's been wounded," he remarked. "Does it hurt?" He pressed on the swollen part gently with a finger.

"Ouch, damn you," she yelled, pulling back. "Of course it hurts. I stubbed it on a rock."

Glancing toward Henry, she said, "Which paw is it?"

"Right front."

The lion was completely absorbed in gnawing a large bone and didn't even return Clover's glance. It would be dangerous to approach him now. Turning, she started to walk toward some high rocks jutting behind the tipi. She would sleep there. The thought of returning to the stifling tipi and lying there, in a fever of passion, was almost nauseating.

She had taken three steps from the tree when he caught up with her and grabbed her by the forearms. Spinning her around, holding her arms tightly to her sides, he taunted, "Now tell me why you *really* came outside."

Pinioned by his two brawny arms, she stared up into laughing gray eyes. His face was much browner than she remembered, and he reeked of sweat and Henry's musky scent. There was a small cut in his lower lip, the kind a person gets in the desert heat. She longed to kiss it. His hair was full of sand. It stood up in little spikes all over his head, making him resemble a blond devil.

Yet she wanted him at this moment more than anything else in the world. Her head was spinning, there was a loud pulsing noise in her ears, and his laughing face eclipsed all else in her brain.

With a small moan, she swayed toward him. Releasing her arms, he pressed her to him, and, grasping a handful of thick black hair, he tilted her head back.

"Now tell the truth, Clover Sinclair, why did you come out here?" His tongue whipped out to lick his dry lips and stayed there as he regarded her intently.

Maddened by the flicking tongue, Clover wailed, "I came out to—" but unable to blurt out the shameless truth, she started to cry.

Grimly, he tugged her even closer so that his erection pressed into her soft lower body. "Stop those blasted tears, woman," he said sternly. "Let's have it straight from your sweet, adorable, ravishing lips. Why did you come out here?"

"I couldn't sleep, I thought a breath of air would cool me off." She sucked in her breath. "Dammit, I *was* worried about Henry, too."

He bristled. "Do you think I would let the pesky beast die after I risked my neck to get him back for you once again? If you only knew the trouble we had—sheepmen jumping out from behind every tree with rifles pointing, Molly coughing up her life's blood. We had to cut off the harness, which had dug into his flesh."

Warming to his subject, Lake exploded. "Then Pedro kept nagging me to forget the lion. 'Let nature take its course,' he said."

He stopped for breath. A wicked gleam came into his gray eyes. "Good idea, that Indian had. Let nature take its course."

"I could not agree more, Mr. Emerson."

Standing on her toes, Clover reached up to silence him with a kiss. Then, taking him by the hand, she led him behind the tipi, stopping at a deep, smooth place between two high rocks. Still without a word, she flung off the furry skin, laying it on the ground, then smoothing out the wrinkles and tucking it up against the rocks until it formed a snug bed.

"Now let's make love," she said simply. "We'll worry some other time about whose money it is." Laughing, she added dryly, "Actually, it all belongs to the bank, doesn't it?"

Gazing down at her alluring figure in the cotton nightgown, dazzled by her blazing black eyes, Lake felt like a fly being drawn into a spider's web. If he succumbed to her wiles, he would be caught forever in her female trap. Now is the time for decision, an inner voice nagged. If you take this woman, you,

Lake Emerson, will be no longer free. Marriage, kids, a house, the lion, God only knows what else.

Forever, until you die.

Hesitating, he glanced over the top of the rock toward the yucca tree. Henry was still munching bone, then he would sleep. Shrugging his shoulders, Lake muttered, "Hell, the bloody lion can't live forever."

"Well, how long must I wait," Clover asked tartly, lifting up her arms in a gesture of surrender. "If you do not like what you see, I assure you there are others who are not so reluctant."

"Gray Falcon, for instance?" he sneered.

Those were the last words either of them uttered for some minutes, as Lake fell upon her with a groan, and, lifting up the gown, spread her thighs with his strong liontamer's hands. He thrust inside her almost cruelly with a force that left her breathless. She was moist and ready, and as she moved her hips to accommodate him snugly, he exploded inside her with an oath.

"Sorry," he muttered into her ear. "But I've wanted you for so very long."

Glorying in the feel of him in her arms, Clover waited, her hands feeling the power of the sinewed muscles of his back. Her fierce desire was quiescent for the moment. She was a woman possessed by the man she adored. What more supreme happiness can there be in this world, she reflected.

He was so quiet, with his dear head on her breast, that she became alarmed. "Don't you dare fall asleep, you scoundrel. I must have my fulfillment, too, damn you."

Rearing up, Lake leaned on his hands against the rabbitskin. "Sleep?" he grinned, his teeth flashing white in the gray light of dawn. "Not much chance for that, with a beautiful volcano under me ready to erupt."

Rolling off her body, he pushed his hands beneath her to push her up and on top of him. "Okay, woman, I am at your mercy."

With a cry of delight, Clover sat up on his haunches. It was like the first time in that Ragtown blacksmith shop, she thought, when he had been covered with poultices. She knew exactly what to do and went about it with gusto.

His chest was bare, but his denim pants were a problem. Untying the cord belt, she pushed them down as he lifted up to allow her to slip them off. Bending her slim, voluptuous body, Clover dangled her firm breasts so that he could plunder them as before. As his warm lips enveloped first one long, erect nipple then another, she moaned with ecstasy, feeling the skittering sensations in her womb.

When she could bear no more caresses on her breasts, Clover lifted up his hard hips so that their bodies touched. Almost instantly, his limp shaft began to stiffen, and, responding, she rained kisses on his face—his ears, his nose, his cheeks, his mouth.

She was insatiable, it seemed to Lake, greedily devouring his manhood with her feverish hands to appease her spiraling passion.

When Clover's insides were a ball of fire, she

reared up again, and, taking his shaft in her hands, brought it to full erection once again.

"Now," she commanded, in a throaty, almost guttural voice, "you, Mr. Liontamer, are going to be ravished."

Lake lay supine, letting her work her will on him. Never in his life had he even imagined such passion in a woman. Freedom be hanged. He'd even put up with a jealous lion to have this woman to himself for the rest of his life.

Inserting his rigid shaft into her moist, waiting, feminine canyon, Clover threw back her head, arched her back and began to move, rhythmically in a circular fashion until all of him seemed to become a part of her. Her buttocks hardened as she strained to bring them both to ecstasy. Her hands tightened on his back, her sharp nails digging hurtfully into his flesh.

But Lake loved the pain. His breathing quickened to match hers, his eyes gazed at the face of a woman who was all women wrapped into one. Her hair swirled about her sweating face, and her breasts jiggled violently up and down with each thrust. Her breathing grew hoarse and labored.

Lake ran rippling fingers along her satiny inner thighs, feeling the quickening movement of her strong female muscles. Determined to withhold his own explosion until she spasmed, Lake held back with a painful effort. Suddenly she cried out, as if in agony, and he felt her entire body shake, like a sapling in a windstorm.

With a loud, agonizing cry, she collapsed in exhaustion upon him.

For a long, delicious time, she spasmed against his body. Lake felt a lightness of head and body that wiped out all traces of the long, tiring desert journey. All his fears of the future evaporated as he exploded within her once again.

Feeling his pulsing masculine love fill her body, Clover's exhaustion also vanished. She felt an exhilaration beyond imagining. Every nerve, every muscle, every drop of blood in her body was dancing with life.

Whatever tomorrow brought—if Molly died, if Lake were taken back to prison, if Gray Falcon demanded that she be his squaw forever—she would have this moment to remember.

For always.

Chapter Thirteen

Clover awoke to full daylight. Loath to leave the delicious feel of Lake's warm body under hers, she lay perfectly still, studying the line of his tanned face and neck as he lay sound asleep. Supremely content, she listened to his steady breathing, loving the rise and fall of his broad chest under her breasts.

The already hot Nevada sun caressed her naked back and thighs. Noises came from the village, which was busily astir. Women called to their children in shrill voices and the pungent smell of breakfast fires drifted into her nostrils.

Instantly, she was startled by a chorus of high-pitched giggles from the other side of the rock crevice in which she and Lake were lying. She lifted her head in horror. A woman with a basket of clothing on her back and the two children with her were peering over them. As Clover met their eyes, they broke out in fresh laughter and ran off toward the stream.

"Oh, my God," Clover breathed, looking down at herself. Her cotton gown was in a roll around her neck. Her breasts, belly, thighs — all were blatantly visible. Lake lay exposed in all his manliness. The woman had seen everything. How many others had gazed at her and Lake as they slept?

With trembling hands, Clover pulled the gown down to cover herself. Her reputation was ruined. Indians were very private about their lovemaking, married couples often resorting to special tipis to be together. The news of her tryst with her white lover was even now being spread about at the bathing stream. Soon, the cuckolding of Gray Falcon would be the scandal of the Shoshone camp, as well as all of Eagle Valley. Within hours, the gossip would have reached the Paiute village.

Burning with shame and remorse, Clover shook Lake awake by both shoulders. As he reluctantly groaned his way into consciousness, she tugged at the rabbitskin blanket beneath him.

Rising quickly, Lake stretched luxuriantly, blinking in the sun. He yawned several times before Clover impatiently yanked at the rabbitskin, nearly knocking him off his feet.

"Woman, wait—"

"Can't wait," she mumbled.

Bending swiftly, Lake scooped up the skin and

lovingly arranged it around her shoulders, bending to kiss her as he did so.

Clover backed away, frowning. "No time for any more foolishness," she said crossly. "Go see to Henry, keep everyone away from him. I've got to see how Molly spent the night."

Clicking his heels together, and putting hand to brow in a mock salute, Lake barked, "Yessir, Captain, right away."

She did not return his mocking smile as she moved off to her tipi. Lake started off toward the yucca and Henry, whom he fervently hoped was still asleep after his meal of cougar. So she was cross, he mused, as he tied the cord around his trousers. He was cross, too. She had awakened him from a wonderful dream of the two of them touring England with Henry in a bright blue circus wagon. They were happy and carefree, making love every night in a tent pitched on a verdant meadow.

There were no Indians anywhere in this dream. Lake Emerson, Englishman, had no particular grudge against the native Americans, but they seemed to be interfering severely with his love life.

Hastily dressing in her tipi, Clover moved into the village, to the lodge of Pedro's friend, Raging Waters, expecting to see Molly. She needed desperately to talk to Molly. Molly would advise her how to deal with the coming scandal.

But Molly was not there.

"Two of Raging Waters's wives have taken Molly to a remote place in the mountains where the air is pure and cold and she will be kept totally quiet," a yawning Pedro informed her.

"I must see her," insisted Clover. "It is urgent."

He shook his head. "Nobody but the women know exactly where the place is. It is a small hut near a hot spring and is totally hidden from sight by trees and brush."

Frustrated, Clover walked a little way into the hills, trying to think. The sensible thing would be to run away with Lake. Immediately. She must forget about preaching peace. As an adulterous wife, her very life would be in danger. Who would listen to a brazen woman?

The sun was high in the sky when she returned to Lake and Henry. Her mind was clearer now. Running away from trouble was no solution. She had sworn to old Red Hawk to preach peace. That mission must go on, regardless of the consequences to herself.

The whole story of the bank money—how much of it was left and where it was hidden—would have to wait until the women decided to bring Molly back to society. Trying to find the secret healing hut would be a waste of time. Some of those places were almost inaccessible—known only to the nursing women, who handed down the secret from one generation to the next.

More important than the money was the matter of the trip to see President Grant. Eighteen seventy-six was an election year; Molly's old pal would not be president much longer. But Molly herself was in no condition to travel. Pray God that Brant's scheme to evacuate the valley would not come to fruition before Grant could be reached, Clover thought. Perhaps she herself could go to the nation's capital and plead the cause of Eagle Valley. Why not? Molly had always described him as a wonderfully sympathetic man, humble and understanding.

Agonizing over what to do—to stay or leave, to visit Grant, to flee with Lake to England—Clover returned to the yucca tree. She found Lake sitting cross-legged a few yards from Henry's slumbering body, eating fried bacon and corn cakes and coffee brought him by the old woman who had given Henry her freshly killed cougar.

Clover's escort of four warriors sat in a circle at a distance, also eating and talking softly. Nothing on the weeks-long journey had even remotely threatened their charges, and they had been bored, anxious to return to their tribes. But now they had a genuine African lion to gaze at, a lion that many of the Indians regarded as sacred. What grand reports and stories they would tell their comrades around the fire at night in years to come.

A small ring of awed spectators, mostly children, gaped at an even further distance at the massive form of the sleeping lion.

Lake seemed unperturbed that they had been seen together. "If the women start throwing stones at you as an adulteress, I'll turn Henry loose on them," he grinned.

She told him that Molly had been spirited away.

"Good," he exclaimed. "Total isolation from everyone, including her precious daughter, is precisely the cure that your mother needs."

He shoved a large wooden bowl of steaming coffee into her hands. "Drink up, you look like you need it."

Clover sipped distractedly. She'd missed Molly so terribly the past months, and had looked forward keenly to the kind of long talks they used to have. Her lover, Lake, who should have been a bulwark, was no help at all.

"As for the money," he continued blandly. "I've decided that it's a divisive element in our relationship. It can only cause trouble. Molly put it in a San Francisco bank where it has accumulated a lot of interest. She has promised me half or all of it."

"Oh, really?" Clover arched a brow. "Don't be so sure about that. My father stole it and carried it away."

"Precisely," Lake snapped back. "The money was *stolen*. Those lovely gold double eagles belong to the bank and its depositors. I intend to return the cash to the authorities in Illinois." He scowled. "With interest, if they insist."

Clover paled. "But if you do that, you'll be hanged for escaping."

He shook his head. "Don't think so. I may have to finish out my term, though, five or six years, maybe time off for good behavior."

"How can you be so sure they won't hang you?"

"Because I'm innocent of the killing. Molly has a

letter your father wrote, absolving me from blame for the robbery as well as the killing. I'm sure the courts will show leniency. After all, I was only a kid, not even dry behind the ears."

The words were out before he realized what he was saying. He had vowed never to tell her of her father's perfidy. His heart beating with remorse, Lake studied her face to see how she was taking it.

She swayed backward as if struck on the chest, but, pulling herself erect again with an effort, she said calmly, with only a hint of a tremble in her voice, "I suspected as much. My papa was a desperate man. His longing to return to England was so intense he would have done anything, anything— even kill a man."

"You didn't think so when Brant first told you about the robbery," he reminded her.

"I've grown up," she replied with a sad smile. "These past months have taught me that nothing is certain in this life. Not even love."

She shifted her gaze to Henry, but despite her wise words, Clover's lovely face was white as chalk, and the pain in her dark eyes was almost palpable. Sliding over to sit by her side, Lake took her hand in his. "Clover, Clover, darling, I love you, I hate myself for causing you pain. I'll devote my life to making it up to you."

He broke off, as a running girl called out Clover's name. In a moment, Mia stood over them, gasping for breath. "A message has come by fast runner from Gray Falcon. You are to return immediately to your home village." She inhaled. "The runner says that Gray Falcon is very angry."

Biting her lip, Mia continued. "Gray Falcon says that you must turn the lion loose, out into the desert."

Clover looked grim. "And if I refuse?"

"Then you will be a disobedient squaw." Mia glanced at Lake. "Adulterous, too. Your husband will have the right to kill you."

"With a knife in the heart," Clover said tonelessly. "And my body will be thrown to the dogs"— she glanced toward the desert—"or maybe the coyotes. I know the custom well."

Shivering, the fearful Mia put her hands over her eyes. "Do not go back, it is suicide."

Sighing, with a last, long look at the desert beyond the rocks, she got to her feet. "I cannot flee. It is best to return. Chief Red Hawk will protect me from the wrath of his son Gray Falcon."

As she and Mia bustled about the camp, alerting their escort to prepare for travel, and filling their saddlebags with food and water, Lake followed them about like a puppy who fears being left behind.

He kept up an unceasing argument.

"Clover, this is madness. You are riding to certain death. That man is an Indian, you are white. Molly is well cared for, Pedro is happy, you and I can leave with no pangs of conscience."

"You are free to do as you please," she retorted, shaking off his hand on her arm. "I am not."

"Idiot, you're not really married to that man—"

Furious, she turned on him. "This has nothing to do with Gray Falcon." She paused. "Or you, either." Putting her hand on the silver eagle totem, she said firmly, "I swore to a dying Red Hawk that I would dedicate myself to keeping war from shattering his beloved valley."

"Nonsense," Lake exploded. "Not even Molly could accomplish that impossible task. Who do you think you are? God? Or the president of the United States?"

Clover was mounted by now on her gray mare, and Lake, suddenly inspired, tried one last gambit. "You and I can take the train to the East, we can see the president. Grant is known to be concerned about the Indians' plight."

Looking down at the face that filled her heart and the desperately pleading gray eyes, Clover urged, "Good idea, why don't you go yourself?"

He backed off, his nostrils flaring with anger. "Just what do I do with your precious lion whom you claim to love and whom you're deserting without a qualm?"

"Take him along, you've traveled with him before." Clover grinned. "I've heard that Sam Grant just adores animals of all kinds." She dimpled, enjoying her joke. "Henry may well save the day for you."

Digging her bootheels into the mare's flank harder than she intended to, Clover sped away from the sight of Lake's pleading face. He was absolutely right, of course. She was mad to be leaving him just when they had found each other again. The ecstasy of last night's lovemaking rushed over her with overwhelming force. How could she risk losing such joy?

Her hands tightened on the reins to keep from turning back. But sense returned quickly. Even if she could forget her vow to Red Hawk to return to him, she could, under no circumstances, run away without Molly. If there was a war, Molly's life would be in danger from the cavalry, who knew her to be an agitator for the Indians.

No, she thought. Her path was clear. There must be no war. Whatever the cost — if she lost the man she loved, or even if she herself had to die — Clover felt a divinely appointed mission to do what she could to keep the peace.

If, for no other reason, she owed it to Molly, who lay helpless, maybe dying. Freedom for Eagle Valley was Molly's life's dream.

Clover's mare was swift, and she set a furious pace for Mia and her four braves as they set out for the Paiute village of Red Hawk.

Lake stood statuelike in the clearing, allowing the dust of the galloping horses to surround him like a cloud. Thoroughly disgusted, he swore profusely at the top of his lungs in English and American epithets. Three woman carrying linens down to the stream to wash looked up, amazed, then started to giggle.

Returning to Henry's side, the angry young Englishman stretched his long form on the rocky ground. He rested his head on Henry's warm flank, pouring out his frustrations to the still-sleeping lion.

"I should have known, blast it, a woman as passionate as that one is probably looking forward to tossing around in a tipi with that musclebound Gray Falcon. Dedicate herself to keeping peace, indeed! Bullshit. I offer her England, travel abroad, a life of ease and comfort. What's Eagle Valley to her anyway? She'll never see it once we are married."

Tears were close to the surface. Lake felt them gather behind his eyes to well up in his throat. With great force of will he swallowed them. Blast, he refused to weep for a silly woman, who loves one minute and leaves the next. Captain Lake Emerson could get any girl he wanted in his bed, anytime, anywhere.

"What do you think, Henry?"

Rolling over on his stomach, Lake jiggled the lion's ear, begging him to listen.

But Henry was oblivious, his heavy, steady breathing indicating that he was sound asleep. The lion's rejected trainer was forced to nurse his wounded ego in silence. After a dip in a nearby cold spring and a brisk run along the banks, Lake decided that life must go on, with or without Clover Sinclair. He was stuck with the lion, and might as well make the best of it.

It was past midnight on a moonless, cloudy night when Clover and her party arrived back at the Paiute village of Chief Red Hawk. Mia repaired to her dead mother's lodge for some much needed sleep, but Clover rode directly to Red Hawk's tipi. Light blazed from inside and voices rang out, as if in heated argument. Finding the flap tied back, Clover walked in.

The large space was filled with men, some in full regalia complete with feathered headbands. Beyond the blazing fire she saw Gray Falcon seated in Red Hawk's old armchair, apparently holding powwow.

At his side stood Brant, arms folded, legs spread out in his usual arrogant posture. Next to Brant stood Indian agent Aaron Parker, talking earnestly, his mouth close to Brant's ear so that he could not be heard. Both were dressed in buckskin shirts and pants, in an attempt to seem more friendly to their Indian hosts.

Brant was smiling, obviously pleased with what the man was telling him. Spotting Clover before the others did, Brant roared, "Well, look who's here!" He poked Gray Falcon in the ribs with his elbow. "I do believe your errant wife has returned for her punishment, Chief."

The tipi became silent as all the warriors stopped to listen. Hooded eyes gazed avidly at the woman who had so boldly entered a powwow of warriors uninvited. News of her behavior was now common knowledge. She had spent the night with her white lover, brazenly, in the open air. She had preached to the tribes against going to war to save their land. She was working hand in hand with Ralph Brant, their sworn enemy.

Clover Sinclair, also known as Flying Bird, was

marked for death.

"Here is my knife, newly sharpened," one called out, springing forward to brandish the gleaming weapon in Clover's face.

Backing off, Clover shrieked, "Where is Red Hawk?"

Arising from the armchair, Gray Falcon advanced toward the fire, where he loomed tall and forbidding in full battle regalia. Red and yellow symbols covered his massive chest. On his head sat a band of pure-white eagle feathers and strapped on his broad back, a quiver of newly made arrows reared sharp crimson points.

"The old buzzard Red Hawk is dead at last," he said grimly. "His body lies in his burial hut, awaiting the burning feast."

His hawkish face split in a wide grin as he thrust his head toward Clover. "As his eldest son, I am now chief."

The warrior with the knife thrust it at Gray Falcon. "Here, son of Red Hawk, slay the adulterous one."

Pushing the man aside with a vicious hand, Gray Falcon gritted, "I will deal with my own woman as I please. Laughing Dog." A cold smile split his lips. "A knife in Flying Bird's traitorous heart is too quick. Much too merciful."

The man with the knife looked angry at being rebuffed. Seeing discontent in the eyes of others, Gray Falcon hastened to appease. He swept the circle of warriors with his eyes.

"I spoke too quickly, in husbandly pride. Though I can devise many ways to punish this female, I welcome any suggestions from my loyal braves for ways to make her wish she were dead."

Boisterous laughter greeted his invitation. Lewd suggestions were heard: "Give her to any man who will taste of a white woman." "Nail her to the rocks and let the eagles pick out her eyes." "Give her to a rutting bull to mount."

The small place was in an uproar. His green eyes dancing with evil pleasure, Gray Falcon let his braves have their sport.

Though her body was wracked with terror, Clover forced her face to be impassive. She ignored the cold sweat that covered her body beneath her dusty traveling garments. To admit fear would be to invite even harsher punishment. If she must die, she would do it with dignity.

But she was determined to live. The heavy pressure of Red Hawk's totem in the dark place between her breasts brought hope and reassurance. She invoked the image of the old chief as he had prayed for her, arms uplifted to the Great Spirit.

Lifting up her head, Clover called out loudly, "Why are the betrayers Brant and Parker here in the tipi of the Paiute chief? Have Gray Falcon and his warriors given up their land to these greedy men?"

She narrowed her black eyes derisively. "Are you women that you will not even protest at this rape of your valley Wun-i-muc-a?"

Quickly stepping out of the shadows, Parker held

out a letter to Clover. "Despite your strenuous efforts to make the tribes behave peaceably, my girl, the natives of Eagle Valley are ready for war against the Great White Father in Washington. So they are to be punished like the disobedient children they have proved themselves to be."

As he spoke, Clover read the contents of the letter. It was from the Bureau of Indian Affairs, informing the Indian agent for northern Nevada to proceed with migration from the valley to specified reservations. Exceptions could be made for those proven to be peaceable — at the discretion of the agent.

Six months was the time allowed for the evacuation. Anyone who defied the ruling would be imprisoned.

Parker spoke again. "I am here to warn these men that if there is even one shot fired at a white man, the order to migrate will take effect immediately."

With some trepidation, he glanced at the ring of warriors. "If necessary, the United States cavalry will be called out."

There was growling among the men. They stared at Gray Falcon, who was strangely silent. Obviously, all of this was a big surprise to them. They had come expecting to be told that their chief would go to battle for them.

White-lipped, Clover stared at Parker. Forgetting her own very real danger, she burst out, "But that is not possible. These people have done nothing of a hostile nature. Yet," she added with a sidelong glance at the warriors.

"Pray, tell me, why are they dressed for battle?" Parker asked, sweeping a hand toward the Indians. "We came here in peace."

This can't be happening, Clover thought wildly. Running to Laughing Dog, she beat him on the chest with her fists. "Your new chief has betrayed you. He is in league with the evil one who wants your land to dig the silver out of."

She pointed an accusing finger at Brant, who remained in the shadows by the tipi wall, a smug look on his face.

With an oath, Gray Falcon grabbed Clover by the shoulders, shaking her violently. "Woman, this is none of your affair." He sniffed, flaring the nostrils of his long nose. "You smell of horse and lion and the sweat of travel. Go wash in the stream. I would bed you tonight."

Laughing uproariously, he addressed his men. "Her punishment begins. She may not rise from the nuptial mat."

Pointing to the man who had offered the knife for killing the adulteress, the new chief ordered, "Go with her, Laughing Dog, and guard her well."

Sheathing his knife, the Indian eagerly stepped toward Clover. But breaking loose from Gray Falcon, she ran around the fire in a circle, screaming, "Your new chief has betrayed you. He pretends to want war, he paints himself in battle array, prepared to fight for you. But he is in league with the white man Brant. They traveled together from the North. I was taken by force and given to him as reward for his help to the great thief Brant." She paused for breath, her dark eyes glittering with rage and excitement.

Murmurs arose from the warriors. Pushing toward the fire, they encircled Gray Falcon, their faces grim. Parker scuttled out of the open flap looking scared.

An arrow flew after the fleeing man. Then another.

"Stop," Gray Falcon roared, flailing out his arms. "The woman lies. Killing the agent will only bring disaster upon you more quickly. The mighty cavalry will descend upon us without delay and burn your lodges. Your women and children will be cut down like dogs."

But his words were lost in the general rush out of the tipi. Fearing for her life, Clover ran like the wind toward the bathing stream. As she stripped off her pants and shirt and plunged into the icy water, she heard the sound of guns being fired. All was lost. Even if Molly rose from her bed tomorrow, she could do nothing to stop the forced migration now.

Despairing, Clover plunged beneath the waters, trying to blot out the noise of guns and shouts of the battling men. After swimming a bit, she emerged from the stream and listened intently. All was silent. Gray Falcon had stopped the foolishness, thank God.

Hearing a rustling in the nearby trees, Clover reached for her clothes. But instantly a voice called out, "We want you naked, slut."

White Feather stood before her, her beautiful

haughty face twisted with hate. Whirling, Clover started to run but instantly found herself caught by two women, who placed their hands beneath her armpits and dragged her upstream between them. White Feather ran ahead.

Stopping at a thicket of thorn bushes, the women pushed her forward. "Here is the slut, naked as a babe."

Clover faced a group of women lined up in two facing columns. Each held a heavy club or stick with nails. Several brandished leather whips. Clover's blood ran cold. She was going to be run through the dreaded gauntlet, an ordeal from which few came out alive.

White Feather, apparently the leader, stood in front of Clover, sneering. She filled her mouth with saliva and spat into Clover's face.

"Our mutual husband, Gray Falcon, will never mete out the punishment you deserve, you whoring slut. Your wiles have made him soft as a newborn babe. Not only have you lain with your white lover in the sight of all, but you have gone about preaching peace. You have urged our men to be cowards so that they will not fight for their land."

"It's not true," hissed Clover. "Chief Red Hawk commissioned me to preach as I did. Going to war will only make things worse for your people."

White Feather spat again, this time at the place between Clover's breasts, where Red Hawk's totem hung on its thong. She took out her knife and viciously cut the silver eagle from its band.

"Red Hawk was an old fool, babbling in his second childhood. Did you comfort him, too, with your lust?"

The women were growing restless. Clover recognized most of them as belonging to Sweet Briar's lodge, where she was hated.

"My babe at home needs the breast. Let us do this thing quickly," one said.

Another called out, "Sweet Briar waits for word that the one who betrayed her son is dead. The old one will have us flayed if we do not bring her the slut's body."

The women began to shriek, jumping up and down impatiently. They sounded like a pack of coyotes, Clover thought, closing in on a flock of sheep. The two who had dragged her from the stream got behind her and pushed her into the flailing clubs. A heavy blow struck her shoulder, and she sprawled upon the thorny ground. Strong hands lifted her up for more.

Clover prepared herself to die. "Good-bye Molly," she breathed silently, "and Lake, my darling, whom I truly loved."

But the hands that held her fast were not a woman's. They were powerful and brown and belonged to Gray Falcon, whose angry voice roared out, "You will all be punished for this insult to your chief."

Her Indian husband threw Clover to the soft riverbank, free of the gauntlet. As she lay there, stunned, her bruised shoulder throbbing with pain, she saw Gray Falcon grab White Feather by the shoulders.

"You have defied the wish of your chief that this woman's life be spared. It is you who will be put into the gauntlet." He pushed her at the women, but they all threw down their clubs and sticks and folded their arms, glaring at their chief defiantly.

"Your old mother Sweet Briar bade us punish the whoring white one," White Feather screamed at him. "She will be angry, she will curse you and bring down the wrath of the Great Spirit on you as chief. The bastards this slut will bear you will be two-headed and slobber like sheep."

At mention of his mother's name, the new young chief seemed to hesitate. He seemed bewildered for a moment, gazing vacantly at White Feather. Then, with a curse, he put his hands on her again and pushed her to the ground, delivering a vicious kick to her abdomen.

"May you never bear a child, you jealous, scheming bitch of a female."

Groaning in pain, White Feather turned to her side and retched. The women ran to her and lifted her up. Supporting their vanquished leader, they moved off in silence.

Returning to Clover, who had got to her feet, Gray Falcon said, "Come, woman, I wish to conceive a child tonight."

The moon had slid out from behind the shifting clouds, and his green eyes glittered as if fired from within. "Tomorrow I may be dead. I would not depart this earth without my seed in your womb."

Puzzled by his change of mood, but grateful that he was no longer violent, Clover followed him, naked, to the now deserted tipi. In the clearing in front of the tipi lay three bodies. Two were Indians, the other, Agent Parker. Nobody else was in sight, all apparently having gone to their homes in terror.

Stepping around the lifeless forms, Gray Falcon strode through the open flap. Clover followed quickly, throwing herself upon his sleeping mat.

But Gray Falcon did not follow her, going instead to a shelf behind the velvet armchair where he kept his whiskey. The man's silence troubled her. Was he nourishing his wrath, building it up to fever pitch? What kinds of fiendish sexual torture was he imagining?

"Tonight her punishment begins," he had told his warriors.

Clover steeled herself for the worst—a beating, perhaps, followed by all-night rape.

Hoping to soften his violence, Clover began to talk. "I am grateful to my husband for saving me from the vengeful women. I am an unfaithful wife and do not deserve such kindness."

He did not reply, but, standing by the mat, he offered her a drink from the whiskey bottle. "It will soften the pain of your shoulder," he said.

"Thank you."

Lifting the bottle to her lips, Clover drank sparingly, not wanting to get drunk as she had the first time with Gray Falcon. Instantly, the liquor eased her pain. She watched as Gray Falcon drank half the bottle, swallowing gulp after gulp as a thirsty man will drink cool water.

Sitting on the edge of the mat, his long legs extended in front of him, Gray Falcon began to talk. "So it has come at last. Eagle Valley will no longer belong to my people. No longer will this green place be a refuge for them."

He sobbed. "They will be as the coyote, wandering from place to place, they will be despised—"

With a convulsive movement, he bent his head into his hands and wept, loudly, uncontrollably.

Rising up, Clover touched the grieving man on the shoulder. Suddenly she realized why he had spared her life. He needed someone to talk to. The burden of his remorse was too heavy for him to bear alone. No full-blooded Indian would properly understand his grief.

"Have faith, son of Red Hawk," she said gently, but with conviction. "We will find a way to keep the enemy Brant from stealing the valley."

Writhing from her grasp, he got up, began to pace back and forth in the small space. He spat into the fire. "You do not understand. I have betrayed my people. Brant has promised me two acres of ore-rich land for my part in making my people look warlike to the Indian agency. I set my warriors to making war so that the migration would come about sooner."

"It is against the law for Indians to mine for silver," she reminded him.

"I am not an Indian," he said heatedly. "The law

does not apply to half-breeds."

Throwing back his head, Gray Falcon shrieked to the heavens. "I am the one to be despised." Racing to the armchair, he picked up his white-feathered war headdress and slipped the band over his brow.

Then, whooping madly, he danced around the fire, leaping like a crazed monkey.

Thoroughly frightened at his antics, Clover realized she must calm him down or he might kill her in his madness.

But as suddenly as his mad dance had begun, it ended. He came over to her again, still in the headdress, and said, bending low to place both hands on her abdomen. "My people will be happy on the reservation, don't you agree?"

She nodded. "They will receive food, clothing, their children will be sent to school."

"Yes. I knew you would agree. You are white, as I am. We who are white do not think as the red man does."

"No." Compassion filled Clover's heart. Gray Falcon, friend of her youth, was only half-white. Like many of mixed blood, he was tortured in the crucible of not belonging completely to white or red. His white soul coveted gold and silver and comforts of civilization, yet his Indian soul also screamed out for recognition of its own worth.

Abruptly rearing up again, he strode to the fire, gazing into the dying embers as if seeking wisdom, and cocked his head, as if listening intently. "Yes, it must be," he said finally, answering a voice that only he could hear. "The woman must die."

Striding back to the mat, Gray Falcon drew out a long, gleaming skinning knife and held it high above his head. His face was contorted, more in pain than in anger, she thought, as he murmured, "You are very beautiful, but your body is a snare. As long as you live, I cannot be master of my soul."

Terrified for her life, Clover whispered, "I am your slave, mighty Chief Gray Falcon, you are my master."

She could not escape. If she moved to flee, the deadly knife would surely come down to plunge itself into her heart.

As if frozen in time, the man stood with the knife held high overhead. His breathing became erratic, his hard belly seemed to writhe in agony, as ripple after ripple passed over the sinewy muscles.

"I want you, Gray Falcon, I am yours," Clover said in utter desperation. She spread her legs wide, invitingly, put her hand on her feminine mound. She must live, she told herself, whatever the price.

"So beautiful, so beautiful, so soft —"

His words were choked and strangled, as if torn from an unwilling spirit. "I will have you one last time. My seed will be burnt with your body."

"Your seed will live and grow within me," Clover responded. "My womb will nurture a strong-limbed boy-child for Gray Falcon."

After a pause, she added, "But only if I, the mother, live. A dead tree cannot bear fruit."

As her sensible words sunk in, the pain seemed to

leave the man's face. His eyes cleared, and, lowering the knife, he tossed it aside. It fell into the fire, where the wooden handle began to burn.

With a shout, Gray Falcon threw off his feathered headdress and mounted Clover, plunging his shaft between her widespread legs. Putting two hard-nailed hands beneath her buttocks, he raised her up and entered her. Seeking only to cooperate and save her life, Clover wrapped her slim legs around his hard hips.

Vigorously, Gray Falcon began to pump, gasping for breath and arching his back. Sweat poured from his face and chest onto her body. For several minutes he labored to harden his manhood, but it was obvious that nothing was happening.

With an oath of disgust, he rolled his body to the side. "Caress me," he commanded. "I would have you bring me to hardness."

With a disgusted sigh of her own, Clover put her hands on his flaccid shaft. He lay quietly supine, his legs spread out, his breath sounding hoarsely in his throat.

Before she had executed a single stroke, however, she became aware that her mad lover's breathing had slowed to a steady, if shallow rhythm. Glancing up to his face, she saw, to her enormous relief, that he had fallen into a drunken stupor.

Suppressing a shout of joy, Clover rolled Gray Falcon's heavy body onto the dirt floor of the tipi. Then, reaching for a sheepskin beside the mat, she curled up in its wooly warmth and fell promptly asleep herself.

She was alive. The first battle in her war to survive had been won.

Chapter Fourteen

When Clover awoke to a chilly autumn dawn, Gray Falcon was gone. He had apparently slept on the floor all night. She looked around. He had taken his eagle-feathered headdress but not the whiskey bottle. That meant he was bent on serious business with his warriors at another village.

The fire was ashes, and the tipi was icy cold. Wrapping herself tightly in the sheepskin blanket, Clover sleepily tried to make plans for the immediate future. Beyond that she did not dare to think.

"Let each day's trouble suffice for the day," Molly had often said. *Molly!* Clover smiled to herself. That was one worry she could forget about for the moment.

How her life had changed, Clover marveled. A few short months ago, she had been a naive, sheltered young girl looking forward with trepidation to her bridal night. The mere thought of living without Molly's loving care had nearly frightened her out of her wits. She had even feared becoming Spike Brant's wife, of having him at her side every night, possessing her body. What a silly goose she had been.

That innocent girl had been plummeted violently, literally overnight, into womanhood. She was bound to one man, but loved another. She had known the ecstasy of true love as well as the degradation of being raped. Yet her eighteenth birthday had just barely passed—without a celebration, too, she thought wryly.

I should be scared to death, she mused. I should jump off a cliff and be done with life. But somehow Clover felt instead a sense of exhilaration, of living life to the fullest. Paradoxically, she felt no fear of the future or of the leadership role she had been thrust into among the Indians.

Smiling more broadly now, Clover tucked her hands behind her head, pleased with herself. "You've raised your daughter well, Molly Robinson," she murmured. "I may never marry that rich man you had in mind for me, but at least I'll be my own woman. I'll make you proud of me."

At first, her thoughts tumbled over each other randomly, but, gradually, as her senses cleared, things tumbled into place. Clover began to think more clearly.

No matter what happened, even if the whole United States Cavalry threatened to shoot her, she could not possibly leave Eagle Valley without Molly. Lake would simply have to understand that. Her heart lurched, and her optimism flagged. After the abrupt way she had refused his plea to flee with him, she had probably lost his love completely. Once again, she had put her loyalty to the Indians before her love for him.

Molly needed her, too. She could be in trouble. Because of her strenuous activities on behalf of the Indians in the past, she would be first on the list to be evacuated. No matter how securely hidden in the hills, the cavalry was sure to find the healing hut.

Molly had told her many times how thorough the Great White Father's soldiers could be when chasing the native red man from his ancestral land. Many Indians had no place to live, no place to die.

Second, since Gray Falcon was clearly mad, his irrational behavior might pose a danger to his people. Judging from the remorse he showed last night for betraying his people to Brant, Clover doubted that the confused young man could stand by and allow the soldiers to point guns at the Indians forcing them to march north. There would undoubtedly be a confrontation in which many innocent people would surely be killed.

Much as the thought tore at her very being, she would have to remain as Gray Falcon's squaw. Only she could forestall a bloody massacre brought about by the unstable chief's unpredictable actions. Only she, the woman he both hated and loved, could control her childhood friend. If that meant submitting to his savage lovemaking, she would do it. Not gladly, but willingly.

If for no other reason, she would do it for Molly, who had saved her life so many years ago, and who had loved her as if she had actually borne her in pain of childbirth. Clover could not allow this wonderful woman to die without seeing her life's dream fulfilled — that the last of the Paiutes and Washos be granted a place of their own.

Grand and glorious thoughts, Clover reflected as she threw off the sheepskin and slipped off the mat. The air inside the tipi was stale and deathly cold so she began to dance around the firepit, flailing her long, slender arms about, kicking wide and high with her legs, and running her fingers through her long black hair, working out the tangles.

Suddenly the flap opened and Mia entered. The girl laughed. "Don't bother with the war dance, Clover. Everything is peaceful in the village." She sighed. "For the present, anyway. That battle last night has scared everybody." Holding out a doeskin garment, she added, "You'd better put this on. I took it from your saddlebag." Removing a bowl from the whiskey shelf, she filled it with hot coffee from the pot in her other hand.

With a single, lithe movement, Clover slipped the garment over her head. Taking the bowl of coffee, she downed it in two gulps. She held it out for a second filling.

"I know this coffee comes from Brant's store," she commented sourly, "but it still tastes awfully good."

"Mr. Brant is very kind. He has the welfare of the Indians at heart," responded Mia firmly.

"You know my feelings about the man," Clover said caustically. "Let's drop the subject."

"Gladly. Your husband had a splitting headache this morning when he stopped by my lodge. You two must have spent the night in riotous lovemaking."

Clover nodded with a sly smile, but said nothing. Not even Mia must suspect that she and Gray Falcon were anything but devoted husband and wife.

Squinting at Clover's belly, Mia arched a brow. "If you continue these wild nights, that nice flat belly of yours will be swelling out before spring."

"Perhaps," Clover said weakly. "It's all in the hands of the gods." Revolted, she stared down at herself. In her eagerness to help the Indians, she had forgotten that it was possible for Gray Falcon to impregnate her during one of his savage violations of her body.

Impulsively, Clover reached out to hug the girl who seemed so concerned about her. "You're like a sister to me, Mia," she exclaimed.

Clover dressed and braided her hair, tying it back with the beaded headband. Mia busied herself cleaning out the ashes and lighting a new fire with sticks brought from outside, talking as she worked.

"Your husband has gone to meet with other chiefs, who are gathering in the lodge of the Shoshone chief, Raging Waters. They plan to fight to the death, I am

297

told, but many mistrust Gray Falcon."

"Why?" Clover asked, peering out of the flap into the clearing. The bodies of Parker and the two Indians were gone, people moved about, children played. Everything looked as usual. Nobody seemed to be aware that disaster loomed.

Putting a pan on the fire, Mia started frying bacon. "They think as you do, that he wants to hasten the date of migration so that he can get his silver lands more quickly."

"My husband's actions are very strange," Clover said quietly. She sat down on a chair beside the chief's armchair, chin in hands, thinking. Mia was quiet as she removed the bacon and poured piñon batter into the hot fat. "Promise me, Mia," Clover said suddenly, "no matter what happens between me and Gray Falcon, you will not lose faith in me."

The girl looked up, shocked. "Why should I do that?" she asked. "You are my sister in the heart."

"Sisters often quarrel. Promise, cross your heart and hope to die."

Solemnly, Mia crossed her heart. But as she did so, her dark eyes dropped from Clover's intent gaze. A shadow crossed her own heart. A fearful presence seemed to enter the cozy tipi. This seemingly loyal companion will someday betray me, she thought.

After they had eaten breakfast together, Clover remarked casually, rising from her chair, "I think I'll travel to the lodge of Raging Waters to be at my husband's side. He will need me."

"No, you must not. He left strict orders that you remain here." She peered at Clover with narrowed eyes. "Besides, if you visit the Shoshones, all will think you are meeting your white lover, the liontamer."

Clover reddened. "I'm sure the Englishman is many miles from the valley by now. With his lion." Her eyes grew merry. "You heard how angry he was when I refused to flee with him."

"Uh, huh. I heard." Mia's pretty face darkened. "That man is big trouble for you. Stay away from him."

Tending to her physical needs was not all that Gray Falcon had commanded her companion to do, Clover thought. The girl was told to spy on me, she was certain, and to report if I go to bed with Lake Emerson. Or any other man.

The day turned out to be glorious—cold but sunny, and Clover spent the afternoon with the older women who were hard at work roasting the bountiful pine-nut harvest. The delicious and nourishing fruit of the pine tree that covered the nearby slopes were a staple in the Paiute winter diet.

Fire had been lit in a large clearing behind the dwellings, and choosing from a stack of tightly woven reed baskets, Clover filled it with ripe brown nuts. With a metal shovel, she lifted some hot coals into the basket and began to turn and bounce them vigorously, keeping them in constant motion to prevent the basket from scorching.

When the nuts hissed and popped, becoming soft and translucent, Clover flipped out the coals and placed the nuts on a flat stone for shelling. This was done with another grinder stone.

The rhythm of the winnowing, and the warmth of the autumn sun, was like balm to Clover's soul. The world of war and soldiers and lost lovers melted away. The old women gossiped and laughed in shrill voices, chatting about their children and grandchildren, making big plans for many years to come in Wun-i-muc-a, their paradisal Eagle Valley.

"Next autumn, when the pine nuts are in, my son will build a bigger lodge, all of wood and with a stone chimney," one woman boasted. "His wife has twins in her womb."

Clover's heart sank. It was plain that the old women refused to believe that anything could drive them from their homes.

When the day ended, and all went home to supper fires, the chief's young white squaw had winnowed three times as many nuts as the others combined. The women's old eyes widened in admiration. "Gray Falcon has chosen well," they exclaimed. "Molly's daughter will bring us luck."

Tired but smiling, Clover replied modestly, "My mother has taught me well the art of winnowing the pine nut."

"Ah, blessed Molly," they murmured, "pray the healing art of Raging Water's women will restore her to us. While Molly is among us, no harm can come to our people."

During the next days, determined to win love and respect from the village women, Clover moved from place to place, mingling, sharing the often grueling work of providing food and garments for the inhabitants. She skinned and gutted the desert jackrabbits with the younger girls and helped repair some of the weather-damaged skin and reed dwellings.

All but those in Sweet Briar's lodge, where White Feather ruled, began to speak of the new chief's wife with warmth. There was no need for Mia to prepare meals, for the old women brought cooked and smoked meats and cakes to the tipi of Clover Sinclair. One weathered old crone named Brown Squirrel presented a bottle of whiskey, unopened.

"My warrior husband left it with me many years ago when he died," she said, "I give it to Gray Falcon's squaw to warm her blood in her husband's absence."

After three days away, the Paiute chief rode into the village at dusk, accompanied by his braves. Clover lay on the mat in her tipi, pleasantly exhausted from her labors. She had not washed, and her doeskin was smeared with dirt and leaves from carrying firewood from the forest with the maidens.

Gray Falcon loomed tall over her, his bronzed face stony, his green eyes inscrutable. Anxiously, Clover rose up to face him. "Welcome home, husband, I trust your powwow went well."

"Whiskey," he muttered, turning away abruptly.

"Bring me to drink, wife."

Moving to the armchair, he sank into its velvet depths, obviously weary in mind and body. He flung back his head, lifting the long black hair from his neck to fall over the chairback. His long arms dropped limply to his sides, the powerful hands resting on the chair arms.

Fetching the still-unopened gift of Brown Squirrel, Clover handed it to him. Lifting off the cap eagerly, he asked, "Where did this come from?" He grinned slyly. "One of your lovers, no doubt."

Ignoring his jealous jibe, Clover replied smoothly, "The old one called Ground Squirrel gave it to me in friendship."

After he had swallowed a tremendous gulp, Gray Falcon commented, "I have heard that you work well with the women. That is good. You are a good wife."

"Thank you," she said simply. "I am trying."

As she cut thick slices from a cold smoked lamb leg that had been given her also by Ground Squirrel, Clover's Indian husband told her the news from the powwow. There would be a reprieve from marching north because of Parker's death. It might take a month or more to appoint a new man from Washington City, he said. Without a local Indian agent to work out the details, the cavalry cannot be summoned, no action taken.

"Where is Brant?" she asked.

"In Carson City, where he will remain until the evacuation is completed." He made a contemptuous sound in his throat. "The man is a coward. After the skirmish when Parker was killed, he fears for his life."

Turning his startling green eyes full upon her, Gray Falcon continued. "It is best that you and I make the trek with the Indians to the Pyramid Lake Reservation. Later, maybe in the spring, when all are gone, we can return and start working the land Brant promised me as reward."

Clover bit her lip in anger and frustration. Once again her childhood friend had forgotten his tribal loyalty. Once again he had reverted to his white blood and become a greedy, grasping person. Was he such a fool that he thought she would remain as his wife once they were gone from the valley?

Then, amazingly, paradoxically, Gray Falcon said heatedly, "The government will investigate Parker's killing. We must protect and defend anyone who is accused, hiding him if necessary."

As he ate, Clover stood by silently listening to his talk of matters concerning Eagle Valley. Like the old women, he talked of the future, as if no dark cloud hung over them, as if no letter had ever come from Washington City, as if Ralph Brant, landgrabber, had never existed.

Like many mad people, Gray Falcon had lost all sense of time and logic. His often brilliant mind had become a morass of confusion.

Handing her his empty wooden bowl, he said, "Go wash yourself, I would conceive a child on you tonight." Smiling, he lifted the whiskey bottle to his lips.

As she opened the tipi flap to walk to the bathing stream, his mocking voice followed her. "By the way, your white lover has left the valley, taking his lion with him."

That night Gray Falcon took her three times, hurling her to the mat and violating her body with savage force. Clover made no attempt to pretend desire, and he did not demand it, wanting her supine and compliant. As the crazed man plundered her nipples, raining biting kisses on her lips and face and neck, he muttered, "You can never belong to another, you filthy slut."

Clover was tempted to inquire why he would want a son from a slut, but the knife he had laid on the floor by the mat terrified her into silence. In the morning, bruised and humiliated, she bathed in the icy stream and went about her duties in a daze.

After Clover and Mia had left him unceremoniously at the Shoshone camp, Lake prodded a sleepy Henry into action for the promised noon performance. The animal's injured foot was still sore, but he managed to execute a few simple routines. Henry rolled over, played dead, took his trainer's head into his big maw with pretended savageness. Rearing up on his hind legs, he shook the trainer's hand. He roared, many times on demand, crouched as if to attack, then submitted meekly to Lake's stick of authority.

The Indian audience was enthralled, showering Lake with gifts of food and money.

Next day, Lake began a tour of the various camps and villages, collecting gifts of clothing, rugs, wicker baskets, food, and cash money as he went. There were even gifts of silver, both ore and ornaments. After every show, comely Indian maids approached him boldly, offering themselves to the handsome lion-tamer, with or without promise of marriage. Lake declined one and all politely.

Overjoyed at his new luck, the Englishman resolved to leave this blasted Nevada forever, once he was sufficiently prosperous. He would take a train for San Francisco, riding with Henry in the baggage car, and there take a ship for his native England, putting Clover Sinclair and her fickle love behind him forever.

Taking the bank money back to Illinois—as he had promised Molly—and surrendering to authorities was not part of his revised life plan. Clover and her Indian husband were welcome to the money. Coveting the loot had brought him nothing but misery.

"From this day forward, it's just you and me, old boy," he told Henry at dusk one day after an especially rewarding show in a Washo camp. His strong but gentle hands stroked the luxuriant mane which he had once again brushed to dark, gleaming glory. Henry stretched his neck with pleasure, but did not make the contented throaty noises that Clover always brought from him. All traces of the lion's desert and mountain ordeal had vanished under the liontamer's expert care. Clean and shining, Henry looked superb.

"My British countrymen will love you," Lake exulted. "It'll be just like old times with the Grandiose Circus."

He burst into a hearty laugh, but somehow it sounded hollow to his ears.

One morning, a week after his return from powwow, Gray Falcon said to his wife, "We must make ready for my father Red Hawk's funeral. You must work with my old mother Sweet Briar and the other women in my family."

"Is it not customary to wait a full year before the ritual burning," Clover asked, surprised. She dreaded visiting the women's lodge, where she had been so cruelly mistreated. She did not want to face White Feather again.

"Yes, but the thing must be done quickly before the soldiers come. My father's ashes must rest in the ancient burial ground here in the valley of Wun-i-muc-a where he lived many happy years."

Obediently donning a clean doeskin garment, Clover walked to Sweet Briar's lodge. It was a cold and drizzly early November day, and the air smelled of snow. This part of the valley was high, snow came early and lay thick on the ground for months.

Nobody was outdoors; all were in by the fires. The high voices of children came from inside the long wooden lodge along with the busy murmur of women's voices. Pausing at the door, Clover thought of her suffering during those first hard weeks. She had not seen White Feather since the night Gray Falcon had kicked her in the stomach as she lay on the riverbank by that terrible gauntlet. Mia had reported that the girl was ailing.

Pulling her blanket tight around her slim shoulders, she put a hand to the eagle totem at her neck. With fresh courage, Clover knocked firmly — two long, two short, the signal of a friend.

The door was flung open by a child. Entering quickly, Clover stood smiling as sudden quiet descended. Everyone stared at her curiously until White Feather emerged from the hearth where she had been sitting at Sweet Briar's knee.

The girl's walk was painfully slow, and her beautiful face was marked by pain. One hand pressed against her abdomen. But the hatred blazing from the dark eyes was as virulent as ever.

"The whore of Gray Falcon is not welcome in his mother's lodge," she spat out.

Stony-faced, Clover brushed past the girl, moving swiftly to Sweet Briar, who sat rocking and smoking a sweet-smelling weed. The old woman looked up, but did not greet her new daughter-in-law.

"I have come to talk of your dead husband's ritual burning," Clover said loudly. "Your son, the new

307

chief, has ordered that it be done before the snow lies too thick and the soldiers come to drive us from the valley."

Stolidly, speaking in a faint, trembling voice, the old one announced, "The guardians of the dead world will not receive Red Hawk's spirit until the full year has passed."

Undeterred, Clover persisted. "Gray Falcon orders it. Red Hawk must rest here in the valley. He says we cannot take his old bones on the long march to the north."

Sweet Briar cackled, her wrinkled face breaking into a wide, toothless grin. "Gray Falcon is a child. I, his mother, say so." Waving an imperious hand at Clover, she said, "Go tell the fool his mother has said this."

Standing beside her, White Feather hissed at Clover, "If the burning is done, none of this lodge will come to the burial site. I will see that nobody from this village attends."

Suddenly, Sweet Briar rose up, trembling, her old hands on the chair arms. Her reed pipe fell to the hearthstones. White Feather rushed to keep the old one from toppling over as Gray Falcon's mother shrieked at Clover, "Tell my fool of a son that he must put aside the white whore who shares his mat. Until he is free of her, his father may be burned a hundred times and his spirit will not be at peace."

The woman seemed near collapse, wheezing and coughing to catch her breath. Her eyes rolled back in their sockets.

White Feather stormed at Clover, "Leave us before the old one's heart bursts with grief."

"The old bitch," Gray Falcon fumed when Clover reported her failure with Sweet Briar to him. "We'll hold the burning without her and her silly women. I declare it to take place one week from this day."

Privately, Clover was relieved that White Feather would not be at the burning to cause trouble. Aided by the "women of death" who had inherited from their mothers the ancient lore of the burning herbs, she set to work with enthusiasm. She had loved Red Hawk, and vowed to make his burning an event that would go down in legend, to be told in song and story as long as a single Paiute remained on earth.

Red Hawk's tipi, where she and Gray Falcon now dwelt, would be torn down and burned on the funeral pyre, along with the old chief's armchair and some of his favorite household possessions. A new dwelling would be constructed for Gray Falcon and his squaw. Clover and Mia removed themselves to Mia's ancestral lodge, where the girl's numerous female relatives worked feverishly on Clover's ceremonial costume for the burning.

That very day, Gray Falcon disappeared to mourn privately for his father, he said, and to seek wisdom from the spirit world for his new chiefdom.

A week later, the funeral day dawned clear and cold. Clover emerged from Mia's lodge, resplendent in a heavily fringed short doeskin dress worked to feather softness. Scarlet leggings fitted her long legs tightly and on her thick, unbraided hair sat a glorious headdress of eagle feathers dyed crimson. Silver bracelets adorned her bare, tanned arms, and many chains hung around her neck.

A vast throng accompanied the chief's squaw on the half-day journey to the ancient burial ground in a limestone pit where the primordial Anesazi — ancestors of all the Nevada tribes — lay interred. Chief Gray Falcon had not returned from his meditative retreat; Clover expected to see him at the pyre.

As they set out, Clover was thankful for the finely tooled leather boots sent by Ralph Brant, along with many gifts of cloth and food for Mia and her family.

They reached the site, a large hollowed-out portion in the limestone and basalt shale. People from many tribes awaited them, the chiefs standing rigidly at attention in a wide circle around the pit. Black-hooded shamans danced and chanted in circles, holding aloft lighted torches of pine.

Atop a large pile of rocks stood the tall funeral pyre burdened with Red Hawk's bones, his dead horse and dog, his tipi, and many other provisions for his journey to the spirit world. Mourning women covered with ashes squatted nearby, keening in sharp voices. But children played among the tumbling rocks, young people flirted, making cow's eyes at each other, choosing mates.

Life goes on amid death, mused Clover.

A murmur arose as she waited for Gray Falcon to

appear to light the torch with her. She turned. Sweet Briar was being carried to the pyre on a litter by her women. Dressed in ceremonial garb, White Feather walked proudly at her side.

Happily, Clover rushed to greet the dead chief's wife. But before she reached Sweet Briar, an eerie cry split the air.

"Ai-ee-ee—!"

It was Gray Falcon, who broke through the circle of chiefs, striding to the pyre without a glance at anyone. Except for a bare scrap of loincloth across his sinewy thighs, he was naked. His usually neatly groomed shoulder-length black hair blew in tangles around his head in the bitter wind. A primitive stone tomahawk hung on a thong around his narrow waist.

"Ai-ee-ee!" he cried again, snatching a burning torch from a shaman. As the next shaman danced near, he snatched another, extending it to Clover, who ran from Sweet Briar's side.

A wild chant went up from the throng as the new chief and his young white squaw extended their torches to the tinder at the base of the pyre. Suddenly, like an omen, eagles swarmed overhead, dipping and circling gracefully, as if summoned by an unseen power to witness this great occasion.

Gray Falcon's torch caused a blaze, but as Clover leaned forward to apply her torch, a shrill, blood-curdling scream came from behind. She felt a violent thrust in the small of her back and fell to the rocks by the already burning pyre, clutching the torch.

311

A crazed White Feather snatched the torch from Clover's hand. "I am the son of Red Hawk's true betrothed. It is I who must light the funeral pyre in the name of Sweet Briar."

The Indian girl touched the pyre with the torch, now in full, consuming flames. As Clover rolled down the rocky slope away from the searing heat, she heard an enraged Gray Falcon roar, "The blasphemer must die."

As Clover sprawled below, she saw Gray Falcon draw the tomahawk from his waist and lift it high above White Feather's head. The girl made no move to escape, but appeared to be eagerly waiting for death.

Several chiefs ran up to stay the son of Red Hawk's murderous hand. As his stone weapon was snatched from his hand, Gray Falcon seemed to crumble like a dead leaf in autumn. With a cry of pure anguish, he flung himself out of the burial place.

The trembling voice of Sweet Briar rose up in the shocked silence. "The white whore has driven the son of Red Hawk mad."

As she struggled to her feet, Clover saw White Feather bearing down on her. Grabbing her by both shoulders, the insanely jealous Indian girl pushed Clover toward the blazing pyre.

"This one must die for her great sin," she shouted.

The chiefs who had prevented the son of Red Hawk from murdering White Feather now tore the vengeful girl away from Clover. Weeping, the girl crawled on hands and knees back to Sweet Briar's litter.

Lifting herself up by her elbows in the litter, the woman spat at the pitiful girl. "You have acted foolishly, White Feather. If you would become my son's squaw, you must put aside your vengeful ways and prove your worth in honest battle."

The crawling girl rose up, astonished. "Old mother, your brains are addled. Paiute women do not go into battle with guns and arrows."

Pointing a gnarled finger at Clover, who was fitting her fallen headdress on her streaming black hair and preparing to leave for home, Sweet Briar hissed, "There is the one you must fight and defeat before Gray Falcon will take you to bed."

A wild, hyenalike laugh ripped from White Feather's throat. "With pleasure, old one." Whirling, she walked toward Clover. "Come, whore, your mother by marriage would have us fight each other." The girl laughed again, raising two fists into the air.

More amused than shocked at the idea of hand-to-hand fighting with her clearly insane enemy, Clover backed away. But Mia, who had sidled up, said quietly, "You swore once that you two would settle your differences by single combat. Do it now, and be rid of this hateful girl forever."

"Yes," Clover breathed. The thought of slamming her fist into the spiteful face before her made the blood flow faster in her veins. "But not here in this hallowed burying place while Red Hawk still burns

313

on his pyre."

With hardly a glance at her challenger, who was now crouching on all fours and breathing heavily through flared nostrils like an animal, Clover addressed Sweet Briar. "Gray Falcon's mother speaks wisdom. I will fight White Feather when she is fully recovered from the injuries suffered at the hands of your son."

Her tanned cheeks red with excitement, Clover started back down the trail to the Paiute village, Mia and many others following behind her. The wails of the mourning women and the eerie chants of the shamans echoed in her ears. The old ones would remain here until the old chief's ashes were cold and ready for interment in the rocks.

Chapter Fifteen

As she and Mia walked rapidly through the forested terrain, Clover could not help glancing back over her shoulder to see if the mad White Feather was following them. Halfway back to the Paiute village, Clover stopped at an ice-choked stream to rest. After drinking handfuls of the cold water, she picked up two chunks of ice and held them to her burning cheeks. The stormy events of the morning had left her emotionally drained.

The two young women sat down on the leafy ground against a bare cottonwood, the small group with them following their example. Sighing, Clover remarked to her companion, "I cannot do battle with that foolish girl. It is obvious that she is not well. I would never forgive myself if I should do her permanent harm."

Mia snorted. "It is my opinion that her pain is a

mere posturing. She means to garner sympathy for herself so that all will turn against you."

"You may be right," Clover sighed. "I also fear that if I don't accept her challenge I will appear cowardly to the people whose respect I have worked so hard to earn."

The cold but bright sun had disappeared and gray woolly snowclouds took their place. Shivering, Clover rose. "Let's resume our journey before we get caught in a snowstorm."

Turning to the old woman who had given her the whiskey, Clover asked, "What do you think, Ground Squirrel? You are wise and have seen much. Is White Feather pretending illness?"

The answer was prompt. "Mia, who is called Little Chicken, has spoken well. White Feather suffers from an inward cancer that is eating out her heart. It is called jealousy. She envies your kind way with the people and Gray Falcon's great love for you."

Leaving the cottonwood grove, Clover said firmly, "That settles it. If White Feather persists in challenging me, I will fight."

They had not gone more than a few yards when the noise of a great crowd of people was heard behind them. Clover turned to face White Feather, who grinned evilly into her face.

"There are no chiefs to save you now, slut," the enraged woman gritted, taking a large handful of Clover's unbraided hair with one hand and yanking off the eagle headdress with the other. Twisting her arm with surprising force, she forced Clover to the ground.

Her eyes smarting with pain from the girl's steely grip, Clover lay motionless. "I will not fight a sick woman," she hissed between clenched teeth, "though you pull out every hair of my head."

The challenger yanked again, and Clover winced but did not cry out. Kneeling at her side, Mia spoke in Clover's ear. "You must fight her. Get up and knock her down quickly."

Clover struggled to rise, but White Feather kicked her viciously in the side. Immediately the voice of Ground Squirrel was heard in the shocked silence. Rushing up to White Feather, she grabbed her arm. "Loosen your hold, girl. You took your opponent unaware. If you must do this fighting, do it fairly."

The girl obeyed, backing off. Bounding up, Clover quickly shed her ceremonial doeskin and bent to remove her leather boots.

"Leave the boots," yelled White Feather. "Kicking is greater sport with sharp leather."

"No," shouted Ground Squirrel, who, by common consent, had assumed the role of referee. She shook her blanket-covered head. "No boots. Both must be naked as babes." Picking up a fallen cottonwood branch, she brandished it before the two combatants and declared in a loud voice, "When I touch you with this stick on the shoulder, the fight must stop. My decision will be final."

No one came forward to question Ground Squirrel's authority and the two young women squared off, naked, feet spread wide, arms on hips in a half-crouching position. Both stared at the old Ground Squirrel, waiting for a signal to begin.

A few snowflakes were swirling out of the woolly clouds, but Clover felt no cold. Her blood was heated to fever pitch. Images of Lake and Henry passed through her mind. She imagined she heard Henry's wonderful roar. She had been prepared to die when she faced the gauntlet and now she might well die at the vicious hands of White Feather. The girl had powerful arms for a woman, developed from chopping and hauling firewood long distances.

The crowd was deathly silent, numbering at least a hundred, she thought. A group of men had stopped to watch. Thankfully, Gray Falcon was not among them. He would most certainly have stopped the battle and Clover was determined to give the sullen Indian girl a lesson she would never forget.

"No kicking in the stomach." Ground Squirrel spoke again. "Gray Falcon's squaw may be with child."

This brought a loud guffaw from White Feather. "A babe of hers is better off dead. How would we know if it be our chief's or her white lover's bastard anyway?"

Ignoring the vicious jibe, Clover doubled up her fists and prepared to fight. When the signal came — "begin" — she rushed forward with fists flailing. Cleverly, her opponent turned sideways and hurled the full weight of her tall body against the onrushing Clover, knocking the wind out of her.

Sprawled once again on the gnarly roots, Clover lay helpless as the Indian girl sat on Clover's hips and rained punishing blows on her head and breasts and neck. Dimly, Clover heard the crowd yelling at her to get up and fight.

"Clover, get up, she's murdering you" came Mia's clear, high voice.

"Molly, help me," Clover prayed, just as she used to do when she was a child and fell on the rocks. Molly's dear, caring face swam before her vision. Suddenly, new strength seemed to pour into her battered body, and with a supreme effort of will, she lifted up from the waist and hurled the Indian girl from her body.

Both were on their feet now, facing each other squarely. Clover felt blood trickling down her face from her swollen left eye. Her upper body felt as if it had been tightened in a vise. Every muscle was in agony. But a new kind of rage, far more deadly than any she had ever experienced, now consumed her.

"You're no sicker than I am, you bloody fraud," she screamed. Then, lashing out windmill fashion with arms and legs moving in all directions at once it seemed, Clover Sinclair went at her enemy, the girl whom she had once felt sorry for. She felt the satisfaction of connecting with White Feather's soft flesh time and time again.

All her pain forgotten for the moment, she felt

light as a feather. A single thought possessed her. She would make this spiteful girl sorry she had ever tangled with Molly Robinson's daughter.

The hot blood was pounding in her ears, the cheers of the crowd exhilarated Clover so that she never heard Ground Squirrel's call to quit or the sudden silence in the forest until she felt the sting of the stick on her shoulder.

Dazed, Clover stumbled back. Her breath came in quick, hurting gasps. She faced Ground Squirrel angrily. "Why did you stop us? I was winning." She glanced at White Feather, who sat hunched over on the ground a few feet away, her head hanging down between her knees, retching painfully.

Clover smiled triumphantly. "So my brave challenger has yielded."

The old Indian woman waved her stick toward the edge of the crowd. "The wife of Gray Falcon has visitors. The liontamer and his lion have come to visit. I do not think you wish to have them witness your brutal battle."

Wiping the blood from her swollen eye, Clover gazed where the stick pointed. There, big as life, and more beautiful than ever stood her sweet lion Henry. Beside him, with the widest grin she had ever seen on anyone, Lake Emerson lounged against a tall tree trunk, holding on to Henry's leash.

In the amused silence, Henry lunged toward her, uttering a low, rhythmic "uh-uh" that indicated he was very happy. A soft command by Lake held him

320

back, but his long tail with the bush at the end wagged back and forth so vigorously it nearly knocked down several children who had come too close.

Darting forward, Mia slipped the doeskin over Clover's head, cloaking her nakedness. Shrugging off a proffered blanket, Clover ran eagerly to Henry, taking his massive head in her arms and laying her bruised and battered face against his thick, warm, fragrant mane.

"Oh, my sweet lion, I've missed you so," she murmured. "Please forgive me for leaving you. I'll never, ever do it again, I swear."

Cries of "the sacred lion has returned to dwell among us" ran through the spectators. Ground Squirrel's clear old voice rang out, "It is an omen from the Great Spirit. Now all will be well among us."

Standing now at Henry's side, Clover stroked his broad rump, rhythmically, firmly, murmuring softly to him all the while. The restless crowd was making the animal nervous.

Clutching the leash tightly, Lake stepped forward to face the crowd. "Stand back, everybody, please. Give the lion room. He is tame but nervous, and might decide to run off. He is a massive animal and needs much breathing space."

As if just now aware of his presence, Clover lifted her eyes to meet Lake's gray-eyed gaze. Their glances locked for a brief moment, but all she said was,

"Thank you for bringing Henry back to me. I have missed him sorely."

A tiny muscle worked in Lake's bronzed cheek, and his nostrils flared in brief anger. *Goddam it, you went off and left him,* he wanted to yell at her, but knowing this was not the time for an argument he nodded. "He misses you too, terribly. I had thought to take him on the road again, doing shows, perhaps join up with the Grandiose outfit again." His eyes clouded, and he seemed lost in her steady gaze. "They're in winter quarters now, I think, somewhere in the West."

Clover looked astonished. "You mean to tell me that you intended to just leave — with my lion? Without even telling me first?" Her voice rose to a squeal of outrage.

"Our lion," he corrected sternly but with a twinkle in his eyes. The crowd was slowly drifting away, since there was no more excitement, the lion just standing there being petted like a big dog. Moving to Henry's other side, Lake began to stroke him also, while continuing to talk to Clover.

"Actually, Henry settled the matter for me. He pined away for you, only picked at his food. Once he ate only half of a fat, juicy beaver." He twinkled. "It's his favorite food, as you know. We did a few shows for the Indians, but his heart wasn't in it."

Walking away, Lake stared at the snowy sky. The ground had a thin layer of white on it, and everything looked peaceful. "Nosirree, without his Mary

Anne, this contrary lion isn't much good at anything. Sleeps all the time, wakes up grouchy."

This sad description fit the trainer more than the lion, Lake was well aware, but he would cut his tongue out before he told this fickle girl that *he* had missed her, too.

Turning back, he met her amused glance, and Clover saw in his eyes the longing denied by his flippant words. "You've been lonely, too," she said boldly, "as I have."

Suddenly conscious that the remaining Indians were staring at the two of them with great interest, and that most of them understood the white man's tongue perfectly, Lake shrugged off the romantic mood. Breaking into a wide grin, he remarked, "I can see, however, that you managed to find ways to amuse yourself. You were boxing—or was it wrestling?—with that poor girl when I showed up. Was it a game, or perhaps a performance for pay?"

He glanced over at White Feather still under the tree prone and still. Her friends still hovered over her. Two young boys were fashioning a litter from some chopped-down saplings.

Turning a brilliant red, Clover dropped her eyes and mumbled, "It's a long story. Things are not really what they seem."

Lake's brow furrowed. "She seems to be terribly hurt. You play rough, Clover Sinclair."

Clover bristled, her black eyes shooting fire. "I repeat—things are not always as they seem."

323

She was in no mood for lengthy explanations. At least not here in full sight of a crowd of avidly curious Indians. Remembering her opponent's great strength during the fight, Clover did not go over to the girl to see how badly she was hurt. Clover was certain that, once again, White Feather was playing the sympathy role to the hilt.

Sighing, Lake commented, "I beg your pardon for showing up so unexpectedly and spoiling your game." He grinned wickedly. "If I were referee, I'd say you had won, hands down."

His wide, sensual mouth trembled in a barely suppressed laugh. Raking her from head to foot, he commented, "Aside from that beauty of a black eye, I'd say you were in fairly good shape."

Ground Squirrel, admiring the lion respectfully from a few yards away, had been shamelessly eavesdropping. Now she called out loudly, "The two young women were fighting to see who will be Gray Falcon's chief squaw. It is a quarrel of long standing between them."

The look of sheer amazement on Lake's face was almost comical, but, rallying quickly, he bounded to Henry's other side to grab Clover's hand. He shook it energetically. "Well, then, congratulations, Miss Sinclair. I admire a woman who goes after what she wants. I hope you and your green-eyed Indian chief will enjoy many happy years together."

Amazed, the Englishman shook his head. "It's a fortunate man indeed whose woman will fight for him," he exclaimed, his face wreathed in merriment. "Such a thing would never happen in quiet old England."

"As I said before, things are not always what they seem," Clover responded icily, conquering a desire to punch him in his smug, grinning face. Throwing Ground Squirrel a withering glance, she added, "One must be careful not to believe the idle gossip of old women."

Tugging Henry's leash away from him, she lashed out stiffly, "I must return to my village. If you care to follow, I will explain the whole affair in detail." She tightened her lips. "At a more opportune moment."

Bowing low, Lake fixed her with a mocking gaze while relinquishing the leash. "I look forward to a rattling good story, madam."

Henry had been sitting contentedly on his haunches, but now he grumbled excitedly and bounded up, anxious to be moving from this place.

"You'll get your story, sir," Clover spat out as she started off at a good clip. Following behind at a distance, Lake soon found himself surrounded by a gaggle of young Indian maids who had been watching him covertly as he had talked with Clover. Their high soprano voices mingled with Lake's deep baritone as they flirted outrageously with the handsome white man with the funny accent.

An hour later, all arrived at the Paiute village to

325

great excitement and distress. Indian scouts on near hilltops had reported that columns of blue-clad cavalry were advancing toward the valley on fast horses. The Paiute chief, Gray Falcon, had not yet returned from his father's burning, from which he had flung out in apparent despair. Not one of the many young village warriors could be found. After much searching, it was discovered that all of the able-bodied men had vanished, leaving old men, women, and children.

All the villagers looked to Flying Bird for guidance. "Should we prepare to flee for our lives, or should we stay here and fight for our homes against the cavalry?" they asked.

Inside her tipi, Clover sat on a chair while Mia bathed and dressed her swollen eye with cooling herbs. Touching Red Hawk's totem around her neck, she prayed for guidance.

"If the soldiers come as they say, we will march north," she said to Mia. "We cannot fight without our men. I am positive they are with Gray Falcon, preparing for battle elsewhere in the valley."

"You battle so well yourself, maybe you should join your husband," Mia joked, but she seemed jittery, accidentally jabbing Clover in the eye with her finger, and when Clover jumped, dropping the bowl of water. Wild with impatience and worry, Clover leaped from the chair.

"You idiot," she barked, then, contrite, murmured, "What is it, girl, are you ill?" She placed a comforting arm around Mia's shoulders.

"No, I mean, yes, I think so. I stood too much in the cold back there at the fight . . ."

Wrenching from Clover's arms, the girl started to weep uncontrollably. "Please don't be angry at what I have to tell you. Please try to understand. You are in love yourself." Turning back, she gazed directly into Clover's eyes. "I will not march with you and the villagers. Mr. Brant will arrive here soon, at any moment, according to his spies among us. I intend to return with him to Black Springs. He has offered me a job in his house."

Astounded, Clover gasped, "In love, did you say? You foolish girl. The man has a perfectly good wife already."

Mia's lovely face turned a fiery red. "I am well aware of that. But they don't do anything, I mean — it is a marriage in name only, he tells me."

"Oh, dear God, Mia, you're headed for a broken heart." Taking the girl by the shoulders again, Clover shook her vigorously. "What about your young man who is in prison?"

"I-I've forgotten about him. He'll be there for years." Lifting her head defiantly, Mia cried, "Seems to me the pot is calling the kettle black. You've made love to a man who is not your husband."

"I was forced into the marriage," Clover said defensively. "It is not really valid—" Breaking off, she threw out her arms and drew Mia into an embrace. "But let's not argue, dear friend," she continued softly. "Let us part in peace."

Clover's black eyes looked vacantly at Red Hawk's old armchair. "I have learned from bitter experience that love may be brief, and must be taken when it is offered."

Smiling through her tears, Mia said haltingly, "There is something else you should know. Mr. Brant has been appointed as the new Indian agent, replacing dead Mr. Parker. The telegram has just arrived from Washington City. This means that he has power to order the evacuation at once."

"How do you know all this?" Clover asked.

"A runner spoke to me as you and White Feather were fighting."

An hour later, after cleaning the tipi with care, Mia departed for her mother's lodge to await Brant's arrival. Impatiently, Clover ran outside. Henry was tied securely to a tree and was consuming a chunk of fresh-killed meat. A few yards away, Lake was surrounded by a group of giggling maidens.

Crossly, Clover approached them. "Go to your lodges and make ready for a long journey. Take all your blankets, for the nights will be bitterly cold. Pack water and food for three days at least until we reach the Walker Lake Reservation at the western edge of the desert. We will stop over there for a night."

Brushing the rapidly falling snow from her face, she gazed at the western ridge. "Our only blessing is that winter is here and the desert temperature will be bearable." Facing Lake, she snapped, "As for you, Englishman, you can help by keeping everyone away from Henry." Whirling back to her tipi to pack, she threw over her shoulder sarcastically, "And kindly leave my maidens alone during the journey."

"Not so fast, heap big lady chief," Lake exploded, running to catch her and turn her around by the shoulders. "Why is a chit of a girl like you left in charge here? Where's that warrior husband of yours that you battled so valiantly to win for yourself?" He cocked a blond brow. "Must you fight his battles for him now?"

Struck dumb for a moment, Clover ran a distracted hand through her fall of black hair that she had not braided since the burning. She looked exhausted, Lake thought, but more beautiful than ever in her rumpled doeskin with snowflakes glistening on her long lashes. Resisting the impulse to scoop her up in his arms and run with her as fast he could away from this incredibly dangerous place, he repeated urgently, "Well, where is Gray Falcon?"

"Our chief is off gathering his forces for battle," she said quietly. "The son of Red Hawk, despite what he has said in the past, will not surrender his valley without fighting to the last warrior."

She tried to wrench loose, but he tightened his hold on her shoulders, and she became still again. "Please let me go, Lake. The Indian men may return at any moment, and I am anxious to leave this place before the soldiers come and there is shooting. Bullets and arrows don't discriminate between a fighting man and a child or old woman."

Unconsciously, Lake's strong hands began to knead Clover's slender shoulders under the doeskin. Briefly, they swayed toward each other, their mutual longing almost a physical presence between them in the cold November afternoon. Clover's arms lifted halfway up to draw her lover to her breast, but, quickly, she dropped them again to her sides.

Groaning, Lake dropped his own hands from her shoulders. "I'll travel with you for a time, taking care of Henry."

"That would be very kind of you," she said hoarsely. Her eyes dropped to the revolver at his waist. "You and your weapon can be of help in providing fresh meat for the women and children."

He smiled broadly. "I'm a crack shot, but I wouldn't want to meet up with any United States cavalry. I don't enjoy killing people, and I'm already in trouble with the authorities."

A group of maidens walked toward them. "You might also help by keeping the silly young girls amused," she commented acidly. "Just keep your hands off them. Indian men don't take kindly to having their virgins despoiled."

Throwing up his hands in mock horror, Lake returned to Henry, who was noisily gnawing at a bone. Squatting a short distance away, he chuckled to the lion, "She may be married to that green-eyed brave, Henry, old pal, but her heart still belongs to me.

330

Only a woman desperately in love can be that wildly jealous."

By early dusk, the snow had stopped, leaving the air clear and sharp. Despite the approaching dark, Clover decided to start the journey. A pale moon already gleamed overhead, and they could easily make much progress by moonlight. They would most likely meet the cavalry approaching, but if they were on the way, out of the valley, the soldiers would not bother them. The old and nursing mothers would ride on mules, Sweet Briar and the sick, including White Feather, would be borne on litters. All able-bodied women would carry filled willow baskets on their backs, including Clover.

When all were gathered around her tipi, their absent chief's squaw addressed them solemnly. "We go to prevent a bloody battle in which many of us might be slaughtered. When Molly Robinson is well again, she will petition President Grant and you will return to your valley."

Placing her hand on her heart, Clover swore, "I, Flying Bird, who became one of your tribe by adoption, promise you this on my life."

Raising up from her litter, White Feather shrieked, "Do not listen to her empty words. She is in league with Ralph Brant, the landgrabber. I will not go. I would rather die here from a bullet than freeze to death in the desert night."

Sitting upright, supported by two women, the Indian girl yelled, "Who is with me?"

Nobody responded, but from her own litter, old Sweet Briar spoke. "Be still, foolish girl. Flying Bird is chief in my son's absence. She is wise, and she has her holy lion to protect us."

Obligingly, Henry let out a small roar, bringing smiles to the faces of many. The children clapped their hands delightedly. Thinking himself back at the circus, no doubt, the lion roared again until Lake commanded him to stop.

Everything's going well, reflected Clover as White Feather fell back down again on her litter, defeated. But suddenly the sound of horses was heard, and Ralph Brant, accompanied by a small troop of soldiers, rode into the village.

Pushing through the women, Brant spoke to Clover. "I see you're being smart, young lady."

"We leave only temporarily," she replied testily. "You have won a skirmish, Brant, the final victory will be ours."

Ignoring her remark, Brant faced the villagers. "Once you pass through the desert, you will rest at Walker Lake. Provisions await you there — warm clothing, woolen blankets, and food for your journey through the mountains. You have absolutely nothing to fear. The Great White Father in Washington City loves you as his children and has instructed me to treat you with all kindness."

"If he is so kind," Ground Squirrel shouted, astride her mule with two of her grandchildren riding behind her, "why does he force us from our homes?"

332

"The nation needs the silver that is buried in this valley," Brant replied smoothly, "and by law, you Indians cannot mine it."

Clover whirled, aghast. "But you promised Gray Falcon some ore-rich land."

Waving a dismissing hand, Brant said lightly, "Oh, that. I had to get him on my side. He will be given some rich bottom land for farming, but since he is half Indian, he will never be allowed to stake a silver claim."

In one horrifying instant, all became clear to Clover. Gray Falcon must have discovered Brant's perfidy. That would at least partially explain her husband's change of heart about the man.

White-faced with fury, Clover gritted, "Gray Falcon will kill you, you cowardly weasel. He will rip off your scalp and hang it from his tipi flap for all time. At this moment, he is marshaling his braves for battle. There will be men from every tribe in Eagle Valley who will vastly outnumber your few soldiers here."

His handsome face crinkling up in a sly smile, Ralp Brant pulled a cigarette from his pocket and, after lighting it with a sulfur match, inhaled, then exhaled a cloud of smoke before replying.

"These paltry few soldiers are for escorting your women and children through the desert," he said, waving his arm to the men behind him. They are not prepared to fight. Ten times this many are waiting outside the Shoshone camp where Gray Falcon and his warriors are headed." An ugly laugh erupted from his throat as he gazed up at the darkening sky. "If my calculations are correct, the two armies should be clashing right about now." He winked at Mia, who came running up with a loaded wicker basket on her back. "Isn't that so, my dear?"

"Yes," the girl responded in a whisper, without looking at Clover. "That's what I have heard."

"So you really are a traitor," Clover hissed at her friend and trusted companion, who swiftly mounted a waiting horse by Brant's side. She gazed round at the other women. "I wonder how many more have betrayed us."

"None," Mia said. "No one but me."

Brant reached out to pat the girl's knee as she sat on her horse. "Pay no heed to her, dear child, she's grumpy at having lost her little war against me."

Loud rumbles from Henry drew Brant's attention to the animal by Lake's side at the edge of the column of women. "So we meet again, liontamer," he sneered. "Like your big cat there, you apparently have nine lives. Congratulations on outwitting those two idiots, Luther and Slade; haven't seen hide nor hair of either of them since."

Sweeping his hand to a soldier at his side, Brant barked, "Take this man into custody, Lieutenant. He is wanted for murder and escaping from prison in Illinois."

Accompanied by two of his men, revolvers in their hands, the lieutenant dismounted and walked toward

Lake. At a soft command from his trainer, the lion bared his teeth and growled. His ears flattened back against his massive head and he assumed a charging position. Bending low, Lake put a restraining hand on the tawny flank, which was trembling violently.

The soldiers backed off quickly, sliding their guns back into their holsters. The lieutenant swore roundly, then exclaimed, "Damn it, sir, my West Point training covered just about everything but dealing with raging African lions."

"One step more and I let go this leash," Lake growled. "A bullet may hit me, but one or more of you will be mincemeat before I hit the ground."

"Shoot the damn lion," Brant gritted, pulling out his own pistol.

Clover, who had observed silently but with a little smile on her face, now drew out her own gun, one of several Gray Falcon had kept in his tipi.

"If that happens, Brant, I will shoot you dead without a qualm." Her voice was cold and deadly, and nobody doubted that she meant what she said.

An angry murmuring arose from among the women. Several young boys drew arrows from quivers on their back, fitting them to their bows. The situation was getting nastier than Brant had anticipated.

"Leave it for now, Lieutenant," Brant muttered, reholstering his gun. To Lake he yelled, "This isn't the end, Englishman. I'll get you yet, one way or the other. A man never forgets his son's killer."

"Let's move out of here," the lieutenant gritted, looking nervously at Henry, who continued to rumble menacingly. Wheeling his horse around, he ordered his men to follow. Patiently, with stoic looks on their faces, the Indian women shouldered their baskets and prodded their loaded mules with sticks.

They had barely started when a shriek from White Feather rent the air. "Look, our warriors are here." The Indian girl sat up in her litter, pointing with both hands to the northern hillside. All turned to gaze in astonishment at a line of warriors on horseback in war paint and feathered headdresses outlined against the twilight sky. As they watched, a second line appeared over the brow of the horizon. In the stunned silence, shrill war cries could be heard.

"Ai-ee-ee," White Feather screamed, opening her mouth wide in her own war cry. Many of the women shrieked also, imitating their men.

Wheeling around, Clover shouted, "Everyone into hiding. Go to your tipis and lodges before the warriors get here and there is shooting."

Frightened by the eerie calls from the bluff, pandemonium ensued. Mothers carried their children to safety. The mules scattered everywhere, some running to the cottonwoods and willows by the stream, while others remained, impassively unaware of the impending battle.

Seemingly paralyzed, Clover remained still, wanting to make sure that all were out of the place before she ran to her own tipi.

"Clover, get the hell out of here," Lake yelled, moving toward her. But an excited Henry began to run rapidly toward the stream, following a stream of women. With a backward, anguished look at Clover, Lake was forced to run with the lion.

"Present arms," the lieutenant shouted and the men obeyed, shouldering their rifles. But Clover remained calm. The charging Indians were still out of range, she knew. Once the women were safely in their dwellings, the cavalry would advance through the village toward the hillside to confront the Indians.

Ralph Brant wheeled his horse around, grabbing Mia's reins. "Let's get out of here, into the desert, before the shooting starts."

"Take shelter with the others," the lieutenant snapped at Clover. "You're directly in the line of fire."

As if mesmerized, Clover gazed anxiously at the rapidly darkening hillside swarming with warriors on horses. They seemed near enough to shoot at, but the soldiers continued to hold their fire. Despite her dread of the coming battle, she could not help but feel a deep pride in Gray Falcon. His loyalties were now undivided. He was willing to defend his homeland and his Indian heritage. Apparently, he had his own spies, as did Brant, and had discovered Brant's treachery in time to avoid a confrontation with the massed cavalry at the Shoshone camp.

A scream from Mia caused Clover to turn around. Ralph Brant had tumbled off his horse, a red-tipped arrow in his back. Another followed, sticking in his

337

neck. His mount, a fine chestnut mare, galloped toward the trees.

A bloodcurdling war whoop was followed instantly by the appearance of Gray Falcon from behind his tipi. Because all eyes had been fixed on the hillside, he had been able to sneak up undetected.

A cavalryman pointed his gun at the tall Indian, who stood in front of the troop, unmoving, his arms folded across his painted chest.

"No," the lieutenant barked. "Take him prisoner. Without their chief, the Indians may not charge." Two soldiers dismounted to take the Paiute chief by the arms.

"Take the women away," Gray Falcon said quietly. "All in this village who are not under cover will be slain."

To Clover, her Indian husband seemed curiously calm. Remembering his madness, she was certain that he welcomed his approaching death in battle. The ten cavalrymen and anyone caught in the village in the open would surely fall beneath the arrows of hundreds of Indians on the hillside.

"Go, Clover," Gray Falcon repeated. "Join your lover in the trees. May you be happy, but do not forget your friend from childhood, who loved you truly."

"I will not go without Mia," she responded, turning to the girl, who had fallen on her knees near Brant's bleeding body. A soldier rolled the body over, putting his ear to the wounded man's chest. After a few moments, he rose up and announced, "He's dead. The first arrow pierced his heart, the second got his jugular vein."

A grief-stricken Mia cradled Brant's head to her chest. As Clover drew near, she raised her contorted face. "You murderer. You knew Gray Falcon was hiding. Now the man I love is gone forever."

Falling to her knees beside the weeping girl, Clover tried to comfort her. "I am truly sorry. But Ralph Brant turned all the Indians against him. It was bound to happen, if not by Gray Falcon's arrow, then another."

But Mia would not be consoled. "I will get revenge for this, Flying Bird." She glanced toward the trees. "I swear by my lover's body that I will see your own lover murdered." She bared her teeth in a fiendish grin. "One way or the other, as you have said."

Chapter Sixteen

Gray Falcon broke loose from his captors and rushed to Clover and Mia. Grabbing each by a strong arm, he drew them away from Ralph Brant's body, then pushed them toward the trees. Laughing wildly, he administered a kick in the buttocks to each of them in turn, yelling, "Now get the hell out of here, you foolish women."

Thinking their prisoner was himself escaping, a soldier pulled his trigger, hitting the Paiute chief directly in his painted chest. The sound of gunfire came from the village and Mia ran into the sheltering trees. With an anguished cry, Clover fell beside Gray Falcon's fallen body, laying her head on his chest just as Mia had done with her lover Brant.

Blood was bubbling from his mouth, and when he tried to speak, his eyes rolled back in agony. Mutely, he placed his arm on hers so that their wrists touched, in silent memory of the mutual blood they had shared as children. Then his hand moved to her abdomen, and, pressing gently, he gasped, "A child . . ."

Clover waited, but he said no more. After a long, agonized shiver, the stalwart body was still forever.

From the village came the bloodcurdling sound of guns and battle cries, and, choking back her sobs, Clover ran like the wind away from the battle into the trees.

Lake met her, his tanned face full of distress. "I lost your lion again," he moaned as he gathered her into his arms. "When he heard the first shot, he broke loose and ran off toward the ridge."

"Don't fret," she murmured, holding him close. "The strongest man on earth cannot hold back a scared lion." Lake was alive, and nothing else—not even Henry—mattered now.

Turning anxious gray eyes to the hills, he groaned, "Our lion is right in the middle of the battle; he could get a bullet or an arrow in him and die out there all alone."

Kissing Lake quickly, Clover reassured him. "Henry has proved many times over that he can handle himself in the wild. As for getting lost, we feared that before, and he always popped up very close by. You found him easily enough at Ragtown. A lion raised in captivity cannot live without human beings he has loved."

The women who had hidden by the stream gathered around them, and Clover informed them that Ralph Brant was dead.

"Hallelujah," Ground Squirrel exclaimed.

After a pause, Clover continued sadly. "Gray Falcon has fallen, too. He died in my arms."

Ground Squirrel fell to her knees, and, squatting, began a mourning song in a loud, piercing voice. Others joined her, and soon the air was filled with their cries. "He was a brave chief," one said, "yet many of us doubted him."

Turning her tear-streaked face toward Clover, Mia snarled, "Our dead chief's squaw does not mourn for him. See how the faithless one clings to her lover."

Clover reddened, but did not defend herself to the girl. The eyes of others stared at her and Lake with undisguised hostility. The women had obviously forgotten her courage in trying to lead them out of the village peacefully, risking her own life.

"Let's move away from the women," she muttered to Lake.

Walking swiftly to the water, they chose a deserted place upstream and sat on the banks of the ice-choked river. Lake put his arms about her shoulders, but she drew away.

"Please, not now," she said stiffly. "I do not wish to offend the villagers."

Lake himself stiffened, and grated, "Which of your two men takes first place in your heart, Clover? I wonder sometimes."

"I love only you," she replied in a strangled voice. "But I loved Gray Falcon also, in a vastly different way. It's not easy to break the bonds of true friendship." Sobbing openly now, she bent her head into her hands.

Bounding to his feet, Lake began to pace up and down the frozen banks. "I saw you holding him in your arms as he died," he said brokenly. "I had come out of the trees, thinking to snatch you from danger and become a hero in your eyes." Dropping to his knees beside her, he muttered, "Like your heroic Indian chief, whom you obviously prefer to me."

"That's not true," she replied angrily, placing her hands on his shoulders. "Don't let your jealousy twist your mind." After a pause, she added, "Your jealousy is dangerous to you. You even fear my love for Henry."

"I want you so," he groaned. "I've been denied so much in life." He pulled her to the ground beside him. With a cry, Clover strained against him, feeling the length of his virile body on hers, and when he bent to kiss her, she met his lips with all the passion in her being.

When they drew apart, she pressed her lips to his ear, holding his blond head in her two hands. "I'll spend the rest of my life proving that I love you," she crooned. "My feelings for Gray Falcon have nothing to do with you. The man was torn; he suffered much in his short life."

Heedless of possible staring eyes upon them, Clover lay on the ground with her lover. "As for being a hero, I have failed more than you have in that regard," she continued. "I tried to play Joan of Arc and save Eagle Valley for the Indians." She chuckled. "Single-handed, mind you. When their chief seemingly deserted them, I pridefully thought I could take

343

his place."

He laughed with her. "Anyone would admire you for trying, my darling, though I must confess your supreme dedication to your Indians made me almighty angry." He grinned. "You seem to have so many other loves."

"You will always be first," she said mildly. "But it is very sad that beautiful Eagle Valley is lost forever. In a year its green slopes and streams will be ravaged for silver. Ralph Brant may be dead, but others will move in with their horrible mining equipment."

"Surely, there is hope," he commented. "Can you not appeal to the government to relent?"

She shook her head. "No, the odds are against it. They had the cards stacked against them as it was, with Brant's falsified charges. And now, with this battle, they're finished."

Sighing, Clover touched her lover's brow with her lips. "Even President Grant can't save the valley now." Despite the happiness she felt in Lake's arms, her heart was sore for the Indians she loved. She had failed them and dreaded having to tell Molly the sad news.

"Hmm, I suppose you're right," he said quietly. But there was a thoughtful look in Lake Emerson's English eyes. He vowed inwardly to find a way to solve the problem of the displaced Indians . . .

"The shooting has stopped" came the voice of Ground Squirrel, who had crept up silently. "The soldiers have told us we may return to the village to tend our wounded and burn our dead."

When Clover and Lake arrived back at the village moments later, an appalling sight met their eyes. Bodies of both Indians and cavalrymen lay everywhere. The lieutenant and two of his soldiers had alone survived the bloodletting. No Indian men could be seen walking about. All had apparently been killed or had run away. Women walked despondently among the dead, searching for husbands, fathers, sons.

Sweet Briar, her old head covered with ashes, stood in the midst of it all in front of her lodge, her withered arms stretched to heaven. At her feet a hysterically weeping White Feather was bent over the body of Gray Falcon. As Clover drew near, the Indian girl leapt to her feet, and drawing the dead man's tomahawk from his belt, lunged at Clover.

"This time there are no chiefs to save you," she screamed. Swiftly, Lake came between them, catching the girl's arm before the weapon fell. Twisting her hand in a powerful grip, he forced her to drop the tomahawk. Others came forward to lead the grieving White Feather into Sweet Briar's lodge.

Her eyes filled with tears of shame, Clover threw herself against Lake's chest. "Not only have I failed to save these people, but I seem to be leaving none but enemies behind me."

Placing one strong arm under her legs, Lake immediately scooped her up into his arms and began to run out of the village. "Your mission to the Paiutes is finished, Joan of Arc," he grunted as he ran. "You are not compelled to save a whole nation. Now it's time you started playing the role of plain citizen Clover Sinclair again."

"Put me down, you coward," Clover hissed, struggling to free herself from the liontamer's brawny grip. "We can't just run out like rats from a sinking ship. There's work to be done, wounded to care for—" She pounded her fists on the back of his neck. "What kind of man are you, anyway?"

"A man who wants his sweetheart to himself," he retorted. "Clover Sinclair belongs to me, not to a passel of Indians."

They had reached the wood again, and making his way through the many horses and mules who had wandered here before and during the battle, Lake placed Clover in the saddle of a fine chestnut mare.

"This is Ralph Brant's mount," he said, smiling broadly. "He has no more use for it, and we do."

Leaping onto the horse meant for Mia's flight with Brant, Lake started off toward the trail leading out of the village. "We'll stop off at the Shoshone camp," he called back, "to provision ourselves for our journey and to inquire after Molly. If she's still in the healing hut in the care of Raging Water's wives, I advise you to leave her there until the dust settles around here."

"Aren't you going to search for Henry?" Clover asked meekly, somewhat bewildered at Lake's new brisk air of command. "You were so worried about him before."

"I'm blasted weary of chasing after that pesky animal," he replied snappishly. "You said yourself that he'd come back himself."

346

Her horse dutifully following Lake's, Clover said no more. She was content to leave everything to this new bossy Lake. She might as well get used to being ordered about by a husband, she mused. According to everything Molly had ever told her, that was a wife's fate. Ruefully, Clover recalled the fierce resentment she had felt when engaged to marry Spike, how she had flared up when he had ordered her about. But now she felt only a joyous expectation of being cared for by a masterful Lake Emerson.

The snow had begun to fall again, and she shivered in her doeskin. The blanket covering she'd put on for the journey north had fallen off when she'd fled into the trees after Gray Falcon's death.

Within, Clover felt drained, physically and emotionally. The intensity of the past months' events had used up all her strength. In the beginning, when she'd fled to Eagle Valley with Henry, it had seemed so simple. Molly had been strong, then, and determined to save the valley. Now all the poor woman's dreams had gone to bitter dust. In July, after that wonderful centennial day when her lion had come back into her life, Clover had been confident that she and Henry would spend many happy years together.

Now her lion was gone again, perhaps forever. Lifting her face to the hills, she murmured, "Bon voyage, Henry dear."

The sight of Lake's broad, plaid-covered back on his horse in front of her reassured her that he truly was a bulwark against all danger. And he was so tall and strong and so good-looking. His white-blond head was frosted with snowflakes. Like a halo on an angel, she mused. Her heart melted. She was a very lucky girl to have such a man. She wondered how he could still love her after all that had happened. He had seen her weeping over Gray Falcon and still wanted her.

"It must be true love, Molly," she murmured again, louder than she thought, for Lake turned around and smiled. "Cold, darling? Bear up, Clover, I'll get you ten blankets when we get to the camp."

"No matter," she replied, lightly. "I like the cold. It makes me feel I'm still alive and healthy."

About halfway to their destination, they saw an arrow lying among the roots of a shaggy-barked tree. A little farther on, Henry sat in a half-frozen stream, his haunches submerged in the icy water. His long leather leash floated in the water. At Clover's shout of joy, the lion splashed out onto the bank, wagging his big tail like a pet dog who had been left behind and now sees his master returning for him.

While Clover ecstatically cradled the big head against her breast, weeping into the thick mane, Lake examined the slight arrow wound. After sniffing the area, he announced, "The cut is clean as a whistle and I detect no smell of poison."

He patted Henry's cold, wet flank with his strong hand. "Jungle instinct told him to stop to knock the arrow out against that tree and jump into the icy water to stop the bleeding."

"And love made him wait for us," Clover caroled happily.

Although it was past midnight when they arrived at the Shoshone camp, the place was wide-awake. Women and children moved about, men lounged outside the lodges talking in loud, excited voices. Blue-clad cavalrymen stood with guns cocked at every dwelling. As Clover and Lake dismounted and tied Henry to the yucca tree behind which they had made love, Pedro ran up to greet them.

Hugging Clover briefly, the Indian shook Lake's hand with vigor. "Welcome and farewell, my friend," he said. "You must take Clover from this place at once. The cavalry has orders to take her into custody."

"What for?" Lake exclaimed, drawing Clover into his arms protectively. "She may have married an Indian, but she is full-blooded white and has done nothing against the law."

Anxiously glancing over his shoulder, Pedro hissed, "She is charged with inciting riot and causing the death of the Indian agent Brant and many others yesterday at the Paiute village."

"That's an outrageous lie," Clover stormed, breaking loose from Lake. "I was ready to march the women into the desert to the Walker Lake Reservation when Brant showed up with the soldiers. I tried as hard as I could to avoid confrontation." Her voice rose to a shriek. "Everyone knows that I've done nothing but preach peace for weeks."

"Shh, not so loud, you'll bring the soldiers," Pedro cautioned, looking over his blanketed shoulder again. "Eyewitnesses say otherwise."

349

"Who falsely accuses me?" Clover demanded, although she half guessed the answer.

"White Feather, Sweet Briar, and your traitorous companion, Mia," Pedro answered sadly, counting on his fingers. "They have spread word that you started the whole affair."

Clover's heart sank to her boots. Would she ever escape the wrath of her enemies?

The clatter of horses in the moonlit dark was followed by the appearance of an officer and two soldiers who reined in close to Lake and Clover.

Grinning down at them with obvious glee, the officer said, "Damn if I haven't caught my two jailbirds without half trying. You two can be nobody else but the infamous Indian lover Miss Sinclair and her paramour, the English liontamer who killed Ralph Brant's son."

Drawing a folded paper from the pocket of his woolen greatcoat, the officer shook it open and read with obvious enjoyment, "It also seems that the warden of an Illinois prison is becoming very impatient to see a certain Mr. Emerson back behind bars." He pocketed the paper again. "Everyone in Nevada is looking for you, liontamer."

"Military personnel are not empowered to arrest civilians," Clover exploded, moving to Henry's side. "If you try to take either of us into custody, I'll order Henry to charge."

Obligingly, Henry crouched with giant forepaws extended and bared his teeth menacingly. He roared, twice, in quick succession. A crowd formed. The officer drew his horse back, swearing roundly. Becoming skittish in the presence of the growling lion, the horse began to neigh and prance about.

"Call off your lion or I'll shoot him dead," the officer shouted, drawing his revolver from its holster. The two soldiers with him also aimed their guns.

With a cry, Clover stood in front of the lion, arms and legs outstretched like a windmill. "You'll have to kill me first."

Picking up a fallen branch, Lake stood tall and erect in front of Henry, branch extended high in the attitude of command to keep the animal from attacking the soldiers.

"Thunderation," the officer exploded, putting up his gun with disgust. Sweeping off his cap, he distractedly ran a hand through a crop of carroty hair. "Nobody at home is going to believe this. It's a goddam comic opera. A chit of a girl, a cockeyed Englishman, and a genuine African lion in the middle of the Nevada desert. Ten years fighting the Sioux was child's play compared to this mess."

The cavalryman squinted at the snow-filled sky, apparently seeking wisdom from above. The two soldiers, who had also holstered their guns, were having difficulty suppressing their laughter. Their faces twitched with merriment, and their hands covered their grinning mouths.

After a few moments' silence during which Henry continued to growl and rumble, the soldier pointed a gloved finger at Lake. "Will you and your lady friend kindly get the hell out of my sight?" His arm swung west toward the desert. "And take your damned lion with you. I've no stomach for killing such a splendid animal."

A grim smile crossed his face. "If the governor of Illinois wants his English jailbird back, he can damn well come out here and get you himself, Emerson. The United States Cavalry has far better matters to occupy its time."

Grinning at Clover with genuine warmth, the officer added, "As for you, young woman, marry the fellow and stay away from the Indians. My men and I intend to forget that we ever set eyes on you." He winked at the soldiers with him. "Is that clear, men?"

"Yessir," the soldiers chorused, wheeling around and following their officer back into the camp.

During the conversation, Pedro had gone to fetch filled waterskins, and now returning, he silently hung them on the saddles of the two horses. There were also woolen blankets, extra rabbitskins, piñon cakes, dried rabbit meat, and ammunition for their weapons, which he and Lake stuffed into saddlebags.

Gazing after the departing cavalrymen, he advised, "Now go quickly, before the lieutenant has a change of heart."

Untying Henry from the tree, Lake mounted, knotting the leash to his reins. But Clover hesitated, gazing with anguished eyes to the hills. "I can't leave without seeing Molly," she cried.

The faithful old Indian put both gnarled hands on her shoulders. "Your mother is in good hands. Raging Waters' nursing women have sent word that she is

352

improving. I will see that she comes to no harm from the soldiers. When you leave here, I will travel to the place where I think the healing hut to be. I will search until I find it."

"The cavalry will find you, and Molly, too," Clover wept, tears streaming down her face.

"Never," vowed Pedro, hugging her and kissing her on the brow.

Setting out instantly, Clover and Lake rode until dawn, spurring their horses to a near gallop. Henry kept pace, appearing to enjoy the half-run. When the horses slowed down at a treacherously rocky place, the lion heedlessly forged ahead, like a cub just freed from its mother. The desert was beautiful in winter garb; flowers of many delicate hues appeared unexpectedly in patches where the snow had fallen and melted. Birds filled the sky and small animals darted boldly about, seemingly fearless of predators.

Reining in at a meadow covered with masses of purple flowers, where a large clump of tall yucca trees provided shade, Lake and Clover fell upon a wide, smooth rock beneath the tree. The sun was in the middle of a cloudless sky, but the air was delightfully cool. They had met no other travelers along the way, except a platoon of cavalrymen headed toward the valley who ignored the pair of white riders.

"The Indian Bureau is determined to evacuate the Indians," Clover said sadly. "I still feel terribly guilty at just running off and leaving them.

Taking her into his arms, Lake murmured, "I thought we left Joan of Arc behind."

"You did," she dimpled, "but I can't change over-night."

Minutes later, Henry was happily devouring two fat jackrabbits, which Lake had felled easily with two shots. The fleeing lovers partook sparingly of piñon cakes and water, Lake being reluctant to start a fire to cook rabbit for themselves.

"Time is of the essence," he quipped as they sat side-by-side beneath the tree on the blanket-covered rock. "Any one of those cavalry officers riding by may be bearing down on us with arrest warrants."

"We have Henry to fend them off," she joked.

"Hmm. Maybe not. A trigger-happy soldier could kill our lion before we could snap our fingers. I won't rest easy until we're all on board ship for England."

"Me, too," she replied. "I can't wait to see England."

Turning her face to his, Clover murmured archly, "Is there time for love?" She pressed her lips to his warm neck, loving the feel of his unshaven chin.

"Always."

Sighing happily, Lake pushed her back with his hands until she lay flat on the rock. He knelt over her, his broad shoulders blocking the sky from her view. His powerful liontamer's chest filled her vision. Slowly, as if they had all the time in the world, Lake kissed her brow, her nose, her neck, coming at last to her mouth. There he lingered, as their lips joined and their warm tongues explored.

Drawing back, he crooned, "Well, is everything still the same?"

She grinned. "If hot, racing blood is any indication, I'd say everything has improved immensely."

Wantonly, she lifted up, and grabbing the hem of her doeskin with both hands, drew it up, along with her homespun cotton shift. Raising her head, she drew the garments over her head, exposing her full breasts and enticing feminine mound in its forest of glossy black hair.

Lake stood up and started to draw off his denim trousers.

"No, let me," she cried, leaping up. "I love to undress you."

"Not this time," he grunted, unbuttoning his plaid cotton shirt quickly and pushing her gently back down again on the blanketed rock. "We don't have time for all those lovely games you like to play."

She pouted. "You mean that I can't sit on top of you as we used to do?"

He was already spreading her legs apart. "We'll save those delightful diversions for a later time."

Clover's feminine mound had begun to throb at his touch, and she felt the moisture building in her dark female tunnel. The blood was pulsing in her ears, and she felt her face and neck grow hot.

"I'm ready for your conquest, liontamer," she gasped. "Do the deed quickly, sir."

Bending his blond head to her breasts, he took her nipples into his mouth, each in turn, kneading with his tongue to stimulate her desire. But she repeated impatiently, "Stop that, I am more than ready for you."

Without so much as a brief glance at his huge erection, Clover feasted her eyes instead on his handsome, aquiline face as he instantly placed both hands under her buttocks, lifting her high to his manhood. Her back arched steeply, and her black hair spread about her as she lay on the rock. She was being ravaged, savagely, and was enjoying the experience. Gray Falcon had also ravaged her, but with a kind of cruel hatred. Lake loved her, she loved him. She wanted nothing more than to be possessed, entirely, body and soul, by this marvelous man.

His manly, forceful entrance sent shivers of ecstasy up and down her spine and, arching wantonly, she felt him fill her so completely she lost all sense. Instinctively, her legs curled tightly around his buttocks so that their union was sealed off from all the world.

When he began to move in and out, first slowly, gently, then more fiercely, with all his masculine power, Clover could only groan and wait for the fulfillment to come. His grunts of intense physical effort, his labored breath, his twisted, sweating face, brought her own desire to fevered pitch.

"Now, please," she panted when her spirals of sensation became unbearable. "Please."

"Now," he panted back, immediately releasing his own explosion to match hers. Never before in all their lovemaking had Clover's lower muscles writhed so fiercely, so wildly, never before had she been so devastated. The violent storm within her seemed to go on forever.

Limp and exhausted from their brief interlude of

passion, the lovers dozed on the rock, Lake's blond head on Clover's breast.

Sometime later, a sudden rumbling from Henry brought them wide awake. He growled again, watchdog fashion, as a thin column of about ten people moved swiftly toward them through the desert. All were on horses or mules.

Bolting up, the lovers dressed quickly. As the group drew near, Clover exclaimed, "They are Indians, Paiutes from our own village, I think."

Irritated, Lake frowned. "It is no longer your village," he gritted, clearly annoyed.

A rider broke from the group and galloped toward them. It was Mia. "Clover, I'm so glad I found you," she gasped, sliding out of the saddle and throwing herself down on the rock. "There is trouble—much trouble—back in the village. Gray Falcon did not die from the bullets but lies only wounded. He is directing one of his brothers to lead a revolt against the cavalry. The soldiers are threatening to shoot all their prisoners and burn the lodges and tipis if there is any more resistance."

"Are there any able-bodied fighting men left?" Lake asked, astonished. "So many fell in the fighting already. Clover and I saw a multitude of bodies after Gray Falcon was slain."

"More men have come from outlying camps and villages. Some foreign tribes have sent braves from Utah and Idaho. The village teems with men in war paint. Many see this battle for Eagle Valley as a last stand against the white man in Nevada."

"Well, then they are fools," Lake responded grimly. Turning to Clover, who had been listening with horror, he ordered curtly, "Let's continue our journey, Clover. None of this concerns us."

"But it does," Mia pleaded, falling to her knees and hugging Clover's legs. "Please, Clover, only you can talk reason to Gray Falcon. He is mad, and the warriors revere him as a god."

"Mia's right," Clover said tonelessly. "The disastrous battle I have always feared has come to the valley Indians." Her tormented dark eyes dwelt on Lake's stony face. "I've got to go back; it's just possible I can change Gray Falcon's mind." Her voice was low and filled with urgency. "You see that, my darling, don't you?"

"It's some kind of trick," he said stonily. "The girl Mia hates you. She's set a trap for you."

"It's you she vowed to kill," Clover said, "as she bent over Brant's body."

"I spoke those evil words in anger," the Indian girl wept. "I didn't mean it." She stretched out her hands. "See—I have no weapon."

"Get up, Mia," Clover said tensely. "We'll go back for what help I can render."

"Speak for yourself, Clover," Lake flung out as he ran to untie Henry from a tree and hitch him up again to his horse's harness. "I can't take a chance on being arrested by some eager lieutenant and sent back with escort to Illinois. Besides, Henry and I are basically cowards. We have other plans for our future." An ugly laugh escaped from his throat. "You

358

know how Henry hates gunfire." He grimaced. "Almost as much as I do."

Clover blanched with shock. "How can you do this to me, Lake Emerson? The village is only a few hours' ride from here." She peered at the sky. "We'll be there before dark. All I need is a few hours with Gray Falcon, to cajole him into being peaceable until the women and children are safely marching north."

"Suit yourself, Joan of Arc," Lake sneered, bending in a mocking bow. Mounting his horse, he pointed west. "You've made your final choice, Miss Sinclair. May you and your Indian chief make heap big peace together," he lashed out sarcastically, "and anything else you want to share. I'll send you a postcard from merry old England."

Her black eyes brimming with scalding tears of humiliation, Clover watched the man she so desperately loved gallop out of her life. She knew with dread certainty that he was never coming back. How ironic, she thought gloomily. She had gloried in his manly domination of her in love, but in real life, in a crisis, she did not really want to be possessed so totally.

Mia had been bidding farewell to the others in her party, who were continuing on their journey north. They seemed to be extremely well provisioned, with blankets and plenty of food and water, as well as healthy-looking mules. Turning back to Clover, Mia tried to console the weeping girl. "Your lover will come back," she said. "He's in a huff right now. Want to bet he'll be chasing after us within the hour?"

Mounting her horse, Clover shook her head. Suddenly feeling chilled to the bone, she wrapped the heavy woolen blanket around her shoulders and rode alongside Mia toward Eagle Valley. When they arrived, all was dark and quiet. Soldiers marched about on sentry duty, but there were few Indians about.

"Gray Falcon lies in his mother's lodge," Mia said, leading the way to Sweet Briar's dwelling. "The old one has covered his wound with an ancient infusion, which has stopped the bleeding and brought the fever down."

Tying up their sweat-lathered horses, Clover ordered two boys to rub them down, then entered the lodge. The long room was ablaze with light. Sweet Briar sat in her rocking chair by the fire, while White Feather sat on the hearth at the old woman's feet. She walked among the sleeping mats, searching for the wounded Gray Falcon, while Mia stood by the door, smiling enigmatically.

Puzzled, she returned to the hearth. "Where have you taken my husband?" she inquired of Sweet Briar.

"He lies in his tipi, ready for the ritual burning," the old woman cackled, puffing on her pipe.

After a moment's shock, Clover realized that she had been tricked, just as Lake had warned. Suddenly frightened for her own life, she cried out, "Have you brought me here with lies to slay me?" Instinctively, she moved toward the door, but Mia was there before her.

"It was all my idea," Mia burst out, her words tumbling over each other. "I swore on my lover's body to kill your precious Mr. Emerson but knew that I would be imprisoned for such a deed."

White Feather interrupted. "Killing is too easy for such a wicked one as you."

"That's right," Mia continued. "Now you will feel the agony of living without the man you love, not because he is dead, like my Ralph, but because he has deserted you." She clapped her hands together in glee. "I saw him ride away without a backward glance."

Stunned, Clover stood immobile as White Feather rushed to stand close, spouting hateful words into her face. "You will live out your life knowing that your liontamer is in the arms of others. You are a fool, Flying Bird, to think that you could stop an Indian war." The Indian girl laughed madly. "You vanquished two good men with your wiles, but now you are alone, abandoned, forsaken."

Enraged more at herself than at the vengeful women who had tricked her, Clover flung out the door, brushing a grinning Mia aside. Securing a fresh horse, she rode to the Shoshone camp, and the lodge of Raging Waters. She needed Molly now, she would demand to be taken to her.

But Pedro, who answered her knock on the door, shook his head. "Molly must remain until the healing women say she is well enough to come back to us."

The Indian opened up his arms, and Clover poured out her grief to him, as she had so often done as a child.

"You have been foolish," Pedro commented when

the storm of weeping had passed, "but your life is not over. Whether or not your Lake Emerson returns, life has much to offer you."

She was welcome to remain with the Shoshones, Pedro assured her. There would be no further threats from Mia or White Feather, he was certain. A cot was given her in the crowded lodge, and a corner of her own to sleep in.

"There is much work here," the Indian said. "Make yourself useful." He grinned. You've always said you wanted to live among the Indians."

The cavalry remained in the Shoshone camp, as well as in other parts of the valley. But no action was taken to evacuate the Indians. The redheaded officer who had chased her and Lake and Henry out into the desert explained, when she questioned him the day after her arrival, "The Indian Bureau feels that it would be bad publicity to march those poor Indians north during the winter months." He paused. "It may happen in the spring."

The officer scowled at her. "As for you, young woman, just stay out of my way and out of trouble."

Obediently, Clover settled down to a waiting game. She knew she should take the train to Washington City to plead with President Grant on the Indians' behalf but doubted that she could work the miracle without Molly's help. It wasn't a simple matter to see a President. Spring was many months away. She'd worry about it then.

Chapter Seventeen

Once through the desert, Lake Emerson spent a full week in the high Sierra Nevada mountains, following trails with Henry, killing his own meat, cooking it over a fire at night from saplings and branches of large trees he chopped down himself with his hunting knife. He was loath to return to civilization; the struggle for survival in the bitter cold thrust his miseries out of his mind. At times, when Clover's beautiful face loomed to taunt him, he stripped off his clothes and jumped into an icy stream until all maddening thoughts and tormenting desires left him. In the starry nights, stretched out under the tall trees, wrapped cocoonlike in a thick rabbitskin, he slept like a dead man.

As the days passed, the lion became restless, and several times growled at his old master, as if anxious to be somewhere other than this lonely wilderness of ice and snow. Henry spent long hours moping about. His old eagerness to hunt for himself seemed to be gone. When Lake dropped a fresh-killed juicy rabbit or possum in front of him, Henry merely picked at it.

One fine cold morning Lake woke up knowing that he was cured of his depression. He was ready to rejoin life. A plan had been forming in his brain during his retreat, without his really being aware of it. He would become the hero that damned girl Clover Sinclair seemed to require of the man she loved. Despite his angry words when they had parted in the desert, Lake knew instinctively that they would someday be together again.

"She's just confused," he chatted to Henry as they packed and moved out to descend to more temperate climes. "Thanks to her adoptive mother, she has an exaggerated sense of duty and loyalty to the Indians."

As he pondered the matter, though, Lake had to admit that the plight of the Nevada Indians was real. On his travels he had come across many a pitiful group of wandering redskins. On questioning them, he had found that they all seemed to be without a permanent home. The children, by and large, looked emaciated. The Indian's traditional hunting grounds had been usurped by the railroads or gold and silver miners. Many had once been proud owners of prosperous farms and sheep ranches. Others had fled the reservations where the food and land promised them by the United States Indian Bureau had been stolen from them by corrupt officials.

"The government agents are thieves," one old man told him. "And the Great White Father in Washington City seems not to care."

"But he does," Lake responded. "President Grant

cares very much but simply has not been told the truth about what's been happening."

With a plan to visit Grant, Lake arrived at Virginia City early in December, where the Grandiose Circus was wintering, waiting for the mountain roads to be clear of snow before they resumed their tours of small mining towns in the West.

The ringmaster was overjoyed to take Henry off his trainer's hands. "We've been picking up a little cash just holding weekly shows, but business has been poor without a lion," he lamented. "Even without a trainer to put him through his routines, that huge beast of yours will draw crowds just pacing around in his cage, looking fierce."

Feeling conscience-stricken at deserting his long-time companion, Lake bade farewell to his lion. "I'll be back in a month or so, old pal," he said, "once I've carried out my mission to be a hero."

To Lake's surprise, Henry didn't even glance up as his master walked away, so absorbed was he in consuming a large chunk of fresh beef thrown into his cage by the animal keeper. In fact, as he departed, he had a distinct if uneasy feeling that the blasted animal looked happy for the first time since they had left Clover in the desert.

The next part of his plan was not so easy. Lake was penniless, having left behind in Clover's saddle-bags the cash and silver he had collected during his brief tour of the Indian camps with Henry. He sneaked into Black Springs at night to escape possible detection by a lawman who had seen the Illinois poster. Once he had explained the dire situation at

Eagle Valley to Samson at Molly Robinson's stage-house, the Chinese cook willingly lent the young liontamer enough money for railroad fare to Washington City.

"It's from the dining-room grocery money," the cook explained, "but please don't tell Molly." The little man shivered in anticipation of his boss's wrath.

"If she were here, Molly would gladly give it to me," Lake assured the man. "I'm doing something she longs to do herself, but cannot." He grinned. "If my scheme succeeds, she will amply reward you for helping me out."

In the absence of both Molly and Clover, Samson had been operating the stagehouse himself with the help of two local boys. But there was little to do, business, as with the circus, being poor in the winter months. "We are lucky if we get five customers a day," Samson mourned, shaking his pigtailed head. "Bad news, bad news."

About midnight, after his talk with Samson, Lake climbed up Superstition Hill and took Cedric Sinclair's letter of confession out of the gilt box. He wasn't quite sure exactly how it would be of use to him but he folded it carefully in a watertight bit of sheepskin and tucked it into his trousers pocket.

At dawn, he took the coach for the depot, and began his transcontinental train journey. The trip to the nation's capital usually took a mere six days, barring accidents. But four days out, somewhere in southern Ohio, the speeding train which bore Lake Emerson on his heroic mission stopped dead. The young Englishman, who had been sleeping much of the time, luxuriating in a crimson plush reclining seat, looked out the train window. He saw a wooden platform and a high water tower set in the midst of what looked like a harvested wheat field. It had been raining off and on ever since the train had left the western plains, but here it was clear, with a mild, winter sun. The passengers were disgruntled and demanded to know why they could not go on.

"There's floods up ahead," the conductor informed them, "debris on the tracks. It'll be hours before we can proceed."

Most of the passengers left the stuffy, overheated coaches to walk nervously up and down the platform, consuming sandwiches provided by the train's dining service. Although it meant more delay in fulfilling his plan, Lake tried to be philosophical about it. Even if he obtained an audience with the president and got the needed reprieve for the Indians of Eagle Valley, chances that any of the unfortunate redskins he was trying to save were still alive were not very good. A big war had been threatening when he had left the valley.

He chuckled at the irony of it all. He might become a hero, but nobody would be left to care. His heart lurched. Clover might even be dead or in federal prison for loving Indians. He refused even to think about it.

Hearing his chuckle, a trainman with a swinging lantern came up to him. "Glad to hear you're not grumpy like the rest of 'em," he commented. "I hear our great president himself is stuck on the rails up ahead. He's on a branch train that came from northern Ohio where he's been visiting his hometown of Galena. It's supposed to join up with your train right at this point."

Lake's mouth dropped open. "You don't say," he exclaimed, peering at the small train of three coaches about a hundred yards east of their own. The news had apparently spread rapidly, for already a small crowd had gathered around the presidential train, hoping for a glimpse of the national hero, General Ulysses S. Grant.

"Why don't you go up there with the others and get a glimpse of the president for yourself?" the trainman suggested.

"Good idea, why not?" Lake responded, marveling at the coincidence. Literally bumping into Grant was an answer to a prayer he had not uttered. A blasted miracle. The young Englishman felt lightheaded as he ran toward the crowd, now yelling and chanting for the hero of the War Between the States to come out and say a few words to them.

"Come out, Sam, I fought with you in the big war," said one. "I was at Shiloh," called out another. A rhythmic clapping began, and when Lake arrived, breathless and exhilarated, old Sam Grant's graying head was sticking out of a window, smiling and waving at the crowd.

But he's old and tired was Lake's first thought. Elbowing his way to the front, so close he could touch the steel side of the coach with his hand, he saw faded blue eyes that were still alert, and a swift, intelligent gaze that darted over the crowd of admiring citizens.

Grant's mouth and chin were entirely hidden by a

368

neatly cropped grayish beard streaked with its original rust red. There was a wart on his cheek. Lake had seen portraits of the man called "savior of the nation" and had somehow expected him to be in full blue Union Army regalia, complete with medals. But this old man wore a rumpled brown suit, there was a cigar in his mouth, and in his hand he cradled a glass of golden whiskey.

"The man's a marvel, but he's a drunk," Molly had told him once.

Yielding to his public, the president gave a speech, filled with jokes and banter, mostly about the "damned rain," and how he kind of liked sitting here, far from his desk in Washington City, with nothing to do but play cards.

Laughter and foot-stomping greeted this sally, and in the tiny pause while Grant drank from his glass, Lake shouted out, "I've a message for you, from Molly Robinson, Mr. President."

The glass froze in midair as Grant turned to stare at the bold young man. "Did you say Molly Robinson, from the glorious state of Nevada?"

"Yessir," Lake responded. "The same. She's in trouble and has sent me to seek your help."

The president's smiling face became abruptly serious. The crowd grew silent, waiting, gaping at Lake. "Come inside, Englishman," Grant ordered Lake, instantly withdrawing his head from the window.

An awed conductor ushered Lake into a plush, elaborately decorated smoke-filled parlor car. Three men were seated at a table in the carpeted aisle laid out with cards, waiting for the president to rejoin them. In a wooden-sided booth, four ladies sat with needles clicking. Their talk was low and chatty, and Lake recognized the plump figure of Mrs. Grant from newspaper pictures. She glanced at him curiously but said nothing. Lake felt out of place in his dusty, rumpled plaid shirt, denim trousers, and scuffed leather boots.

Noting the young man's discomfort, Grant laughed. "My wife is accustomed to my strange visitors, no matter what they're wearing." He led Lake to the far end of the car and sat down in an empty booth containing facing upholstered seats separated by a little table.

"Now, tell me quick, is Molly okay?" Grant asked, placing both elbows on the table and speaking in a low voice so as not to be overheard.

"Not exactly," replied Lake. "She's very ill, maybe dying."

Grant's fist pounded the table until it rattled. "It's those damned weak lungs of hers," he muttered angrily. "I always told her they would be the death of her."

"She's had a hard life," Lake said.

The presidential eyes clouded. "I wish like hell it could have been different with the two of us. I was real fond of Molly, some might even call it love. And I know she had a soft spot for me, too." His still-broad shoulders heaved in a great sigh. "But I'd been married just a year when we met in California. I loved my wife, too. I was miserable and Molly Robinson cheered me up."

He stared out the window, a distant look in his

eyes. "She saved my life once, did she tell you?"

"No, but I'd like to hear the story."

"Later, perhaps," Grant said, accepting more whiskey from a waiter and pushing it in front of Lake. "You look like you need this, young fellow," he grinned.

Lake sipped, swallowed, then stared into his glass, still shaken at his extraordinary good luck. It might have taken him weeks in the capital to get admitted to the presidential office.

"Did Molly ever get married again?" Grant asked. "She lost a child and always wanted kids in the worst way."

Lake shook his head. "Don't think so, but she adopted a little girl whose wagon went over a cliff nearby. Molly has devoted her life to Clover."

Grant twinkled, puffing out a string of smoke rings. "Clover, eh? She must be the girl you are in love with."

Coloring, Lake burst out, "How did you know?"

Heads turned in their direction. "Shh," cautioned the president. "I want to keep this conversation just between ourselves."

Then, winking broadly, he poked Lake in the chest. "It's the way you say her name, kind of soft and tender like."

One of the card players walked down the aisle to their booth. "Will you be much longer, Sam?"

Grant waved him off.

"Now what kind of trouble is Molly in?" he asked Lake.

Briefly, the liontamer outlined the situation with

371

the Indians of Eagle Valley, including Brant's perfidy in petitioning with false documents and the imminent eviction of the natives from their ancestral land.

Abruptly, the president rose up and shouted, "Hey, Luke, fetch your notebook. And find that fellow who wants to take my photograph for his newspaper."

The card player who had approached them earlier now raced down the aisle and stood at attention, pencil poised. In short, efficient sentences Grant dictated a telegram to be dispatched at the next stop, addressed to the governor of Nevada. "Stop all action at Eagle Valley until further notice from Indian Bureau."

Grinning at Lake, Sam Grant added, "I'll make sure that Molly's Indians will keep that valley in perpetuity." He sighed. "Though God only knows what'll happen to them after I die."

Moments later, as they walked outside for the photograph-taking, the president lamented to Lake that he had not done all he could to ease the plight of the American Indians. "A Chief of State has so many burdens," he sighed.

Slinging a still-burly arm around Lake's shoulders, he struck a pose for the photographer, who had set up his tripod outside on the wheatfield. "Thanks to you, young man," he chortled, "I can redeem myself to a small extent for neglecting the Indian issue. I've also repaid my long-standing debt to dear Molly. I'll have my secretary make sure this story gets into all the newspapers."

Two hours later, photographs completed, the president invited Lake to a sumptuous meal in the presidential dining car, with all the Havana cigars and whiskey he wanted. Declining the cigars, Lake consumed more whiskey than he should have, and when he finally returned to his own train, he fell promptly into a dreamless sleep.

During the meal, Ulysses Grant had exhorted the young Englishman to think of something—anything—he as president could do for him.

Although Dr. Sinclair's letter of confession was almost burning a hole in his pocket, the liontamer replied simply, "Nothing, sir, nothing. I have not pled this cause for a reward."

It would have been an easy matter, Lake mused next morning as he switched trains at Cincinnati to head back out west, to have obtained a presidential pardon for the crimes against him in Illinois. But what kind of hero takes the easy way out?

After personally seeing the important telegram dispatched, Lake Emerson boarded a train for Illinois. Until now, the whole experience with Grant had been like a dream, but now he had to face grim reality once more.

On a snowy late-December day, more than a month after Clover's return to Eagle Valley, she opened the door of Raging Waters' lodge to see the beaming face of the red-haired cavalry lieutenant.

Thrusting a piece of paper into her hand, he said proudly, "It gives me great pleasure to inform you, Miss Sinclair, that the order to evacuate the valley has been rescinded. Permanently." Handing Clover the military order, he shook his head in amazement. "Seems the president himself has intervened with a telegram to the governor of the state."

Stunned, Clover read the military order. It was quite clear the miracle had happened. "But who could have seen the president?" she asked Pedro later as they sat by the fire, discussing the wonderful news. "Molly had planned to travel to see Grant. Lake and I talked about it." She paused, a hopeful gleam lighting up her eyes, "You don't suppose that Lake could have gone to Washington City, do you?"

The old Indian shook his head. "Not likely, considering how little he seemed to care about the plight of the valley Indians. He left you cold, don't forget, when you turned back to help prevent a catastrophic battle."

"I'll never forget," she replied somberly. The pain inflicted by Lake's abandonment was as sharp as ever. There had been no word from him, though several Indians who had come south through the mountains in the past week reported seeing him and the lion. Apparently he was still in the area; he could easily have returned to see if she were alive or dead.

"You're right," she replied to her Indian friend. "My liontamer who swore eternal love is no longer interested at all in me or anything I do." Despite her calm words, Clover's heart ached with a pain as fresh as the day it had been inflicted.

Within days, the valley was free of blue-clad soldiers, and life returned to normal. The Shoshones tended their flocks of sheep, the Paiutes and Washos fished in frozen streams, antelope deer and cougar were hunted and bagged throughout the green slopes. Women dried rabbit and deerskins on racks, children shouted at their play, maidens made eyes at young braves who went to them in snug tipis. Clover went about the villages, tending the sick and old. Her heart began to heal. Only at times, when she saw the love transfiguring the faces of the newly wedded maids, did her pain engulf her. Only at night, when the muted roar of a cougar drifted over the village, did she allow herself to think of her lost Henry.

Word was sent to the healing hut where Molly had been hidden for months, and one fine January morning the sick woman was reunited with her daughter. Molly was very thin, but the bleeding from the lungs had stopped.

"If she remains with us in Wun-i-muc-a, the healing women admonished Clover, "she may live many happy years."

Molly had no desire to return to her Black Springs stagehouse. "My life there is over," she said contentedly. Her Indian friends built a snug log lodge for Molly and Clover. Despite Clover's vehement denials, all were convinced that she was responsible for the message of freedom from President Grant.

"I am happy with the Indians, and wish to remain here always," she told Molly. "I can't bear to return to Black Springs where there is so much to remind me of . . ."

She hesitated, hand over mouth, unwilling to say her lover's name.

"Go on, say it," Molly snapped. "Where you met Lake Emerson, the man who loved you and left you.

You can't hide forever, Clover, like a gopher in a hole. You'll never forget him if you're afraid even to mention his name."

When Molly continued on the mend, Clover reluctantly agreed to go back home long enough to handle the transaction of selling the stagehouse to Samson if he wanted it.

"Stay a while, you may change your mind about living in Eagle Valley," the older woman scolded. "Don't let one man's disloyalty ruin your life. Don't let bitterness shrivel your heart. To my eternal regret I did just that."

"I'm through with love," Clover gritted, hardening her beautiful black eyes and tightening her soft, sensual mouth into a grim line. "It hurts too much."

Molly was certain that Samson would jump at the chance to be owner of the business. "The little Chinaman has a good head for business," she insisted, "and can cook rings around me." She chuckled. "Besides, I happen to know that the rascal has salted away a pile of money through the years."

When Clover inquired about the bank account in San Francisco founded on the stolen bank money, Molly shook her head. "I haven't quite decided what to do about that," she said. "Lake's obviously skipped the country for England, and returning the money at this late date won't do him any good. Let it be for now."

"I'm sure he's back in his native land with Henry," Clover mused. "He often spoke of touring the British Isles and Europe with his marvelous lion."

* * *

On a hot Fourth of July, 1877, the ill-gotten loot in a San Francisco bank was far from Clover's mind as she sat in the stagehouse dining room drinking strong coffee and enjoying the dinner lull after midday. Though she sorely needed ready cash, she couldn't touch it without Molly's signature. She had traveled back to Black Springs in May, only to be told by Samson that, much as he would like to, he could not purchase the stagehouse.

"I send all my money to China to my family there," he wept. "I poor as Job's turkey."

Resignedly, Clover settled in once more, and managed to keep the place afloat with the help of Samson and two fresh-eyed Indian girls from Eagle Valley who had returned with her. The girls worked hard and were good company for Clover, who was lonely. Few in town would even talk to her after all that had happened last year. There was much bitterness over Spike Brant's death, for which many blamed her.

Soon after Clover's return to her hometown, one of Molly's old pals from town had given her a newspaper from San Francisco. On the front page was a photograph of President Ulysses S. Grant with his arm around the shoulder of a smiling young blond man named Lake Emerson.

"Ain't that the young man you were so sweet on?" the man asked slyly.

Clover nodded, dropping her eyes to hide the sudden anguish. "Yes, it is. But that's all over now." She managed a smile. "It was really the lion I was interested in."

The headline read, "President Grants Reprieve to Indians in Nevada." The article went on to report this would be Grant's last good deed in office and related the sad story of Eagle Valley, how it was almost lost to the native redmen until a young foreigner, an Englishman on his way home to his own country, brought it to the attention of the President at a chance meeting on a train.

"So, thanks to a man who is not even an American citizen, the story of Eagle Valley has had a happy ending," the reporter wrote. "Ironically, it would seem that only citizens of the United States are oblivious to the misery of our native tribes."

"How the man must despise me," Clover wrote to Molly when she sent the clipping to her mother. "With a bit of good luck and a smile, Lake accomplished what I had failed at so miserably. No wonder he never wrote to me about his good deed. It would be like a slap in the face."

Several other people had also given her the photograph and story, and she hid them in a drawer, taking them out to gaze at when her despair and loneliness proved too hard to bear. Molly's advice to get the man out of her mind by thinking and talking about him was doing absolutely no good.

Having met with such success last year in the little silver town, the Grandiose Circus had agreed to put on a show again this year on Independence Day. Clover had resolved not to go; seeing another lion in Henry's cage would surely break her heart.

But now, as she heard the familiar martial strains of circus music drifting up from town, she tore off her apron, put on an old straw hat, and ran down the rocky path in her denim pants and plaid boy's shirt. Clover had reverted to her old habit of wearing male attire. She no longer wanted to feel like a woman.

The parade was in full swing when she got to Front Street. Crowds lined the dusty street, though there wasn't nearly as much commotion as there had been last year at the Centennial celebration. Nothing would ever compare to that wonderful day, Clover knew.

Listlessly, she watched the leopards, the monkeys, the belly dancer, the cavorting dogs. Everything seemed somewhat jaded to her eyes. She was not the eager girl she had been last year. Even the blue-painted lion cage looked the same, with its chipping paint and gilt legend, "Grandiose Circus," as it rattled around the bend and headed her way.

Tensing, Clover closed her eyes, not wanting to look. But quickly, she opened them again, in full anticipation of pain. *I'll just let it wash over me,* she thought. *Like a dose of Epsom salts or a bad dream.*

But joy and amazement washed over her instead as she heard a roar that could belong to no animal but her own Henry. There he stood, filling the old cage with his massive four hundred pounds, wet black snout pressed against the cage bars, just as it had been last year when they had seen each other so unexpectedly.

The lion wagon stopped, to give everyone a chance to gape. Racing into the street, Clover grabbed the bars and kissed the warm black whiskery face, reaching far inside to stroke the lovely, tawny mane. The animal's answering grunts of contentment brought applause from the crowd, many of whom knew well the story of Clover Sinclair and her lion.

"So Lake abandoned you, too," she murmured to her lion. "Don't worry, darling. I'll buy you from the circus, and this time nobody can stop us."

A clipped English voice sounded at her elbow. "I wouldn't be so sure about that, young lady."

Whirling, Clover came face-to-face with Lake Emerson, glorious in his snug, revealing liontamer costume. Before she could speak, he flipped off her hat with his bronzed hand, sending it skittering into the wind. His laughing gray eyes bored into hers, as he lifted a thick strand of her black hair. "God, how I've missed you."

Bending swiftly, he kissed her in front of all, evoking titters and applause from the crowd.

"They think it's all part of the act, I suppose," he grinned, lifting her up and setting her down on the buckboard beside him. "Now keep quiet until we finish this parade."

Struck dumb with shock, Clover was forced to watch the man she still loved with all her heart strut and preen and flex his brawny muscles for the special delight of admiring women and girls.

Had he been pardoned? she wondered. Why else was he taking such risks of being arrested and sent back to the Illinois prison? Out of the corner of her eye, Clover saw the marshal from Carson City surrounded by his deputies. He was laughing and clapping like the rest. Surely he knew about the bounty on Lake Emerson's head.

Happy as she was to see Henry perform again, sitting through the performance beyond the town on the flats seemed an eternity to Clover. But at last it was over, and putting Henry in his cage, Lake turned to Clover at his side.

"He looks happy in there, doesn't he? I don't think he really enjoyed all that romping around in the mountains. He likes his cage, he likes the circus life."

Later, after a hearty dinner of lamb and potatoes and hot piñon cakes, Lake and Clover walked upstairs to her bedroom hand in hand. Stripping off his shirt with unseemly haste, Lake reached to draw her into his arms.

"Not so fast, Englishman," Clover cried, running into a corner. "There's a lot you have to tell me. I've read all about your heroic exploits in the newspaper, of how it was you who saved Eagle Valley. But are you still not wanted by the governor of Illinois?"

She dimpled, as he leaned both hands on the walls imprisoning her. "Or did the president grant you a pardon when you told him about Eagle Valley?"

He shook his blond head, "No, I did it the hard way, the way a true hero would. I surrendered to the warden at Joliet, and gave him your father's letter in which he absolved me of the killing and planning the robbery. Just to make sure, he telegraphed Molly at Eagle Valley to verify my story."

"Molly never told me," Clover said thoughtfully. "I think she wanted me to forget all about you."

"Well, no matter," she said. "You're here." Unable to keep her hands off him any longer, she caressed his broad chest with her trembling hands, shivering at the warm feel of the thick blond mat of hair.

"The warden's a good-hearted fellow, and when he learned what I'd done for the Indians, he begged for leniency to the judge who presided over my hearing. When I told them where the money was, I was acquitted of the original crimes but given six months for escaping."

"But that's not fair," she protested. "You were innocent."

"Not entirely," he said soberly. "I was guilty of complicity in the robbery."

Counting on her fingers, Clover said, "Hmm. So you came directly here from prison." She pouted. "Why didn't you write me? I was miserable."

He cocked a blond brow. "Prison's no paradise, either, but I wanted you to miss me like the devil before I—"

Wildly impatient, Clover reached up to capture his lips in hers. After a long, passionate kiss, Lake lifted her up and threw her on the bed.

"Now undress me," he grumbled as he straddled her lower body. "Slowly. Then we can begin some of those games you're so fond of."

There are some times in a woman's life when words simply get in the way, Clover decided, as she started to untie the cord around the belt of Lake's snug liontamer tights.

HISTORICAL ROMANCES BY EMMA MERRITT

RESTLESS FLAMES (2203, $3.95)

Having lost her husband six months before, determined Brenna Allen couldn't afford to lose her freight company, too. Outfitted as wagon captain with revolver, knife and whip, the single-minded beauty relentlessly drove her caravan, desperate to reach Santa Fe. Then she crossed paths with insolent Logan Mac-Dougald. The taciturn Texas Ranger was as primitive as the surrounding Comanche Territory, and he didn't hesitate to let the tantalizing trail boss know what he wanted from her. Yet despite her outrage with his brazen ways, jet-haired Brenna couldn't suppress the scorching passions surging through her . . . and suddenly she never wanted this trip to end!

COMANCHE BRIDE (2549, $3.95)

When stunning Dr. Zoe Randolph headed to Mexico to halt a cholera epidemic, she didn't think twice about traversing Comanche territory . . . until a band of bloodthirsty savages attacked her caravan. The gorgeous physician was furious that her mission had been interrupted, but nothing compared to the rage she felt on meeting the barbaric warrior who made her his slave. Determined to return to civilization, the ivory-skinned blonde decided to make a woman's ultimate sacrifice to gain her freedom — and never admit that deep down inside she burned to be loved by the handsome brute!

SWEET, WILD LOVE (2834, $4.50)

It was hard enough for Eleanor Hunt to get men to take her seriously in sophisticated Chicago — it was going to be impossible in Blissful, Kansas! These cowboys couldn't believe she was a real attorney, here to try a cattle rustling case. They just looked her up and down and grinned. Especially that Bradley Smith. The man worked for her father and he still had the audacity to stare at her with those lust-filled green eyes. Every time she turned around, he was trying to trap her in his strong embrace.

Available wherever paperbacks are sold, or order direct from the Publisher. Send cover price plus 50¢ per copy for mailing and handling to Zebra Books, Dept. 2936, 475 Park Avenue South, New York, N.Y. 10016. Residents of New York, New Jersey and Pennsylvania must include sales tax. DO NOT SEND CASH.

HISTORICAL ROMANCES BY VICTORIA THOMPSON